On Her Own
Two Feet

By Pam Evans and available from Headline

A Barrow in the Broadway
Lamplight on the Thames
Maggie of Moss Street
Star Quality
Diamonds in Danby Walk
A Fashionable Address
Tea-Blender's Daughter
The Willow Girls
Part of the Family
Town Belles
Yesterday's Friends
Near and Dear
A Song in Your Heart
The Carousel Keeps Turning
A Smile for All Seasons
Where We Belong
Close to Home
Always There
The Pride of Park Street
Second Chance of Sunshine
The Sparrows of Sycamore Road
In the Dark Street Shining
When the Boys Come Home
Under an Amber Sky
The Tideway Girls
Harvest Nights
The Other Side of Happiness
Whispers in the Town
A Distant Dream
On Her Own Two Feet

Pam
EVANS

On Her Own
Two Feet

headline

Acknowledgements

Many thanks to my lovely editor Clare Foss who continues to be a pleasure to work with, and to all the team at Headline who make my stories into such well produced and attractive books. Thanks also to my agent Barbara Levy who has lost none of her enthusiasm for my work over the years. A special thank you to Leonardo Lopez who provided me with some information I needed for an aspect of this story.

Chapter One

Celebrations were well under way all over London to mark the Silver Jubilee of King George and Queen Mary and the street party in Pearl Road, Chiswick was in full swing on the afternoon of May the fifth 1935.

In the mood for a 'good old knees-up', the residents were out in force, jolly and sociable, while neighbourhood stalwarts organised the event with an air of affable authority. Patriotic flags and bunting waved in the breeze; the children had feasted on jelly, blancmange and other traditional party treats and were now being entertained by young resident Mollie Fisher and her twin brother Geoff who were arranging some races for them.

'All right, kids,' said Mollie, whose maiden name was Potts; she had lined the children up to start in the road outside her family's residence in the row of Victorian terraced houses of which the street was made up. 'When I say "Go," run as fast as you can to Geoff who is waiting by the next lamp post to judge the race.' She looked

1

towards her brother, a slim young man wearing grey flannels and a sleeveless knitted pullover on top of his shirt. 'Ready Geoff?'

'You bet.'

'Right then, you lot,' she said to the children. 'On your marks . . . get set . . . go!'

Off they went; the fast, the slow and the barely moving. Mollie gave a helping hand to a couple of stragglers and got them to the finish – eventually.

'Well done to the winners; Geoff will give you your prizes,' she told them. 'And there will also be a little something for everyone who took part because you entered into the spirit of this very special day and, as you all know, taking part is just as important as winning.'

'No it ain't,' said a round, freckle-faced boy with ginger hair, flaming cheeks and fiery blue eyes. 'Winnin' is the 'ole point.'

'Well yes, but there is more to it than that.'

'Such as?' he queried with a swagger.

'Without competitors there would be no race so everyone who takes part matters,' she said patiently. 'It's all about something called sporting spirit.'

'Never 'eard of it but I don't mind gettin' somethin' for losin',' said the aggressive child, causing the other youngsters to erupt into laughter, at which point Mollie ended the discussion and moved on with the proceedings.

'Shall we have the three-legged or the sack race next, Geoff?' she asked as the children drifted away.

'Oh, we haven't finished yet then?' he groaned with good-humoured regret. 'That's a pity.'

'After just one race? Don't make me laugh; you know me better than that.' She grinned.

'Don't I just.' He was smiling though. His sister was one of the most energetic people he knew and he sometimes had difficulty keeping up with her.

'And if you're not careful I'll get the adults to have a go as well,' she added.

'Thanks for the warning.' The twins were nineteen and, although not technically identical, they did have a special emotional bond and certain similarities in appearance. One thing they shared was a sense of fun and enthusiasm for life. 'I shall make myself scarce if you start that malarkey.'

'I'll find you wherever you are hiding, don't worry,' she kidded him. 'Now let's get these children organised.' She glanced across the street to where her mother was standing outside their front gate by a shiny, upright black pram. 'Before that baby of mine wakes up and wants feeding.'

'Yes, madame,' he said with a mock salute and they both laughed.

'You'd never guess that Mollie had just had a baby would you?' observed the twins' mother Madge, watching her son and daughter enjoying themselves together, Mollie a petite brunette while Geoff was taller and had a thatch of light brown hair.

'You certainly wouldn't,' agreed Madge's mother Nora, a perky pensioner with bright blue eyes, a clear complexion and white curly hair. 'She's as slim as a reed and full of beans; and little Esme only a few weeks old. Some women take ages to get back on their feet with their figure intact after lying-in.'

'She's always been a very energetic and agile girl as you know,' remarked Madge, who had brown eyes and dark hair with a few touches of grey.

'Ooh, not half; she was very good at gym and games when she was at school as I remember; captain of the netball team, no less?' Nora said proudly. 'Perhaps that has something to do with her getting her figure back so soon; her being so supple.'

'Could be,' agreed Madge. 'I think she missed all that sort of thing when she left school.'

'She's bound to have done; there's not much opportunity for sport and physical jerks when you start work,' remarked Nora. 'She's certainly a credit to you though, Madge, the way she's knuckled down to motherhood . . . er, considering the circumstances.'

Madge's brow tightened into a frown at the reminder. 'Yeah, she is doing well, though it was very upsetting for us all when the pregnancy first came to light. Every mother of daughters' worst nightmare and not what I would have chosen for her at all. Still, it seems to have turned out all right.'

At that moment Mollie appeared beside them.

'Talk of the devil,' said Madge.

Mollie looked at them quizzically, half smiling, her rich brown eyes shining. 'Should my ears have been burning?' she asked. 'Are you saying what a terrible

4

mother I am for leaving you to look after my little daughter while I'm off enjoying myself.'

'As if we would. Quite the opposite, in fact,' her mother assured her. 'Your gran was just saying what a cracking little mum you've turned out to be.'

'Thanks, Gran.' Mollie bit her lip. 'Can I push my luck even more and ask you to watch Esme for a little while longer? I have to organise the three-legged race.'

'You go ahead, love. You should know that we don't mind; we enjoy looking after her,' said Madge. 'Anyway, you are contributing to the celebrations. Someone has to keep the kiddies entertained.'

It would never have occurred to Mollie to ask her husband Syd to look after their baby, even for a few minutes, because she'd been brought up to believe that babies were exclusively a woman's responsibility along with all things domestic. He was here at the party, though, standing nearby with her father Len and some neighbours. She noticed that they had done what all the men she knew usually seemed to do at any social gathering: they had formed an all-male clique, their conversation interspersed with guffaws of raucous laughter. She caught Syd's eye and waved, smiling. He responded with a grin and she positively glowed with adoration. He was her hero, her soul mate and the love of her life.

'Come on, Mollie,' called her brother. 'The kiddies are getting fed up with waiting.'

'Just coming.' She turned to her mother. 'Call me if she wakes up, Mum,' she said and hurried away, a skinny, nimble girl wearing a summer frock and sandals, her dark hair falling loose to her shoulders.

The party showed no sign of abating. It did become a little more adult towards evening, though, with music from a wind-up gramophone, alcoholic drinks and savoury snacks, such as sausage rolls and cheese straws. Some of the smaller children became fretful and were taken indoors to bed but Esme was still at an age to be conveniently portable so Mollie took her in to feed and change her then put her down in her pram outside so that she herself could join in the celebrations with her baby close by.

'Are you enjoying yourself, Syd?' Mollie asked her husband as they jogged around together in the road to the grainy sound of Fats Waller singing 'It's a Sin to Tell a Lie'. Her mother and gran were sitting on the wall by Esme's pram with some female neighbours peering in admiringly.

'Yeah, it's not a bad do,' approved Syd, a builder's labourer who had chestnut-brown wavy hair and gorgeous hazel eyes. Undeniably handsome, he had firm features and a good physique, all of which he was very well aware of.

'Better than just not bad I would say; the residents have done a really good job in organising it,' she said. 'I'm having a lovely time anyway.'

'You grew up in this street and you know everybody, that's why,' he said airily.

'So you're not enjoying it then.'

'Yeah, course I am,' he said, sounding bored. 'But maybe not quite as much as you are, having lived here all your life.'

'I don't know everybody. Only the close neighbours,' she said. 'That's why it's so good to have a do like this every once in a while because it brings the whole street together and reminds us that we are a community.'

'Mm.'

'Anyway, you are part of the neighbourhood now.' She and Syd were living with her family until they could afford to set up home in a place of their own. Their marriage had been swift and unexpected on account of Mollie being so smitten with Syd that she had found herself pregnant. It had been a major calamity at the time and her parents had been absolutely furious. But as Mollie – although deeply ashamed and full of remorse for upsetting them – hadn't been prepared to give up either her baby or Syd, a wedding had been arranged with all possible speed to avoid any scandal. 'So this is a good opportunity for you to feel part of things, isn't it?'

'Yeah, I suppose so,' he agreed.

'Don't overdo the enthusiasm,' she chided him.

He looked at her and smiled. 'Mollie. If we were all as keen about everything as you are, London would probably explode from an overload of enthusiasm.'

'I'm not over-keen about everything,' she said. 'You make me sound gormless.'

'That's the last thing you are,' he assured her. 'I just meant that you are very upbeat about life in general.'

'Why wouldn't I be when I have everything a girl could possibly want: a handsome husband and a beautiful baby daughter?' Her tone became more serious and a little emotional as she leaned back slightly and looked right into his eyes. 'Honestly Syd, I am so happy with our life together I could cry with the joy of it. You and me and Esme. I can't imagine ever wanting anything more.'

Seeming rather uncomfortable, he cleared his throat and drew back from her.

'There's no need to be so embarrassed about it,' she said affectionately. 'We are married, remember, so it's how I should feel and I'm not afraid to say so.'

'Yeah, yeah, I know,' he said just as the music came to an end and the dancing petered out.

Being a very warm and tactile girl, she put her arms around him impulsively and held him close.

He responded with a brief hug then said, 'I'm just going inside to answer a call of nature. Won't be long.'

'They'll put another record on in a minute so hurry back and we can dance some more,' she said warmly. 'I'll pop over to have a chat with Esme's fan club while you're away.'

'See you in a minute,' he said and strode towards the house while she headed for her mother and her cronies.

Having ascertained that Esme was sleeping through the rather noisy celebrations and that there was more than enough help on hand should she awaken, Mollie went to have a dance with her brother.

'No girlfriend tonight, Geoff,' she observed as they moved to the tune of 'Blue Moon'.

'There's nobody special at the moment.'

'Ooh, you need to put that right sharpish,' she said jokingly.

'There's no hurry,' said Geoff, who had velvet-brown eyes like Mollie's, despite their different hair colouring, and the same warm smile. An amiable man with a keen sense of humour, he was very well liked in the area.

'I'm sure someone special will turn up before long.' Her brother was popular with the opposite sex which wasn't surprising as he was boyishly handsome in an understated sort of way, unlike Syd who made the most of his dazzling good looks and was an avid user of the wardrobe mirror.

'We'll have to wait and see, won't we?' He smiled at her. 'Look at you though; an old married woman and still glowing like a newlywed.'

'I can't help it because it's the way I feel,' she told him. 'I was just telling Syd that I couldn't possibly be happier than I am now, with him and Esme.'

'He's a lucky man to have you.'

'As I am to have him,' she said, slightly on the defensive because Syd had been out of favour with the family for a while after what had happened, and she sensed that he still wasn't too popular with Geoff.

'As long as you're happy,' he said in a neutral tone.

'I know it seemed like a complete disaster when I got

pregnant and Mum and Dad were so angry about it, especially with Syd. I was none too pleased either at the time. But they were really supportive once they got used to the idea and I'm very grateful. As it happens, Syd and I were made for each other so it all turned out for the best anyway.'

He nodded.

'So how are your ambitions lately?' she asked because her brother wanted to make something of himself as a chef eventually and had a job in the kitchens of a large hotel in the West End of London. He'd started as a kitchen porter, washing up, peeling potatoes, cleaning and taking care of all chores and mundane food preparation. Nowadays he'd moved up a notch and helped the other chefs, followed recipes and created some of his own, prepared salads and was learning about working to a budget.

'Still very much alive and kicking,' he replied. 'Hard work and initiative are the key to success if you don't have money behind you and I'm giving the job plenty of both. Watch and learn is the head chef's advice and that's what I've been doing ever since my first day there. I'm working my way up and one day I'll have my own kitchen, Moll, maybe even a restaurant at some point.' He looked thoughtful and his attitude became serious. 'Of course I know that I'm lucky to have work of any sort. Plenty of men are on the dole, especially in other parts of the country.'

She nodded in agreement. 'How come you're not at work now? Hotels and restaurants in the West End will be busy tonight with the Jubilee celebrations.'

'I worked all over Easter so they let me have tonight off,' he told her.

'I'm blowed if I know where you get your ambitious streak from,' she said. 'It's certainly doesn't run in the family. Dad is happy driving a tube and Mum enjoys making a bit of pocket money from sewing at home, dressmaking and alterations. Both perfectly content with their lot.'

'We don't know that, do we?' he pointed out. 'They might have had all sorts of aspirations when they were younger but they had to have money coming in so they discarded them.'

'That's true.'

'It's all comes down to opportunity,' he said. 'Dad was unemployed and he had a family to support so getting a job as a tube driver probably felt like heaven to him at that time. He might have harboured all sorts of ambitions for all we know.'

Mollie laughed. 'Maybe Mum wanted to be a fashion designer,' she suggested lightly.

He smiled at the unlikely suggestion. 'We all have our dreams. At least mine are realistic. I want to do well at something I enjoy, which just happens to be cooking. I'd like to become known for creating interesting new dishes as well as delicious versions of the old favourites. Now is the time to go for it while I'm young and free. Once you get married and have kids, a decent wage packet every week is the only thing that matters. My pay is low at the hotel as I'm learning my craft but as I'm single I can manage, and I could earn good money later on as a head chef.'

'You certainly have a talent for it, judging by the meals you've produced for us at home,' she complimented him. He often took over from their mother in the kitchen on his day off. 'I don't have any special gifts that I know of.'

'I wouldn't say that. You had a real talent for games and gym at school,' he reminded her.

'Yeah, but all that finished when I left and is no use to me now,' she said. 'Still, all I want is to be a wife and mother so I'm quite happy as I am.'

'That's what girls are destined to be.'

'It's the way things are, I suppose, for people like us anyway,' she agreed. 'The men earn the money and the women look after the home and children. It seems to work.'

'It's just as well it is what you want because it's what you'd get anyway.'

'By the time you have kids you'll be a millionaire; is that the plan?' she asked.

'It isn't about money, you know me better than that,' he said. 'Though, of course, having a few quid in my pocket would be nice. I hope I can provide well for any nippers that might come along in the future, though I'm not planning on that being at any time soon.'

'Neither was I,' she said with a wry grin. 'It was the last thing I wanted at that time. These things happen and I'm very glad it did now because Esme means the world to me.'

'Steady on. I don't even have a girlfriend.'

'Don't mind me. I want my daughter to have a cousin of a similar age; someone for her to play with.'

'You can count me out on that one,' he smiled.

She nodded. 'Oh well, she's enough to keep the family happy for the moment.'

When the music ended she looked around. 'Syd is taking his time indoors. I can't see him anywhere.'

'He's probably having a crafty sit-down and I don't blame him either.'

She smiled. 'You men always stick together.'

'The pubs will be open by now,' Geoff reminded her. 'Perhaps he's slipped down to the local.'

'No, he wouldn't do that; not without asking me if I mind anyway.'

'He wouldn't be the first man to slope off for a quick one during a party. Dad's usually the first to go.'

'That's different. Mum and Dad have been married for donkey's years,' she reminded him. 'Syd and I are young and in love and he wouldn't have gone without telling me. So I'll pop indoors and hurry him up so that we can enjoy the rest of the party together.'

'Talk about love's young dream,' teased Geoff. 'The poor bloke doesn't stand a chance.'

Although Mollie knew that Syd was just being 'one of the boys' by leaving the party and heading off to the pub, she was feeling a little hurt when she came back outside, having failed to find her husband indoors.

'Why the long face?' her mother enquired.

'Syd isn't in the house so I suppose he must have gone to the pub,' she replied.

13

'Is that all?' said her mother lightly. 'You'd better get used to it, girl, because it's what men do. He's beaten your dad to it and not many people do that.'

'That's nothing to be proud of.'

'Cheer up, love,' urged Madge. 'He isn't doing any harm. I expect your father will be going down there soon. They don't stay long. Usually just have a quick one.'

'But why do they go at all when there is plenty to drink here?' asked Mollie.

'They enjoy the atmosphere of a pub,' suggested her grandmother. 'They like to get away from women and indulge in men's talk without having to watch their language. Your grandfather was just the same. Escaping from their wives is almost a sport with them.'

'But Syd is only twenty,' Mollie pointed out. 'That's what old married men do.'

'So, Syd has started early,' Madge put in with a wry grin. 'It's really nothing to worry about so stop fretting and enjoy the party.'

'You're right,' said Mollie, deciding that she was being far too sensitive and making a determined effort to cheer up. She didn't want to become a possessive wife.

The music didn't resume because the needle on the gramophone had broken so Gran, who was an accomplished pianist, was asked to step in and get cracking on the piano which had been brought outside earlier from one of the neighbouring houses.

Mollie sat on the front wall with Esme in the pram, listening to the music and singing along in a soft tone to 'Red Sails in the Sunset'. Her mother was over by the piano with Gran, shining a torch on the music for her. The weather was mild and the atmosphere warm, though darkness had now slipped over the festivities. Soon she would take Esme inside for the night but for now she was enjoying the atmosphere of the party in the neighbourhood of her birth, the soft amber glow of the street lights creating a feeling of homeliness which imbued her with a sense of belonging.

Her father had now disappeared, presumably in favour of the pub, and she knew she must be adult about Syd going there too. Part of her was pleased that he was with the men because it meant that he had been accepted by them, which had taken a while since he was a bit flashy for down-to-earth types like her father and brother.

But an immature part of her was niggled. They hadn't been married for more than a few months and naturally she relished every minute they had together, expecting him to do the same though she was beginning to suspect it might be different for men. Never mind, he'll be back soon, she reminded herself. Esme stirred so she wheeled the pram into the hall and lifted her out.

Although the houses in Pearl Road – which was a turning off Chiswick High Road – were tightly packed terraces, they were roomier than they looked from the outside with a good-sized bedroom in the attic and a bathroom recently built on at the back beyond the kitchen. All were rented out by the same landlord at reasonable rents for working-class people; there were two reception rooms downstairs, one of which was the best sitting room at the front. Mollie and Syd had her old bedroom, Geoff was in the attic and Gran had the room next to Mollie's parents.

Mollie had just put Esme down in her cot when she heard some movement downstairs; the noise outside seemed to have abated too. It looked as if the party was winding down and the others had come in. She could hear male voices so guessed that the men were back. Expecting Syd to bound up the stairs at any minute she was pleased when she heard someone coming.

'Is everything all right up here, dear?' asked her mother in a whisper with respect to the sleeping baby.

'Yeah fine. I've just put her down after her feed,' she said, disappointed not to see Syd.

'Are you coming downstairs then? You can leave the bedroom door open so you'll hear her if she cries. I'm just going to make some cocoa.'

'I'll be down in a few minutes, Mum,' she said. 'Meanwhile can you ask Syd to come up please?'

'He isn't down there.'

'Not down there,' she said, puzzled. 'But I thought I heard men's voices.'

'That's your dad and Geoff.'

'Where's Syd then?'

'I've no idea,' her mother replied, unconcerned. 'Probably outside in the street. There are still quite a few people out there talking. Come downstairs and have some cocoa.'

Leaving the door open slightly, Mollie followed her mother down the stairs.

'Did Syd come back with you, Dad?' asked Mollie, having been outside and seen no sign of her other half.

'No, Moll, he didn't,' replied Len, a man of stocky build with brown hair greying at the edges.

'He stayed in the pub then, I suppose.'

'He wasn't in there,' said her father.

'What, not at all?'

'I didn't see him.'

'Where is he then?'

'He must have gone to one of the others,' suggested Len casually. 'We're not short of pubs round here.'

Now Mollie really was upset and worried. 'He's been gone for ages,' she said miserably.

'He'll have got talking somewhere, I expect,' decided her father 'You know how it is when there are celebrations going on. People lose track of the time. Are you sure he isn't outside?'

'Positive,' she replied, her voice high and anxious. 'Something awful must have happened to him. He wouldn't have just gone off somewhere.'

'Go and find him, Len, and put the girl's mind at rest,' suggested Madge.

Len emitted an eloquent sigh. 'The man will come home when he's ready,' he stated impatiently. 'He doesn't need a search party out looking for him.' He caught his

17

wife's commanding look. 'But I'll go and look for him anyway, just to please Mollie.'

'And come straight back,' said his wife. 'No staying till closing time.'

'As if I would,' he said with a wicked grin.

Mollie had only taken a sip of her cocoa when the demanding sound of Esme in full voice wafted down the stairs.

'I'll finish my drink later,' she said to her mother and hurried up the stairs.

She had just finished feeding her daughter and was sitting on the edge of the bed giving her a cuddle when she noticed something on her pillow, a folded piece of paper, the same colour as the white bed linen which was why she hadn't noticed it before. Intrigued, she put Esme on to her shoulder, unfolded the note and read the scribbled writing.

Sorry to let you down, Mollie, but I have to leave and by the time you read this I'll be well on my way. Marriage just isn't for me. I've tried hard but I just can't do it anymore. I'm too young to be tied down with a wife and child. It's nothing personal to you, I promise; just bad timing for me. I'm moving away from the area so there's no point in your trying to find me. I've left a few shillings which should keep you going for a while and I'll send more money when I can. Take care of yourself. Syd

This couldn't be real. Syd wouldn't leave her. They were in love; newlyweds, a happily married couple. Then she saw two half-crowns on the pillow and the awful reality of the situation began to register; creeping through her body, a deep and all-consuming emotional ache.

'Your cocoa is getting cold so I've brought it up,' said her mother, coming into the room and seeing her daughter sitting motionless on the bed holding her baby. 'Whatever is the matter, Moll? You're as white as a sheet.'

Mollie handed her the note.

'We'll soon see about this,' boomed her father, having returned from his search and been presented with the note, the family assembled in the living room. 'Doesn't want to be married indeed. Bloody cheek! How dare he walk out on my daughter? Too young to be tied down. He should have thought of that when he got her in trouble. Well he won't know what's hit him when I get my hands on him. Come on, Geoff, let's go after him.'

'Calm down, Len,' said his wife, clamping a restraining hand on his arm. 'Violence never solved anything.'

'He's gone anyway,' said Mollie in a dull tone; she was perched stiffly on the edge of an armchair near the hearth. 'Left the area, so he says, so you won't find him.'

Had Mollie been older and more experienced she might have handled this differently, rather than have the family take over and upset her even more by criticising Syd. But she was hurting so badly she didn't have the strength to take control.

'He couldn't have moved away already; he would have to have somewhere to go.' Her father thought this over. 'Not unless he planned it, of course . . .'

Mollie thought she would choke as the possibility of this registered; the thought that her beloved Syd had been planning to leave her while she had been head over heels in love and showering him with it.

'How could he bear to leave his little daughter?' she said, almost to herself.

'The man is no good, that's how,' stated her father, far too angry to choose his words. 'That's the answer to that. I always knew he was a wrong 'un.'

'All right, Dad,' said Geoff, seeing his sister wince at the criticism and feeling her pain. 'There's no point in ripping him apart. That won't solve anything.'

'He's gone to get away from me,' said Mollie, her voice distorted by emotion. 'Not because he's a bad person. So it's all my own fault.'

'Don't get daft ideas like that, dear,' said her grand-mother, sitting on the arm of the chair and putting her hand on Mollie's shoulder. 'Of course it isn't your fault.'

'He doesn't want to be with me, Gran,' said Mollie, stricken with a lacerating feeling of rejection. 'And I thought we were so happy. All the while he didn't want to be there.' She clutched her head. 'How could I have been so stupid?'

'There is nothing stupid about you,' said her brother, going over to her. 'You are a very bright girl.'

'So bright I can't even keep my husband.'

'Syd is selfish and immature and he can't cope with

20

the responsibility of marriage and fatherhood,' said Geoff. 'It isn't you he wants to get away from; it's being married. That's what it seems like to me anyway.'

'If he really loved me he would have stayed and tried harder to get used to it,' she said.

The undeniable truth of her statement produced a painful silence then Nora eased the tension by saying, 'Things aren't always quite as cut and dried as that, dear. Syd might be regretting his actions as we speak. Just because he doesn't feel up to the job of being a husband and father, it doesn't mean his feelings for you have changed.'

But they all knew these were just empty words.

'All this talk about love,' exploded Len. 'Marriage is a commitment; it's about pulling together and putting each other first. You don't run away when it's hard going.'

'Why was being married to me hard going?' asked Mollie, genuinely puzzled.

'It wasn't,' said her mother quickly. 'Some men find being married to anyone difficult.'

'He'll know what difficult is when I get my hands on him,' declared Len.

'Come on, Dad. Let's go round to his parents' place and see if his folks know anything about it,' suggested Geoff because he guessed his father was making Mollie feel worse while he was so angry and lashing out.

Somewhere beneath the weight of pain and rejection, a flicker of spirit stirred within Mollie. 'No, don't do that,' she said. 'I don't want to be with someone who doesn't want to be with me so let him go and do what he wants.'

'But what about his responsibilities?' asked her father.

'He's left some money and says he'll send more when he can,' said Mollie.

'Huh, I'll believe that when I see it,' Len exploded.

'If he doesn't send anything, I'll manage somehow, Dad,' she assured him. 'I'll earn money if I have to.'

'You shouldn't have to worry about those things,' seethed her father. 'That's supposed to be his job. Ooh, wait until I get my hands on him.'

'You and I are going for a walk, Dad,' intervened Geoff, putting a firm hand on his father's arm. 'You need to calm down.'

'Don't drag him out on my account,' said Mollie, needing to be alone suddenly. 'I'm going to bed anyway.'

Her mother looked worried by this. 'You don't want to be up there on your own,' she said.

'That's exactly what I do want right now, Mum,' she assured her. 'Don't worry about me. I'll be all right. Anyway I won't be on my own. Esme will be with me.'

'She's just a baby,' said Madge. 'She can't help.'

'Oh, I think she can.' She stood up, feeling shaky but managing to hold herself together. 'Goodnight everyone. We'll talk about it tomorrow.'

And she left the room and made her way upstairs.

'You don't think he's gone off with another girl, do you, Mum?' said Madge to Nora when they were in the kitchen clearing up. 'He's a good-looking boy; he probably gets plenty of offers.'

'Don't let Len hear you say that, for Gawd's sake,' warned Nora. 'The mere idea of that will send him off on another tirade.'

'Yeah, I know. I was praying he didn't think of it himself and upset Mollie even more by saying so.'

'Well, according to the note there's nothing like that involved,' said Nora. 'But he could have just been trying to soften the blow, I suppose.'

'Still, the reason isn't as important as the fact that it has happened,' said Madge, whose maternal empathy was in full flow and extremely painful.

'Exactly. We'll have to concentrate on doing what we can to help Mollie get through it,' said Nora. 'No one can stop her hurting and we're going to have to go easy on the sympathy or damage her pride even more. But plenty of support is definitely needed.'

'Not half,' agreed Madge.

Mollie lay in the big double bed staring at the lacy pattern on the ceiling made by the street light shining through the net curtains from a gap in the drapes. She was consumed by images of Syd: his smile, his lovely eyes, his strong hands, the way she felt when he touched her. Not being with him and knowing she wouldn't be at any time in the future was a physical pain, as though she had been bruised inside. She loved him so much and his leaving her hadn't changed that.

She turned on to her side, pulled the covers over her head and sobbed. She was soon joined by Esme, who wanted feeding and let her mother know in the only way she could. Mollie lifted her out of her cradle, took her into the bed and put her to her breast. 'It's just you and me now darlin'', she said in a whisper. 'Daddy won't be coming home.'

Mollie was in pieces; broken by Syd's betrayal and almost unable to function. She vowed that she would never allow herself to become this vulnerable again over a man. It wasn't in her to be cynical and, in retrospect, she could see that she had never held back. Her behaviour had been dictated by the strength of her feelings for him and he had obviously found it overpowering. The humiliation of this realisation was awful.

But somehow she knew that, no matter how low and terrible she felt, she would keep going for her daughter who was her purpose in life now.

One of the good things about being a Londoner, thought Syd Fisher, as he undressed for bed that night, was the ease with which you could disappear without going very far. All you had to do was move to another neighbourhood on a different bus route and tube line and no one from your original area would ever see you. You just became one of the crowd.

Nobody from Chiswick was ever likely to come to North London. They would have no reason to so he could get on with his single life without interference from the past. He turned the light off and got into bed, glad to be rid of the sight of the room which was worse than shabby and in a dilapidated and smelly boarding house on the outskirts of Tottenham, the best he could do without notice.

He didn't feel good about leaving Mollie. She was a great girl and he supposed he had loved her once in that he couldn't get enough of her, if that was what love was. In fact he had been besotted until everything had changed. His ardour had dampened when the pregnancy had become dominant and disappeared altogether when Esme arrived.

As passion killers went a baby was at the top of the list for him. As far as he could see there were no benefits to be had from being a father since all the child did was demand attention and generally rule the roost. Their lives revolved around her. And as for the breast-feeding; he could hardly bear to look when Mollie was doing that which seemed to be practically all the time. It turned his stomach as did the baby sick and the awful smells which didn't seem to offend Mollie in the least.

Anyway, he decided that there was no need for him to spoil his freedom by feeling bad about leaving because he had done the right thing by Mollie when she got pregnant; he had married her and saved her reputation. A deserted wife might be the subject of gossip for a short time but didn't even come close to an unmarried mother in terms of scandal. That stigma really would have been hard for her to take. So he wasn't going to allow conscience to bother him for a second. After all, it wasn't as though Esme had come about as a consequence of rape. Mollie had been as keen to do the deed as he was if his memory served him correctly.

The burden of married life and the responsibility of fatherhood had been suffocating him and holding him back so he'd had to get out. Of course, he hadn't planned to do it in the middle of a party but seeing Mollie adoring him so obviously when they'd been dancing had made him feel trapped and fraught with panic so strong he had left on the spur of the moment, throwing a few clothes into a bag and leaving through the back gate and hurrying unseen down the alley. It wouldn't have been fair to Mollie to stay and let her get even fonder of him.

Now that his mission was actually accomplished he could think about the future and his plans to get out of the building trade. Things were changing in some parts around the London area and with manufacturing in the new industries booming there were fresh opportunities to be had for someone like him with plenty of savvy and the gift of the gab. Sales was the thing to get into and, now unencumbered by responsibility, he planned to find out how to do it. Tomorrow he would start a new life.

Chapter Two

'Oh, not again, Cora,' groaned Grant Parker with a pained expression, over dinner at their house one evening in June. 'What happened to cause it this time?'

'I have absolutely no idea,' replied his wife haughtily; they were seated at the dining table by the bay window overlooking the Thames in Chiswick Mall. 'The wretched woman went off in a huff for no reason at all and said she won't be coming back, ever, and her husband will be round to collect the wages we owe her.'

'She wouldn't have stormed out for no reason, dear. So, what did you do to upset her?'

'Absolutely nothing,' she stated categorically.

'You must have said or done something to offend her,' said Grant, who knew how vicious his wife could be when she was in a bad temper. 'People don't just walk out of a job unless there is a good reason, because they need the money.'

'They are so damned sensitive, these domestic workers,' she ranted. 'Why can't they realise that I pay their wages

27

so they do what I tell them without question? If I say the floor polishing isn't up to scratch and needs doing again with more elbow grease she should have done it without any sort of fuss. But oh no, she gave me a load of cheek then stormed off without finishing her work. She didn't even clean upstairs and I had to prepare the vegetables for our dinner myself.'

'Well doing the vegetables isn't too much of a hardship, is it?' he suggested.

A tall, shapely woman of twenty-four with mid-brown hair worn shoulder-length and immaculately waved, her vivid grey eyes were bright with temper. 'That remark is typical of you,' she said. 'Why do you never take my side?'

'Because every domestic help we've ever had leaves on bad terms with you and the agency will no longer deal with us because of your attitude towards them, so what else am I to think but that you upset her?'

'I suppose you'd be happy if I set to and looked after the housework myself.'

He shrugged. 'I certainly don't think it would do you any harm but I'm quite happy to pay for someone to do it if you can find anyone you can get along with.'

'A man in your position allowing his wife to do her own housework, wouldn't that be embarrassing for you?'

He looked at her with a serious expression. 'Surely you know me better than that, Cora.'

Didn't she just? Twenty-five years old with brilliant dark eyes and curly black hair, her husband was his own man and well known for what people called his good nature but she saw as weakness. A partner and the managing director of a successful department store in Chiswick High Road, which his father had started as a bric-a-brac market stall before Grant was born, he made a point of being on friendly terms with the staff and insisted on being told if anyone was ill or in trouble. If they were really short-staffed he would get behind the counter and serve customers himself. The whole thing was ridiculous in her opinion and probably the fault of her father-in-law, who also treated the staff like equals and had apparently made Grant work for a spell in every department, including the warehouse, before taking him into the business as a partner.

'Unfortunately, yes I do,' she said now. 'And it's all very well your being down-to-earth and a man of the people but you have a position to uphold and you don't take enough advantage of it.'

'To hear you talk anyone would think we were part of some sort of upper class,' he pointed out.

'We are well off.'

'Comfortable is how I prefer to put it and the reason we are is because of hard work and initiative on my father's part all those years ago.' Herself the daughter of a self-made man, Cora was used to the good things in life and demanded nothing less. Her father had turned his craft of cobbling into shoemaking before she was born and had built a successful business; now he had a large factory and workforce making shoes sold in shops all over the country.

'Maybe but you do your share now to keep the firm running successfully,' she pointed out.

'Yes but it was all set up for me. You and I are both extremely fortunate to come from such enterprising stock.' Grant's beloved mother had died of pneumonia when he was just eight years old and he was still very close to his father who had raised him. Grant held him in high esteem. His rules for life were simple: do your best and respect others less able to make their way. 'It certainly doesn't give us the right to ride roughshod over people.'

'So you're saying that I treat these women who come to clean for me badly.'

'You may not mean to,' he said, softening the truth with a little diplomacy. 'But I can't think of any other reason why every single one of them leaves on bad terms with you. After all, they must need the money to be doing the job at all so wouldn't walk out unless they were seriously upset.'

'I have to tell them if I'm not pleased about something, surely you can see that,' she said.

'Of course but there are ways of doing these things.'

'And I'm so ignorant I don't know how to do it. Is that what you are suggesting?'

He sighed. 'Of course not. Whatever else you are, you are certainly not ignorant.' Actually, although he'd been married to her for four years, she still often felt like a stranger to him. He had certainly never felt close to her as a husband should. There was a harshness about her that he didn't seem able to break down no matter how hard he tried. She had no friends, almost no contact with her family and seemed to be permanently angry

30

with the world in general. Fortunately he was able to provide her with a good standard of living and knew that she wouldn't have married him if she hadn't been absolutely certain of that. They had this lovely house and she could have whatever she wanted in the way of furnishings, clothes and jewellery, which would surely make most women happy.

But it was obvious that she wasn't and he was beginning to think that it was beyond him to make her so. The only living thing that did seem to please her was her pet poodle Peaches and she absolutely adored her. 'You just seem to get so cross about things and this could affect your attitude when dealing with people.'

'Is it any wonder that I get angry when I have slipshod workers to cope with,' she blasted. 'I really wish you would take my side occasionally.'

Wondering if perhaps he was being a little too hard on her he said, 'Would you like me to put an advert in the local paper for a daily help?'

'Yes please,' she said, brightening. 'And I'll put a few cards around in some of the shops in the High Road. That way we should get some sort of a response.'

He wanted to suggest that she tried to hang on to any future staff by being more considerate towards people in general but now wasn't the time; not while she was so fired up. He'd have to try and get her to change her attitude at some point though or they would be having this same conversation all over again in a couple of months' time. These quarrels with the cleaners happened far too regularly.

Sometimes he felt as though he'd been closer to his wife when they were courting than he was now, and he had certainly been happier then. She'd been good company in those days and seemed keen on him. They had met through their fathers who were both members of a businessmen's association. Grant had gone to a function with his dad and she was there with her parents who had made no secret of their pleasure at seeing him and Cora getting on so well. He'd had no real objection to being set up; that was how these things were often done among families of similar circumstance and she'd seemed like a nice girl.

Cora wasn't exactly beautiful but she was very attractive with her smoky grey eyes and curvaceous figure. They'd got on well so had courted and an engagement and marriage had followed quite soon as a matter of course. They had no reason to wait. It wasn't as though money was a problem.

Her enthusiasm for him had faded soon after the wedding and he realised early on that she wasn't in love with him. In the cold light of everyday life there was no magic for him either by that time, but they were married for better or worse so they carried on without ever discussing the situation. He wondered if perhaps it might be like this for other married couples after a while, a kind of domestic partnership with sex, though she made it abundantly clear that the latter was merely endured by her so the occasions were few and far between.

Still, somehow, they managed to co-exist and he had no plans to change anything. He did need to get that advert in the paper though. She would be absolutely unbearable without someone to clean for her.

Later that same evening Cora walked by the river with her beloved white poodle Peaches. The weather was fine and the air soft with early summer, the river tinted olive green in places by the setting sun and gently lapping as the tide began to ebb revealing the muddy river bed.

This was one of her greatest pleasures in life: walking with her dog on her own, which couldn't be right. Surely her happiness should lie in being with her husband. But it didn't. Grant never suggested coming with her when she took the dog out; as though he sensed she didn't want him along. He was considerate like that; seemed to know that she needed her own time.

He was a good man and she respected him; was even rather fond of him. She wondered if she might have actually fallen in love with him if she had been given time to let things develop naturally. But she had been desperate to leave home and the only way to do that was through marriage so she had used her feminine charms to hurry things along. Her parents had wanted her off their hands too and made no secret of it; they had never enjoyed having her around. She'd been born late in their lives when another child was the last thing they wanted so she had always been the nuisance of the family, unlike her older sister whom they adored and who could do no wrong in their eyes.

Maybe jealousy had made her bad-tempered. She had

no idea; she only knew that she had been like it as far back as she could remember; tetchy and prone to spitefulness. Now she rarely saw the family. She'd done what they wanted and got married so she stayed away and guessed that that suited them.

As she entered the verdant sweep of Duke's Meadows, she let Peaches off the lead and turned her mind to her husband. He should be a very easy man to fall in love with. All the right ingredients were there: he was good-looking, articulate, strong and rich. She guessed that she was envied by other women for managing to bag him but he didn't have that special something for her. She wasn't sure what it was she thought she should be feeling because she had yet to experience it but she knew she would never feel it for him. Still, she had a comfortable life with him and she valued that so she would continue to make the best of things.

Loneliness was a problem for her though because Grant was very absorbed in his business and involved with several charities, so out quite a lot. What she really needed was a female friend but there was little opportunity for her to meet new people. The neighbours were all much older and the women of her age she saw around the town all had babies or young children. They were in their cliques out walking with their prams in the afternoons. She wasn't good at making friends anyway; she'd never seemed to come across anyone with whom she'd felt a connection.

She knew she lacked warmth but it was something that couldn't be manufactured. Even if she did meet the requirements by getting pregnant she probably wouldn't fit in with the other mums. If being the operative word. Four years and still no babies, which wasn't surprising as she and Grant hardly ever did the deed. Her fault, not his. She really didn't like it so avoided it whenever possible.

The subject of sex was strictly taboo but she had read somewhere that some women could be frigid and guessed that must be her problem. It felt like a stigma even though no one else knew about it. There was no solution that she knew of so when she simply couldn't get out of it she faked it and tried to make the occasions as infrequent as possible.

She guessed that Grant was disappointed with that side of their life together and she knew he would like a family. But he hadn't made an issue of it; that wasn't his way.

It would be nice to have some female company of a similar age, though, to have some girl talk. Grant had mates who he saw regularly and of course he was very close to his father. Still, she had Peaches and that helped. She smiled at her pet trotting along sniffing at every blade of grass or weed and yapping at the ubiquitous pigeons and any other dogs they happened to pass. She sat down on a bench near the empty bandstand for a while, watching the river shining through a gap in the trees, then put the dog back on the lead and set off for home.

They were still a good distance from the house when Peaches sat down in front of her, looking up pleadingly.

'No, I am not carrying you the rest of the way,' she said. 'You're a full-grown dog, not a baby.'

Her round black eyes stared at Cora and she stayed put where she was. The dog was very pretty; almost doll-like, and practically irresistible.

'Come on now, Peaches,' she said, struggling to stay firm. 'I am not falling for it this time.'

But the animal refused to move. So with a tut and a sigh she picked her up and headed home. 'It's a good job you are only little or I wouldn't be able to carry you and you'd have to walk,' Cora went on. 'You must be the laziest dog in London.'

She knew it would be wise to put the dog down before they reached the house or risk a lot of ribbing from Grant about the way she pampered her pet. Grant thought it was ludicrous and wrong for her to carry Peaches when she'd taken her out for the exercise. Although she might not admit it, she knew it too. It wasn't natural. But the little dog was spoiled and Cora couldn't refuse her anything.

The awesome responsibility of bringing up a child without the support of a husband was something that Mollie took very seriously and it proved to be her salvation in that it motivated her to rise above the leaden inertia caused by her broken heart.

Just a few days after Syd left she was out looking for a job because she had no intention of sponging on the family, and Syd couldn't be relied on to provide. A man who could walk out on his wife and daughter without warning certainly couldn't be trusted to offer them any sort of support in the future.

Finding a job proved to be difficult. Married women, it seemed, were unemployable, especially ones with a child. Even the firm which had employed her as a clerk before she got married had turned her away because it wasn't their policy to employ women of the married kind.

As a result she had been forced to turn to employment of a different sort, which actually suited her better because of the hours. She worked from five thirty in the morning until eight o'clock cleaning local shops; this meant she got to spend most of the day with her daughter though Mum and Gran were willing to have her for longer if she could get more hours, which she really needed because her current earnings wouldn't be enough when the five shillings from Syd ran out.

The work was physically demanding because there were large areas of floor to be scrubbed but she was young and fit so it wasn't a problem for her though her knees got sore sometimes.

'I'll have housemaid's knee if I carry on with this sort of work for too long,' she said jokingly one day in July when she got home and was giving her daughter a cuddle and having a cup of tea with her mother.

'You will and all. It isn't right that you have to go out cleaning, especially so early in the morning,' said Madge sympathetically. 'And you wouldn't have to if that wretched Syd had done his job properly.'

'There's no point in harking back to that,' said Mollie, who still didn't like people to speak ill of her husband even though she knew in her heart that he deserved it. Two months on from his departure and he was still on her mind for most of the time; she still longed to be with him but hated him too and found it hard to believe that she had meant so little to him. At the time it had felt as though she was the world to him as he was to her. 'It's good honest work and the only kind I can get so I have to get on with it. Anyway, it isn't so bad, Mum. It's very good exercise and I like the idea of getting it over early and having the rest of the day to myself, though I need to find some more cleaning jobs. The money I get at the moment isn't enough.'

'You'll be worn out, especially as you still have to get up in the night to Esme.'

'I'm nineteen, Mum,' she reminded her, 'and very healthy. Anyway, I won't always have to get up in the night to Madam here.' She was holding her daughter, now a chubby three month old who could smile and gurgle and be awake for a while without crying. Mollie plonked a kiss on her head.

'I know all that, dear.' It broke Madge's heart to see her daughter struggling to make ends meet and she was sure she was still pining for that rat who had let her down so cruelly. She was so damned independent too. Madge and Len had told her on several occasions that there was no hurry for her to find work but she was out there right after Syd left trying to get fixed up.

'I'm lucky because I have such marvellous family

support,' she said. 'A lot of women in my position don't have a mum and gran on hand for babysitting.'

'We're only too happy to help.'

'Where is Gran anyway?' asked Mollie.

'She's nipped down to the paper shop,' replied Madge.

'Oh, doesn't she usually get the paper when we go out shopping?' A trip to the High Road together to get food was a regular daily ritual for all the women.

'Yeah, she does, but for some reason she wanted to go early today; she didn't say why.'

Just then Nora came in clutching the newspaper and seeming pleased about something.

'We were just wondering why you were so keen to go to the paper shop so early,' said Madge.

'I saw a card in the window after the shop had closed yesterday. It said "apply for details within" and I wanted to get there early in case someone else saw it and snapped the job up. That's why I didn't say anything.' She handed Mollie a piece of paper. 'They wrote the particulars down for me. I thought it might be better for you than shop cleaning, dear. You wouldn't have to go out so early in the morning.'

Mollie cast her eye over the paper. '"Daily help required. Pleasant house by the river. Congenial surroundings. Four days a week. Hours to be arranged."'

'Mm, it might be worth a try,' she said. 'I'll go round there later on. The address is here and it says call at the house between eleven and twelve weekdays.'

'Good for you,' said her mother, looking at the paper

and noting the address. 'As your gran says it will be nicer than shop cleaning. Chiswick Mall eh! It's lovely round there. Classy too.'

'What's this, Gran,' said Mollie, reading something else written on the piece of paper. '"Keep-fit class for women of all ages and sizes. Make new friends while keeping fit and healthy. St Mary's Church Hall Wednesday mornings Eleven to twelve. Fourpence a session."'

'Oh yeah, I saw that too and thought that would be perfect for you,' explained Nora. 'You're very good at that sort of thing so I thought you would enjoy it.'

'But I'm looking for work, not fun, Gran,' Mollie reminded her. 'I can't afford luxuries.'

'It would be my treat.'

'Absolutely not,' said Mollie. 'Do you really think I would let you do that?'

'It's fourpence a week dear; hardly a fortune,' Nora pointed out. 'Your grandfather left me with a bit of insurance money and I'm sure he would want me to treat you every now and again.'

'It's a lovely thought and I really appreciate it, Gran,' said Mollie, 'but work is my priority at the moment. If I did happen to get this job I'd be working at that time.'

'You know what they say about all work and no play . . .' said Nora.

'They also say "needs must when the devil drives".'

'Fair enough,' said the older woman. 'But if you do get the chance and you fancy an hour off once a week, the offer will stay open.'

'Thanks, Gran, and thanks for getting the job details for me, you're a love.'

'I have my uses,' said Nora, beaming.

It was certainly in a lovely spot, thought Mollie, as she approached the large, elegant white house with black gables and latticed windows . Only a fifteen-minute walk from home too. It would be a nice place to work in even if it was charring. But she mustn't get her hopes up because there would probably be strong competition for a job like this; much more competitive than shop cleaning with its unsocial hours.

She lifted the heavy knocker and it fell with a dull thud.

The woman who answered the door was much younger than Mollie had expected and looked to be in her mid-twenties. Mollie had assumed that the residents of this salubrious part of town would be getting on in years before they could afford this sort of accommodation. So this must be the daughter of the house.

'Good morning. I've come to see Mrs Parker,' she announced with a hesitant smile.

'I'm Mrs Parker.' She was tall and fashionably dressed in a smart grey day dress and carrying a small white poodle.

'Oh. I'm here about the job,' explained Mollie. 'My grandmother saw a card in a shop window in the High Road.' When the woman stared without replying, Mollie added, 'Is the position still available?'

She nodded. 'Come in,' she invited.

★   ★   ★

Quite early on in the interview, Mollie wondered if she actually wanted this job, should it be offered to her. The house would be lovely to work in, being so elegant and spacious, but Mrs Parker was conspicuously snooty and Mollie wasn't sure if she could cope with that for long without exploding.

'So what about you?' asked Mrs Parker when she had given her a rough idea of what the job entailed and taken Mollie's name and address. 'What attracts you to domestic work?'

'Necessity. There are very few jobs for married women in the traditional workplace,' she replied with determined candour. 'And the part-time hours suit me because I have a baby.'

Up went Cora's brows. 'Oh. I am looking for someone reliable,' she said in a tone of obvious disapproval.

'If you are implying that I won't be reliable because I have a baby, and yes they are unpredictable so I can understand your concern, I can assure you that I have very good help at home,' she explained. 'My mother and grandmother look after my daughter and they take over when it's time for me to go to work.'

'Go to work; so are you already in employment?'

'Yes I do shop cleaning first thing.'

'Oh, and are you planning on giving that up if you come to work for me?'

Mollie met her gaze steadily. 'Not necessarily,' she said. 'It would depend on the hours here. I have finished at the shops by eight o'clock.'

'The hours here are nine till twelve four days a week,' Cora explained.

'That would work out very well then,' said Mollie. 'I can fit them both in.'

'Hmm.' The other woman mulled this over. 'I wouldn't want someone coming to clean for me who is already too exhausted to give of their best.'

'I'm nineteen, Mrs Parker, and as such I have plenty of energy. I need both jobs to make ends meet.'

'What about your husband?'

Mollie gave her a dark look. 'I don't see how my husband is relevant to this interview.'

'Oh.' Cora was clearly surprised at Mollie's temerity. 'No, he isn't, I suppose. I was just taking an interest.'

'He walked out on me if you must know,' she blurted out. 'Which is why I have to go out cleaning other people's houses instead of looking forward to a house of my own.'

'I see.'

Suddenly the other woman's attitude throughout the entire interview triggered Mollie's fury. 'Look, I'll be straight with you, Mrs Parker,' she burst out spontaneously. 'I need this job but if something ever came up that meant my baby needed me at home then that's where I'd be. There would be no contest. Also I cannot absolutely guarantee that I will never feel a bit tired when I'm on duty here because I am a human being and not a machine. And just one last point, doing domestic work does not make me any the less intelligent or worthy than you which is the impression your attitude is giving me.' Her cheeks were burning from the outburst but she was surprisingly calm even though she'd ruined her chances of getting the job. 'So having got that off my chest I'll be on my way.'

'Yes, I think you had better,' Cora said stiffly and rose and led the way to the front door, scowling.

'Thank you for seeing me,' said Mollie with icy politeness before leaving and striding out along the garden path.

Well, the bare-faced cheek of the woman, thought Cora, watching Mollie walk away, head held high and shoulders back. What was the world coming to when a servant had the audacity to speak to a potential employer in such a way?

There was something about her, though, that Cora couldn't help admiring, even envying. The frock she was wearing looked as though it had been laundered more times than was good for it, her dark hair was unstyled and hanging casually around her shoulders and there wasn't so much as a smidgeon of cosmetics on her face but she still managed to look beautiful. So self-assured too. She wasn't slow in speaking up for herself.

It was odd because she appeared to have nothing: no money, prospects or a husband. But seeing her march away, she seemed to have everything and Cora had no idea why. Oh well, she mused, let's hope things go better with the other candidates.

★   ★   ★

It was Geoff's day off and he had made the evening meal for the family: a traditional meat pie with vegetables and gravy followed by a jam sponge and custard.

'It's a wonder you're not fed up with cooking, working in a kitchen,' said Mollie who had put the baby to bed so was able to have her meal in peace.

'I sometimes get a bit bored with doing the donkey work, preparing the vegetables and weighing up the ingredients and general duties but I never get tired of the actual cooking. Making meals for you lot is good practice for me and I really enjoy it,' he said.

'I'm not complaining because I get a holiday,' his mother remarked.

'You've certainly got the gift, Geoff,' said Mollie. 'This sponge just melts in the mouth.'

'So my sponges don't then,' said Madge.

'Sorry Mum, I didn't mean . . .'

'Just kidding,' laughed Madge.

'So tell us more about your job interview,' urged Geoff with interest.

'There's nothing much else to say really,' said Mollie, who had already given them a brief outline of events. 'The woman was very uppish with me and I lost my rag and that was that. I couldn't work for someone who is looking down their nose at me all the time. I know we have to take what comes if they are paying your wages but there is no need for that sort of attitude. At least with shop cleaning, you are left to get on with it with no one breathing down your neck. You do your job and get paid and that's that.'

'Some old hag was she?' Geoff assumed.

'No, she isn't a great deal older than me; early to mid-twenties I'd say and smart and well turned out but a real dragon,' Mollie told him. 'I didn't even stay long enough to find out what the rates of pay were. Silly of me really as I need the job. I suppose I should have held my tongue.'

'Something else will turn up,' said Nora. 'We'll keep an eye on the local paper and noticeboards.'

'You're not so desperate you need to work for someone who will make you miserable,' put in her father. 'You make enough to pay your way by doing the shop cleaning.'

'Only just, Dad,' she said. 'But I'll need to get clothes for Esme soon and that will be something I'll have to budget for regularly so I do need more hours. Still. I'll keep looking. Meanwhile is there any more sponge going?'

'Yeah, help yourself,' said her mother.

A knock at the door interrupted the conversation.

'I'll go,' offered Geoff. 'Don't eat all the sponge while I'm gone though.'

'You'd better be quick then,' said Mollie, teasing him.

'I'll save you a bit,' said Madge.

Mollie was just pouring some custard on to her sponge when her brother re-entered the room.

'Someone to see you, Mollie,' he said. 'It's Mrs Parker. I've shown her into the front room.'

'Blimey,' said Mollie and headed for the door.

'Sorry to disturb you while you're eating,' said Cora, perched rather stiffly on the edge of an armchair near to the piano. Net curtains adorned the windows and, this being the barely used best room, there was a three-piece suite and carpet with polished lino around the edges.

'That's all right,' said Mollie politely, puzzled by the visit and slightly unnerved by it. 'Is something wrong? Did I leave anything at your place this morning?'

'No, nothing like that.' Cora paused; it wasn't easy for her to climb down from the high ground. 'I was, er, just wondering if . . . that is, I have just come round to tell you that the job is yours if you want it.'

'Oh,' said Mollie, astounded.

'So, do you want it?'

'Well no, not really,' she said bluntly.

Cora was infuriated by her attitude but not surprised by it. 'I thought you were looking for a job,' she said.

'I am, obviously, or I wouldn't have applied,' Mollie confirmed. 'But it was clear to me this morning that you and I wouldn't get along so my working for you would be a disaster.'

'Perhaps I was a little er . . .'

'Arrogant,' Mollie finished for her.

'Was I that bad?'

'I thought so,' said Mollie.

She made a face. 'It's just my way,' she tried to explain.

'And my way is not to accept that kind of treatment,' Mollie informed her. 'So, as much as I need that job I really must decline.' She moved towards the door. 'But thank you for coming round anyway. I hope you find someone suitable soon.'

Cora stood up but she made no move to leave. 'Are you going to make me grovel?' she blurted out. 'Isn't it enough that I came round here?'

'I'm not sure I know what you mean,' said Mollie. 'Are you playing some sort of game?'

'Not at all.'

'So why . . . I mean you must have had plenty of applicants for the job.'

'Yes, I've had quite a few,' Cora said. 'But I want you to come and work for me.'

This was very peculiar indeed and Mollie wasn't certain that she liked it. 'Why me exactly?'

'I'm not entirely sure myself but maybe it's because you are in a similar age group to me and it will be nice to have someone young around the house. All the other ladies who applied were a good bit older.'

'It seems very strange to me; you wanting me in particular,' Mollie opined with a puzzled expression. 'Especially after what happened this morning.'

'I'm willing to put that behind us if you are.'

'But you have seen what I'm like,' said Mollie. 'I won't stand for being talked down to and you are the sort to do plenty of that so it wouldn't be a good idea.'

'I shall have to change my ways as far as you are concerned then, won't I?' Cora said.

'If you want me to stay, yes,' Mollie confirmed.

'I'll pay you more than the going rate.'

'Oh!' This did change things because Mollie wasn't really in a position to refuse this new offer so she said,

'All right, I'll give it a try. When would you like me to start?'

'Could you manage tomorrow?'

'I'll be there nine o'clock sharp.'

'I'll see you in the morning then,' said Cora, and headed for the door.

Mollie followed and showed her to the front door and off the premises with a brief 'goodnight'.

Cora thought she must have taken leave of her senses to almost beg someone to come and work for her and she reflected on it as she walked home. She wasn't normally an unpredictable person but she'd acted entirely on impulse over this. Grant was out on business this evening and she had been thinking back on the interview with Mollie. Then, before she'd even thought it over properly, she'd been looking for her address in the bureau and walking through the streets of Chiswick to Pearl Road, having to ask a passing stranger for directions. She hadn't even waited for her husband to drive her there in his Austin Cambridge. There was something about the girl that appealed to her. She was the sort of woman it would be nice to have as a friend.

She reined in her ambitious thoughts. The woman was going to clean for her, not go to the pictures with her or have cosy chats and joke around like women friends did when they got together. Cora didn't get on well enough with anyone to have them as friends anyway, so she was sure that Mollie Fisher would be no exception.

Besides, making friends with staff wasn't the done thing, which just went to show how desperate she was.

Well, she'd offered her the job now so she'd have to give her a try, damn and blast it. How could she have made herself so vulnerable?

All eyes were on Mollie as she re-entered the room.

'Well,' said her mother, 'what did she want?'

'We're dying to know so don't keep us in suspense,' added her gran.

'She came to offer me the job,' Mollie announced.

'Good for you,' said her father.

'That's a turn-up for the books,' added Madge,

'And did you take it?' asked Nora.

'Eventually,' Mollie replied.

'You didn't fall at her feet by the sounds of it,' said her father, grinning.

'No,' Mollie confirmed. 'I think we both know where we stand with each other now.'

'Thank goodness you won't have to go out at the crack of dawn cleaning shops anymore,' said Madge.

'I'm not giving up the shop cleaning, Mum,' Mollie explained. 'I shall do both jobs. That's the whole idea. To earn some more money. Not the same.'

'So you'll go straight from one job to the other,' pointed out her mother disapprovingly.

'No, not exactly. I shall come home for a break in between,' she explained.

'That's something I suppose.'

50

'And Mrs Parker won't need me on Wednesdays apparently. And I'll still have all the afternoons free to look after Esme and take her to the park.'

'That's good,' said Nora. 'You'll be able to go to the keep-fit class, too. That's on a Wednesday morning.'

'Oh Gran, you know how I feel about that,' she objected.

'You'll need some relaxation more than ever with all this extra work you'll be doing. I told you that I'd treat you to it. And I'll look after the baby if your mum is busy.'

'And you know how I feel about taking money from you.'

'We'll see,' said Nora knowingly.

'Oh, I think you'd better get your plimsolls out, Moll,' said her father. 'Your gran won't take no for an answer when she uses that tone of voice.'

'Let's wait and see how I get on with the job, shall we?' suggested Mollie, sitting down at the table. 'Mrs Parker and I will probably fall out on the first day and that will be the end of that.'

'Don't say that for goodness' sake,' said her father. 'That's not the right attitude to have when you start a job.'

'Just trying to be realistic,' she said. 'But of course I'll do my best to get along with her.'

'You're very quiet all of a sudden, Geoff,' observed his mother. 'Are you all right?' asked Mollie.

Geoff was gazing into space and didn't respond.

'He's miles away,' said Len. 'Penny for 'em, boy.'

His son shook himself as though returning from some distant place. 'What's that?' he asked.

'Good news about Mollie's job isn't it?' said Madge.

'Er, yeah, very good,' he agreed vaguely, having managed to grasp the gist of the conversation despite his preoccupation. 'Well done, sis.'

'What is the matter with you, Geoff?' asked his mother. 'You seem to be in a dream.'

'Just thinking about work,' he fibbed because he couldn't tell his mother the truth about his thoughts which concerned a certain Mrs Parker. To him she was the most beautiful woman he had ever seen. A tall, smoky-eyed goddess, she stirred him like no woman ever had before.

'Thanks for saving my sponge for me,' said Mollie.

'We wouldn't dare to steal it from you,' grinned Geoff, forcing himself back to the present with reluctance.

Chapter Three

Compared to scrubbing shop floors, Mollie's duties at the Parker residence could be considered light work. There was plenty for her to get through during her shift, though, because it was a large property with ornate furnishings that needed a lot of polishing and thick carpet that collected the dust. But much to her delight there was a vacuum cleaner, which was a novelty because they didn't have one at home. Mollie's duties included general cleaning throughout, washing and ironing of clothes – mercifully the bed linen went to the laundry – and preparing the meal for the evening, some jobs divided over the days.

So when her employer produced tea and biscuits about halfway through her first shift and suggested that she take a break Mollie was forced to say, 'Thank you but I won't stop if you don't mind because I want to finish on time. I'll drink the tea as I go along.'

'Five minutes won't hurt surely,' Cora insisted. 'You'll get indigestion if you eat while you are working.'

'Just a few minutes then,' agreed Mollie and sat down at the solid wood kitchen table which stood on a quarry-tiled floor.

Cora sat down opposite her, looking all set for a chat. 'Do your babysitters get angry if you are late home then?'

'Oh no, not at all,' Mollie assured her. 'They love having her. Because we live at Mum's, Esme is a real family baby and will go to anyone. You know how it is with families; she probably gets spoiled rotten.'

Cora didn't know how it was with Mollie's sort of family and couldn't begin to imagine but she said, 'Yes, I expect that's bound to happen.'

Mollie sipped her tea and nibbled on a digestive biscuit. 'I like to finish work on time so that I can have the rest of the day free to be with her,' she explained.

Impressed by the fact that Mollie seemed intent upon finishing her duties rather than leaving on the dot of twelve regardless, Cora said, 'You don't get much time to yourself then.'

'Being with Esme is time to myself,' she responded.

'Er, yes, of course I suppose it would be,' said Cora quickly. 'I meant actual free time.'

'You say goodbye to all that the instant you become a mum,' said Mollie cheerfully. 'But I am really enjoying her. She wasn't planned but I'm very glad she happened. I couldn't imagine life without her now.'

Cora nodded.

'Anyway, I'd better be getting on,' said Mollie, finishing her tea and rising quickly. 'Thanks for the tea and biscuits, Mrs Parker.'

'You're welcome.' She paused. 'Look, as we're of a similar age, I think we'd better drop the Mrs Parker. It makes me feel old. My name is Cora and I'd rather you called me that.'

'Oh.' Mollie found this rather odd. The other woman's attitude had changed from offensive haughtiness to down-right matiness which meant Mollie was uncertain where she stood with her. 'If you wish certainly, er, Cora.'

'That's better.'

Mollie nodded and hurried upstairs to continue with the vacuuming.

'It's a lovely house,' Mollie told the family over dinner that night. 'But was I glad of the vacuum cleaner for all that thick carpet. We could do with one here, Mum. They are really good and some ordinary people are beginning to get them now.'

'Not many in this street,' said Madge.

'We'll have to save up for one,' suggested Mollie.

'If I was to get a nice big sewing job; all the dresses for a wedding, for instance, I could put the money I earn towards one. Meanwhile, what you've never had you don't miss so we'll manage with the broom for now.'

'What's she like, Mrs Parker?' Geoff enquired.

'Cora, if you don't mind,' laughed Mollie. 'Mrs Parker makes her feel old apparently, which she clearly isn't. But I find her a bit strange. She was as nasty as anything at the interview but now she seems to want to be friends. So I'm a bit wary of her, wondering if she'll get on to her high horse again at any moment. But it's a job and I'm glad of it.'

'What about her husband?' ventured Geoff.

'I don't know anything about him,' she replied. 'I don't suppose I'll ever see him because he'll be out at work when I'm there. There's a wedding photograph on the piano, though, and he's a nice-looking man with dark curly hair.'

'A woman like her is bound to get a good-looking bloke,' said Geoff.

'What do you mean, a woman like her?' wondered Mollie.

'Beautiful; smart,' he said.

Beauty must definitely be in the eye of the beholder in this instance because it certainly hadn't struck Mollie. 'She's smart, certainly,' she said.

'You didn't think she was good-looking?'

'Not especially, no.'

'You want your eyes testing then.'

'Sounds as though someone was impressed,' said Nora.

'She looks like a film star to me,' said Geoff.

'Steady on; that's going a bit far,' said Mollie.

'The rest of us didn't see her so we can't judge,' Madge mentioned.

'She's just a woman I work for anyway,' Mollie reminded them. 'Her appearance is of no importance whatsoever.'

'Exactly,' her father agreed.

'I actually think she might be quite nice once I get to know her and find out which is the real her,' said Mollie, 'the high and mighty Mrs Parker or the amiable Cora.'

'Probably a bit of each,' suggested her mother, who usually tried to see the best in people. 'Most of us are changeable.'

'Not you, Madge,' proclaimed her husband. 'You are the most consistent person I know. The same whatever circumstances you are in.'

'Am I, oh well.'

'I still think Mrs Parker is gorgeous,' said Geoff. 'Not that it makes any difference what I think.'

'It certainly doesn't,' confirmed his mother. 'She's a married woman.'

'A cat can look at a queen,' he reminded her.

'Not too closely though or you'll have Mr Parker coming after you,' said his mother.

'I'll risk that,' said Geoff.

'You won't get the chance,' said Mollie. 'Because she won't be coming around here again.'

'I suppose not,' he agreed lightly.

'Right ladies, let's start by walking around the hall with head up, shoulders back and keep those arms swinging to get us going. Tummy in, remember your posture at all times. Keep in time with the music. Very good. Now let's turn and walk the other way.'

It was the first day of the new term at the keep-fit class and Mollie was here to please her grandmother who seemed to think it was some sort of a panacea.

'You need a break from mothering as well as cleaning,' she'd insisted on a regular basis throughout the summer.

'One hour a week, that's all. Just try it once to please me and don't go again if you don't like it. You might as well make the most of something for women to do outside of the home. There was nothing like that for me or your mum when we were young married women.'

As it happened neither of them would be out of place here today, Mollie noticed, as the age range of the women was very extensive.

After the walking they did more arm swings and sways and some rather neat footwork which came easily to Mollie but caused much hilarity among the others as they went wrong and giggled with embarrassment. The teacher got them working on tummies, thighs, posture, arms, legs, even feet and hands and all done in time to music from Peg on the piano.

The hour shot by and after the lesson there was tea and biscuits for anyone who wanted it, made by a volunteer from the class. Some people slipped away and Mollie guessed they wouldn't come to class again but the majority were full of enthusiasm and she found herself enjoying the social gathering at the end.

'Mollie, isn't it,' said Rose the teacher who looked to be in her thirties, had blond hair, the most wonderfully toned figure and spoke with rather a posh accent.

Mollie nodded. 'Thank you for the class,' she said. 'I really enjoyed it and will definitely be coming again.'

'Excellent,' approved Rose. 'I suspect that you have done this sort of thing before. You're very good.'

'Thank you,' said Mollie, smiling with pleasure. 'I haven't done anything exactly like this before. In fact

I haven't done any sort of instructed exercise since I left school.'

Rose's brows rose. 'Really! You must have a natural aptitude for it then.'

'I was always good at gym at school. I used to fly over the vaulting horse and excel myself on the sports field. Just as well really, as I never shone at anything else.'

'Did you enjoy our style of exercise?'

'Very much,' said Mollie.

'More fun than just bending and stretching and touching your toes.'

'I love the gracefulness of it,' said Mollie, full of enthusiasm. 'It seems quite gentle but I feel as though every bit of me has been stretched.'

'Yes, that's what our classes are all about. We are hoping to spread the word and open more centres,' Rose told her. 'We really believe in what we do.'

'You'll certainly have a supporter in me,' Mollie assured her. 'All being well I shall be here next week.'

They chatted for a while. Mollie told her about Esme and eventually Rose drifted off to mingle and Mollie joined in another conversation with other class members. She was enjoying herself so much she had taken her eye off the time, unheard of for her when Esme was being looked after. She ran most of the way home and fell in the door full of apologies.

'Did you enjoy it, that's what we want to know?' asked her mother.

'I loved it,' effused Mollie. 'Thanks, Gran, for treating me and making me go.'

Nora beamed. 'I've got all the thanks I need seeing your joyful smile.'

Mollie turned her attention to her daughter, who was in her high chair. She lifted her out and danced around with her making the child chuckle. Mollie felt completely revitalised; as though she could cope with anything. Already she was looking forward to the class next week.

Cora had been a lot more cheerful lately, her husband noticed, and mentioned it one autumn evening as they sat in their sumptuous sitting room with mint-green armchairs, best quality Axminster and the windows draped with elaborate lace curtains. He was reading the newspaper, she was nursing the dog.

'What did you do today?' asked Grant, lowering the newspaper and looking at her. He always made a determined effort to take an interest in his wife in the hope of improving their lifeless marriage.

'Usual things,' she replied. 'I took Peaches out for a walk and went for a look round the shops after that.'

'Did you let the dog walk or did you carry her?'

She made a face. 'A bit of both,' she said, fondling the poodle's head.

He raised his eyes. 'That dog is so spoiled, she'd never be able to fend for herself if you weren't around.'

'That applies to all domesticated animals,' she pointed out. 'We've made them reliant on us.'

'Yes, but you take it a stage further with that dog,' he said.

'That's because I love her so, don't I, Peaches?' she said, lifting her up and kissing her.

'Did the cleaner come today?' he enquired.

'Yes, why do you ask?'

'Because she seems to cheer you up,' he said. 'You're usually happy when she's been.'

'No I'm not, not especially,' she denied, a touch haughtily because it wasn't easy to admit that she relied on her cleaner for company.

'Oh, I thought you seemed a lot more cheerful since she's been coming.'

'Well, of course I'm glad to have someone come regularly to clean for me. It saves all the bother of having to do the work myself.'

'But you like her, don't you?'

'She's a good worker.'

'I presume you get along with her as she hasn't left yet,' he suggested. Anything that made his wife happier made his life easier. She wasn't a sociable woman, so tended to isolate herself.

'We are getting to know each other better now,' she told him. 'But she's wrapped up in her own life; her baby and her family.'

'Which is only natural,' he said. 'She comes here to work, not to socialise.'

'Of course, but I insist that she takes a break. As soon as she's finished her tea, she's off flying around the house to get finished so she can leave on time. She's just a slip of a thing really but she has such energy.'

'Oh well, as long as she stays, that's the main thing.'

'Quite.'

Cora wasn't going to admit this to her husband but she knew she had to watch her behaviour with Mollie or they would lose her; she'd made that very clear from the start. But much to Cora's surprise she found her to be pleasant company and enjoyed hearing anecdotes about her home life, which was very different to her own when she'd lived with the family. It sounded such fun, all of them together in a little house, joshing and chattering. Unfortunately, Cora didn't get to hear enough because of Mollie's self-imposed time limit on her break.

Recently, apparently, she'd joined some sort of an exercise class and Cora wanted to know more about that but she could hardly follow her around the house while she was working asking her questions. So she would make do with scraps of information during their tea break.

The keep-fit class soon became the highlight of Mollie's week. No matter how tired or harassed she felt – and as a working mother of a young child this was inevitable at times – the class energised her and lifted her spirits, the effect lingering into the rest of the week.

She liked the other class members too. They were a mixed bunch; some unmistakably middle class, others ordinary like Mollie, a few rough and ready but all good fun. One or two brought their babies with them and left them in their prams in the vestibule while they exercised. Social status and age were irrelevant here; as long as you came to class you fitted in. Mollie made new friends and got on very well with Rose the teacher, who took several other classes during the week at other places in and around London, one or two in the evening.

Esme was thriving and the Parker job was going well for Mollie too, much to her surprise. She had expected Cora to cause trouble long before now. But over time she had got to know her better and rather liked her in a wary sort of way. She was aware that she wasn't a woman to cross though, and guessed that she was sometimes just a heartbeat away from her high horse. She hadn't been annoyingly condescending yet, though, probably because of Mollie's outburst at the start.

Mollie had discovered that Cora's husband – whom Mollie had never met – was one of the Parkers of the eponymous store in Chiswick High Road, which was tantamount to fame locally as it was a very well-known store.

Her employer had a tendency to want to chat and Mollie suspected she needed a friend; this was awkward because Mollie didn't have time during her shift for long conversations. Although the work was congenial, there was plenty to do to earn her money, especially now that it was winter and she had to clean the hearths and light the fires. Anyway, there was too much of a class divide for them to have a friendship. It was nice that she felt comfortable working there though.

One good thing was that Cora never criticised her work or stood over her. She told her what to do and let her get on with it and in as much as she hadn't sacked her Cora must be pleased with what she did. So now, as the winter took hold, things were better for Mollie than they'd been in the aftermath of her husband's departure. Life was more demanding for her than it had been when Syd was around but she felt stronger in herself now. As long as she could pay her way and support her daughter, she wouldn't complain.

'So are the exercises very hard?' asked Cora during Mollie's tea break one morning near to Christmas.

'Not for me but you do need to concentrate on the teacher's instructions.'

'Is it bending and stretching, that sort of thing?'

'That comes into it, of course, because it's an exercise class, but there is much more to it than that,' said Mollie, exuding enthusiasm as she talked about one of her favourite pastimes. 'We learn routines and just when you think you've got it off by heart, the teacher starts teaching you a new one. There is a certain amount of bending and stretching and swinging and swaying and toe-pointing, but it's great fun and very graceful.'

'Do you wear ordinary clothes?'

'Oh no, that would be far too inhibiting,' replied Mollie. 'We wear black shorts and a white blouse which you can buy through the association although it isn't compulsory. Some people wear their own shorts, especially when they are new and haven't decided if they will continue. Others make the uniform. But we'd get too hot if we wore anything too heavy.'

'What sort of people go?' asked Cora.

'A mixture really,' she replied. 'There are a few posh ones like yourself but mostly they are just ordinary like me. We all have a common interest so we get along.'

'Hmm. Interesting.'

'Anyway,' said Mollie, finishing her biscuit and rising. 'It's time for me to get back to work.'

She headed for the sitting room to finish the vacuuming, her thoughts full of keep fit. She was quite unprepared for what Cora had to say to her at the end of the shift.

'I was wondering,' she began as Mollie put on her coat and gloves. 'If I could give the class a try.'

Mollie was taken aback. 'Well yes of course; all are welcome, provided you are female, of course.' She wanted others to experience the joy the class gave her and Rose wanted more members, but *not Mollie's employer*.

Sensing Mollie's reluctance and misunderstanding it, Cora said hesitantly, 'Are you afraid I might tell the others that you clean for me?'

This infuriated Mollie. 'Of course not. I'm not ashamed of what I do,' she made clear. 'I earn an honest living to support myself and my daughter. Why would I worry about people knowing? I've probably mentioned it to some of them anyway.' She wanted to say to Cora: 'Aren't you afraid I might tell people that you sit around all day doing bugger all but coddling your pet dog when you could make yourself useful to some charitable cause?'

'All right, don't fly off the handle. I sensed reluctance on your part for me to join, that's all,' said Cora.

'No reluctance about your joining, none at all,' said

65

Mollie. 'I get so much from it I want others to feel that too. But when you mentioned it I knew that I would have to make one thing clear which is probably what you noticed in my expression.'

'And that something is . . .?'

'When I am here, I am your employee; at your beck and call,' she began. 'Outside of this house we are on an equal footing and I am independent. I thought I needed to mention this because, until recently, people like you and me would never mix outside the workplace and it's still quite unusual.'

'What do you think I'm going to ask you to do, Mollie?' asked Cora. 'Help me get changed and tie my shoelaces for me?'

Despite the sarcasm, Mollie was quite impressed with her answer. At least it showed she had a sense of humour. 'I wouldn't put it past you,' she said in a tone of banter.

'I wouldn't dare,' Cora said.

'I'm glad we understand each other.'

'Understand each other,' said Cora. 'I'm frightened to death of you.'

'Oh . . .' Mollie was shocked.

Then suddenly, somehow, they were both laughing and Mollie knew that they had passed through some sort of a test in their relationship and a spark of warmth had been created.

'It's the last class of term tomorrow,' said Mollie, still smiling and only too pleased to help now that the rules had been set. 'Why don't you come along and meet Rose the teacher and have a peep at what we do. If you think it's for you, then you can join when class starts again in January. It wouldn't be worth starting tomorrow because we've been working on the routines all term.'

'I might do that,' said Cora, looking pleased.

'This cleaner of yours must be quite something if she can persuade you to do that,' said Grant that evening when Cora told him about her plans. 'A keep-fit class; I didn't know there were such things.'

'It's quite a new thing apparently.'

'I can hardly believe that you would go to something like that,' he said with a wry grin.

'What makes you say that?' she asked. 'I can bend and stretch with the best of them.'

'I know that,' he assured her. 'I was thinking more of the fact that you'll probably have to mix with the hoi polloi.'

'So what?'

'You're usually such a snob about such things, dear,' he told her truthfully and without any malice.

'Mollie said there are a few posh ones in the class.'

Grant laughed heartily. 'I rest my case,' he said.

'You're twisting my words,' she said. 'Of course I shall try to mix with everyone and not just the posh ones.'

'Good. I'm pleased that you're making an effort to mix with someone other than that hound of yours,' he said amiably. 'I hope you stick with it because it will do you the world of good.'

'Peaches isn't a hound,' she objected, stroking her beloved pet who was in her usual position, on her lap.

'It doesn't get a chance to be anything resembling a normal dog because you are always pampering her,' he stated. 'She needs to be running around in Duke's Meadows sniffing around trees and barking at other dogs.'

'She doesn't like to do anything like that,' Cora told him.

'You mean you don't like her to do anything like that,' he corrected.

'I take her out for regular walks and she sniffs around then,' she reminded him.

'And you carry her most of the way back,' he said in a tone of gentle admonition. 'It's no wonder she wants to sit on your lap all day. She knows nothing else.'

'You bought the dog for me so why don't you let me decide what's best for her,' she suggested. 'I treat her well; she wants for nothing.'

'Except time to be a dog.'

'All right, stop going on about it,' she said irritably. 'I'll try and make her walk all the way home in future.'

'Good, but make sure you do.'

She nodded.

'So when is your entry into the world of the ordinary woman and exercise?' he asked.

'I'm going to watch the class tomorrow and if I like the look of it, I'll start at the beginning of the next term sometime in early January.'

'I hope you do go ahead,' he said, because he genuinely wanted his wife to be happy. He wasn't in love with her but he did care about her in a responsible sort of way. It was his duty as her husband to do so.

They were certainly all shapes and sizes here, thought Cora, the next morning as she watched the keep-fit class in progress. There were the tall, short, slender and downright chubby; at various levels of ability too. Most could follow the instructions, some didn't have a clue and others were wonderfully graceful and lovely to watch. Being small Mollie was at the front and she shone out from the others with her faultless execution of the routines and the elegance with which she moved her body.

One thing that all these women had in common, Cora noticed, was joy in what they were doing. If someone went wrong nobody minded. There was a general feeling of unity. She could feel it and she wasn't even involved. She wanted to be though, very much. She slipped out of the hall before the end because Mollie had told her they socialised for a short time afterwards and she wanted to wait until she was a member before she took part in that. It would be hard enough joining something new without having to meet the others before she'd even taken her first step. She was very pleased she had come though, and couldn't wait to join in January.

Syd Fisher watched another satisfied customer drive off the forecourt in the Morris that he'd just sold him and felt very pleased with himself. The day had got off to a good start and this latest sale would provide him with a nice healthy commission and, added to the other sales he had made this month, his wage packet should be nicely bulging. Especially handy with Christmas almost upon them.

How glad he was that he'd got out of the building trade when he had. His life had completely turned around since he'd left Chiswick. These days he went to work in a suit and had a decent amount of dough in his pocket. He'd managed to get out of that tatty boarding house and had a couple of comfortable rooms with cooking facilities now. He even had a car for personal use provided by the guv'nor, a businessman who had seen the potential for used car sales and opened a showroom on the outskirts of Tottenham.

Syd had first met him in a pub and they had got into conversation. He'd been looking for someone who could sell cars at the time and Syd had just moved into the area and was looking for work, so they made the perfect team. The boss looked after the management and paper-work and left the selling to Syd. If he'd known he had such a gift for it he'd have gone into it before. Still, better late than never and the sky was the limit for him now. He'd have a proper flat of his own before long.

The Christmas decorations that adorned all the shops in the parade opposite gave him a sudden pang as he realised that he'd be on his own this year. He daren't show his face over Chiswick way as he'd made such a success of disappearing, so he wouldn't even get to see his mum and dad.

Still, it was only one day. There was a nice crowd in his local pub and he had plenty of pocket money so he could go there on Christmas Eve and Boxing Day. They might even open for a short time on Christmas Day.

A feeling of unease was trying to insinuate itself into his high spirits and spoil things for him. Should he send Mollie some money now that he was doing well? He'd sent nothing so far. But he had his own expenses to take care of; his rent and food and, of course, his beer money. The fact that Christmas was a time for children came into his mind. But what was the point of sending anything for Esme. Babies didn't know anything about it. She'd probably be screaming all over Christmas anyway, as per usual.

No, he wasn't going to send anything at all. After all, he got nothing from the marriage now – no home comforts or sex – therefore why should he pay for nothing? So that was settled. He would keep what he earned for himself and rightly so. He wished he didn't have a stupid feeling of guilt about it though. Still, that would disappear after a few pints tonight. Meanwhile there was an interested party on the forecourt looking at the Austin.

'Good morning sir,' he said smiling at the man, ready to launch into his spiel. 'Lovely little motor, isn't she? Only one owner and the engine is as sweet as a nut . . .'

There was a pleasantly festive atmosphere after class that day. Rose had brought some mince pies for them to have with their tea and everyone was exchanging cards and talking excitedly about the forthcoming holiday; shopping not yet finished, baking still to be done and presents to be wrapped up.

As the gathering began to disperse and people were putting their coats on, Rose took Mollie aside. 'I've been wanting to have a chat to you,' she began. 'Do you have a few minutes?'

'I can't stay long because of my little girl . . .'

'I understand and I'll keep it short for now.'

'Oh dear, what have I done wrong?'

'What could my star member possibly have done wrong?' said Rose, who had a very warm smile and gentle blue eyes. 'Quite the contrary in fact.'

'Really.'

'Yes. I've been watching you work all through the term and, as I have already told you on several occasions, you are very good; excellent in fact. We don't often come across anyone with such a natural aptitude. You're very good with people too.'

'Thank you,' said Mollie, glowing with pride. 'It's very nice of you to say so.'

'The fact is, I was wondering if you might consider training as a teacher.'

Mollie was so flabbergasted she gawped at her in silence for a few moments. 'A teacher, me,' she gasped at last. 'I can't do anything like that. I left school without any qualifications.'

'That doesn't matter. You would get qualifications from us. It takes two years, the training course.'

This was the most exciting thing that had ever happened to Mollie and she was truly honoured even though she knew such a thing wasn't possible for her. 'I'm very thrilled to be asked, Rose,' she said, 'but as much as I would love to do it, it's out of the question for me. I work and I have a baby to look after so I couldn't possibly take it on.'

'Hmm, I thought that might be your answer but the course isn't full time and a lot of the work can be done at home,' Rose explained. 'There is a fair bit of studying as well as the practical element: biology, anatomy and so on. Most of the course that you would need to attend is at weekends so would be outside of the working week.'

'It would be impossible to study at home with a baby around,' said Mollie as the unfeasibility grew even stronger. 'As much as I would love to do it, and I really would, I shall have to say no. Anyway, there would be the cost. Such things don't come cheap.'

'Indeed they don't but ours is very reasonably priced and you would earn your fees back when your classes got under way. You won't make a fortune as a teacher, after you've paid for the use of the hall and the services of a pianist, but you should make enough to pay back your fees over time and have some money in your pocket. None of us go into it for the money but because we enjoy it and believe in its benefits. But we are entitled to be paid for our work and that's what happens once your classes get going. You would start with one class, of course, and see how it goes from there. If it does well, and I'm sure it would, you could open another.'

Because Rose was obviously not short of a bob or two, she didn't seem to understand how things were for people like Mollie who had no access to extra money at all. She wasn't going to spell it out for her, though, because it was too embarrassing.

'It's really kind of you to ask me—' she began.

'I'm not being kind, Mollie,' Rose cut in. 'I want you to do it because I think you'd make a fine teacher. We need people like you in our association.'

'Sorry but . . .'

'Will you just think about it over the holiday?' she asked. 'There's a course starting in January. I could probably get you booked on to it if you did decide to go ahead.'

'But I . . .'

'Talk to your family about it.'

'I will but it won't make any difference,' Mollie said. 'I don't have a husband to support me so things aren't easy.'

'Yes, I'm sure,' Rose said, seeming to understand at last and looking disappointed. 'It's such a pity though.' She sighed. 'Oh well, never mind. Later on perhaps. You're still very young.'

Mollie nodded. 'But thank you for asking me. It's the best Christmas present anyone could give me.'

'Really?' Rose looked surprised. 'Even though you're not in a position to take it on?'

'Yes, even then,' she said.

The other members wanted to know what the teacher had been talking to Mollie about.

'Nothing special,' she fibbed because she didn't feel like going through her negative circumstances again so soon. It might spoil the positive aspect of having been asked. Her self-esteem had taken a real dive when Syd left and this had boosted her confidence no end. She wanted to enjoy it while it lasted because it really was an enormous compliment to be asked. 'See you all next term. Happy Christmas, everyone.'

'Happy Christmas, Mollie,' came a chorus.

Walking home, Mollie was positively glowing. She was so pleased that Mum and Gran had nagged her into joining the class. She felt part of something special when she was there. They were such a nice bunch of women too; the combination of the exercise and the company really refreshed her and helped her to cope. She quickened her step, eager to get home to the family and her beautiful daughter.

Chapter Four

Christmas was as traditional as ever in the Pottses' house; Mum in the kitchen all day Christmas Eve, the house fragrant with fresh-baked mince pies, sausage rolls, cheese straws and various other culinary delights for the big day. Esme wasn't old enough to understand any of it but she was very entertaining now, sitting up on her own and doing lots of smiling. With brown saucer eyes like her mother's and a mop of dark wavy hair, she was very cute.

Geoff was at work on Christmas morning because of the festive lunch at the hotel but the chefs were allowed to leave a cold buffet for the guests in the evening which would be served by a skeleton staff so he was home in time for a very late family dinner. Since he always cycled to and from work the lack of public transport due to the holiday didn't affect him.

They sat around in the evening after Esme was in bed, having a drink or two, talking, playing cards and telling jokes. It was very enjoyable but Mollie couldn't help remembering last year when she and Syd had been together and absolutely mad about each other, or so she had thought at the time. You didn't stop loving someone when you found out that they didn't love you back and she still missed him even though she had learned to live without him.

She was hurt rather than angry that he hadn't sent any money, more for Esme than herself. She could work to keep them both but found it hard to understand how he could just abandon all responsibility for his daughter. How he could not want to see her was quite beyond Mollie.

The sound of her grandmother's voice asking for everybody's attention recalled her to the present.

'Listen up everyone,' she was saying. 'I've got something to say and I want to tell you while we are all together.'

'That sounds a bit ominous, Nora,' said Len, grinning. 'Have you found a man?'

She tutted. 'Don't be so rude, Len,' she admonished.

'What's rude about that?' he asked lightly. 'You're a good-looking woman for your age. Some bloke might be glad to have someone like you, especially if he can't see very well.'

'Stop teasing her, Len,' admonished his wife. 'It's very disrespectful.'

'Don't worry about me, Madge,' said Nora who bantered with her son-in-law on a regular basis. They had a running joke about him wanting her to move out so that he could rent her room but it was all done in fun and they were actually very fond of each other. She knew she was welcome here. Madge had told her that she and Len loved having her to live with them and were glad to see her enjoying life after the miserable existence she'd had with her late husband. 'I can stand up for myself against him, don't worry. I'm used to his nonsense.'

'So, don't keep us in suspense. What is it you want to tell us?' asked Geoff.

'Well, you know how proud we all were when Mollie was asked to train as a keep-fit teacher.'

'Not half,' said Madge. 'It's such an awful pity that she can't take it on.'

'But I think she can,' said Nora, her voice rising excitedly. 'If I lend her the money there's no reason why not.'

There was a surprised silence. Then Mollie said predictably, 'No Gran, I can't take your money. Thank you for offering. It's very kind of you but I wouldn't dream of it.'

'I did say lend and not give, dear,' emphasised Nora, who knew there was no chance of her granddaughter accepting it any other way than as a loan. 'You could repay me gradually when your classes get going. The teacher said you would eventually earn the money for the course fees back so you could give me so much a month when you can afford it. I've still got some of your grandfather's insurance money left and it would really please me to do this for you.'

'You won't have the money left for much longer if you keep giving it to me,' Mollie pointed out. 'You're already paying for my classes.'

'As I have just said, this would be a loan,' Nora reminded her.

'But it will take me two years to qualify and then I need time to build up membership to my classes so it would be ages before I could even start to pay you back.'

'It's very good of you to offer this, Mum,' said Madge and turning to her daughter added, 'I think you should at least consider it, Mollie, as your gran has been kind enough to suggest it.'

'But Gran might need that money before I can pay it back,' Mollie responded worriedly.

'That's very unlikely, dear,' Nora assured her. 'I wouldn't have offered if I wasn't as sure as I can be of that.'

Mollie was actually tingling with excitement at the thought of what this would mean to her life in the future but, even apart from the financial side, there were too many problems. 'But how would I get the chance to study?' she asked. 'What with working and the baby.'

'After Esme is in bed at night, when she's having her nap, any time you can fit it in,' suggested her mother. 'I'm not saying it will be easy but neither will it be impossible.'

'What about when I have to go to headquarters for the training?' she asked. 'You and Gran already look after Esme while I go to work and class. I can't expect you to have her while I do that as well.'

'I don't mind,' said her mother.

'And I wouldn't have offered to lend you the money if I wasn't prepared to help out with Esme,' said Nora. 'And I have thought about it.'

'I can lend a hand with Esme when I'm at home if you're stuck,' offered Geoff.

'And I'll give backup support when I'm not at work,' said Len. 'There are more than enough of us to make sure one small child is looked after.'

Mollie was overwhelmed with emotion at their love and generosity. 'You're all so good to me,' she said tearfully. 'I'll be forever in your debt.'

'You can take your time paying me back,' said her grandmother. 'Whatever you can afford every so often; and not until your classes start to earn for you.'

'Thank you all for everything,' she said and burst into tears.

Mollie didn't think it would be appropriate to tell her plans to anyone outside the family until she had informed Rose of her change of heart about the course. So she got to class early on the day they started back and gave Rose the good news. She was absolutely delighted and, much to Mollie's surprise, announced it to the class at the end.

'I'm sure you all wish her well in her teaching course,' she said in conclusion, 'and if anyone else is interested in our training scheme please talk to me afterwards and I'll let you know if you might be suitable. We do have very high standards and I'm sure you will all have noticed how naturally talented Mollie is but you don't have to be as exceptional as she is to make a good teacher. What you do need is a good general ability, a sense of rhythm and dedication to our method of exercise.'

'Good luck, Mollie,' said a class member and it was echoed throughout the room. Mollie felt truly blessed.

One person who wasn't so pleased about Mollie's new plans was Cora, though she kept her feelings well hidden while socialising with the other class members during which time Mollie introduced her to everyone and generally tried to make her feel welcome.

Cora could see that Mollie was the centre of attraction here and she couldn't help feeling a bit out of things. Even though she knew that was only natural as this was her first time, she guessed she would never be as popular as Mollie. Some people just had something about them that drew others to them.

'This is Cora,' was how Mollie made the introduction. 'In another life, outside of keep fit, she is my boss. I clean her house for her.'

People were far more interested in Mollie's new venture within the association than her employment arrangements outside of it but Cora guessed she had made it known deliberately to prove that it didn't embarrass her.

'I hope your training to be a teacher doesn't mean you will leave this class when you get one of your own,' said someone.

'Of course not,' she assured them. 'I'll be teaching at mine, working. This will be my relaxation.'

'That's all right then.'

When the gathering broke up and they all went their separate ways, Mollie said to Cora, 'Well, did you enjoy the class?'

Cora looked doubtful. 'Not enjoy exactly because I didn't really know what I was doing but I think I might like it better when I get used to it. I wasn't very good.'

'It isn't about *being* good, it's about *feeling* good and enjoying yourself,' said Mollie. 'You'll improve with time. There's a lot to take in at first.'

'I did like the sense of dance in the routines and look forward to actually being able to keep up.'

'That's the spirit,' enthused Mollie.

Cora hesitated, wanting to tell Mollie about something that was worrying her.

'I must go because of Esme,' said Mollie, crushing the opportunity. 'See you tomorrow.'

'Yes,' said Cora and watched her fly down the street, half running in her haste.

'You seem a bit quiet today, Cora,' remarked Mollie as she sat down at the Parkers' kitchen table to drink her tea in her break the next morning. 'Is there anything wrong?'

'Er . . .' It wasn't like the outspoken Cora to be hesitant but she was much less arrogant with Mollie than anyone else because she knew the girl wouldn't stand for it.

'It isn't my place to pry, of course,' said Mollie, sipping her tea. 'So forget I said anything.'

There was a brief hiatus. 'There is something bothering me actually,' she began uncertainly.

'Well why not get it off your chest.'

'Er . . . I was wondering if I'm going to have to find another cleaner now that you have new plans.'

'Not as far as I'm concerned,' Mollie assured her. 'I'll need the money I get working here more than ever while I'm doing the course with extra travelling expenses and so on.'

'What about after you qualify and start your own classes?' Cora queried.

'I shall still need to earn money, for a good while anyway,' said Mollie. 'And here is as good a place to work as any.'

Smiling now, Cora said, 'That's good.' Annoyed with herself for becoming so reliant on Mollie for company and fearing that this would give her the upper hand, she decided to tone it down by adding, 'You get used to someone when they come regularly. I don't really want the bother of looking for anyone else.'

'It's just as well you won't have to then, isn't it?' said Mollie cheerfully, picking up a rich tea biscuit.

'Indeed,' said Cora, more relieved than she ought to be about the fact that Mollie would be staying.

With careful management of her time Mollie found the training course manageable. Rose had told her that the association had to make it practically possible or no one would sign up since most people had other commitments.

Because babies were so unpredictable and Esme still required a lot of attention and Mollie wanted her to have it, she seized any opportunity that presented itself for studying: during Esme's afternoon nap, after the family had gone to bed at night, when a member of the family was keeping her baby entertained, very early Sunday mornings before Esme woke up when she didn't have to go out cleaning shops. Whenever she saw a chance she settled down at the kitchen table with her books, learning about the technicalities of teaching exercise which she found enthralling. She only had to go to headquarters in central London for lectures and tuition once a month and Mum and Gran stepped into the breach with Esme then as they had promised.

The process of studying opened her eyes to another side of herself; a part that could actually absorb facts, retain them and be interested in them. She was so engrossed in this and her daughter, her family, her keep-fit class and her jobs that important events outside of her own personal concerns registered with much less impact than usual. The death of King George V in January seemed to pass her by emotionally as did the abdication scandal at the end of the year even though everyone was talking about it.

'I don't know how you can concentrate on your studies with us lot all clattering about,' said her mother one day.

'Neither do I but I can,' said Mollie. 'I rather like having things going on around me; everybody in and out and you cooking. I think I'd feel too isolated if I shut myself away somewhere, even if there was anywhere to do that.'

'When you put it like that, it's just as well you can be a kitchen-table student then,' said her mother wisely.

'There is the bonus of having the first rock cake out of the oven,' said Mollie with a grin.

The feeling of detachment from the outside world was stripped away from her completely one day in January 1937 when something happened that she felt with such intensity it shocked her.

She went to the Parker residence one Monday morning to do her cleaning shift as usual and knocked at the door. Instead of it being opened by Cora as she expected, a man greeted her.

'Hello there,' he said, smiling and offering his hand. 'You must be Mollie.'

'Yes, that's right,' she said, taking his hand which he pumped vigorously.

'I'm Grant, Cora's husband,' he informed her. 'Come on in.' He opened the door wider and waved his hand towards the hall. 'Cora has had to take to her bed, I'm afraid. She isn't very well at all. I had to call the doctor out to her last night.'

Mollie recognised him from the photograph on the piano but that black-and-white image gave no indication of how stunning he was in reality. That thick black hair framing his square-shaped face, and such gorgeous eyes, a kind of black with a hint of blue with long dark lashes. 'Oh, I'm sorry to hear that,' she said, trying not to gawp at him too openly. 'What's the matter with her?'

'A heavy cold that's gone to her chest,' he explained. 'Nothing serious but she's feeling rotten. The doctor gave me some medicine for her so that should clear it up.'

'So . . . you'd rather I gave the cleaning a miss today then, would you?' she assumed.

'Oh no, not at all,' he said. 'She'll go into a complete decline if the cleaning isn't done. Very house-proud, my wife.'

'But what about the noise?' Mollie queried. 'I don't want to disturb her.'

'The sounds of cleaning will be music to her ears,' he said, giving her a lingering smile. 'So you carry on.' He paused, his depthless eyes resting on her. 'Actually I have a favour to ask you.'

'Anything I can do to help, I'll be only too pleased.'

'I have to go into work for a couple of hours so wonder if you could look in on Cora every so often to ask if there is anything she needs,' he explained. 'The dog is up there with her. I'll take Peaches for a walk later but she might need to go outside before I get back. I'd be very grateful.'

'Of course I'll do that. No trouble at all,' she said, smiling at him. 'I'll give Cora some company too if she's up to it.'

'Thank you. I understand you've been a good friend to her.'

'I'm not sure about that,' she said, surprised by the exaggeration. 'Basically I just work for her.'

'You persuaded her to join the keep-fit class and it's done her a lot of good.'

'I didn't persuade her,' Mollie explained firmly. 'I happened to mention that I go and she seemed interested and asked a lot about it then said she wanted to join.'

'Because you'd spoken about it with such enthusiasm, I expect,' he said. 'She said you are very keen.'

She smiled. 'Yes I am and I probably did go on about it. I do tend to enthuse about things that I enjoy.'

'I was pleased anyway. I'd been telling her for ages that she should go out and make some friends,' he said. 'But up until now there hasn't been anywhere for her to go as she isn't the type for things like the Townswomen's Guild. She isn't really much of a mixer at all.'

'She doesn't seem to have a problem at keep fit but they are a very friendly group.'

'I'm glad she has you as a friend anyway.'

To say that she and Cora were friends was a gross overstatement but, thinking about it, Mollie realised that she and Cora did seem to have forged a kind of companionship, mostly instigated by Cora but Mollie rather enjoyed it too. In an odd sort of way they needed each other; Mollie was reliant on the job and Cora seemed to need her friendship. Somehow they had defied the class divide though it did hover from time to time in as much as Cora could afford luxuries that were barely heard of by Mollie and reminded her that they lived in different worlds.

One of the strengths of their odd association was in Cora knowing that Mollie wouldn't take condescension so she didn't talk down to her. The peculiar thing was that Mollie always felt that she was in the stronger position rather than the other way around as it should have been since Cora paid her wages. She suspected that Cora would like them to do more things together; go to the pictures or shopping. But Mollie made it known that she was fully committed. Cleaning and keep fit, that was as far as it went even though she had grown to rather like her employer.

She was recalled to the present by Grant saying, 'Well, I'll get off now if that's all right.'

'Oh yes, yes of course,' she said, sure she must seem gormless but experiencing such a strong reaction to him she was certain he must have noticed.

'I'll see you later then,' he said. 'I'll be back before you go. If not she'll be all right on her own for a while.'

'That's fine.'

Why was it that he made her feel as though she was doing him a huge favour by being here when he was paying her wages? She answered her own question. Because he was a true gentleman, that was the reason. It was generally known locally that the Parkers were good to their staff. Now she had met him she could believe it. Rumour had it that his father was a self-made man. Maybe that had something to do with his down-to-earth attitude.

What she did have trouble working out was her own physical reaction to him. She was still quivering inwardly from it and she wasn't sure it was quite decent, him being a married man. It wasn't like anything she had experienced before, not even for Syd. Still, at least it proved she was still alive and functioning again as a woman. She'd thought all that sort of thing had died when Syd left. But apparently not!

Grant was having similar thoughts about Mollie. She was lovely! So petite and pretty with those huge brown eyes, shiny dark hair and such a warm smile. He was instantly attracted to her. Cora had told him she'd been deserted by her husband; the man must have been out of his mind to do a thing like that. But Grant tried not to judge anyone because you never knew what went on in other people's lives, especially a marriage. He and Cora probably seemed ideally suited to the outside world when nothing could be further from the truth.

However he was married to her so there was no point in lusting after another woman. He was smiling at the memory of Mollie, though, as he got into his shiny black Austin. He sat for a few moments thinking about her then started the engine and drove away towards the town.

Cora clearly wasn't going to suffer in silence.

'I feel terrible,' she said mournfully to Mollie when the latter went into her bedroom to see if she wanted anything; the dog was settled beside Cora on the bed. 'I'm really ill. I think I might be going to die.'

'You have a heavy cold. That's all,' Mollie said, trying not to smile. 'I know it isn't very nice for you but you'll be up and about again in a few days.'

'Do you really think so?' Cora said, sniffing into her handkerchief.

'Most definitely,' said Mollie. 'If I had what you've got I'd probably be out working, not in bed being pampered by that lovely husband of yours.'

'I can't help your circumstances, Mollie,' she said woefully.

'Course you can't,' agreed Mollie. 'I'm just trying to make you realise that you are not at death's door.'

'I feel as though I am.'

'Mm, I can see that,' said Mollie. 'Is there anything I can get you, a hot drink perhaps?'

'I think perhaps I could manage a cup of Bovril,' she said weakly. 'I don't fancy anything sweet.'

'Coming up,' said Mollie. 'Do you want me to tidy your pillows before I go?'

'Yes please,' she said, sounding tragic.

Mollie smiled at the other woman's overemphasis as she gently plumped the pillows and straightened the covers while Cora groaned at every movement

'Cor, you don't half pile on the agony,' said Mollie. 'I bet you have that gorgeous husband of yours running up and down the stairs every five minutes.'

'He doesn't mind.' She seemed to forget her illness for a moment. 'What do you mean by gorgeous?'

Mollie laughed. 'Have you been married to him for so long you've stopped looking at him?' she asked lightly.

'I don't know. I hadn't really thought about it but yes he is quite good-looking.'

'That's an understatement if ever I heard one,' said Mollie. 'I bet he makes a few hearts flutter at that store of his, among the shop girls.'

'Do you think so?'

'Absolutely,' confirmed Mollie. This sort of banter made her feel better about her own lustful thoughts. 'There are some pretty girls working there too.'

'I shall have to keep my eye on him then if he's got female admirers,' Cora said in a less feeble voice, as though forgetting how ill she thought she was.

'I would if I were you,' said Mollie, wondering what Cora would have to say if she knew about the effect her husband had had on her. 'I'll make you some Bovril then get started on the cleaning. Would you like some bread with it?'

'I think I could manage a thin slice.'

'Good,' said Mollie. 'You'll be up and about in no time, if you can manage to eat.'

'Thank you, Mollie,' said Cora. 'For being so kind.'

'Kind, me?' she said in surprise, not wanting compliments she didn't think she deserved. 'I thought I'd been a bit hard on you, actually, kidding you on and suchlike. Anyway I'm paid to be here, remember.'

'Even so . . .'

'I'll be back in a few minutes,' said Mollie and hurried from the room because she felt oddly emotional. This was just a job and she didn't want to get too involved with the Parkers, but was beginning to feel that it was somehow inevitable.

★   ★   ★

91

Cora lay back on the pillows mulling over Mollie's comments about Grant and wondering why she didn't see her husband with the same eyes as other people. Why, when he was clearly so attractive, did she not particularly fancy him and never had? He had simply been her means of escape from home. Even so, he was clearly desirable so surely she should have had a normal reaction to that. It must be because she was frigid, as she had suspected before, she thought miserably; there was no other explanation.

But there was something very satisfying in knowing that he was admired by other women because it made her feel envied and that worked wonders for her confidence. Not that she felt very envied at the moment while she was so ill and looking such a fright. Still, it was nice having people running around after her and she was really looking forward to that Bovril. Good old Mollie, she really was a brick.

The strict discipline of Mollie's life since she had taken on the course sometimes got too much for her and made her tired and irritable, especially as she was already plagued by guilt for the amount of time she spent away from her daughter.

This happened one day in the spring of 1937 not long before Esme's second birthday, when Mollie had been doing a lot of extra hours at the Parkers' house because of the spring cleaning.

She had not long been home from work and was

trying to drink a cup of tea, unsuccessfully because her daughter was being clingy and bad-tempered, which was unusual. Esme was normally such a happy child.

'What's the matter, darling?' asked Mollie when her daughter threw her teddy on the floor and started to cry, her huge brown eyes wet and soulful. 'Come on; come on Mummy's lap.'

She lifted her up but the child screamed to get down then started to throw her toys about and went into a tantrum, crying so hard she was bright red and tear-stained, her beautiful dark hair damp with perspiration. This went on intermittently all afternoon.

Mollie, Madge and Nora all tried to coax her out of it but to no avail. She just wouldn't stop crying. Suddenly the continuous piercing screams set Mollie's nerves on edge and she stood up and let rip at her daughter.

'Shut up, will you, shut up,' she yelled, clenching her fists for fear she might come to the end of her tether and pick her up and shake her. 'Shuuuut up.'

'All right Mollie, that's enough, calm down now,' said her mother, 'the child is obviously very distressed.'

Esme stopped briefly then sat on the floor sobbing quietly and hiccupping.

Mollie was crying too when she picked her up and tried to calm her, dabbing at her wet eyes carefully, the child eventually becoming calmer. She cradled her for a long time, until she was happy again and wanted to leave her mother's lap to play with her toys.

'I'm so ashamed, Mum,' she confided later when her daughter was in bed and she herself was, at last, able to drink a cup of tea. Gran was upstairs in her room. 'I don't know what came over me, screaming like that at her. I lost control.'

'You were just being human,' said Madge. 'Most mums lose their temper with their children sometimes. I did it a good few times with you and Geoff when you were little.'

'I know that, Mum, and I've been cross with Esme plenty of times before, naturally. *But not like that.* I was beside myself,' she said. 'I don't remember ever feeling that way before.'

'Perhaps you're tired love, and it's making you irritable,' suggested her mother sensibly. 'You do have a lot on your plate at the moment with the course as well as work, and you are up very early in the mornings.'

'Unavoidable I'm afraid because I need the money,' she said. 'Needs must and all that.'

'Yes I realise that,' said Madge. 'It's a pity we don't know where Syd is. You could write and ask him to face up to his responsibilities and send you some money as he should so that you could at least give up one of your jobs; then you wouldn't be so exhausted.'

Mollie still couldn't bring herself to speak ill of Syd and didn't like it when other people did. 'Or I could give up the course,' she suggested quickly.

Madge was shocked. 'Surely you're not thinking of doing that,' she said. 'What on earth would that achieve?'

'I wouldn't always be chasing my tail to find time to study and more importantly I'd get to spend more time with Esme.'

'And bang go all your plans of running your own classes,' said Madge.

'Yes but I *have* to work because I need the money,' she said. 'I don't have to continue with the course so if something has to go that's the obvious choice.'

'I can't believe I'm hearing this,' disapproved Madge. 'You love your course and really believe in the benefits of the exercises you'll be teaching once you've qualified.'

'That's true but if I'm going to be cross and losing my temper with my daughter then something has to change and I can't afford to give the jobs up.'

'I think you're making a mountain out of a molehill,' opined Madge. 'Put what happened today behind you. Esme was being difficult and you got cross. So what! It's all part of the rough and tumble of bringing up a child.'

'Yeah, I suppose you're right,' Mollie finally agreed. She was still concerned though. The last thing she wanted to do was give up the course but she'd do it if she thought Esme was suffering because of it.

In the early hours of the next morning Esme became ill. She was very feverish, had a chesty cough and was sick. Mollie nursed her and put a damp flannel on her forehead to cool her but nothing seemed to help.

'I should have known she was sickening for something when she had that tantrum yesterday afternoon,' Mollie said to her mother. 'It's so unlike her I should have guessed.'

'You couldn't have done anything about it if you had suspected it,' Madge pointed out. 'You can't nurse a child better until it is actually ill and she wasn't then.'

'I've been too preoccupied with the course and work and everything,' she said. 'That's why I didn't realise.'

'It doesn't matter so shush for Gawd's sake,' said Madge. 'Let's concentrate on giving the little one some relief, not harking back to yesterday.'

'Yeah of course.'

Nothing seemed to give Esme any comfort; she cried consistently and her cough was frightening. She was obviously a very sick little girl. The whole family was up and when dawn broke they were all so desperate that Geoff headed off for the doctor's house and they waited at home with bated breath.

After examining her thoroughly, the doctor pondered for a while then muttered something about pneumonia at which point Mollie thought her legs would give way beneath her because that illness was known to be lethal; a man in this street had died of it recently and Mollie remembered a girl in her class at school suffering the same fate.

'Keep her temperature down as much as you can with a cool damp flannel and give her plenty of liquid,' he said. 'I'll be back after morning surgery.'

'Does she need to go into hospital?' asked Mollie.

'I'd rather she wasn't moved at this stage but will review the situation again when I return later,' he told them, 'but yes, it might be necessary.'

'Is she?' Mollie began, barely able to speak the words. 'Is she going to die?'

He didn't answer right away; he seemed to be choosing his words and Mollie was trembling. Then he said, 'I won't lie to you, she is very sick and we all know the seriousness of this disease but I don't give up on patients without a fight and I'm certainly not going to give up on her so stay with her and do what I say until I come back.'

For the whole of that day Mollie left her daughter's side only to go to the bathroom. The doctor decided not to move her into hospital so with the assistance and support of her family Mollie nursed Esme; she cooled her skin and held her hand, talked to her softly and prayed hard.

Tea was consumed in large quantities by Mollie because her mouth was parched but she was unable to eat so much as a morsel of food.

'We don't want you getting ill from lack of food,' said her worried mother. 'You need to keep your strength up for Esme's sake.'

'My mouth is too dry, Mum,' she said. 'The tea will keep me going for a while.'

The doctor came again after evening surgery and said that if she worsened during the night to come for him whatever the time. And so it went on. Mollie insisted that the others went to bed and they were all too exhausted to argue. Mollie herself was forced by weariness to lie on the bed next to Esme. But she didn't close her eyes for long.

Then, as the silence of the night closed in on the house, Esme's condition changed. She became still and silent with her eyes closed. Mollie thought they had lost her.

'Oh my God no,' she whispered. 'Please no . . . please . . .'

'I'm thirsty, Mummy,' said the little girl and Mollie wept with joy and gratitude.

'Here, have some of this, darlin',' she said, holding a cup to her lips while she drank some water.

Esme slept through the night after that, with her mother beside her, staying close. There was quiet jubilation in the house the next day, everyone relieved and happy. It happened to be a Wednesday, Mollie's keep-fit morning at Rose's class, but she didn't want to leave Esme's side. Her daughter would need careful treatment over the next few days.

The doctor called and was delighted with Esme's recovery and made the family even happier by only charging for one visit though he had actually made several.

That evening after they had finished their meal and were sitting around the table chatting and Esme asleep upstairs, Mollie made an important announcement.

'I'm giving up the course,' she told them.

'Oh, no,' said her mother. 'I thought I'd talked you out of that daft and unnecessary idea.'

'It isn't a daft idea,' claimed Mollie. 'It's the right and proper thing to do.'

'What on earth has brought this on?' asked her grandmother, who hadn't heard about her comments on the subject the day before.

'I'm getting irritable and preoccupied and Esme is suffering because of it,' she explained. 'So I need to re-arrange my life so that I can spend more time with her and give her my wholehearted attention.'

'In what way is Esme suffering?' her grandmother wanted to know.

Madge took it on herself to answer. 'Esme was being a bit fretful yesterday and Mollie got cross with her and agonised over it afterwards. She also thinks she should have known Esme was going down with something, though what good that would have done I have no idea,' she said. 'I told her she's got the whole thing completely out of perspective.'

'Let the girl answer for herself,' suggested Len. 'So, tell me Mollie, what actually is the trouble? I thought you were enjoying the teaching course.'

'I am, Dad, but I have too many things going on in my life and, as I can't get rid of the cleaning jobs, the course will have to go,' she told him.

'But you've worked so hard, dear,' said Nora, 'and you are well over halfway. It does seem an awful pity to give up now.'

'Sorry Gran. I'll pay you back the money as soon as I can out of what I earn cleaning,' she said. 'It might be slow but I promise I'll do it.'

'I'm not worried about the money,' Nora informed her. 'But I am concerned about you giving up something that means so much to you when there's no need.'

'Esme means more to me than any training course.'

'That goes without saying but this isn't a competition,' said her grandmother. 'I can't see why one isn't compatible with the other as you have plenty of support with Esme.'

'Does your brother know about this?' asked her father; Geoff was at work.

'No.'

'He'll be as disappointed as we are,' said Madge 'He loved the idea of you having this chance. You know how Geoff feels about seizing any opportunity that arises. There aren't many of them for people like us.'

'Let's get this straight, Mollie dear,' began Nora in a kindly tone. 'You are going to give up the course because you think Esme is suffering. So that must mean that you're not satisfied with the way your mother and I look after her.'

Mollie was shocked that her decision had been misinterpreted in this way. 'Of course it doesn't mean that, Gran,' she tried to assure her. 'You know that I really appreciate what you do and I'm only giving up the course and not the jobs so will still need you to look after her while I'm out at work.'

'It seems unnecessary to me,' said her father. 'But I suppose you're old enough to know your own mind.'

'Exactly,' said Mollie.

'Humph,' snorted her mother.

'A child needs to be with its mother whenever possible,' said Mollie. 'Isn't that what they say? Isn't that why women stay at home to look after the children and are expected to stop work when they marry?'

'Well yes, I suppose there is something in that,' her mother was forced to agree. 'But everyone's circumstances are different and there are exceptions to every rule. There's no law against a woman, a mother, making the most of her chances that will benefit her child in the long run.'

'How will Esme benefit exactly?'

'Because after you qualify you can actually get on with the job of teaching instead of studying. You will be a more content person because you'll be doing something that pleases you and that will rub off on Esme. Also if the classes go really well you might be able to afford to give up the early morning shop cleaning so you won't be quite so tired.'

'I'll still have my mind on other things besides Esme, though, won't I?' she said.

'Do you think I only ever thought about you and Geoff when you were little?' asked her mother. 'Of course I had other things on my mind. My sewing work for a start. I used to do a lot of it then to help make ends meet.'

'Yeah I know, Mum, and I know everything you are all saying is for my own good but my mind is made up on this one I'm afraid. I have to do what I think is best.'

There was a general sigh of disappointment, and then Mollie got up and began to clear the table.

★   ★   ★

101

'Had a good day, Geoff?' asked Madge when her son got home from work later on.

'Not bad thanks,' he replied. 'Chef was in a foul mood though. He's been shouting so loud my head is still throbbing from it.'

'That's nothing new is it?' said Mollie because Geoff had told them how the head chef yelled at everyone if they were the tiniest bit late getting the food ready and out to the customer because it was bad form to keep customers waiting and also because he wanted the food to reach them before it had a chance to get cold.

'Not really,' he said. 'But he's been an absolute bugger today. It is annoying for him when the food is freshly cooked and then it's left to go cold and cause complaints because the waiters are held up but my God does he make a noise. I reckon the guests on the top floor must have heard him tonight.'

'You'll probably be like that when you're in charge of a kitchen,' his sister suggested.

'Very probably. It's par for the course really,' said Geoff. 'Cooking is a delicate art and everything has to be done with split-second timing or the food spoils so tempers are bound to run high in a professional kitchen.'

'I'll make the cocoa,' said Madge, yawning rather theatrically. 'I think we all need an early night after all the worry we've had about little Esme.'

'I'll take mine up to bed I think,' said Nora.

'Good idea, we'll do that too, won't we Len?' added Madge, more as an order than a suggestion.

'Will we?' He looked at the clock on the mantelpiece.

'It's a bit early though, love.' Madge and Nora rested their gaze on him and he finally caught on. 'But yeah, I am tired now that you come to mention it.'

There was a flurry of activity and within the space of a few minutes the twins had been given cocoa and the others had all disappeared.

'So what was that all about?' asked Geoff. 'Do I sense a conspiracy?'

She gave a wry grin. 'I think the idea is for you to talk me into changing my mind about giving up the course. They have all tried without success so they think you'll do the trick. They know that if anyone can do it, you will.'

'Give up the course,' he said in surprise. 'Why on earth would you want to do that?'

She told him.

'Hmm. I can understand why you might feel like giving up but I don't think you should use Esme as an excuse.'

'Esme an excuse!' she said, astonished. 'That's the last thing I would do.'

'Consciously, yes it is,' he agreed. 'But subconsciously you just might.'

'You couldn't be more wrong,' she insisted. 'I thoroughly enjoy the course and had such plans for the classes I was going to run and gradually open more.'

'I remember going through a similar thing myself when I started at the hotel working as a kitchen porter, doing all the boring and back-breaking jobs and being yelled at by all and sundry. I thought, I've had enough

103

of this; I'll give it up and try and get an easier job some-where else. There were times back then when I would have cleaned the streets rather than work in that kitchen for another day.'

'I didn't know you ever felt like that, Geoff.'

'I kept it to myself because I didn't want to admit it to anyone and at the back of my mind I always I knew that if I kept going, sooner or later, I would progress beyond that hard, tedious graft to something more interesting.'

'And you did.'

He nodded. 'I'll never forget when I first moved on to preparing and cooking vegetables and following recipes, making salads and helping the other chefs. There is something so exciting and rewarding in cooking, espe-cially when you are at that early stage in your career. One more step up for me and I'll actually be putting dishes together and working out menus.'

'And you nearly gave it up.'

'On several occasions.'

'But that was something personal to you because you were doing that awful work,' she said. 'It's different for me. I'm giving up the course because of Esme.'

'I suppose if you tell yourself that enough times you'll begin to believe it.'

'Geoff, you know I'm not a quitter.'

'Yes I do know that,' he told her. 'I also know that the studying must be getting difficult at this stage, espe-cially when you have other calls on your time. It probably feels like a chore at times. Concentrating on your books takes a lot of self-discipline and you and I don't have that sort of a background so it comes hard to people like us.'

'So you think that's why I want to chuck it all in, because I can't cope with it.'

He swallowed the last of his cocoa. 'In your heart you know that Esme is fine with Mum and Gran and that none of us, including you, would ever let her suffer. So I think you've got a serious case of cold feet and without realising it you are passing the buck to Esme.'

'That's a horrible thing to say,' she objected.

'I don't mean it in a bad way. I know that Esme is everything to you. But we're twins, Mollie, and I know you nearly as well as I know myself. We're two of a kind. I've gone into cooking, which is a world away from what a lad like me was expected to do. People would have thought I would drive a bus or train or work as a welder so I have to prove myself. Similarly, I don't know any other young mums of our sort who are about to embark on a career as a keep-fit teacher and I think the whole thing has got on top of you. But just think ahead to how you'll feel when you've qualified and are working out the exercises to make up your class and deciding on the best music to suit it and please the members.'

'Yes but I'll still be preoccupied with the classes, won't I?' she pointed out. 'It won't be like my cleaning jobs that require no thought from me whatsoever when I get home so that I can give Esme my full attention.'

'Come on, Moll, that really is a feeble excuse. You're more than capable of having something else besides your daughter to consider. This opportunity is tailor-made for you. You know you'd make a good job of it.'

She looked into the distance. 'Yes, I suppose I do really,' she said. 'I was looking forward to it.'

'You still can,' he reminded her. 'You haven't actually told them you are giving up yet, have you.'

'No, not yet,' she confirmed.

'It's your decision, of course, but if I were you, I would at least give it some more thought.'

'Mmm. You're right in what you said just now,' she admitted. 'I have been finding the studying difficult at times. There's a lot to learn and teaching someone how to exercise their body is a big responsibility. I don't want people putting their backs out or straining muscles because I'm not doing the job right.'

'You won't do that,' he said. 'You're far too diligent.'

'I certainly try to be.' She drained her cocoa cup. 'Of course, it doesn't help that married women are so strongly discouraged from taking on anything outside of the home. I've had a good few digs about the course from some of the neighbours.'

'Surely you are not going to let them influence you,' he said. 'You're better than that.'

'I suppose I should be but it is a bit off-putting.'

'Promise me that you'll think about it some more before you do anything official.'

'All right, I promise to think about it, I'll say no more than that,' she said. 'As usual it's taken you to make me slow down and think things through.'

'It's what we do for each other.'

'Can you do something else for me?' she asked.

'Of course. As long as it's legal.'

'Would you go round to the Parkers' for me tomorrow morning before you go to work and tell Cora that I won't be coming into work for the rest of the week. I want to be with Esme as it's such early days. Tell her what's happened and say I'll be back at work next week, all being well.'

'Yeah. I'll do that. No trouble,' he said.

Mollie was far too preoccupied with her own concerns to notice the broadness of his smile.

To Geoff she seemed to shimmer when she opened the door, a vision in a red dress, a poodle at her feet.

'Hello, Mrs Parker,' he greeted her. 'I'm Mollie's brother.'

She gave him a studious look. 'Yes, I recognise you,' she said with a worried smile. 'I came to your house one day, you might remember.'

Would he ever forget the impact she'd had on him that day, and seeing her again he was even more impressed.

'I am expecting Mollie this morning,' she said. 'Your being here means that something is wrong.'

'I'm afraid it is,' he confirmed. 'Esme has been very poorly. In fact she gave us all a real scare. We thought we were going to lose her at one point.'

'Oh dear, that's awful.' Cora was frowning. 'I thought something might be wrong when Mollie wasn't at the keep-fit class yesterday. Is the little girl all right?'

'She's come through it and seems better now but

Mollie wants to be with her for the next few days just to be on the safe side so she asked me to call in and tell you that she won't be coming into work until next week. She's very sorry to let you down and hopes to be back on Monday.'

This was infuriating news for Cora who wanted her cleaning done. But she heard herself saying, 'Tell her not to worry at all. She mustn't think of coming back until she's happy about leaving her little girl.'

'I don't suppose she's ever happy about leaving her but I'll pass on the message.'

'Tell her,' began Cora, hardly able to believe what she was about to say, 'that I'll pay her the same as usual for this week.'

He was surprised too. 'That's very good of you, Mrs Parker. I'm sure my sister will be delighted,' he said, giving her a smile that she noticed was very much like Mollie's. 'Thanks very much on her behalf.'

'That's quite all right,' she said, struggling with the effect he was having on her. 'I do hope Esme continues to improve.'

'Me too but she will I'm sure, now that she's over the worst,' he said. 'We're a tough lot in our family.'

'I'm sure.'

'I'll be off then, ta-ta.'

'Cheerio.'

She watched him stride down the path and was still at the door when he got to the gate and turned and gave her a wave. She'd been too preoccupied with eating large amounts of humble pie from Mollie when she'd met him briefly that first time to pay much attention to him. But she had certainly noticed him now and she liked what she saw very much indeed: a tall, slim young man with warm brown eyes, a wide smile and a boyishness about him that she found very attractive. In fact she fancied him like mad. So perhaps she wasn't frigid after all. Quite the opposite if her current feelings were anything to go by.

Chapter Five

'Can we have a bit of hush here, please folks?' requested Len, tapping a spoon against a glass to gain attention until the party racket abated. 'I won't hold up the festivities for longer than I need to but I just want to say how proud Madge and I are of our twins who have now officially come of age. Twenty-one today and doing fine. It doesn't seem five minutes since they were giving Madge and me grief by screaming their heads off in the middle of the night. If one started the other soon joined in. What a din.'

There was a communal 'Aah' from the guests, who were made up of relatives, neighbours and friends of the twins, everyone gathered in the front room with Nora seated at the piano.

'But they've grown up to be a couple of smashing adults,' he continued. 'They still have that special twin bond but are both pursuing their own ambitions. Geoff is working his way up in a hotel kitchen and Mollie is training as a keep-fit teacher. I'm sure you all wish them well.'

Cheers and whistles filled the room.

'So can I ask you all to raise your glasses please to Mollie and Geoff,' he said.

There were roars of approval and chinking of glasses. Nora belted out 'Happy Birthday to You' on the piano.

As the notes died away and conversation resumed Mollie was thankful that her father had been able to mention her ambitions in his speech because she had so nearly quit after Esme's illness a few weeks ago. Ultimately the decision had had to be hers. She had listened to the opinions of others and Geoff's pep talk did have a powerful effect on her but the decision to continue with the course had been hers alone.

She had thanked God for Esme's recovery and decided to make the most of the special opportunity the likes of which were few and far between for working-class women such as her. Looking back on her time of uncertainty, she suspected that she had passed a turning point in her life. Since making her decision she'd felt as though she had added strength to cope with her responsibilities and that included the course.

In hindsight she could see that she had got the whole thing out of proportion in her mind. Her mother was right when she said that most mums got angry with their kids at times. When weighing up the pros and cons she had also taken into account the fact that when she qualified she would only be teaching part-time which was hardly going to make Esme a deprived child. So she would make the most of the talent she had thought she would never use again and eventually build up a network of classes.

Gran launched into 'Just One of Those Things' and people started jigging around. They were dancing and singing in the hallway too. No one paid any attention to the lack of space because making merry in a confined area was normal for them.

'You didn't invite the Parkers I notice,' observed Geoff when he and Mollie were talking in the corner.

'Are you mad, Geoff?' she replied. 'Of course I didn't.'

'But I thought you were quite friendly with her these days,' he said.

'I am at work but that's as far as it goes.'

'You do the keep-fit class together and she gave you a lovely birthday present.'

'Yeah, she was generous and it was very kind of her.' Cora had given her some expensive perfume and a huge box of chocolates.

'So why didn't you invite them?'

'Don't be dim, Geoff,' she said. 'Can you imagine the Parkers at a do like this?'

'More comfortable at the Dorchester, eh?'

'Exactly,' she replied. 'Anyway, I hardly know her husband. I only saw him that once when she was ill. This sort of a do would probably frighten them half to death,' she went on, having to shout to make herself heard over the noise of talking, singing, laughing and Nora thumping away on the piano.

'They say that he is quite down-to-earth,' he mentioned, deliberately casual.

'Not far enough down for a party at the Pottses', I

suspect,' she said, laughing. 'Been doing a spot of detect-
ive work, have you?'

'Of course not.' He knew his interest in Cora was
pointless but, try as he might, he couldn't stop thinking
about her. 'The Parkers are well known around here
because of their store so naturally people talk about them.
As you work for her, I am more aware of them than I
would be otherwise.'

'Mm, I suppose you would be. They live in a different
world to us though,' she said thoughtfully. 'Can you imagine
Cora's reaction if she was here and Dad had one too many
to drink and started telling his embarrassing smutty jokes.'

He laughed. 'It doesn't bear thinking about.' He looked
at her with affection. 'Anyway, happy birthday, Moll.'

'Same to you, Geoff,' she responded.

When anyone came to see Madge about sewing work
they were taken into the front room where her treadle
sewing machine nestled among the soft furnishings and
highly polished coffee table and piano.

'Did you say that this outfit is for you to wear at your
youngest daughter's wedding, Dot?' asked Madge chattily
one day in the autumn as she worked with pins on a
blue crepe dress she was fitting for a woman who lived
in Pearl Road.

'Yeah, last one, thank Gawd,' she replied. 'It's a relief
for mothers of daughters when they are safely married
and can't get into trouble.'

113

'Mm, I suppose it is.'

'The expense of it is crippling though,' she went on. 'It's nearly all up to the bride's parents; the groom's lot get off practically scot free. But you'll know all about that as you have a daughter, won't you?' She thought for a moment. 'Still, Mollie didn't have a big do, did she?'

'No, she didn't.'

'How is Mollie?' asked the woman. 'She hasn't had much luck, has she, what with a rush do of a wedding then her husband going off and leaving her.'

'Mollie is fine,' Madge assured her.

'Somebody was telling me that she's doing some sort of a course with the idea of teaching exercises. I told them that they couldn't be right as Mollie has a little girl.'

'They are quite right I'm proud to say,' Madge announced through gritted teeth.

'Oh really,' said the woman. 'I must say I'm surprised at your attitude, Madge.'

'Are you? Why is that?' she asked, though she knew perfectly well what the woman was getting at.

'I should have thought that was obvious. A mother's place is with her child and I heard that she already goes out working in the mornings.'

'She has to as she doesn't have a husband's wage supporting her.'

'Mm, I suppose so,' the woman agreed reluctantly. 'But surely that's enough for anyone. Most women would be glad to be at home with their child after that; not taking on something else as well.'

'Mollie is very talented at anything to do with exercise;

always has been. I'm pleased she's being given the chance to use her ability.'

'Oh well, each to their own I suppose but I wouldn't encourage any of my girls to do something like that. Oh no. You have kids, you stay home to look after 'em, that's my rule. It's how I was brought up.'

'Let's hope that none of your daughters ever find themselves in a position where they need to work and call on you to look after their kids then,' said Madge.

'Ouch,' shrieked the woman, flinching and rubbing her arm. 'What are you doing sticking pins in me?'

'Sorry,' said Madge. 'My hand must have slipped.'

'That isn't like you, Madge; you're usually such an expert at what you do,'

I'm also Mollie's mother and I don't like the way you are talking about her, you malicious old cow, Madge's inner voice said. You're lucky I didn't dig it in deeper. One more crack about my daughter and you'll have pin marks all over you and you can take your dressmaking elsewhere. But she actually said, 'How does that feel? Have a look in the mirror. If you want it more fitted I'll move the pins in a bit.'

'That's about right I think,' said the woman, looking in the long free-standing mirror with a polished wooden frame.

Because Mollie was cautiously optimistic about passing her exams in December and becoming a qualified teacher, she began to put plans into place to start her classes in January.

She could be tempting fate, of course, but she went ahead anyway, preferring to have a positive attitude.

A provisional booking for a hall just off the High Road was made. It was only vacant on a Monday evening so she decided, having discussed it with Rose, to take it. This would suit single women who were at work during the day and mums who couldn't get the children looked after until the evening when their husbands got home from work. She put notices in local shop windows and one on the noticeboard in the library and post office, announcing that the classes were to begin at seven thirty on the first Monday in January.

There was no shortage of support at home. Mum offered to look after Esme, who would be in bed anyway. Dad said he would do it if Madge wanted to go to the class at any time. Gran offered to play the piano, free of charge, and Rose was on hand with plenty of advice.

'Always start with a march,' she said when Mollie told her that she and Gran were going to look through her music and choose suitable pieces. 'As most teachers start the ball rolling with some strong energetic walking, a march is ideal. Something rousing, to get everyone in the mood.'

The biggest surprise came from Cora who seemed very eager to help and was planning on going to Mollie's class as well as Rose's.

'Would you like me to take the money and do the register for you?' she asked one day during Mollie's shift at her house, in the tea break.

'That would be really helpful but you'd miss some of the class because of latecomers,' Mollie pointed out.

'I don't mind that.'

'You'd get your class free in return,' Mollie told her.

'You won't make a profit if you do things like that,' said Cora. 'So absolutely not!'

'It's quite usual,' Mollie told her. 'Rose does that for the woman who does her reception. It's very helpful to the teacher to have someone to take care of that side of things while she prepares for the class and doesn't have to stay at the desk for the stragglers. There are always some of those as you know.'

'I'd still rather pay.'

Mollie put her cup down forcefully. 'Cora,' she began in a determined manner. 'When I am here in this house you make the rules because I am paid to do what you say. But at my class I will be in charge. Suggestions will be welcome but I will have the final say on everything.'

'Oh, well; I'll take the free class then since you're being so stubborn about it.'

'Good! I'm glad we understand each other.'

'I'll never understand you with your damned pride and determination,' said Cora.

'You don't need to understand me to come to my class,' said Mollie laughing. 'You just have to do what I tell you.'

'Watch it or I'll have you scrubbing the kitchen floor with a nailbrush,' Cora riposted.

'You'll be lucky,' Mollie came back at her.

They were both laughing as they finished their tea. They each recognised that theirs was a peculiar bond but they did have a rapport of sorts.

Mollie had qualified and was all set to go. Excitement and the jitters were present in equal measures on the Monday night of the first class due to start at seven thirty. She was at the hall early, running the broom over the floor and checking that all the chairs surrounding the walls were pushed right back to avoid an accident; all the while she was mentally checking the exercise sequences she had worked out.

Cora was sitting at a desk in the lobby with a large book in which to write names and amounts paid and a tin for the money. There were also membership forms to be filled in for people who wanted to commit to membership, usually after the class when they had decided if it was for them.

Mollie knew she wasn't the only one who was tense. Gran was studying her music rather too ardently and Cora repeatedly tidied the desk. There was a large round clock on the wall and Mollie was drawn to it. She knew from experience that people often arrived early but twenty past seven came and no one had appeared; twenty-five past and two women arrived; friends apparently. It was a relief and Mollie hoped that their appearance might be the catalyst to get things moving.

But no one else came so at seven thirty Mollie started the class, as advertised, with just two people plus Cora who joined in after she had abandoned all hope of anyone else turning up and closed the book. With Gran at the piano, Mollie launched into the warm-up and then taught the routines she had worked out as though she had a full class. The disappointment was painful but no one could have guessed how shattered she actually felt. After a while, though, she forgot she had so few people and enjoyed the class for its own sake.

'Well done,' said Gran when the two people had left and Mollie and Cora were changing out of their kit into their warm winter clothes. 'It couldn't have been easy with an almost empty hall. But you were really good.'

'Excellent,' added Cora.

'It must have been the weather that kept people at home,' suggested Nora.

'It isn't raining or snowing, Gran,' Mollie pointed out.

'No, but it is cold.'

'If that's going to put people off, I'll have no one come all winter,' she said miserably.

'It's bound to take time to build up,' suggested Cora.

'I suppose so,' said Mollie but she was worried. She'd borrowed money to train as a teacher and it needed to be repaid. Tonight she wouldn't so much as break even after the hall was paid for. It was fortunate that Gran gave her musical services free or she would be even more in debt.

★　★　★

When the three women came out of the hall there were two men waiting for them: Geoff and Grant Parker, who seemed to have got to know each other.

'Why didn't you come inside out of the cold?' asked Mollie.

'What, with a hall full of women,' said Geoff. 'Not likely!'

'We didn't think we'd be allowed,' added Grant.

'The class is for women only but men aren't absolutely banned from the premises,' Mollie said with a grin. 'I know we've got the vote now but we wouldn't take things that far.' She turned to her brother. 'What brings you here?'

'I got home from work early so I thought you might need me to walk home with you as you'll be carrying money,' he replied.

Mollie's sense of humour underwent a revival and she burst out laughing. 'We only had two paying customers,' she told him. 'Not exactly cause for an escort.'

'Oh dear,' he said. 'It didn't go well then.'

'A complete disaster,' she confirmed and told the men what had happened.

'That's such a shame,' said Grant. 'I suppose it might take time for people to get to know about it.'

'I put cards in as many shop windows as I could find,' she said, 'and told everyone I spoke to about it. What else can I do? It's expensive to advertise in the local paper.'

'If you make a few good-sized posters, I'll put them up around the store, if you like,' he offered.

'That's a good idea,' Cora approved. 'I don't know why I didn't think of it.'

'Thank you, Mr Parker,' said Mollie brightly. 'That would be really helpful.'

'No trouble,' he assured her. 'And the name is Grant.'

'I'll remember that next time.'

'Anyway, it's cold standing here,' he said. 'The car is just across the road. Can we give you a lift?'

'Thank you but we're only a few minutes from home and I need to walk off my frustration,' said Mollie. 'Geoff and Gran might like to go in the car with you though.'

'Thanks, mate,' said Geoff. 'But I'll walk with Mollie.'

'Me too,' added Nora.

'It's just us then, Cora,' he said. 'It was nice to see you all. Don't forget about the posters, Mollie.'

'Don't worry, I won't,' she said. 'And thanks ever so much.'

'A pleasure.'

They said their goodnights and he took his wife's arm as they crossed the road. Cora was a very lucky woman to have him, thought Mollie.

'Handy having friends in high places isn't it?' remarked Nora as the three of them walked home. 'Having your posters in Parker's store should help to spread the word. Most women go in there quite regular even if it's only for a reel of cotton in the haberdashery department. If he puts a notice near the entrance the customers won't be able to miss it.'

'Yeah, that's given me a real boost. I would never have dreamed of asking to put a notice up in such an esteemed store but as he's offered and suggested big posters rather than postcards it just might work. I shall get some paper to make them with tomorrow. I think perhaps I was expecting too much too soon. It's bound to take a while to get going.'

'Nice people, aren't they,' remarked Nora. 'Especially him. I thought you said that she was a bit of a madam, Mollie, but she seems all right to me.'

'She can be very snooty if she gets half a chance but she doesn't do it with me, not since I told her I wouldn't put up with it,' she said. 'But for all her airs and graces she's turned out to be a good friend and is very supportive of my class.'

'What did you think of them, Geoff?' asked Nora.

Geoff was miles away dreaming of Cora. Seeing her with her husband had brought him down to earth slightly but not entirely because she was just his fantasy woman and most men had one of those. 'I thought they were all right. He's a really nice bloke,' he said with a casual air, thinking that his gran would probably clip his ear if she knew what he really thought of Cora.

'Lovely family, the Pottses, aren't they?' Grant remarked to his wife in the car on the way home. 'There's something so special about twins, don't you think?'

'Mm,' she said absently, her thoughts all of Geoff. 'There's certainly something special about those two.'

'Yes there is,' he agreed, remembering Mollie's laughter despite having had such a huge disappointment. She was so full of vitality, he was entranced by her. 'They seem very close.'

'I think twins usually are,' she remarked. 'I suppose you are never lonely if you are a twin because you always have each other.'

'Maybe. I've never really thought about it,' he said. 'Probably because they are the only twins I've ever met.'

'Me too,' she said as the car rolled into their drive. Seeing Mollie and her brother together made Cora feel stupid about her attraction towards Geoff. They were both so appealing. He could have the pick of the girls. Cora was older than him and married so the whole thing was pathetic.

'Can we go through that again please, ladies,' instructed Mollie from the stage. 'It's four steps forward and clap, four steps back then two steps right then left, arms movements as we have learned. Don't forget your posture: tummies in, shoulders back.'

Mollie wasn't sure if it was the homemade posters in Parker's department store or word of mouth or a bit of both but the numbers for her classes had increased. Two became four, then ten and now at the beginning of the summer term, more than thirty people had turned up. Teaching had slipped into her life as though she was born to it and, with the encouragement of the association and the family, she was planning on opening another evening class in the autumn.

Looking at her class now from the stage to see the rows of women in black shorts and white blouses, all pink-cheeked and dishevelled from the exercise, their enthusiasm palpable, she was very proud of them and thankful that she had been given this opportunity, so nearly lost because of an exaggerated sense of duty. Not only did this work give her pleasure, it made her feel fulfilled. She also had an income from it now and had started paying the loan from her grandmother back.

'That's much better, everyone,' she said to the class. 'Let's go through that once more with the music and then I'll let you lie down and do the floor exercises.'

There was a ripple of laughter and they stood poised waiting for the music to begin.

Mollie had something to tell the family one day soon after the beginning of the new term. She waited until Geoff's night off and told them over the meal.

'There is going to be a keep-fit display at Wembley Stadium in early September; a big important event with teams from other countries performing,' she began. 'It's been in the planning for ages and Rose has put together a team to represent West London, and the girls have been rehearsing for a while. She told me ages ago that she would like me to be in the show and I turned it down because of other commitments but now a couple of the girls have dropped out and she's desperate to have me so I said I would talk to you about it before I give her an answer.'

'What a lovely opportunity,' said her mother, 'but why do you need to talk to us before accepting it?'

'Because I will have to go to rehearsals and it means leaving Esme and asking you to look after her again. It won't be a permanent arrangement though. Only until after the show.'

'I'm sure we can manage that between us,' said her mother. 'She's no trouble and you don't want to miss an experience like that so go ahead and tell Rose that you're in.'

'Thanks Mum,' she said excitedly. 'Cora will be pleased too. She's offered to take part and she's hoping I'll do it to give her some moral support. The team will be made up of members from several classes so we'll be working with some strangers.'

'They won't be strangers once you start rehearsals,' Nora pointed out. 'You'll soon get to know each other when you are working together.'

'I know but Cora, for all her money and superior attitude, lacks self-confidence at times; it's strange.'

'She'll be all right with you,' said Madge. 'I hope we can come to see the show.'

'I'd be disappointed if you didn't,' said Mollie. 'I'll order some tickets.'

'It will be a nice family occasion,' enthused Madge. 'Are you coming, Len, to support your daughter?'

'Men aren't allowed are they?' he said.

'Of course they are, to see the show,' said Mollie. 'It's just the classes that are for women only.'

'Count me in then but if there are no other men there I'll come straight home.'

'What about you, Geoff?' asked Nora. 'Do you fancy joining the party?'

Geoff had his own reasons for wanting to go but thought this might be going a bit too far in his admiration for Cora because it would probably be her he would be watching rather than his sister. Admiring her when their paths crossed was one thing; going out of his way to feast his eyes on her quite another and could overstep the mark.

'I'll probably be working,' he said lamely.

'It's a Sunday afternoon, Geoff,' said Mollie. 'I know you work odd hours in your line of business but I'm sure you could get the time off if you ask the chef well in advance.' She looked at him with her appealing brown eyes. 'I'd love you to be there if you can possibly make it.'

What was he doing thinking about some other man's wife when his sister needed his support? 'Yeah, of course I'll be there. You give me the time and date and I'll speak to chef about it tomorrow,' he said. 'I don't think there will be a problem.'

Mollie smiled and he was determined to be there for *her*, not some married woman he happened to have a fancy for.

The day was fine and the turf at Wembley Stadium gloriously green and bathed in sunlight, the stands filled with people; mostly women, but there was a sprinkling of men.

'When is Mummy coming on?' asked Esme for the umpteenth time; she was looking very cute in a pink frock with matching ribbon in her hair. The family were in a prime position in the front row of the stands.

'Not quite yet, love,' said Madge. 'The show hasn't started yet and there are lots of other groups to perform as well as Mummy's team.'

'I want to see my mummy.'

Madge wondered if she was perhaps too little to sit through the show because there were lots of teams due to perform. But they couldn't let her miss seeing her mother in such a prestigious event so would keep her pacified somehow until her mother came on. 'We have to wait for a little while longer.'

'When will it start?' she persisted.

The sooner the better if my patience is to hold out, thought Madge, but turned and asked Geoff to go and get Esme an ice cream from a nearby seller in the hope it might keep her occupied while they were waiting. It proved to be a mistake because she got the ice cream all over her dress then dropped the cornet and started to cry, loudly. They were all at their wits' end trying to pacify her when the show finally started and opened with a group dressed in bright red sequinned outfits.

Not only did Esme stop crying; she seemed transfixed and absorbed in the show which was very colourful with eye-catching costumes and music from an orchestra. Apart from asking when she was going to see her mother once or twice she was quiet so Madge and the family relaxed and enjoyed the show.

Rose's team were the last item before the interval and stage fright in the crowded dressing rooms grew more severe with every second that passed as they got changed in the tiny space allotted to them. There was the heat, the noise of women chattering, the distant beat of the music from the stadium and nervous giggling all around.

'I wish I'd never agreed to do the show now,' said Cora as they waited to go on, the team resplendent in turquoise satin pants and white tops with blue sashes round the middle. 'I'm sure I'll go wrong and put everyone else out of step. Oh dear, I can't do it.'

'Stop panicking. You'll be fine,' encouraged Mollie though she was trembling too. There was a huge crowd out there to please. 'It will probably be me who goes wrong, not you.'

'I very much doubt it,' said Cora as they made their way to the stadium ushered along by Rose. 'My legs are like jelly.'

'Mine too but I think they'll still work.'

They heard the music come to an end and an explosion of applause. Then flush with success the performers came off stage. The compere made her introduction. 'Please welcome Rose Smith and her West London team.'

Cora said she thought she was going to wet herself and Mollie was rooted to the spot. But somehow Cora managed to control herself and Mollie ran into the stadium with head held high and waited for the music to start. After that first step something happened and the frightening ordeal turned to pure joy; her body did everything that was expected of it and all too soon it was over and the applause was all around them.

An extra thrill was the close proximity of the family to Mollie, who was on the outside of the group; just a stone's throw from Esme who was clapping and smiling in the front row near to the aisle. Mollie waved and blew kisses to her. Then the unexpected happened; the little girl escaped from her grandmother and ran out on to the turf, over to her mother who swept her into her arms and smothered her with kisses. This sort of thing was strictly against the rules but nobody seemed to mind. Mollie's own performance was forgotten while she revelled in being the proudest mum in London.

The show ended with a grand finale, an emotional spectacle with all the performers in the stadium together doing a short pre-rehearsed item which didn't require much space. The feeling of friendship and unity with many people she didn't even know was so tangible it brought tears to Mollie's eyes.

When she and Cora had changed into their ordinary clothes and emerged from the building, Grant was standing with Mollie's family with Peaches on the lead, Esme entranced by the little dog.

'Well done, girls,' he said. 'An excellent show.'

'Not half,' added Nora and there was a general chorus

of approval, everyone chatting and getting along. Then,
to Mollie's astonishment and dismay, she heard her mother
inviting the Parkers to join them for a picnic in the park.

It should have been a disaster but somehow it wasn't.
Cora and Grant tucked into egg sandwiches and Tizer
as though they had it every day. After the thrill of that
successful performance and the relief that it had gone
well after months of rehearsals, it would have taken a
catastrophe of epic proportions to dampen Mollie's spirits.
So the sociable atmosphere only enhanced her mood
and was the perfect end to such a special event.

She still thought Grant was gorgeous and their eyes
did meet on several occasions but she didn't read anything
into it; just enjoyed the pleasure it gave her. Life was
good. Even the dismal Air Raid Patrol recruiting posters
that were so ubiquitous in London lately couldn't spoil
her mood today.

Syd was sitting on the grass in a park near to where he
lived. He was with a young woman he was currently
seeing. He was bored stiff but was forced to do things
like going to the park on a Sunday afternoon and taking
a girl to the pictures to persuade her to agree to what
he was really after.

He lay down on his back and closed his eyes, enjoying
the warmth of the sun on his face. Things were going
well for him; he was earning good money, had a nice
flat, a car and never had any trouble finding female
company when he fancied it. Naturally living alone did

create a certain amount of loneliness but it was a small price to pay for freedom.

Something hitting him in the face startled him and he sat up quickly, holding his cheek. 'What's going on?' he grunted and found himself staring at a small girl regarding him gingerly.

'I'm so sorry, mate,' said a man coming up behind the child. 'My daughter got a bit carried away with her new ball. Apologise to the gentleman, Susie.'

'Yes, say sorry,' added a woman he presumed to be the child's mother.

The child's saucer eyes rested on him intently. 'Sorry, mister,' she said shyly.

'That's all right, love,' he heard himself say, handing the ball to the child and smiling at her. 'You carry on and enjoy your game.'

'Thank you,' she said and turned and ran to her father.

'Apologies again,' said the man, holding the child's hand.

'She only had the ball yesterday and got a bit over-enthusiastic with it,' the woman explained. 'You know what kids are like.'

'No harm done,' Syd assured them and they went on their way, the child skipping between them, a picture of family unity.

'I didn't know you liked kids,' remarked his companion.

'I don't particularly but I've got one of my own,' he surprised himself by telling her.

'You've got a child.' She didn't look pleased. 'I didn't know you were married,'

'Separated,' he informed her.

'You're still married though.'

'Technically I suppose I am, yeah.'

'Oh, that's charming that is,' said the woman furiously, scrambling to her feet. 'You've been stringing me along, hiding it from me.'

'I haven't been hiding anything from you,' he said casually. 'I just didn't think to tell you. I haven't seen my wife and kid for years so I didn't think it was important.'

'Not important,' she screeched. 'You're still married and you've no right to be going out with innocent girls like me.'

'Innocent? You? Blimey, that's a good one.'

'How dare you?' she shouted.

'Well you're not exactly Little Miss Pure, are you?'

'That's a flamin' insult, that is,' she said, her voice rising.

'No offence meant.'

'But plenty of offence taken,' she rasped. 'Whatever I am, I don't knowingly go out with married men. So you can get lost, you lying, cheating pig.'

She walked away swinging her hips, a shapely blonde, well endowed up top. Oh well, that's tonight's bit of the other gone down the drain, he thought. It didn't even occur to him to go after her because she meant nothing to him. She was just a random girl he'd got lucky with.

He lay back down to enjoy the sunshine, thinking about the little girl whose ball had hit him and found himself experiencing something he didn't understand. It felt like a pang of regret but it couldn't be because he was glad he'd left his marriage. It must be over three years since he'd last seen his daughter so she would have grown up a bit now. He found himself idly wondering what she looked like as he dozed in the sun.

Chapter Six

'The attendance is good at the new evening class, considering it's only been going a few weeks, isn't it?' Cora mentioned to Mollie during her break one day in the autumn. 'The numbers are a lot better than they were at the first class at the beginning.'

'Yes, they are not too bad at all,' agreed Mollie. 'Maybe it's because keep-fit classes generally are becoming more popular.'

'I think it's more to do with people getting to know about your reputation,' suggested Cora. 'If you weren't such a good teacher they would only come once and they certainly wouldn't recommend your classes to their friends.'

Mollie was unexpectedly touched, 'Oh Cora, that's such a nice thing to say. Thank you.'

'Only saying what's true.'

Over time and especially since opening her second class, Mollie had come to realise that she had a true friend in Cora. She worked tirelessly to help the classes run smoothly. As well as looking after the reception at both classes, she counted and entered the money, kept the register up to date, distributed any leaflets and magazines from head office and listed names of members interested in attending extra events such as fun days. People seemed to like her too. The superior attitude she sometimes adopted was never present at keep fit.

'It's nice to know you approve of the way I do things anyway,' Mollie said, clearing her throat and moving on swiftly to avoid sinking into a vat of emotion. 'I appreciate your contribution.'

I enjoy being involved.'

'Good.' She nibbled a ginger nut and decided to bring things down to earth by talking about the job in hand. 'Your paintwork needs washing down so I'll only take a short break today.'

'You must take your proper break,' insisted Cora. 'You can do the paintwork on extra paid time if you like, though, knowing your busy schedule, I doubt if you'll have time so if you want to leave something else to fit that in, it's fine with me.'

'I'll see how I get on,' said Mollie, glad that things were back on a normal footing after the unexpected compliment.

'Well, stone me, it's Nora. After all these years, we meet again,' said a tall, sprightly man in his sixties with a shock of white wavy hair, warm brown eyes and an expression of pure delight. He'd spotted her coming out of the greengrocer's in Chiswick High Road. 'I always hoped our paths would cross again one day and now they finally have, here in my old home town. How are you, Nora?'

'Wilf Robbins,' gasped Nora, deeply affected by this unexpected meeting and struggling to hide it. 'What are you doing around here? I thought you moved away years ago.'

'I did. But I'm back now.'

'Your going was all very sudden,' she said, remembering. 'You just disappeared overnight. Nobody knew where you'd gone.'

'It was all very sudden for me too on account of it being a moonlight flit,' he explained. 'Mum and Dad were behind with the rent so we ran away under cover of darkness. I knew nothing about it until I was told to get my things together.'

'Where did you go?' she asked, remembering how heartbroken she'd been when he'd vanished.

'The Kent coast. Margate. I was miserable for ages because I missed London and my friends, especially you, but I had to stay because they needed me to work and help pay for the younger kids. Eventually I settled and made a life there.'

'Did you get married?'

'Yeah. I married a local girl and we had a long marriage,' he replied. 'She died a couple of years ago so as I'm on my own and can please myself I decided to come back to my roots. I'm retired now so there are no ties in Margate.'

'No children then?'

'No. Sadly we were never blessed that way.' He paused, looking at her. 'How about you?'

'My husband died a few years ago,' she told him.

'Sorry to hear that.'

'I've been on my own for a while so I'm used to it,' she said quickly. 'I'm not really on my own though. I live with my daughter and her husband, my grand-daughter and her little girl. All in all we are quite a crowd.'

'A good bloke was he, your husband?'

The answer to that was an emphatic *no*. He'd been a bully and made her life hell but he'd been her husband and therefore deserved respect so she never spoke ill of him outside of the family and not even then if she could avoid it. Madge sometimes mentioned him in derogatory terms because she'd hated him. She knew what a brute he'd been at times because she had grown up with it.

But now Nora smiled and said, 'I wouldn't have married him otherwise.'

'Course you wouldn't. I'm glad things worked out for you.' When he looked at her he didn't see a white-haired sixty-something; he saw a pretty young girl with shiny blond hair, blue eyes and a lovely smile. He still saw that girl. Her hair colour had changed and her skin had acquired a few lines here and there but she was still an attractive woman with wonderful eyes and the same brilliant smile. He remembered how upset he'd been when he'd been dragged off to the seaside to live. Since he'd had no choice but to make a new life there he'd concentrated on that and hadn't kept in touch because he'd been told by his father to sever all connections because nobody must know where they were. 'If things had been different we might have ended up together.'

'Who knows?' she said. 'But it obviously wasn't meant to be. We were too young. Not in control of our own lives.'

'Exactly!'

She was unnerved by him because he brought back powerful memories that she'd been trying to bury for over forty years. 'Anyway, it's lovely to see you, Wilf, but I have to go now,' she said, turning to leave.

'Don't rush off, Nora.'

'I'm needed at home,' she fibbed, 'to look after my granddaughter.'

'Let's meet up sometime when you're not in a hurry then, shall we?' he suggested with enthusiasm. 'We've a lot of catching up to do. I want to know all about you.'

'I don't think that's a good idea,' she said hurriedly, looking alarmed.

'Just a cup of tea in Lyons,' he said.

'No, no,' she said.

'I'm in my sixties, Nora, and my seducing days are well and truly over,' he said with a slow smile.

Now she was mortified. It was so long since anyone had thought of her in those terms, let alone spoken the words out loud, she thought he was taking the mick. 'Of course I know that you had nothing like that in mind.' She tutted. 'The very idea, at our age. I might be knocking on a bit but one thing I don't suffer from is self-delusion.'

He frowned. 'I meant no offence, Nora,' he said apologetically.

'No offence taken,' she responded, moving away. 'Now I really must go. Ta-ta.'

'Ta-ta,' he said, watching her hurry away; he was looking very disappointed.

Foolish didn't even come close to how Nora was feeling as she walked home. She'd been married for forty years to a man who had bullied and humiliated her on a regular basis but he hadn't managed to destroy her. Now all of that was behind her, she enjoyed life with Madge and the family. She made her contribution by helping around the house and with Esme and more lately playing the piano for Mollie's classes. So she was happy and in control.

Then an old boyfriend appears on the scene and she behaves like some gormless old bat, makes a complete idiot of herself and her self-esteem crumbles to dust. She thought back to the happy times she and Wilf had had together; he'd been gorgeous back then with thick fair hair and an athletic build. As a boy he'd been a whiz on the sports field. He was still a handsome man for his age and looked to be in very good shape. As the memories came flooding back she found herself smiling. She wondered if he remembered their youthful romance in such detail as she did. It was a very long time ago.

One thing she was sure of: she would steer clear of him in future. At the first sign of that mop of white hair, she would cross the road or dash into a shop out of sight. She couldn't have him coming back into her life and disturbing matters long since put to rest. Oh dear, she really was too old for this sort of carry-on.

Mollie was as disciplined with her time as it was possible to be, given the unpredictability of a young child with their tendency towards sudden illness, grazed knees, awkward moods and occasional anarchy. But she thought she juggled motherhood, cleaning jobs and teaching pretty well, especially now she had been able to give up cleaning shops at the crack of dawn due to the high attendance at her classes. She enjoyed being busy and felt as though her life was on track. Then she received a letter in the post and her sense of security was shattered.

They met on neutral ground: Lyons tea shop in Hammersmith one Monday afternoon. She was angry with herself for feeling nervous but she was inwardly trembling when she saw him sitting at a table near the window.

'Hello, Mollie,' said Syd, getting up and pulling her chair out for her.

'I'm surprised you've got the nerve to show your face,' she said coolly.

'It did take some bottle, I must admit,' he said. 'That's why I sent the letter asking to meet. I wouldn't have dared to come knocking on your door.'

'I should think not,' she said. 'You'd be a dead man if Dad and Geoff clapped eyes on you.'

He ordered tea and buns from the nippy.

'You're looking very well, Mollie,' he remarked. 'Different somehow.'

Up went her brows. 'It is three and a half years since you left so that might explain it.'

He made a face. 'Sorry about that,' he said. 'It all got on top of me: married life, being a dad.'

'So I gathered from the note you left; what do you want with me, Syd?' she said. 'I can't stay long. I've a lot on.'

'Such as?'

'I'm teaching tonight and I like to spend time with Esme before I go out so if you could get to the point.'

Naturally he wanted to know about the teaching so she told him what she'd been doing since he left.

'Blimey, things have changed while I've been away.'

'Indeed.' She gave him a hard look; her nervousness had changed to anger. 'I've toughened up a lot for one thing,' she said. 'I've had to earn a living to support myself and Esme and that soon strengthens you. I'm doing all right. She doesn't want for anything, except a father, of course. But what she's never known she can't miss.'

He bit his lip. 'I did intend to send you some money . . .'

'But you never got round to it.

'Er no . . .'

'Complete disregard of your responsibilities,' she said sharply. 'I don't care for myself but how you could just abandon an innocent child is beyond me.'

141

'It was bad, I admit.'

'Bad! It was brutal,' she said, pausing as the waitress brought the tea. 'But you're the loser because you gave up your beautiful daughter and she gives us all such pleasure.'

He dug into his pocket and took out a wad of notes. 'Perhaps this might help to make up for what I did.'

Mollie wanted to throw it at him but she said, 'I am going to accept this; not for me, I don't want a penny from you, but for Esme. I shall put it away for her.'

He shrugged, looking guilty.

'So can you get to the point please, Syd?' she asked briskly, buttering her bun. 'I really must go when I've had this. Why did you want to see me?'

When he'd arranged this meeting he wasn't really sure why except that he thought it might be interesting to see his daughter again now that she was older. But now that he had seen Mollie he wanted her back. The adoring girl she had been when he left had been replaced by a feisty, self-assured young woman whom he found extremely attractive. Persuading her to have him back wouldn't be easy but he enjoyed a challenge and he would get started right away.

'I know it was wrong of me to leave,' he began as though full of remorse, 'but I've learned my lesson. I've changed and I want you back, Mollie. I want you, me and Esme to be a family.'

Mollie almost choked on her tea.

'You can't be serious,' she exploded.

'I'm very serious,' he said. 'I'm doing well. I'm in used car sales now and I earn good money.'

'Surely you can't really believe that I would consider having you back,' she said.

'As I have said, I've changed. I've got all that freedom nonsense out of my system. I'm ready to settle down now and I can afford somewhere nice for us to live,' he told her. 'You wouldn't have to work. You could get away from the family into a place of our own, as we always planned.'

She looked at him studiously; a reasonably handsome man looking smart in a suit and tie, his hair slicked back. You can't love someone as she had loved him and not feel anything for them but she knew, in that instant, that the magic had gone. The man she had adored, almost worshipped, was just an ordinary bloke who held no particular attraction for her any more.

'No thanks, Syd,' she said.

'But we could have a good life together, get a place with a garden for the little 'un,' he tried to persuade her. 'You could stay at home and be a proper wife.'

'You've got a cheek. You walk out of my life without a care and waltz back into it, trying to take over and telling me to give up work just like that.'

'I thought you'd be pleased not to have to go out to work and you'd have no need to because I earn enough to keep us both,' he went on enthusiastically. 'It would be lovely for the three of us. You could have a nice easy life at home with Esme. I wouldn't want a wife of mine going out to work. That would be an insult to my capability as a provider.'

'It's just as well I have no intention of going back with you then, isn't it?' She gave a dry laugh. 'It was all right for me to earn my own living when you decided you didn't want to be married any more, wasn't it? But now that you fancy some domestic bliss you expect me to give up everything I've worked hard for.'

'But Mollie,' he pleaded. 'We could have such a marvellous life together, you and me and Esme.'

'No we couldn't, Syd.'

'Why not?'

'Because I don't love you.'

He looked stunned. 'Yes you do,' he stated categorically. 'You were always mad about me when we were together. You couldn't get enough of me.'

'Yes I was back then; before you went away I was besotted, I admit it,' she said. 'But I've done a lot of growing up since then and now, seeing you again, I know that the feeling has gone. I'm no longer in love with you.'

'It would come back if were together,' he announced with confidence. 'I'd make sure of that.'

She shook her head. 'I'm no expert on these things but I'm sure it won't. Once those sort of feelings have gone I don't think you can recapture them.'

This was proving to be more difficult than Syd had expected but he wasn't prepared to give up so he'd have to try another angle. 'What about my daughter?' he asked. 'You can't stop me seeing her.'

'You deserted her; you didn't want anything to do with her. Now, when it suits you, you want to start playing Daddy. Parenting isn't a game, Syd, it's a serious commitment. She's a vulnerable little girl, not a toy. You'd persuade her to love you then let her down when the novelty of being a dad wears off and something more interesting turns up.'

'No I wouldn't.'

'I don't trust you.'

'Surely you don't think I would lay a finger on her.'

'Oh no, I didn't mean that.' He was selfish and irresponsible but he wasn't violent.

'That's something I suppose,' he said. 'But she has a right to see her own father. You wouldn't want to deprive her of that. Anyway, I could take it through the courts.'

'I don't think they would be impressed when they find out you deserted her,' she pointed out.

'I'd tell them I'd changed,' he said. 'But surely we can sort this out between us. A child needs a dad as well as a mum.'

Mollie thought of the good relationship she had with her own father and how much joy that had always given her and she knew that he was right.

'I'll think about it and try to work something out,' she said. 'But if I let you see her, it will only be with me there as well.'

'Fair enough.' He didn't mind since it was Mollie he was after. The child was merely a means to stay in contact so that he could persuade Mollie to have him back.

'Meet me in here on Saturday afternoon at four o'clock and I'll let you know what I've decided.'

145

He shrugged. 'Do I have any choice?' he asked.

'Not really,' she said. 'Now I have to go.' She got up. 'I'll see you Saturday.'

'I'll be here,' he said and watched her as she left the café and walked up the street.

She really was quite something now that she was no longer a soppy adoring girl and he was determined to get her back whatever it took.

'I'm so afraid for her,' Mollie told her mother and gran; Dad and Geoff were at work. 'I don't trust him.'

'I'm worried about it too,' said Madge.

'I don't think Syd would actually harm her,' added Nora.

'Not physically,' agreed Mollie. 'But he isn't reliable. His suddenly wanting to be a dad might just be his latest fad and when he's had enough he'll disappear and break her heart. But, on the other hand, I don't want Esme to never know her father.'

'I think the best thing is to take it slowly and carefully,' suggested Madge. 'Take her to see her dad for just a short time. Letting him see her here wouldn't work because we are all so angry with him an argument would probably break out.'

'Some sort of neutral area like a park is probably the best place to meet but it's cold this time of year,' said Nora.

'But you both think I should let him see her then,' said Mollie in an enquiring manner.

They nodded. 'His name is on the birth certificate so I don't see how you can deny him the right to see her. Try it once and if it doesn't go well, think again. She's too young to know anything about the status quo as regards parenting but she will when she goes to school.'

'And all the other kids will have a mum and a dad at home,' said Mollie.

'Most of them I expect,' said Nora.

'Do you think I should take him back to stop her from being the odd one out then?' asked Mollie.

'Of course not,' her mother assured her adamantly. 'That's the last thing you should do.'

'It's what he wants,' said Mollie.

'Now, until family life starts to bore him then who knows what he'll do,' said Madge.

'I don't want him back but if it would be better for Esme I'd do it,' she said.

'Women have been staying with men they don't love because of the kids since marriage was invented but in your case you'd be taking a real risk,' said Nora. 'He's left once, he could do it again then Esme would be even more upset.'

'Mm. That's true,' said Mollie but she was in a real quandary. Esme was no longer a baby; she would be four in the spring and old enough to be hurt. Mollie would do anything to spare her.

When she saw Syd on Saturday she arranged to meet him by the bandstand in Duke's Meadows the next morning for a half-hour meeting with Esme.

147

It was a bright but chilly Sunday morning and Mollie dressed her daughter in her red coat and matching pixie hood. Her maternal pride was all-consuming as she got her ready. Anyone would think she was entering her for a competition rather than taking her to meet her father.

Syd was completely unprepared for his feelings when he first set eyes on the beautiful brown-eyed child who was his daughter, skipping alongside her mother as they walked towards him. She was Mollie in miniature, dark hair falling from beneath her hat and the same unbeliev-able eyes.

'Hello, Esme,' he said thickly.

'Hello. Are you my dad?' she said in a matter-of-fact manner.

He gulped, feeling tears burning at the back if his eyes. 'Yes, that's right.'

'Are we going to the swings?' she asked, jumping up and down as though excited, her cheeks pink with the cold.

'How about we go inside and have a drink first,' he suggested. 'And maybe you might like a bun.'

'I love buns,' she said sweetly. 'Please can I have some lemonade?'

'I'm sure that can be arranged,' he said and the three of them walked towards a small café overlooking the river.

'She's beautiful, Mollie,' he said later when Esme was

running around on the grass outside with some other children who had appeared 'Absolutely gorgeous.'

'Yes, I think so too.'

'You're doing a good job.'

'Thank you,' she said graciously. 'I do my best.'

'She was just a scrap of a thing who was always filling her nappy and screaming her head off when I last saw her,' he remarked. 'I never looked forward to a time beyond that. I can't believe how different things are now that—'

'Now that she can walk and talk and take herself to the lavatory,' she said.

'Yeah, but I meant more that she's a person now.'

'She was back then but I know what you mean,' she said.

'It must be nice having her around.'

'It's wonderful,' she said. 'I love her to bits. She's so funny at times and such entertaining company.'

'How can you bear to leave her to go out to work?'

'It's hard sometimes but I'm used to it as I don't have a choice,' she said. 'Money doesn't just appear; it has to be earned.'

At least he had the grace to look sheepish. 'I should have sent something.'

'Yes you should,' she agreed. 'How did you think I would manage without you to support me?'

'I didn't think about it,' he admitted ruefully. 'I suppose I must have shut it out while I concentrated on building a new life.'

'It's only recently, since my classes have started doing well, that I've been able to give up cleaning shops early in the morning. That was really hard.'

He bit his lip. 'Sorry,' he said.

'It's a bit late for that,' she said. 'But I managed. In a way you did me a favour because your leaving forced me to stand on my own two feet and I've realised that I'm pretty good at it.'

'I'm glad some good came out of it.'

She fixed her gaze on his face. 'I was absolutely heart-broken when you left, Syd. How could you do that to me when you knew how I felt about you?'

'I'm asking myself the same thing,' he told her. 'I had something so good and I walked away from it. What was I thinking?'

'About yourself probably,' she suggested.

'I felt trapped; suffocated by duty,' he said. 'Life had stopped being fun.'

'It's called being an adult,' she said. 'But you certainly chose your moment to walk out on your responsibilities. Right in the middle of a party.'

He made a face. 'It was bad, I know; a rotten trick. Everything seemed to be closing in on me so I just took off.'

'Oh well,' she said, wanting to move on instead of harking back. 'It's all in the past and we've both done well in our own ways. I'm happy with my life as it is now.'

'Is there someone else?' he asked.

'Good Lord no,' she said. 'What chance do I get to meet men? I'm either working or being a mum.'

'So come back with me,' he suggested eagerly, relieved that he had no male competition. 'I could give you and Esme a good life. She'd want for nothing, I promise you.'

'Don't keep bringing that up, Syd,' she urged him. 'I've told you, I don't want to come back to you, so let that be an end to it.'

'Do you think you are being fair to Esme, depriving her of a better life in a proper family unit?'

His words hit home. She could only give Esme so much. According to Syd he could give her much more and, of course, he could provide the standard two-parent family. But could she trust him, and could she live with a man who had betrayed her trust and whom she didn't love? Would that have a detrimental effect on their daughter eventually? Mollie wanted Esme to have the best possible chance in life. If that lay with them being with Syd, should she give him a chance?

'I don't think you are being fair to me by putting that sort of pressure on,' she said.

'No perhaps not,' he agreed, deciding that force wasn't a good strategy. Now that he'd seen them both he wanted family life more than anything and he was determined to get it. It was time he settled down. He could afford to rent a house with a garden. Possibly in one of the new suburbs that were going up on the fringes of London. He looked ahead to a time when he would get home from work of an evening and Mollie would be waiting for him with a meal ready. They could drive out to the country or the coast on a Sunday. Oh yes, he could see it all.

He'd have to get her to give up her outside jobs though. The cleaning shouldn't be too much of a problem because she'd probably be glad to get shot of that. The teaching thing might be more difficult because she seemed very keen on it. He had to box clever and persuade her to agree to come back to him before he made demands or she wouldn't agree to anything. But he would put a stop to it once he had her under his roof. Too damned right he would. He wouldn't permit any wife of his to have a career. That was strictly his domain. He'd be a laughing stock among his mates.

'There's no perhaps about it,' she was saying. 'You're using emotional blackmail to get your own way.'

'Yeah, I probably am. Sorry,' he agreed craftily. 'So let's just see how it goes for the moment, shall we? I'll concentrate on getting to know Esme. With you there of course.'

She gave him a studious look. He'd agreed rather too easily for her peace of mind. Was he up to something? Before he deserted her she had trusted him implicitly. It would never have occurred to her to doubt him. Now she couldn't bring herself to believe a single word he said.

But she said, 'That will be the best thing.'

'Perhaps we could go for a spin in my car sometime, the three of us. Esme might like that.'

Mollie was noncommittal. 'We'll see,' she said.

'Can we go to the swings please, Mummy?' asked Esme, bringing the adults' conversation to a halt.

'Yeah, we'll walk over there, love,' said Mollie and they went to the playground and put Esme on a swing. Syd found the whole family thing hugely appealing and was eager to be a part of it. Or, to be more accurate, he wanted it to revolve around him, as the daddy; the head of the house and the breadwinner.

The following week, Syd was somewhere he'd never been before, engaged in an activity he had never, in his wildest dreams, expected to do. He was in Hamley's looking for something to give Esme as a present. Not for any other reason than he wanted to do it, though he was hoping it would please her and perhaps help her to like him.

There were toys of every kind here: clockwork cars, whips and tops, train sets, marbles, doll's prams, scooters. Then he saw the dolls and knew that was what he must get. Little girls always liked those. He chose the prettiest baby doll he could find, with bright blue eyes that opened and closed and dressed in pink knitted clothes.

He paid for it and left the shop proudly carrying it in a Hamley's bag. Oh yes, only the best for his daughter. He couldn't wait to give it to her.

Naturally Esme was delighted with her gift, and hugged the doll to her as if she would never let it go. She could hardly bear to give it up while she went on the swing but eventually gave her dolly to her mother to hold.

'Syd, I know you are keen to win her over and you probably mean well, but it's still a good few weeks until Christmas and it isn't her birthday until the spring,' said Mollie. 'You mustn't make a habit of giving her presents because she'll expect it all the time. I don't want her to get spoiled.'

'Don't ruin it for me, Mollie,' he said. 'A few presents won't hurt her.'

Mollie was torn. She didn't begrudge her daughter a treat but neither did she want her to become over-indulged because her father was trying to make an impression. 'I don't want to mess up anything for you or Esme but expensive gifts aren't a normal part of her life and I don't want her to get used to it and become a spoiled brat. Christmas and birthdays and occasionally in between but not all the time.'

'I've given her one bloody present,' he objected, 'Anyone would think I'd ill-treated her.'

Maybe she had been too hard on him. He did seem to be trying to make amends. 'I suppose I'm a bit protective of her, which is only natural as I'm the sole parent.'

'Not any more, Mollie,' he said. 'I'm back, so you're not on your own now.'

'I'm not really on my own anyway. I have a lot of family support,' she reminded him.

'You know what I mean,' he said. 'It will be the three of us from now on. I want to take part in her life. Be a proper dad. I didn't think I would ever want that but I do. I know it will take time for you to trust me again but I'll show you that I mean it. All those things we used to talk about – having our own place and being a family – I can make it all come true.'

'It's early days,' she said cautiously. 'We are going to see how it goes, remember.'

He had no intention of waiting too long but it wouldn't be wise to let her know that so he just said, 'Yeah, of course; whatever you want.'

Because the family had seen what Syd had put Mollie through and had been there to pick up the pieces after he left, they were biased against him and worried that he was going to hurt her again which meant that Mollie couldn't really discuss her dilemma with them without causing upset. Of course, she did tell them that she and Esme were seeing him.

Geoff in particular was concerned when he saw his sister seeming worried and preoccupied a few weeks after the meetings with Syd had begun.

'Is Syd Fisher causing you difficulties again?' he asked one night when everyone had gone to bed and they were having a late cup of cocoa together.

'Obviously I'm concerned about what happens next,' she told him. 'As it is now he sees Esme for a short time with me there. He's going to want to have her on his own eventually. He's her father, Geoff, so he's entitled.'

'And there was I thinking you were worrying about whether you should go back to him or not.'

'I am worried about that but this other thing is more immediate,' she explained.

'I don't think he would actually harm her,' said Geoff.

'I was thinking more in terms of her getting used to him being around and then him leaving again.'

'I wouldn't put it past him.'

155

'Maybe he really has turned over a new leaf,' she suggested. 'People do.'

'It is possible,' he said. 'But please don't rush into anything as regards going back with him.'

'If I did it would only be for Esme's sake,' she said 'And I'd have to learn to trust him first.'

'As long as you don't do anything in haste,' he said. 'Promise me you won't.'

'I promise,' she said.

'Good.'

Mollie found herself unexpectedly confiding in Cora who remarked on the fact that Mollie was quieter than usual and seemed to have something on her mind. Prior to this Mollie hadn't discussed her marriage with Cora, only that Syd had walked out on her and Esme. Now, out it all came, about the early marriage and him wanting her back with promises of a better life for Esme and how her feelings towards him had changed.

'I have to do what's best for Esme, whatever my personal feelings,' she said.

'Living with a man you don't love isn't best for anyone,' was Cora's opinion. 'You can't build a happy family that way. Esme would be affected by it in the long run.'

'Do you think so?'

'I don't have children so am not really in a position to say but I should think that any child would sense something was wrong,' she said. 'In a way it's a blessing Grant and I didn't have a family.'

'What are you saying, Cora?'

'I married Grant because I wanted to get away from home and he was a good catch but I was never in love with him, not for a second.'

'Oh, Cora.'

'Don't be so shocked, Mollie. That sort of thing happens every day,' she said. 'Marriage is the only accepted status for a woman so we have to find a man to marry us whether we are in love with them or not.'

'I was head over heels in love with Syd,' said Mollie. 'Absolutely besotted.'

'I've never experienced such a thing in my entire life,' Cora confessed. Naturally she didn't mention her absurd attraction to Geoff.

'But Grant is gorgeous.'

'Yes I know, and he is a good man, but I have never felt a great longing for him; that magic has never been there; if such a thing exists,' she said.

'Oh it exists all right,' said Mollie with a wry grin. 'I had it in bucket-loads for Syd. Not that it did me any good in the long run but I was ecstatically happy when we were together before he left. I wouldn't want to have missed that for all the pain it caused me later. I'll always remember those happy times. It was lovely back then.'

'And it gave you Esme.'

'Yes.' She smiled. 'That in itself made it worthwhile. She's the love of my life now.'

'But he isn't.'

'No, much to my surprise. He's the same man he always was and I wanted to be with him so much before he left us it actually hurt. Now I look at him and can't understand why I felt like that. He's just a man; a good-looking one admittedly but he doesn't shimmer for me anymore.'

'And he wants to play happy families.'

She nodded. 'I'd do it if I really thought it was the best thing for Esme but I think he is attracted to family life and will get bored when he realises what hard work parenting is.'

'So you need to make absolutely sure you don't rush into anything.'

Mollie grinned, introducing a lighter note. 'If I did go back with him, he'd try to make me give up my classes . . . and you would definitely lose your cleaner.'

'That's it then,' grinned Cora, joining in the joke. 'You can't go back to him.'

'I thought that would frighten you,' laughed Mollie.

But she was only laughing on the outside. Inside she was agonising about what she should do. Her feelings were crystal-clear. She didn't want to share her life with Syd. She would do it for her daughter. But could she trust him? That was the thing she had serious doubts about.

Chapter Seven

'Hello again,' said Wilf Robbins when he almost collided with Nora on her way out of Woolworths as he was going in rather hurriedly.

'Oh, wotcha, Wilf,' she responded, caught unawares so unable to avoid him. 'How are you?'

'Not so dusty,' he replied. 'Yourself?'

'Fine,' she replied. 'You look as though you're in a hurry.'

'I am rather.' He smiled. 'I've joined the ARP so that's keeping me busy.'

'That's something to do with the war that we're supposed to be having, isn't it?'

'That's right.'

'So what do you have to do?'

'Attend lectures, help distribute gas masks and various other jobs connected to the preparations for war on the home front. We'll be training in case of the actual event soon. Air raids and so on.'

'Ooh er,' she said, frowning. 'So the government really is expecting it to happen then.'

159

'I don't know about that,' he said, so as not to alarm her. 'But they have to make sure that we are prepared if it does come to be. It's their duty to strengthen our defences and do their best to look after civilians in the event of anything untoward happening.'

'Mm, I suppose so.'

'Don't look so worried, Nora,' he urged her. 'It is just a safeguard, that's all.'

'It's brought the seriousness of the threat home to me, I suppose,' she told him. 'We've all been hearing a lot about the possibility of a war coming but I've put it to the back of my mind in the hope that it won't happen. You're the first person I've come across who's actually involved in the preparations. It makes it seem very real suddenly.'

'War hasn't actually been declared yet so it may not come about,' he reminded her. 'The last thing I intended to do was spoil your day.'

'You haven't, not at all.' In fact, seeing him had brightened her day even though she wasn't prepared to admit it, not even to herself. 'I'll be all right. I'm a tough old bird.'

He smiled. 'You're not so old,' he said cheerily. 'You can't be because you're the same age as me and you won't hear me admit that I'm getting on.'

It was a real tonic to hear such a fresh attitude towards their advancing years. At home she was the senior member, the mother and grandma. By the very nature of things, no one ever thought of her in any other terms. Wilf reminded her that she was still a person as well as an old lady. So maybe she wouldn't try to avoid him after all. A few casual words in passing wouldn't do any harm. As long as he didn't get too friendly.

'Well, I don't have much choice,' she said now, 'since I have grandchildren and even a great-granddaughter. Their existence is a constant reminder. I love them all to bits though.'

'You're lucky,' he said, wistfully. 'I would love all of that.' He paused. 'Still, mustn't grumble. You can't miss what you've never had, can you?'

'I suppose not.'

'Anyway, I must be going,' he told her. 'I want to get some sweets before I head off for my lecture. I'm very partial to a humbug or three.' He looked towards the store. 'Ta-ta for now, Nora.'

'Cheerio, Wilf,' she said and went on her way.

So she had nothing to worry about after all. He wasn't going to pursue her and force her to torment herself about the past. He was occupied with his civil defence work and far too busy to bother about some old dear he had known many moons ago. She was relieved and disappointed simultaneously. They had been such soul mates when they were young and she could do with some like-minded company of her own age.

But they had been little more than kids back then. He'd have different ideas now, as she did. Oh well, maybe she would run into him again some time. Now that she knew he wasn't a threat she did hope so.

★   ★   ★

Wilf was thinking about Nora as he queued up at the sweet counter. The last time he'd run into her she been so eager to get away from him he made sure he hadn't lingered this time. He didn't want her to think he was going to be a pest. It was a pity, though, because he'd like to get to know her again. He'd been very fond of her all those years ago. She'd been full of life, and love, they both had. He smiled at the happy memories.

'Next please,' said the assistant behind the counter.

'A quarter of humbugs please,' he said, returning with a start to the present.

Until a few weeks before Christmas Mollie and Esme met Syd either in a café, the park or Duke's Meadow. But the weather was so cold and sometimes wet now, he suggested picking them up at the house in his car.

'If you're willing to risk the wrath of my father and brother,' she said lightly. 'They're likely to come out and give you a right earful or worse.'

'My back is broad.'

'In that case we'll do it,' she said. 'It'll save us getting frozen or soaked to the skin.'

So it was that she and Esme climbed into a black Hillman one Sunday morning in December, unhampered by any ructions from the family who'd been reminded quite forcefully by Mollie that any arguments in front of Esme would upset her.

'This is a treat, Syd,' Mollie said as she settled into

the back seat with her daughter. 'You *are* doing well for yourself.'

'It's a company car,' he explained. 'It goes with the job so I don't even have to pay for the petrol.'

'Very nice too,' she said.

Esme was fascinated by the whole thing, especially the orange indicator that popped out whenever they turned a corner. When they stopped outside the café she squealed with delight while Syd did it several times especially to please her. Mollie was laughing too. She was having fun almost despite herself. It was lovely to see Esme so happy.

They had a pleasant time in the café. Syd bought himself and Mollie tea, lemonade for Esme and currant cakes for them all. A visit to the playground followed, much to Esme's delight. The atmosphere was so pleasurable Mollie managed to forget their circumstances for a while. But later when he drew up outside the house in Pearl Road things took a downward turn.

'It will be Christmas soon, Mollie,' he said.

'Yes, it's the end of term for my classes next week,' she said chattily. 'I usually finish the first or second week in December. I need the break.'

He wasn't interested in any of that and just got to the point. 'I'd like to see Esme on Christmas Day.'

'Oh, but she'll be with me and the family,' she told him.

'I am her family,' he pointed out.

Sensing a storm brewing she said, 'Esme, love, will you go indoors and I'll be in in a minute. Say bye-bye to Daddy.'

163

The child did as she was asked and ran to the front door where she was swept inside by her grandmother.

'Yes I appreciate that, Syd, but it will be difficult to organise,' Mollie continued. 'Obviously I want her to be at home on that day with me and the people she is used to. Not out in the cold in some park. There will be no cafés open.'

'I have a right to see her.'

'Maybe you do, legally. I don't know the technicalities. But to my mind you gave up that right when you walked out on us,' she said. 'Still, I don't want to be difficult, especially at Christmas. So I can ask Mum if you could join us if you like.'

'And have everyone sniping at me, no thanks,' he said.

'In that case it will have to be either Christmas Eve or Boxing Day,' she told him firmly.

'I remember a time when you would have done anything to please me,' he said.

'That was a long time ago and there were only the two of us then. Things are different now,' she pointed out. 'This isn't about either you or me. It's about our daughter. She comes first.'

'Humph.'

'That's the difference between playing at parenting and the real thing,' she said. 'I want what's best for her; you still want what's best for yourself.'

'Oh, stop being so high and mighty, for Gawd's sake,' he snapped. 'We can't all be perfect like you. I'm still new to it, aren't I? I need time to learn.'

'I think it's instinctive, actually, Syd,' she suggested. 'It was for me anyway, from the very first moment she was born.'

He heaved an irritated sigh. 'Look, I want to be with my wife and daughter on Christmas Day,' he said heavily. 'What's so terrible about that?'

'You were gone for more than three years,' she reminded him. 'You can't come back into our lives and expect to make demands. It isn't fair.'

'I'm not suggesting that we ride around the streets in the car in the cold. I've got a decent flat. I would get nice food in and even put some paper chains up and get a Christmas tree,' he persisted, determined to get his own way.

'Don't make Christmas into a battleground, please, Syd,' she urged him.

He'd grown tired of casual girlfriends and being on his own on Christmas Day. He wanted a traditional family Christmas with *his family*. But it suddenly occurred to him that if he made too much of a fuss about the Christmas issue he might jeopardise his chances of getting Mollie back for good.

'Sorry, Moll,' he said with feigned remorse. 'I got a bit carried away. Perhaps I could see her on Christmas Eve for a little while. I'll be working in the morning but I should be able to get away in the afternoon.'

'That will be fine,' she said. 'We'll make arrangements nearer the time. So now that we've got that settled, I must go.' She reached for the door handle. 'Bye for now. See you next week.'

'Righto.'

Pam Evans

He watched her as she hurried to the front door and went inside without looking back. He remembered a time when she would have stood at the door and watched him lovingly until he was out of sight. He wanted those times back and he was absolutely determined to get them.

'You had a nice car ride then,' said her mother when Mollie got in. 'Esme has been telling us all about it.'

'I don't know how he's got the brass neck to swank around in a car when he doesn't support his wife and child,' disapproved her father.

'It isn't his car, Dad,' Mollie pointed out. 'It belongs to the firm he works for and they pay for the petrol. And he gave me a wad of money when he first came back.'

'I bet it wasn't enough to make up for more than three years without so much as a penny.'

'He should pay you regular now that he's back,' put in Madge.

'But I'm doing fine myself, Mum.'

'That isn't the point,' said Len.

'Dad, maybe I'll ask him to pay maintenance for Esme at some point but not now, so soon after him giving me money,' she said forcibly. 'So can we drop the subject please, for the time being anyway? It makes me feel like a charity case.'

'I like Daddy,' Esme piped up. 'He buys me nice cakes and gave me a dolly.'

Mollie saw a look pass between her parents and grand-mother. She knew they were all worried that she might

166

go back with Syd and get hurt all over again. Things couldn't go on as they were indefinitely, that was for sure.

It was the last class of term and Cora presented Molly with a parcel and a card signed from the whole class.

'From us all,' said Cora. 'We wish you a happy Christmas and hope you enjoy the well-earned break.' There were cheers then Cora added, 'And we also have something for our lovely pianist, Nora.'

More applause as Nora went up on the stage to receive her package. They both opened them to show everyone. Mollie's was a necklace, Nora's was a set of soap and bath salts. They both gave heartfelt thanks then Mollie said, 'I haven't quite finished with you yet so feet apart and stretch those arms up. Up, up as far as they will go, up up, feel that stretch.'

After class there were sherry and mince pies and Mollie, Cora and Nora were full of Christmas spirit when they saw everybody off the premises, talking and laughing, before they left themselves, locking up after them.

'What a super evening,' said Cora as they stood chatting outside the hall. 'They are such a nice bunch of women.'

'They certainly are,' agreed Mollie. 'Thanks for everything you do for me during the term, Cora.'

'No trouble.' There was a toot from the roadside. 'Oops, there is my lift. The ole' man is getting impatient,' she said with a fake working-class accent. 'As I know that you two would rather walk I'll say goodnight.'

167

'G'night,' they chorused, then linked arms and set off for home.

'That's the first term of the new class over then, Gran,' said Mollie. 'I'm pleased with the way it's gone. Most weeks the hall has been full.'

'Yes dear. You've done well.'

'So have you,' added Mollie. 'You are a part of it too; a very important part.'

'I do my best. In fact, I don't know what I'd do without your classes now,' Nora said. 'It's a nice outside interest for me, playing the piano. I look forward to it.'

'I can't imagine life without them now either. I think about them when I'm not actually teaching, in bed and in the bath; I'm planning new routines and so on. Perhaps we can get together over the holiday to sort out some music to go with the new routines when I've worked them out. I have to keep things fresh so that people don't get bored.'

'They'd never get bored with you on the platform,' Nora assured her.

'Thanks, Gran, you're a real pal,' said Mollie, squeezing her arm affectionately.

As she spoke the words she realised that that was exactly what her grandmother was to her: a pal. She'd always got on well with her but the classes had brought them closer; they were colleagues and friends now as well as relatives.

Unnoticed by Mollie and Nora there had been a car parked on the other side of the road from the hall in the shadows. Syd was in the driver's seat. Mollie had happened to mention the hall she used and which night the class was so he thought he would come along. His original plan had been to offer her a lift home but he'd been so angry to see her enjoying herself and obviously in no hurry to get home to their daughter, he hadn't trusted himself to approach her because he knew he would cause an argument and possibly ruin his future plans.

Getting her back under his control had now become urgent, having seen how she carried on. What decent married woman and mother of a child was out on the street at night? Her grandmother too. It was disgusting and he would put a stop to it when he was back in Mollie's life. No wife of his was going out at night without him and that was definite. Drastic measures were obviously needed or this thing would drag on forever. Mollie was still uncertain about a reunion; so he would have to make her realise he was absolutely determined that it *would* happen. How exactly he was going to do this he had no idea yet. Mollie wasn't so easy to manipulate as she used to be. He needed to think of a plan, pronto.

In thoughtful mood, he turned on the engine and headed homewards with the intention of stopping off at his local pub. His brain always served him better after it had been well oiled by a few pints.

Mollie often thought that Christmas Eve was the best part of the whole celebration because of the excited anticipation and the fact that the big day was still to come. She enjoyed the festive scent of fresh baking and Mum and Gran a little harassed but happy in the kitchen for a large part of the day.

Traditionally the house had a special Christmas clean, curtains and paintwork washed, everything polished, especially the front room where the fire would be lit and the family happily ensconced tomorrow. Little dishes of sweets and nuts would be placed around. But that would be done this evening. Now in the late morning, Mollie had finished the cleaning, which she always did on a Christmas Eve because her mother was busy at the oven. Next she would help to prepare lunch then collect Esme, who was next door playing with the children there, ready for Syd who was calling for them at about two o'clock.

Imbued with Christmas cheer, she put the broom and brushes away in the understairs cupboard and headed for the kitchen.

Syd was full of seasonal spirit too but his was of the bottled kind. The boss had put on a celebration at the showrooms and Syd was expected to be sociable. Not that it was a problem for him, especially if there was alcohol involved. Beer was his usual tipple but there had only been spirits so he'd had a few whiskies which had been wonderfully potent.

This was how he liked to feel at Christmas: warm inside and happy. It certainly took the edge off the problem of getting Mollie back, especially as he hadn't come up with a suitable plan to that end yet. Still, it was

Christmas; the time to be merry, and he was certainly that, he thought, laughing to himself about nothing in particular as he got into his car and headed for West London.

'Can we go to feed the ducks on the river please, Daddy,' asked Esme, as she climbed into the back of the car ahead of her mother. 'We've got some stale bread for them.'

'Course we can, sweetheart,' he said full of whisky and good cheer. 'Whatever you like.'

'Yippee,' she trilled.

It wasn't until Mollie got out of the car near the river and Syd opened the door for her and took her arm that she noticed his whisky breath. 'Blimey, Syd, you smell like you've been celebrating in a big way.'

'I had a couple of drinks at work,' he explained. 'Standard procedure on a Christmas Eve.'

'You won't feel the cold then,' she said in a cheery manner. It was the season of goodwill and most working people would be having a few drinks before they finished for the holiday and there was nothing wrong with that. Dad and Geoff would most likely be a bit merry when they got home from work. After Christmas was the time to decide what to do about Syd. Not now!

'I don't know about that,' he said in response. 'It's fresh to say the least.'

It certainly was a cold day with steel-grey skies and a raw wind that skimmed across the river surface as though brushing it with a feather.

'We'll have to walk to keep ourselves warm,' she suggested. 'Don't take too long feeing the ducks, Esme. It's too cold to hang about.'

They walked towards the river's edge with their daughter running on ahead with her bag of bread. This stretch of the Thames near Chiswick Eyot always pleased Mollie, even on a bleak day like this. There was something so relaxing about its serene presence and feeling of open space that gave it a rustic feel in the midst of a busy town.

Such was her mood of exhilaration, she even felt comfortable being with Syd. Just for now she could forget that they were no longer together and enjoy the moment.

'They're coming for the bread, Mummy,' said Esme as a large proportion of the feathered population of the river swam up for the contents of the paper bag.

'Yes, you're doing a good job, darling,' said Mollie. 'They are a hungry lot.'

Absorbed in the here and now, she turned to Syd and said casually, 'Strange how they seem to come from nowhere when you put a bit of stale bread in the water, isn't it? Word spreads fast in the river community but how is a mystery to me.'

'It's nature,' he said.

'Mm, a powerful thing'

It was that all right. It's nature that intends us to be together, you and me, Mollie, he thought, but didn't say anything, not yet. He wasn't so drunk that he couldn't choose his moment.

★   ★   ★

Wilf Robbins took a walk down to the river on the afternoon of Christmas Eve, mostly because he'd fancied some fresh air but also because the flat was awfully quiet with only him in it. He was spending Christmas Day with a childhood pal and his family locally but today he was on his own. Special occasions could be difficult without someone to share them with.

Generally speaking he coped very well with living alone. He had his voluntary civil defence work and he belonged to the British Legion so he could usually find company there of an evening. But the days were sometimes long and lonely. Not that he would even think of complaining; he'd had a long marriage and he wasn't a rich man by any means but neither was he hampered by poverty.

A miscarriage with serious complications had resulted in major surgery for his wife and ended their dreams of a family but they had both come to terms with it long ago. Not that you ever really got over something like that but you did accept that it wasn't meant to be. If they had had children they would be grown up and living their own lives by now, of course, but some grandkids would have been nice. He would love that. Still, his pal included him in things round at his house with his grandchildren so it wasn't as if he was entirely on his own.

As he reached the river he saw a young couple with a little girl walking towards him. The child was the sweetest little thing, skipping along between them. He was just thinking what a handsome couple they made and a happy family unit when they drew near to him and he could see that all was not well between the man and woman. He looked angry; she was obviously worried. They were clearly in the middle of an argument which was halted while he was within earshot.

'Afternoon,' he greeted, in the way that river walkers usually did when passing.

'Hello there,' responded the woman while the man stayed silent, looking grim.

There's a humdinger going on there, thought Wilf as he walked on, hoping instinctively that the child wasn't too upset by it.

'This is neither the time nor the place to discuss our situation, Syd,' said Mollie when they were out of earshot of the old man and Esme had run on ahead. 'Not when we have our daughter with us.'

'It's just an excuse.' Caution thrown to the wind by the effect of the alcohol, he'd been unable to keep quiet on the subject. 'You want to keep me hanging around.'

'I do not,' she objected. 'I have told you all along that I am not planning on going back with you and I have given you no cause to think otherwise.'

'You're seeing me; that could be seen as a positive sign.'

'I'm only seeing you because of Esme; you don't know her well enough to have her on your own yet,' she reminded him. 'You know that perfectly well. I've made it clear.'

'But surely you must know that it would be the best thing, for us all to be together,' he persisted.

'For you maybe.'

'For all of us,' he said, belligerent now as the uplifting effect of the booze wore off, leaving him depressed. 'Am I so revolting to you, is that the problem, Mollie?'

'Shush, Syd. That's adult talk,' she admonished. 'We don't want Esme to hear.'

'She's well out of range,' he said, as Esme was quite a distance ahead of them, happily hopping and skipping intermittently.

'It still isn't the time.'

'So, is that it?' he went on, undeterred. 'You can't bear the idea of sharing a bed with me, only I don't usually have that effect on women. Quite the opposite in fact.'

'It isn't about sex, it's about trust, or rather a lack of it,' she said. 'But I am not prepared to discuss it here with Esme around so shut up about it.'

'But . . .'

'If you don't drop the subject I shall take Esme and we'll walk home,' she stated. 'I mean it, Syd.'

He fell into a sulky silence and they headed back to the car parked in the road near Duke's Meadows. When they got to the vehicle he unlocked it and ushered Esme into the back as usual but as Mollie went to follow her he pushed her aside, locked the door and pulled her roughly by the arm away from the vehicle.

'Right, Esme is inside in the warm and out of earshot so you and I are going to have this out,' he said.

'Oh for goodness' sake, Syd, you're behaving like a spoiled child,' she admonished.

'Only because you've driven me to it.'

175

'I haven't driven you to anything so stop making such a drama out of it,' she said. 'You were the one who walked away from us. You broke us up, not me.'

'I've said I'm sorry.'

Mollie looked towards the car where Esme had her face close to the window and was staring out looking worried. 'This isn't the behaviour of a man who is planning on being a responsible father to his daughter.'

'Is this the behaviour of a man who really does want his wife back?' he said, grabbing her roughly and kissing her full on the lips. He pulled back and looked at her. 'Has that made your mind up for you?'

Feeling only revulsion, she knew in that moment that she could never revive her love for him and a reconciliation for their daughter's sake would be a total disaster and not conducive to a happy and stable life for her. But he was in an explosive mood so she just said, 'Open the car door, Syd, and let me get in with Esme. Take us home please.'

They went over to the car as though he was going to do what she asked. But he got into the driver's seat and locked the passenger door.

'Let me get in please, Syd,' she said, angry now. 'It's freezing out here.' She had spotted her daughter's lip beginning to tremble. 'And Esme is getting upset.'

He wound his window down. 'Esme is coming with me,' he informed her. 'You'll get her back when you agree to have me back as well and not before.'

'Syd,' she shouted, her voice rising to a scream. 'Don't

be so stupid. Either you let me in or her out.' Esme was crying now. 'She's terrified.'

'When you see sense and agree for the three of us to be together you'll see her again and not before. You've got my address; let me know when you are ready to agree to my terms and I'll think about letting you see her.'

He started the engine and revved up.

'Stop this,' she yelled. 'For God's sake calm down and turn the engine off.'

He looked at her. 'You know my terms,' he said.

'I'll call the police.'

'Do what you like,' he said and drove off at high speed with her shouting after him and Esme screaming inside.

'What's happened?' asked a voice at her side and she turned to see the elderly man they had passed by the river. 'I heard shouting. Are you all right, my dear?'

'Not really. My husband has taken my little girl,' she said, sobbing now with terror. 'He's gone off with her driving like a maniac and he says I can't have her back until I agree to have him back. We're separated, you see.'

'Blimey, that's a bit of a shocker but I'm sure he'll calm down and see sense,' he said.

'I need to call the police,' she wept.

'Yes, that would be best, so let's find a call box,' suggested Wilf. 'Here, hang on to me. You look a bit shaky.'

'I have to get her back. She'll be so frightened. She's just a little girl, not even four yet.'

'The police will soon find her.'

'A friend of mine lives nearby and they have a phone,' she said, already starting to run in the direction of the Parkers' house, tears streaming down her face.

'I'll come with you to make sure you're all right,' said Wilf, very concerned about her.

'Thank you,' she said, grateful for his support.

Syd was completely out of his depth and didn't know what to do next. He had acted on impulse and now Esme was snivelling in the back of the car and it was grating on his nerves. Still, he had done the best thing. This would make Mollie realise that he was serious.

'You'll be all right with me, Esme,' he shouted into the back. 'But you'll have to stop crying. It's getting on my nerves.'

'I want my mummy,' she sobbed.

'All in good time.'

'I want my mummy,' repeated the distraught child.

'Well you can't have her just now so stop that silly noise.'

'Mummeee,' she wailed.

'Shut up,' he shouted loudly. 'Or I'll stop the car and give you a good hiding.'

She wept quietly, beside herself with fear and misery.

'It'll be all right, sweetheart,' he said in a kinder tone. 'I'll look after you.'

She was crying silently now, her face sodden with tears, her nose running and she couldn't find a hanky.

Her mother usually wiped her nose when she'd been crying.

Her father put his foot on the accelerator. All he could think of was to get away, out of the area, as fast as he could. He sped along Chiswick Lane and into the High Road, going through a red light and taking a turning which he mistakenly thought was a short cut towards Willesden which would eventually take him northwards.

As the enormity of what he'd done registered he began to cry, knowing in his heart the hopelessness of the situation and the fact that he'd done wrong. It was as though he collapsed inside as he faced the awful truth. There was no way he was ever going to get Mollie back. He'd damaged the marriage when he left her and had now destroyed it completely. The only thing he could do was return Esme to her mother because he didn't have the faintest idea how to handle a distressed child.

'I'll take you back to your mum, Esme,' he said thickly, hardly able to see through his tears. 'I'll turn round as soon as I can find a place. You'll be home soon.'

As eager as he'd been to get away, he now felt the same urgency about getting back. He knew he was speeding in a built-up area but couldn't slow down sufficiently, such was his anxiety pushing his foot down on the accelerator.

Suddenly the car swerved across the road and mounted the pavement on the driver's side, heading towards a high brick wall. He turned the steering wheel as hard as he could to avoid it and slammed his foot on the brake but the vehicle was out of control because of the high speed. 'God Almighty,' he said just before the impact silenced both him and Esme and the car was motionless against a brick wall in a quiet suburban street.

'Oh that's a nuisance,' said Madge, still working at the kitchen table. 'I'm running low on flour and I want to make a few more cheese straws. I'll have to ask Mollie to pop down to the High Road for me to get some when she gets back.' She looked at the clock on the wall. 'I thought she'd be back by now. I know she didn't intend to be out long so I don't know what's keeping her.'

'She'll be home in a minute I expect,' said Nora. 'But I'll go and get the flour.'

'Thanks, Mum,' said Madge. 'That would be a great help.'

'I'll get my coat,' said Nora.

Nora had just come out of the grocer's with a bag of flour in her shopping basket when she found herself face to face with Wilf, looking worried.

'Whatever is the matter, Wilf?' she asked in concern. 'You look as though you've got the worries of the world on your shoulders.'

'Oh hello, Nora,' he greeted absently. 'I've just had a worrying experience, as it happens.'

'Have you? What happened?'

'Well, I saw this young couple with a little girl walking

by the river; they looked as though they were in the middle of a real barney,' he explained. 'Then a bit later on I heard shouting and it turned out the man had taken the little girl in his car; snatched her. The woman was in a terrible state. I went with her to her friend's house nearby to use the phone to call the police. Once I knew she was safe with the people there I slipped away; didn't want to intrude.'

'I'm sure you wouldn't have been but I know what you mean,' she said.

'But I can't stop thinking about it and hoping the little girl is all right,' he went on. 'The woman said the man, who is her husband apparently, drove off at break-neck speed.'

'There no point in upsetting yourself, Wilf,' she said, concerned for him. 'There's nothing you can do.'

'I know that,' he said. 'The people at the house were going to call the police.'

'There you are then. The bobbies will soon get the kiddie back,' she said. 'They have ways and means, our coppers, and they know what they are doing. So you must try and forget about it, Wilf. It isn't your problem.'

'You're right, Nora,' he said, smiling bleakly. 'It's cheered me up no end, seeing you. It's made me feel better talking to someone about it.'

'Glad I could help. Actually we had a minor emergency of our own in the kitchen,' she said in the hope of lightening his mood with trivia because he seemed so upset. 'My daughter ran out of flour before we'd finished the big Christmas bake so I rushed down here to get some more. It would be the end of the world in our house if we didn't bake enough stuff at Christmas to last until Easter.'

He managed a half-smile.

'And I must hurry back because she's waiting for it.'

'I won't keep you then.'

'Happy Christmas, Wilf.'

'Same to you, Nora.'

They stood looking at each other. 'Cheerio then, Nora,' he said at last.

'Ta-ta, Wilf.'

They parted company and as Nora hurried homewards Wilf went to the newsagent's to get the *Evening News*. He had noted that Nora was in a hurry to get away from him again, which was a pity. But at the front of his mind was still the young couple and the little girl; such a pretty little thing too. He did hope the couple managed to solve their differences and that no harm came to the child.

It wasn't until Nora got home to find that Mollie and Esme were still not back and Madge was beginning to worry that Nora began to make a connection. No, it was too much of a coincidence. Of course the couple that Wilf had seen by the river hadn't been Mollie and Syd. It was ridiculous to think the little girl who had been snatched was Esme. She was letting her imagination run wild now.

Why would Syd take her away when he had never

wanted her in the first place? Vengeance was the answer to that. If they'd had a row and he'd wanted to hurt Mollie he might just do something like that. He did have a cruel streak; he'd proved that when he'd deserted his wife and child. Mollie did know people who lived by the river too. The Parkers. Oh dear, this was beginning to seem more likely with every second that passed. She didn't want to alarm Madge unnecessarily. But she'd have to mention it to her. It was no more than her duty.

'About time too,' said Grant Parker, looking out of the window when two policemen arrived at the door. 'It's taken them long enough to get here.'

'You reported a child abduction, sir,' said the officer when Grant, with Mollie and Cora right behind him, opened the door.

'Yes,' said Mollie, rushing forward. 'Have you found her? Please tell me that you have.'

There was an alarming silence. 'Can we come inside please, sir?' asked the policeman looking grim.

'Of course,' said Grant, ushering them inside.

Mollie's face was bloodless as she followed the policemen into the Parkers' sitting room.

Chapter Eight

Mollie's voice was little more than a whisper as she responded to the officer's words. 'A car accident,' she said in nervous staccato tones. 'My husband is . . . dead.'

The policeman cleared his throat. 'The driver of the car was fatally injured,' he explained. 'And we believe the victim to be Sydney Fisher but there will have to be a formal identification of course.'

A silent scream rose within Mollie. She went into a state of such dread that she seemed almost calm as she asked the terrifying question.

'My daughter.' The words stumbled out, her lips trembling with fear. 'Is she . . .'

'The child in the car has been taken to Hammersmith hospital,' he said.

Her hands flew to her head. 'So does that mean that she's alive?' she asked.

He nodded. 'We believe she is unconscious, Mrs Fisher,' he said in an even, noncommittal tone. 'But the hospital staff will tell you more. We can arrange transport if you wish.'

'I'll take you in my car, Mollie,' offered Grant.

The sound of the doorbell didn't register with Mollie, such was her turmoil, but Grant slipped from the room and re-entered with her father looking pale and anxious, having come looking for Mollie following Nora's story and been brought up to date by Grant. Her dad was a welcome sight for Mollie even though he seemed to be on the other side of the cloak of darkness that had fallen over her.

One of the policemen asked if she wanted them to let anyone know.

'The rest of the family need to be told but my mother and grandmother will die of fright at the sight of a policeman at the door,' said Mollie.

'We can call at your place on the way to the hospital,' suggested Grant

'Thank you,' she said through dry lips.

Mollie was deeply distraught but oddly distanced from everything. She felt vague and unreal; people coming and going; nurses, doctors, her mother telling her that Gran had stayed at home to tell Geoff when he got home from work and they would come to the hospital together later.

She sat at her daughter's bedside with her parents, her gaze fixed on the motionless child, head bandaged, her face, normally so pink and animated, now pale and still. Her mother was crying but Mollie was unable to shed a tear. She felt taut and frozen inside.

They had been told by the doctor that Esme had suffered a blow to her forehead when the car hit the wall and she had been flung forward and struck her head on the back of the front seat. The wound had been stitched but there was always a risk of brain damage with such a head injury; however this couldn't be ascertained until she regained consciousness.

So all Mollie could do was wait and hope. She was too frantic with worry about Esme to grieve for Syd just now. All she could feel was anger towards him for causing their daughter's parlous condition. He'd died as he had lived: in pursuit of his own interests.

A nurse appeared with the news that there were some visitors and in walked Geoff and Gran. Mollie rushed over to her brother and flung her arms around him. He was the one person she needed most right now and she wept in his embrace.

'I'd like to do something to help Mollie,' Cora said to Grant. 'I can't just do *nothing*.'

'It's a nice thought,' said Grant, thinking how much his wife had changed since she'd been friendly with Mollie. 'But I don't see what you can do really except hope and pray for Esme. Mollie has her family with her so she has plenty of support.'

'Maybe I could cook them something,' she suggested. 'If they are all at the hospital they won't have had a chance to get a meal. I know that food is probably the last thing on their minds, and they'll have plenty of mince pies and so on at home, but they need a proper meal to keep them going. I've got plenty of stuff in because of the holiday. I'll make something for them to have tonight when they get home.'

'Mollie might have to stay at the hospital overnight,' he mentioned.

'Then she can have hers there, and the others if they stay into the evening. I'll take it if you'll run me in the car. There will be no one in at the house anyway.'

'Of course I'll take you,' he agreed readily. 'It's a very kind thought.'

After making her way through a maze of hospital corridors with a shopping basket containing a pie wrapped in a tea towel, a dish of vegetables and some plates and cutlery, Cora was pleased to see a familiar face.

'Geoff,' she said, seeing him sitting on a chair in the corridor outside the ward. 'I thought I'd never find it.'

'Hello, Cora,' he said with a tired smile.

'I'm not stopping,' she said quickly, almost apologetically, as she put the basket down by his chair. 'I just thought you might all forget to eat because of the worry so I've brought something along. A meat pie for your supper.'

'Oh, that's very kind of you.' He'd never thought of her as the compassionate type so he was surprised. 'That will cheer us all up. Thank you very much.'

'Any news?' she asked.

He shook his head. 'She's still unconscious.'

'I wish there was something I could do to help,' she said.

'We feel that way too but all we can do is give Mollie plenty of support,' he said.

'It's awful for all of you,' she said sympathetically.

'Are you going in?' he asked, looking towards the doors of the ward. 'I've come out for a break so there's room for you if you'd like a few minutes.'

'Oh no, I wouldn't dream of intruding,' she said in a tone that didn't invite argument. 'I'll leave the pie with you if that's all right. My husband is waiting for me in the car anyway.'

'As you wish,' he said and she noticed how pale and drawn he looked.

'Please give Mollie my love and tell her that I'm thinking of her and praying for Esme. If there's anything Grant and I can do please let us know. Anything at all.'

'I'll pass your message on to Mollie. I'll be going back in soon. It's harrowing in there though.' He lapsed into thought for a few moments then looked at her as though seeing her properly. 'Thanks for the food; it's much appreciated.'

'A pleasure,' she said.

Even now, in these terrible circumstances, she still found him very attractive and was ashamed of her physical reaction to him. How could she feel such a thing at a time like this, she admonished herself as she hurried away.

Geoff was wondering how on earth he could have

even noticed Cora in any significant way when his niece was in such a critical condition. But he felt drawn to her even so. Passion, apparently, had no dignity and there was nothing he could do about that, he told himself as he went back into the ward carrying the basket.

It was a few minutes to midnight and Mollie was alone at Esme's bedside, the rest of the family having gone home to bed at her insistence and because it was against hospital regulations for them all to stay. Because Esme's condition had been critical when the ambulance brought her in she'd been admitted straight on to the ward. Had the circumstances been less severe the question of payment would have arisen before admission and could have delayed treatment. Mollie had signed to the effect that she couldn't pay as soon as she arrived.

Now she had her gaze fixed on her daughter but her own lids kept drooping and she would wake up with a start into the awful circumstances. This was the second time she had felt her life crumble around her without warning; both occasions caused by the same person and now he was dead! She forced herself to say the words silently to make it seem real because it was hard to take it in, especially as her mind was focused on Esme.

Maybe she could have prevented the accident. She'd known Syd had been drinking so perhaps she shouldn't have let Esme get into the car. She didn't know many car owners but she'd never heard of any rules about alcohol while at the wheel so presumed there weren't any. It wasn't as though he'd seemed drunk; just determined to get his own way. Anyway there was no point in tormenting herself about it. It wouldn't change anything.

A calamity like this did bring out the best in people though; her family were a wonderful support and the hospital staff couldn't be kinder. Even Cora had shown she cared by sending a meal which the others had enjoyed but Mollie hadn't been able to manage more than a morsel. Her mouth was parched and she felt nauseous while, at the same time, feeling weak and empty. It was kind of Cora to make it for them anyway.

Every so often a nurse would appear to check Esme's pulse and temperature then steal away, her rubber-soled shoes squeaking on the polished floor. Time seemed to stand still. Mollie both longed for this night to end while not wanting time to pass for fear of what the coming moments might bring.

The black hands on the big round clock on the wall kept pulling her gaze towards them and as she watched them turn midnight she realised absently that it was now Christmas Day. Her eyes were just beginning to close again when she heard a small voice say, 'Mummy, where's my bedroom?'

Instantly alert, Mollie saw that her daughter was awake and not just muttering in her unconscious state. 'It's at home, sweetheart, waiting for you,' she said, copious tears of relief dripping down her face. 'You're in hospital and you're safe.'

★　★　★

It was the strangest Christmas Day. Naturally there was elation about Esme's return to consciousness but Syd's death still hung over everything and a hospital ward wasn't the best place in which to celebrate. But they did their best to give Esme a good time; they brought some of her presents in but decided to celebrate Christmas properly when she came home.

Mollie was told by the doctor that there was no evidence of brain damage but Esme would have a scar on her forehead for life. Compared with their worst fears it seemed insignificant but Mollie wondered if when Esme was older it might bother her.

Because of the nature of the accident Mollie was questioned by the police. But they seemed satisfied with her account of events before the car crashed and said that they didn't expect to bother her again. Recounting events to them reminded her of someone else who had been involved in a small way.

'There was a man by the river,' she said to Madge and Nora. 'An elderly gent who was ever so kind when I was in such a state. I wish I knew who he was so that I could thank him and tell him that Esme is all right. He seemed really worried. But he disappeared when I got to the Parkers'.'

'His name is Wilf Robbins,' said Nora and went on to explain how it was that her father had come looking for her at the Parkers'. 'I happened to meet Wilf in the High Road and he told me what had happened by the river and how worried he was about the little girl. It didn't dawn on me until you and Esme didn't come home that he might be talking about you.'

'So how do you know him then, Gran?' asked Mollie.

'I knew him years ago when I was just a girl,' she explained. 'He left the area and recently came back.'

'Was he a friend, Mum?' asked Madge.

There was a brief hiatus. 'Yes, that's right,' Nora replied.

'Can you tell him that Esme is all right and also that I'd like to see him to thank him personally.'

'I don't know where he lives,' she said.

'Oh.' Mollie couldn't hide her surprise.

'We only met briefly and didn't get around to exchanging addresses,' she explained.

'Well, if you happen to run into him again will you tell him I'd like to see him and offer my thanks for his kindness.'

'Will do,' said Nora.

Geoff went with Mollie to Syd's funeral to give her some moral support. Esme was still in hospital so Mum and Gran visited in Mollie's place. It was a miserable occasion, made sadder by the very small turnout: just Syd's parents, a few other relatives and his boss. Syd's devious ways meant he didn't have many friends. The few mourners there stood around the grave with umbrellas up against the steady drizzle.

Mollie had never had much to do with her in-laws because Syd hadn't been close to them, and there had been no contact at all after Syd deserted her until his death when they had called at the house to say they wanted to take care of the funeral arrangements. Mollie thought they were probably ashamed of his behaviour and that had kept them away. But they were Esme's grandparents so it would be nice for her to see them sometimes even if only very occasionally.

'How are you, Mrs Fisher?' asked Mollie after the burial when people were heading away from the grave.

She shrugged, looking bleak, a small, pale woman dressed all in black. 'Much as you'd expect really.' She paused. 'Sorry to hear about the little 'un. How is she?'

'On the mend now, thanks,' Mollie said.

'Good. I'm glad about that.'

Suddenly Mollie could see beyond her own problems and viewed things in a different way. She herself was the estranged wife of the deceased. This little woman had given birth to him and raised him. He must have shamed his parents by disappearing and now he had died under a cloud. Molly was very sad that his life had been cut short despite everything but to lose a son must be devastating whatever his faults.

'You're very welcome to see Esme if ever you're round our way,' she said. 'She'll be coming out of hospital soon,'

'Thank you, Mollie,' she said, managing a sad smile. 'It's good of you.'

Mollie nodded politely.

'Are you coming back to the house?' asked Mrs Fisher. 'You'll be very welcome.'

'Thank you but I have to go to the hospital,' she said. 'I need to get there as quick as I can.'

'Of course. I understand,' she said and her husband took her arm and led her towards the car.

'It was kind of you to say that they could see Esme,' said Geoff as they watched them go. 'As they've ignored her existence for so long, not everyone would be so nice.'

'Life is too short for grievances, Geoff.'

'You're right. Today is a reminder of that.'

'Exactly,' she said. 'Anyway, Esme isn't a possession that I want to keep to myself. She's related to them by blood so as far as I am concerned they have a right. They won't take me up on it anyway, I don't think.'

'That was the impression I got too.'

'It's a pity really. It might have helped them with their loss. Syd was a bugger but he was their son.'

'Mmm,' he agreed. 'Oh well, there's no accounting for people, is there?'

'Shall we go?' she said.

'Yeah let's,' he said and they walked out of the cemetery arm in arm, under an umbrella.

When Esme came out of hospital Mollie's maternal instincts magnified to an unhealthy degree. Now that her daughter was away from the safe medical environment, with trained people on hand day and night, Mollie became excessively protective and refused to leave her under any circumstances. This meant she didn't go to work at the Parkers' and arranged for Rose to take her classes with Gran at the piano and Cora doing the reception as usual.

'I hope you'll come back to work soon,' said Cora one afternoon when she was visiting Mollie. She had become a regular caller at the Pottses' home lately and was on friendly terms with the family. 'I take a dim view of having to do all the housework myself and I don't want to take on anyone else only to have to get rid of them when you start again.'

'I'm very grateful to you for keeping the job open for me but I think you should get someone else because I can't leave her yet,' said Mollie while Esme was playing with her dolls and oblivious to the adults' conversation.

'I'm not getting anyone else because I want you,' Cora stated. 'I just hope you won't be away for much longer.'

'Esme will be perfectly safe with me and Mum,' Madge put in. 'All this fussing over her isn't doing her any good.'

'She's had a bad time, Mum,' Mollie reminded her.

'And so have you which is why you need to get back to normal,' said her mother.

'Most mothers of young children stay at home all day to look after them and no one thinks they are being overly fussy.'

'Probably because they aren't,' said Madge. 'But you are; watching her every move and never letting her out of your sight; it isn't good for her.'

'If you're worried about me paying my way—' began Mollie.

'Now you're being insulting,' Madge objected.

'I think you should apologise to your mother for that

remark, Mollie,' her grandmother put in. 'You know her better than that.'

'Sorry, Mum,' she said. 'I didn't mean it.'

'Apology accepted.'

'I'd better go,' said Cora, feeling awkward as this was a family matter.

'There's no need, dear,' Madge assured her. 'We've had a few words and it's over. There isn't going to be a big row. So stay for as long as you like.'

Cora was fascinated by the Pottses, who were so different to her own family. They spoke their minds and disagreed quite strongly at times but there was never any lasting bad feeling as far as she could see.

'I need to be going anyway,' she said. 'I have to get a meal ready and it's keep fit tonight so I'll have mine early and leave Grant's in the oven for him.'

'Tell Rose I'll be back as soon as I can, and thanks, Cora, for doing the reception.'

'I'd be doing it for you anyway so it's no trouble but we'll all be glad to have you back, isn't that right, Nora?'

'I'll say.'

'The class members always ask about you,' added Cora.

Mollie was consumed with guilt but just said, 'I'll be back as soon as I can but not until I'm confident that my daughter is ready to be left.'

'Anyone would think you'd be leaving her alone on the streets instead of at home with people who love her,' said Madge in a tone of admonition.

The conversation was halted by the sound of the front door opening and Geoff bounded in.

'What's this, the Chiswick branch of the Ladies' Guild?' he asked cheerily.

'We're just trying to persuade Mollie to loosen the apron strings on Esme and go back to work,' his mother explained.

'Oh, that,' he said, frowning slightly because he, too, was worried about his sister.

'I'll put the kettle on,' said Madge, which was her answer to everything. 'Will you stay for a cuppa, Cora?'

'I've already had two,' Cora reminded her. 'I must be on my way.'

'It's my night off so I'm cooking if you'd like to join us later,' said Geoff lightly.

'A busman's holiday eh?'

'That's right but I'm told I'm a very good driver.'

They all winced in an exaggerated manner at his terrible joke.

'I hope you're a better cook than you are a comedian,' said Cora, smiling.

'He is, thankfully,' said Mollie.

'I have a husband to feed so I can't stay any longer but thank you for asking,' she said.

'You're welcome,' said Geoff and went with her to the front door.

In the end it was Geoff who persuaded Mollie to take a close look at her recent behaviour.

'You're smothering Esme with all the fussing,' he said one night over cocoa when the others were in bed. 'She's a little girl, not a china doll. Kids pick up on these things and she'll get as nervous as you are if you keep clucking over her like a mother hen.'

'Honestly, I'm trying to keep my child safe and all I get from you lot is criticism. It isn't as if I'm sponging on anyone. I've earned enough to cover me for the moment.'

'It isn't about money, surely you must know that. We're only going on at you because we're worried about you,' he said. 'Cora can't keep the job open for you forever, and you might lose members if you don't soon go back to your class. After all your hard work you don't want to have to start again from scratch.'

'Rose is a very good teacher, probably better than I am so that isn't even a possibility,' she said.

'Go back for your own sake then,' he suggested. 'You've done the training and built your classes and your reputation so go and get on with it.'

Mollie burst into tears and sobbed her heart out.

'Come on, sis,' he said kindly, sitting on the arm of her chair with his arm around her and offering her his handkerchief. 'I know you've had a rough time but things are better now and nothing is really that bad, is it?'

'I don't know what's the matter with me, Geoff,' she wept. 'I seem to have lost my spirit and I feel strange, sort of frightened all the time.'

'It's probably delayed shock after everything that's happened,' he said. 'It was no small thing, the abduction and the accident and then Syd dying like that but it's all over now. Time to put it behind you.'

'But I feel as though I don't have the strength.'

'So you're using Esme as an excuse.'

'Not intentionally. I really am afraid to leave her but it's more than just that.'

'I reckon you've lost your confidence,' he said. 'I don't know much about such things but I should think the only way forward is to get back out there. You know in your heart that Esme will be safe with Mum, and Gran when she's not at the class with you playing the piano.'

'Yes, I do know that.'

'Then show your trust in them by returning to work and getting back to normal,' he said. 'If that doesn't make you feel better, we'll take you down the doctor's and get you a tonic.'

'That costs money so I'll try to avoid it,' she said.

'Halleluiah,' said Cora joyfully when Mollie appeared at the door a few mornings later. 'Now I know there's a God and he's sent you back to work for me.'

'All right, don't overdo the welcome,' said Mollie jokingly. 'It hasn't done you any harm to do your own housework.'

'Maybe not but I'm delighted to hand the job over to you,' she said, holding her poodle in her arms as usual. 'We're pleased to have you back, aren't we, Peaches?'

'You might have to do it yourself all the time if this war comes to be,' said Mollie. 'We'll all be too busy working for our country to go out cleaning other people's houses.'

'I presume you heard the prime minister's broadcast last night then.'

'Of course,' she confirmed.

'I thought it was scaremongering rubbish, though I didn't listen to it all,' said Cora, who couldn't bear to even contemplate the idea of her comfortable life being disrupted so she closed her ears to the news of events from abroad. 'This talk of war has been going on for ages and it hasn't happened. It won't come to anything.'

'We can't ignore the possibility, though, can we?' said Mollie.

'I can and I do,' said Cora in a definite tone. 'When Grant starts talking about it, I don't listen.'

'Anyway, I found the broadcast interesting and the government has to tell us what's going on.'

'They only do that when it suits them,' said Cora. 'And we don't get to hear it all.'

'Of course not; they're running the country. They have to choose what we should know.'

'It's their job to keep us out of wars,' pronounced Cora.

'Sometimes it's out of their control, I suppose, when other countries pose a threat,' said Mollie mildly. 'And at least they are making sure we are ready just in case. They are distributing a booklet which lists all the services we can join if the worst happens.' Mollie grinned. 'You'd be all right in the Women's Land Army, Cora, digging up spuds and milking cows miles out in the country in the middle of winter in the bitter cold. That would be right up your street.'

'You've got your sense of humour back then,' said Cora taking the joke in good part. 'Thank God for that. And let's have no more talk of war please. Not when I'm around.'

Actually Mollie was too engrossed in her own concerns to worry unduly about any possible war. While she was polishing Cora's beautiful furniture, vacuuming her deep pile carpets and washing the kitchen floor, she was still troubled by the idea that she herself might have been to blame for the accident. If she had agreed to go back with Syd he wouldn't have snatched Esme to try to force her into it and he would still be alive now.

But the reasonable side of her nature reminded her that Syd had been a man who wanted what he didn't have and would go to any lengths to get it. He'd had marriage and he'd wanted freedom so he'd trampled on her feelings to get it; then he'd wanted marriage again when he was bored with being on his own. If she'd taken him back how long would he have stayed? She didn't know the answer but she did think it was time she stopped punishing herself. The accident had happened and Esme had a scar on her forehead as a reminder. Nothing could be changed so she must put it to the back of her mind. Esme had mentioned her daddy a few times but not very often now, living in the moment as children do.

When Mollie had finished her shift, she practically ran all the way home in her eagerness to see Esme. But now it was just the joy of being with her, not the misery of anxiety. Mollie felt much more normal. As usual it had been her lovely brother who had helped her to get there.

Being back teaching her classes was a better tonic than any medicine. She'd had plenty of time at home to work out new routines but making them work for a class of thirty people was rather more challenging.

'Three sways then up on your toes and circle your arms over your head. Do this six times then lunge to the right then to the left. Now let's try it with the music.' She nodded towards Nora. 'Thanks, Gran.'

There was a lot of laughter and hilarity as a few people were out of time.

'All right, everyone,' said Mollie after a few times through. 'We've made a start but we'll go over that again next week. Let's have some more sways now, then we'll work on your balance.'

At the end of the lesson there was a crowd around Mollie, who always made herself available to members by sitting on the edge of the stage. They sometimes had queries about a particular exercise or just wanted say how much they had enjoyed the class. Today they wanted to know how Esme was and to say how happy they were to have Mollie back.

'I'm glad to be here,' she said.

None of them could possibly know just how pleased she was. Teaching the class was her joy and salvation.

★　★　★

One afternoon a few weeks later Mollie had a visitor. Rose had come to see her and Mollie took her into the front room so they could talk on their own.

'I'm after a favour,' Rose explained. 'Sorry to come on the cadge when you've not long been back but my mother has been taken ill suddenly and I have to go and look after her in Essex so I won't be able to take my classes. I've managed to get cover for my daytime sessions but I'm stuck for my evening one in Hammersmith on a Wednesday night and wonder if you could help out. I'm not sure how long I'll be away but it might be a few weeks, depending on how Mum is.'

'Of course I'll take your class for you,' said Mollie at once. 'I'll have to check with Mum that she'll be happy to look after Esme but she'll be in bed so I'm sure Mum won't mind.'

'My pianist will be there so you won't have to drag your gran out at night.'

'Count me in then,' said Mollie. 'I owe you several favours after the classes you took for me.'

Chapter Nine

The signs were all there. Frequent absence from home, meticulous attention to appearance and a faraway look in his eyes. All this could only mean one thing: Geoff had a new girlfriend. The family could usually tell when he had a woman in his life and naturally there was a great deal of joshing . . .

'Oi oi,' said Len on his son's night off one evening in early spring when Geoff was giving himself a final once-over in the living-room mirror that hung over the fireplace, face shaved almost raw, hair slicked into place with Brylcreem. 'Someone's got a date again, I reckon. You've been getting all togged up on your nights off a lot lately.'

'Should I get the best tablecloth out for Sunday tea?' chortled Madge.

'Give over, Mum,' Geoff riposted. 'I won't be bringing anyone home for tea just yet.'

'That's a pity,' put in Nora with a wry grin. 'Because we are all dying to meet her.'

'Honestly. Can't a chap take a pride in his appearance without everyone assuming that there must be a woman involved,' Geoff objected in an amiable manner.

'Not in this house, mate,' said his father.

'We're all far too nosy,' added Nora.

'You're telling me,' said Geoff.

'Leave him be,' Mollie urged them. 'He always looks smart when he goes out, wherever he's going.'

'Come off it, Mollie,' said her dad. 'He wouldn't be going to all that trouble if he was only off to the pub for a game of darts.'

'Well, you lot, I'm leaving now so you can speculate all you like while I'm out,' said Geoff happily as he headed out of the room. 'Don't wait up.'

'Have a good time,' Mollie called after him.

'Thanks, I intend to,' he replied just before the front door closed after him.

'It's time he had a steady girlfriend,' Mollie remarked.

'Yeah, I'd like to see him settled with some nice girl,' said Madge while her husband disappeared behind the newspaper now that the fun was over.

Rose was away for longer than expected so Mollie was still taking her class up until Easter and into the new term as spring got well under way. When Esme had her fourth birthday Mollie realised with something of a shock that the infant years were almost over and she cherished them, knowing that things wouldn't be quite the same when she started school next year.

But for now Mollie enjoyed the pattern of her life, being a mum and fitting her other commitments around it. Rose's class had become like her own in spite of the fact that it hadn't all been plain sailing. The difficulty of taking over another teacher's established class was knowing that in all probability the members would be disappointed not to have their regular instructor. Although all the teachers taught the same method, they each had their own individual style and ideas. Rose's exceptional teaching skills gave Mollie an incentive to work even harder to create an interesting class. But she enjoyed the challenge and constantly strove to do a good job.

This was very much on her mind while she was standing at a bus stop in Hammersmith waiting for the bus home after class one evening in the spring. She was mulling things over and wondering what else she could do to improve her technique when a couple on the other side of the street caught her eye in the gathering dusk. She felt a pang because she didn't have a special someone now and they reminded her of how she and Syd had been together before things went wrong; they were totally absorbed in each other. Mollie still remembered that feeling even though she had fallen out of love with Syd later.

The woman looked up at the man and he leaned down and kissed her. Oh that was so romantic, thought Mollie, then her eyes bulged as she realised there was something very familiar about them. Surely it couldn't be. How was it possible? But as they drew nearer, she saw with shock and dismay that it was Cora and Geoff and instinctively she stepped behind a man in the queue and out of sight so they had no idea she was there.

So it was Cora Geoff had been seeing for all these weeks when she and the family had thought he was going out with some eligible young woman. They'd even been hoping to meet her soon and welcome her into their home. And all the time he had been seeing another man's wife. She recalled how late Geoff had been coming home and how he often went out straight from work. Oh Geoff, how could you?

When she'd calmed down later at home, Mollie thought long and hard about what to do and, indeed, if she should do anything. After all, Cora and Geoff were both adults and it was, strictly speaking, none of Mollie's business. But adultery was no small thing. Grant could afford to pay lawyers. Geoff would be named as co-respondent if Grant divorced Cora and Geoff's name would be dragged through the courts which would upset Mum and Dad terribly as well as ruin Geoff's reputation. Besides, Geoff was her twin brother and she knew in her heart that if she were involved in something untoward he would certainly speak to her about it.

So when he came in after midnight, she was in the living room waiting for him in her pyjamas and dressing gown.

'What are you doing still up at this hour?' he asked. 'Is Esme all right?'

'Esme is fine,' she said tersely. 'Which is more than can be said for me.'

He looked at her quizzically. 'Why. What's the matter? You look a bit cross.'

'Cross, I'm absolutely livid. I saw you, Geoff,' she blurted out emotionally. 'I saw you and Cora together.'

His face tightened. 'Oh, oh I see.'

'So what do you think you're playing at, getting mixed up with a married woman?'

He threw his jacket over the back of a dining chair and sat down opposite her in an armchair. 'I love her, Moll,' he declared. 'It's as simple as that.'

Mollie held her head in despair. 'Simple is the last thing it is,' she said. 'Surely you can see that. She's another man's wife, for God's sake! It's wrong, Geoff.'

'Do you think I don't know all that?' he said, sounding tense. 'But I can't help the way I feel.'

'What about her?'

'She feels the same about me.'

'Has she lost sight of the fact that she's married to Grant then?' she asked crossly.

'There's no need to be nasty about it, Mollie,' he admonished. 'It was love at first sight for both of us.'

'Oh for goodness' sake,' she said. 'I think you must have lost your mind.'

'I suppose I have in a way.'

'Then snap out of it and give her up before people get hurt, especially you,' she told him. 'It can't possibly have a happy ending.'

'I can't give her up,' he told her with candour. 'Or to be more precise, I *won't.*'

She sighed. 'Oh Geoff. Why couldn't you have fallen for a young single girl who is available?'

'You can't order these things,' he said.

She narrowed her eyes on him quizzically. 'How did it start?' she enquired.

'I fell for her the very first time I saw her when she came to the house to offer you the job as her cleaner,' he explained. 'I couldn't stop thinking about her and I felt increasingly drawn to her whenever I saw her after that which wasn't very often until recently. I knew instinctively that she felt the same. There was a very strong mutual attraction between us from the very beginning. It was almost tangible.'

'So when did the affair actually start?'

'After the accident, when she started coming to the house, I had a chance to speak to her on her own sometimes for a few minutes; on the odd occasion when you were all out of the room or when I saw her to the door, we talked . . . you know how it is when you really like someone. One day I just blurted out how I felt about her. We arranged to meet and it went from there.'

'So you instigated it.'

'Yes, I suppose I did, but if I hadn't she would have at some point,' he told her. 'The feelings were overwhelming for us both. We have to be together, Mollie. I feel almost ill when we are apart. I know what we're doing is terrible, and Grant doesn't deserve it but it's the way it is.'

'Where does Grant think she is when she's out with you?' she asked.

'She tells him she's going to see her friends from the keep-fit class mostly. I don't think he's that bothered anyway. They aren't close. They haven't slept together for years apparently.'

'So this is your future is it?' she said. 'Skulking about after dark with another man's wife?'

'We don't always meet at night,' he told her. 'Sometimes she comes into the West End during the day and meets me from work when I can get away.'

'She must be really keen then.'

'She is. But in answer to your question about my future,' he began. 'It lies with Cora. She's going to leave Grant so that we can be together.'

'As man and wife?'

He nodded.

She drew in her breath sharply. 'This will break Mum and Dad's hearts, you know that don't you?' she said.

'Yeah, I do know that,' he said looking sheepish.

'What about your career?'

'As long as the management don't find out the details that will carry on as normal. My private life is nothing to do with them anyway,' he said. 'We'll get a place in London, in another neighbourhood, so that I can stay on where I am. We haven't worked out the details yet.'

'You could lose the job if your bosses find out,' she said. 'Adultery is considered very scandalous.'

'I know that, Mollie.'

'So you are willing to risk everything you care about for a woman who is married to someone else.'

'Yes, that's right,' he confirmed, as though defying her to argue with him.

'But even apart from the moral issue of this whole thing, Cora is used to a certain standard of living that you can't possibly give her at the moment.'

'Not now but I might be able to in the future. A good chef can do well. All right, maybe I'll never be as rich as her husband but I should be able to provide decently for her, given a bit of time,' he said. 'Anyway that sort of thing doesn't bother her. As long as she's with me she's happy.'

For the time being maybe, thought Mollie, but what about later on when the novelty of being with a working-class man wears off? But she kept these thoughts to herself. It was his life and he was entitled to live it as he wished.

'I'm not asking you to understand, Mollie, I'm baffled by it myself. I only know how I feel. But please try and accept that I have to do this and wish me luck.'

'You're going to need plenty of that,' she said. 'But all right, I'll say no more about it.'

'And not a word to the family,' he said. 'I'll tell them when the time is right. I have to find somewhere for us to live first, and don't worry, I'll make sure it isn't anywhere near here so the neighbours won't know anything about it and the family reputation can remain firmly intact.'

'That sort of thing doesn't worry me but I'm glad Mum and Dad aren't going to be embarrassed.'

'So can you and I stay friends even though you disapprove?' he asked.

211

'We're twins, Geoff, so we're stuck with each other however much we disagree or wherever we are.' She got up and went over to him with her arms open. 'I think you're being a bloody fool but you're still my brother no matter what you do.'

'Thanks, sis,' he said, getting up and hugging her.

Geoff wasn't normally a deceitful man and he didn't feel good about having an affair with another man's wife. But then it wasn't just an affair. Cora was the love of his life and they were meant to be together. He absolutely adored her and would do anything for her. Going against the morals he'd been brought up with and hurting his parents, as he knew he would when he and Cora moved in together and the truth came out, didn't come easy. But his love for Cora strengthened him and made him feel able to withstand anything; even hurting his loved ones.

Knowing what she now did, Mollie felt aggressive towards Cora the next day at work and she couldn't hide it.

'You know, don't you,' Cora said at break time.

'I certainly do,' Mollie confirmed. 'I saw the two of you in Hammersmith last night. Talk about love's young dream. You looked like a couple of kids.'

'I take it you don't approve.'

'Of course I don't approve,' she said angrily. 'You're a married woman. You've no right to be messing around with my brother's life.'

'I'm not messing around,' Cora said truthfully. 'I'm serious about him. In love with him. Absolutely hook, line and sinker. I'm not lying to you, Mollie.'

'Spare me the romantic melodrama please,' said Mollie. 'I had enough of that from Geoff last night.'

'You'll know how we both feel then,' said Cora.

'Oh yeah I know all about that all right,' said Mollie. 'And I think you should show a bit more discretion, walking through Hammersmith together as bold as brass. If I saw you, how many other people did too? It could get back to Grant.'

'We were in Hammersmith, not Chiswick,' said Cora. 'Hammersmith being the operative word. We make sure we are never seen together in Chiswick. Anyway, Grant will know soon enough.'

'Better he hears about it from you rather than have everyone at his store gossiping about it behind his back until someone lets it out and he is humiliated. Chiswick people do go to Hammersmith; it's a neighbouring town and people flock there in droves, especially to the Palais.'

Cora gave her a steady look, a determined glint in her eye. 'Yes, I take your point; maybe we were a bit reckless and I can understand your being worried for your brother, especially as he is your twin. But in actual fact he is a full-grown man, an intelligent adult, and quite able to run his life how he wants and see who he chooses, married or otherwise.'

Feeling her steely determination and knowing she was right, Mollie said, 'Yes I realise that.'

'So why not take a step back and let Geoff and me do things in our own way.'

Mollie mulled this over. 'Fair enough, Cora, I'll keep out of it in future but there is one thing I must say.'

'Go on,' urged Cora.

'If you let my brother down or hurt him in any way you will have me to deal with.'

'There's no need to sound so threatening, Mollie,' admonished Cora airily. 'I have no intention of letting him down *ever.*' Her tone softened. 'I absolutely adore him and want to spend the rest of my life with him. I'll look after him, I promise.'

'I do hope so.'

'So are you and I still friends?'

'I suppose so,' said Mollie, reminding herself what a good pal Cora had been during her recent troubles and how much she helped with her class. She was absolutely right, of course! What her brother chose to do was none of her business and she would try to remember that in future. It wouldn't be easy though because Geoff meant the world to her and she couldn't see how he and Cora could have a happy future together.

Madge was making a party frock for Esme because she'd been invited to the birthday party of a child in the street and she was very excited. It was pale blue taffeta with matching soft netting over the skirt.

Esme looked gorgeous in it when her grandmother fitted it before the final stitching, and Mollie was so proud.

'You look just like a princess,' she said.

'Do I . . . really?' said the child.

'You certainly do,' confirmed her grandmother. 'But stand still darlin', or you'll get pins digging in you.'

'Is that about right, Mollie?' asked Madge, standing back.

'I think it needs to come in just a tad more at the waist,' she suggested.

'About there?' asked Madge, making the adjustment.

'Perfect,' approved Mollie.

'Good, I can crack on and get it finished later on today but I've run out of blue cotton so I'll have to go down to the High Road to get some,' she said.

'I'll go,' offered Mollie, easing her daughter out of the garment, careful of the pins.

'Can I come, Mum?' asked Esme.

'Course you can, love.' She turned towards her mother, 'I expect she's hoping to call at the sweet shop.'

Madge smiled affectionately.

'Can I have a sherbet fountain please, Mum?' asked the child predictably.

Mollie laughed heartily. 'Am I a mind reader?' she said.

'No just a mum,' smiled Madge.

Parker's was Chiswick's answer to Selfridges. It was on a much smaller scale of course, but its goods were reasonably up to date and they catered for most needs. It certainly drew the crowds, thought Mollie, as she hurried with Esme towards the haberdashery department.

'Mollie,' said a male voice and she turned to see Grant Parker looking enormously handsome in a dark suit with starched white shirt and waistcoat. 'And Esme as well. Lovely to see you. How are you both?'

'We're fine thanks.'

He leaned down towards Esme. 'You're looking very pretty today,' he said.

'I'm having a party frock and a sherbet fountain,' she informed him.

'Both at the same time. What a lucky little girl you are.'

Mollie explained what Esme meant. 'So we're not going to put your turnover up by much today. Just by the price of a reel of cotton.'

'Every little helps.' He smiled. 'I'm on my way to help out in our menswear department. We're short-staffed due to people being off sick. Some sort of spring flu is doing the rounds.'

'Oh dear.'

He looked at her thinking how gorgeous she was but said, 'You're looking well. I'm glad to see you back on form. I hope you've managed to put that awful business behind you.'

'Oh yes. Well you have to, don't you?'

'Yes, I suppose you do.'

'Anyway, we must be getting along,' she said because their eyes kept meeting and she could feel her colour rising and the attraction growing.

'Yes, me too,' he said. 'Look after yourself.'

Mollie was still feeling the effects of the meeting when she left the store and took Esme to the sweet shop. She felt a mixture of Christmas Eve and the aftermath of a bus almost hitting her; kind of excited and churned up inside.

It was completely beyond her how Cora could possibly want another man instead of Grant but there was nothing more puzzling than human emotions.

'Oh dear. No sherbet fountains,' she said in response to the assistant's disappointing news. 'What about sherbet dabs?'

'Yes, we have those,' she said.

Thank God for that, thought Mollie but said, 'I'm sure that will be fine, won't it Esme?'

'Yes please,' she confirmed.

They went on their way smiling; Esme because of her sherbet dab, her mother for more adult reasons.

Grant was thinking about Mollie as he headed for menswear. As well as admiring her, he was also thinking how much she had helped his wife. Cora was like a different person since she'd got to know Mollie who had introduced her to the keep-fit classes. Not so very long ago he couldn't persuade Cora to leave the house apart from walking the dog. Now she went out several nights a week with her friends. She even left her beloved poodle at home with him and that was progress.

It certainly made life easier for him because his wife was happier and easier to live with. They no longer spent every evening irritating each other because she was often not there. Of course, no marriage should have to rely on

217

the absence of one of the partners to be comfortable but theirs wasn't a normal marriage and never had been. Still, it was a lifetime commitment so he just had to make the best of it and things were a whole lot better now that he and Cora had some evenings apart from each other. As well as it being better for him he was glad for Cora's sake that she had friends to go out with and was happier.

Dear Mollie, the trauma she'd been through would have destroyed some people. But she seemed to have bounced back smiling the same as ever, though he guessed that some of it was just front. You couldn't go through something like that without gaining scars. One thing was for sure; he had a lot to thank her for.

Mollie hadn't mentioned 'the affair' to either Geoff or Cora since she'd agreed to stay out of it. She assumed it was still going on but behaved as though it wasn't and tried not to think about it. She had plenty of other things on her mind anyway, her daughter being her main priority. Now that Esme was growing up she was fun to be with and Mollie enjoyed her company.

There was another call on Mollie's time now too because when Rose returned to London from Essex she selected a team for the Albert Hall display and rehearsals got under way, usually on a Sunday afternoon at the London headquarters. The family were unanimously keen for Mollie to take part and happy to look after Esme while she was out so Mollie entered into it with her usual enthusiasm.

They had a setback quite early on in the rehearsal schedule when themes for routines and plans for costumes had to be changed suddenly. The show, in which teams of members from all over the country and abroad were to perform, had been planned as an international festival but, as a result of the Germans invading Czechoslovakia, which had changed the political climate throughout Europe, it was decided to have a much more modest display without any emphasis on patriotism.

'The situation abroad is really beginning to hit home now then,' said Mollie's father when she told them about the changes at Sunday tea in early May after she'd been to rehearsal. 'Who would have thought that the troubles abroad could affect something as innocent as a women's keep-fit display here in England?'

'It is surprising,' said Madge. 'And rather worrying.'

'There's no point in upsetting yourself, dear,' said her mother but Nora herself had turned pale at Mollie's news. 'If war comes we'll just have to get on with it.'

'And I'm sure we will,' said Mollie.

'Geoff's out again then,' said Len, in a much-needed change of subject. 'That boy is never home lately.'

'He works funny hours, being in the hotel trade, dear,' Madge said defensively.

'I know that but he used to be around some of the time,' he said. 'There's obviously a woman involved. But I can't understand why he doesn't bring her home.'

Mollie concentrated on slicing a wedge of apple pie for Esme and didn't say a word.

'I'm sure he will when he's ready,' said Nora.

'Course he will,' added Madge.

'He never says much about her, does he?' Len remarked. 'It isn't like him to be secretive.'

'He's a grown man,' Madge reminded him. 'He doesn't have to have our approval or tell us about his friends.'

'I suppose not,' agreed Len.

'Anyway,' began Mollie, switching the subject again, 'Rose has to design new costumes for the show now; definitely nothing in red, white and blue.'

'A single colour would be best,' suggested Madge. 'Green perhaps, or yellow. Nobody could possibly take offence at either of those shades.'

'Green would be nice,' enthused Mollie. 'I'll suggest it to Rose the next time I see her.' She turned to her mother. 'Some of the girls will make their own costumes, I expect; others will need a dressmaker to do it for them. Shall I tell them you're available?'

'Not half,' she said, looking pleased. 'I'd give them a very low price; just a bit of pocket money for me, and I'd enjoy being involved.'

'I'll spread the word then.' She lifted the lid of the teapot and looked inside. 'Meanwhile, I'll make some more tea. The pot is almost empty.'

Geoff had found a flat in Fulham for him and Cora and was very excited at the prospect of them moving in together. It wasn't, strictly speaking, a flat. It was actually two rooms and shared facilities but there was a sink and a gas ring in the corner of the living room so they could cook their meals in private.

'What do you think?' he asked when he took Cora to see it. 'Lovely big bay windows and it seems like quite a nice street. The landlord is all right about the dog too.'

'That's good,' said Cora, trying not to show how appalled she was at the idea of living in two furnished rooms in a shared house.

'The lavatory is downstairs.'

'Bathroom?'

'There isn't one of those,' he explained. 'But we can have strip washes at the sink and go to the public baths.'

'Yes of course we can,' she said, trying to inject some enthusiasm into her voice because she could see how thrilled he was.

'I know it isn't a palace but it's a start until I can afford something better,' he said. 'Oh Cora, just imagine being together all the time instead of secret meetings and love in cold alleyways. The rent will take a large slice out of my wages so we won't be able to go out much but we won't need to, will we? We'll have each other all the time.'

'It will be lovely, Geoff,' she said in an even tone.

She was touched by his eagerness. Geoff didn't live in such grand accommodation as she did but the Pottses' house was cosy and comfortable with all home comforts. Yet here he was waxing lyrical about living in two awful rooms in a dreadful house with peeling paint and a sour smell of damp about it, all of which was going to take the better part of his wages. It spoke volumes about his feelings for her. She absolutely adored him, too, but she hadn't lost all sense of reality.

'So, shall I tell the landlord that we'll take it?' he asked. 'I have to pay some rent in advance to secure it.'

'Perhaps we could look at a few more,' she suggested.

'There aren't a few more, Cora,' he told her. 'This is London. We have a housing shortage at the cheaper end of the market. Later on when I'm in a better job I'll be able to afford to get us something better. This is just a starting point for us, just the beginning. But at least we'll be together.'

'Yes of course.'

'So do you want me to go ahead?' he asked. 'I need to know. Someone else will snap it up if we hang about.'

His gorgeous brown eyes rested on her hopefully. She loved the bones of him. 'Yes, you go ahead.'

'Oh that's wonderful,' he said, hugging her and lifting her off her feet in the joy of the moment. 'You won't regret it, Cora, I absolutely promise you.'

'I know, Geoff,' she said in a soft affectionate voice.

Geoff was pleased that Mollie was still up when he got home because he wanted to talk to her.

'You're looking pleased with yourself,' she said, making them both cocoa. 'Have you come into money or something?'

'I know we agreed not to talk about me and Cora but things are happening,' he said excitedly. 'I've found us a flat and we're moving in together.'

Mollie felt the blood drain from her face and she stood with a teaspoon in mid-air. 'Oh, I see,' she said.

'Please be happy for me, sis,' he implored her. 'I love Cora so much.'

She stirred the cocoa and handed a cup to him. 'I really hope it works out for you,' she said, taking her drink through to the living room with him following. 'I know how much she means to you, Geoff, and I can see how happy she makes you so that makes me happy too.'

'What about all the disapproval?'

'It's still there; I can't pretend to think what you're doing is right but I suppose this sort of thing is bound to happen to people sometimes,' she said. 'Rules are bound to get broken. We are all only human.'

'Thanks, sis. You know how much you mean to me and I'd hate us to fall out.'

'We'd never do that in any serious way. We'll always be close even when we go our separate ways.'

'I'm going to tell Mum and Dad in the next day or two,' he continued. 'As I've paid the rent in advance I can move in whenever I want. It's time I left home anyway.'

'Will you tell Mum and Dad about Cora being married?' she asked.

'Oh yes,' he said without hesitation. 'As I'm going to be sharing my life with her, I want them to accept her warts and all, though I realise it might take a bit of time.'

'So will she be telling Grant or will she just leave a note?' she asked.

'I don't know,' he replied. 'We haven't discussed that part of it yet.'

Mollie had to physically restrain herself from telling him that this could only lead to disaster and begging him not to do it. But she just said, 'Oh, I see.'

'I do feel bad about Grant,' he admitted. 'He seems like a nice bloke from the little I know of him and he's always treated Cora right.' He paused thoughtfully. 'But some things are meant to be and there's nothing else you can do but go along with them.'

'I suppose so.'

'Anyway,' he continued, having taken a sip of his cocoa. 'I'm expecting Mum and Dad to be upset until they get used to the idea. Mum will be sad and worried for me but Dad will be absolutely furious. I think Gran might understand though; she's a wise old thing and knows that some of us fall by the wayside because of our feelings.'

'Maybe.'

'So can you keep an eye on them after I've left? I'm almost certain to be banned from the house for a while by Dad so I'll give you my new address so that we can stay in touch.'

'Of course I'll do what I can to help them through it but it will take some time for them to accept it because it goes against everything they believe in.' She paused. 'Here we are predicting their reaction when they might be fine about it.'

'We both know that isn't going to happen by the very nature of what I'm doing but I really hope that later on they might forgive me and give Cora a chance.'

'Geoff, I really hope this works out for you,' she said emotionally. 'I know how much you want it to.'

'Thanks, Mollie,' he said and she could see that he had a kind of glow about him. She recognised it because it was the same sort of thing she had felt in the good days with Syd.

That night Cora couldn't sleep. She was finding it impossible to get the memory of those awful rooms out of her mind. No matter how hard she tried she couldn't imagine herself living in a place like that. Up until now, she had been carried along on a wave of passion, living for the time she spent with Geoff, loving him so much that it hurt. She wanted to move in with him as much as he wanted her to but the reality of living without money was beginning to seriously worry her now.

There were the practicalities to be considered. Here she had huge wardrobes full of clothes. That place had one small clothes cupboard that she would have to share with Geoff. Then there was Peaches; she was used to access to a large garden. There was only a small, concrete backyard at the flatlet house and that was down several flights of stairs.

Geoff worked long hours so what would she do while he was out? Here she had soft sofas to recline on with velvet cushions and glossy magazines to read and lots of rooms to wander around as well as a lovely garden to sit in during summer. There it was just one living room and a solitary brown sofa that was hard and shabby.

Then there was the actual cash situation. She had never had to live without money. Her parents hadn't been warm and loving like Geoff's but they had never kept her short of cash. She'd been given a generous allowance until the day she had got married when Grant had taken over and he had always made sure she had plenty. So she didn't know what it was like to live on a budget as Mollie had to. If she wanted something she had it right away, it was as simple as that.

Geoff talked about saving up for a place of their own which was an alien concept to her and didn't seem possible on the wage he earned at the moment. Of course all that would change when he had a head chef's job, and she didn't doubt that he would do well in his career, but that was in the future and their plans were to take almost immediate effect.

She knew her limitations; she didn't have Mollie's courage or strength of character and the ability to carry on in the face of adversity. She was struggling to be brave enough to lower her standard of living for the man she loved; and there was no doubt in her mind that Geoff was the love of her life. But how long would it be before she started taking her lack of luxuries out on him? How long before she resented what she had given up for him? She was worried about it now so it certainly wouldn't take long for the novelty to wear off.

There must be some way around it because she couldn't bear to be without him. She would talk to him and see if they could come up with another plan. The beginning of an idea was already starting to form.

'So, are you saying that you don't want to move in with me?' asked Geoff the following evening when he and Cora were in a pub outside their area, across the river in Barnes.

'No, of course I'm not saying that,' she assured him. 'I'm just suggesting that we either look for somewhere a bit nicer to live or leave it until you can afford something better.'

'But I've already paid a month's rent in advance,' he reminded her.

'I know, Geoff, and I'm really sorry but I'm certain that I would be miserable there and I'd take it out on you.'

'Why didn't you say so before I paid out all that money?' he demanded.

'Because you were so thrilled I didn't have the heart,' she explained.

'But you have the heart now when I'm a good few quid poorer.' His bitter disappointment had turned to anger.

'I was awake all night thinking about it,' she said.

He put his pint glass to his lips and took a long swallow of beer. 'Personally I think the flat is quite nice,' he said. 'It's about the best we'll get in that price range. We could make it cosy.'

Which highlighted to Cora the vast difference in their expectations. She knocked back her gin and tonic to steady her nerves. 'But why don't we leave it a bit longer until you get promoted and can afford to pay more rent so that we can have something really nice.'

He stared at her coldly. 'What are you saying, Cora?' he wanted to know.

'I'm suggesting that we carry on as we are for a while longer until your pay goes up.'

'So you don't want to be with me properly unless I can give you what you have now?'

'I've never had to rough it, Geoff,' she said in a tone of apology. 'I don't think I'd be very good at it.'

'You could always learn.'

'It isn't in me.'

'So you don't want to try.'

'It would tear us apart, Geoff.'

'So much for your declarations of love for me,' he said, hardly able to speak for bitter disappointment.

'I meant every word,' she said.

'But not enough to give up your comfortable life all paid for by a man you are deceiving.'

'Be realistic, Geoff,' she pleaded with him. 'How can I, or anyone, move into a different kind of life to what I've always known without being miserable?'

'You could always do what my sister does to make ends meet; go out cleaning and earn a few bob then you'd have money of your own.'

'Now you're just being stupid.'

'Yeah, maybe I am.' He was utterly dejected.

'I know that I'm not half the woman Mollie is and I've never pretended to be,' she said. 'I'm spoiled and you have known that from the start. Maybe that was why you fell in love with me, because I'm different to the other women you know. Maybe you like the glamour of someone with the aura of money about them.'

'Who knows? That could have been the initial attraction but it goes much deeper than that now.' He looked at her accusingly. 'Maybe you just wanted a bit of rough on the side.'

'No it wasn't that, not consciously anyway. But whatever originally drew us together doesn't matter. My feelings for you are really serious now,' she said.

'So much so that you can't tear yourself away from your riches to move in with me,' he said sharply.

'It's because I love you that I don't want to do it,' she tried to explain. 'I know what I'm like and I think I'd start being horrid to you because I couldn't have what I'm used to. We are all products of our environment, Geoff, and I can't help being accustomed to certain standards. But we can still be together, like we are now. We've been happy, haven't we?'

'It isn't enough for me now,' he said gruffly. 'I want you in my life properly.'

'And you will, later on,' she said.

'If this is your attitude, there won't be a later on for us,' he said. 'There can't be because I can do well in my chosen profession but I'll never be as rich as your husband. I wouldn't even try to be. That sort of thing doesn't interest me. I want to be comfortable yes, of course, but I want to be a chef because I love it and am interested in cooking and creating new recipes, the whole business of a professional kitchen.'

'Surely if you do well, money will automatically follow, isn't that how it works?' she said.

'Not to the extent that you are used to,' he said.

'All I want is to be able to live somewhere better than that flea-bitten hovel you took me to.'

'And I can't give you that yet.'

'So we carry on as we are.'

He looked at her steadily. 'No,' he said. 'I don't want to be involved in a sordid affair.'

'It's never been that.'

'It will be if we carry on in this way,' he said. 'Pubs and cafés in strange neighbourhoods, meeting in the dark on street corners. No, that isn't for me, Cora, not any more. I want commitment.'

'Give me more time, Geoff.'

'You either want to be with me or you don't,' he said. 'Leaving it won't make me into the man you want me to be; the man you want to share your life with.'

'Geoff please . . .'

'Cora, I understand how you must feel; the penny has finally dropped. I don't expect you to give up your good life for me,' he said. 'But neither do I want to carry on as we are.'

'But you are a talented chef, Geoff,' she said. 'You could do very well.'

'I might, yes,' he said. 'But I don't want to be with someone who has reservations about being with me. I understand that we have different expectations and I certainly have no intention of forcing you to lower your standards.'

'But Geoff . . .'

'I don't want to spend all my time trying to prove myself to you,' he cut in. 'Why the hell should I?'

'You won't have to.'

'Of course I will. You said it yourself that you'll resent lowering your standards and why should you anyway, if it isn't what you want?' he said. 'I'm not prepared to spend all my time apologising for who I am.'

'I promise that you won't have to,' she said. 'Once you start to climb the ladder . . .'

He finished his pint and put the glass down rather forcefully. 'You are missing the point, Cora. I want to be with you more than anything I've ever wanted before.' He paused because this was painful but he knew he must be strong. 'But you have to accept me as I am now, not what you hope I'll be in the future, and that means making a commitment; it means moving in with me now, not later on when I might be better off. You have to take me as I am or it's over between us.'

She was horrified. 'You can't want that, Geoff,' she said.

'Of course I don't,' he confirmed gruffly. 'I want us to be together in a proper relationship. No more sneaking around, deceiving that husband of yours. But unless that is what you want as well, this will just be a sleazy affair. So it has to end.'

'Why can't we . . .?'

'The decision is yours, Cora,' he said, his gaze resting on her face. 'You either commit to me or it's over.'

'Geoff, please,' she implored him, tears welling up. 'Don't do this to me, to us.'

'I'm just being straight with you which is what you haven't been with me.'

'I wasn't not straight with you,' she tried to explain. 'I just wanted to be with you so I lived for the day, for the time I spent with you, cherishing every moment we had together.'

'You must have known it couldn't just go on indefinitely,' he said. 'Surely you knew I wasn't the sort of man who would be content with an affair.'

'I don't know what I thought beyond loving you,' she said. 'You're my whole life, Geoff.'

'Then move in with me,' he said

She stared at him; his lovely open face with not a bit of deceit in him. She had a mental image of those ghastly rooms that he thought were nice and she knew she didn't have the courage to do it.

'Sorry, Geoff.'

He stood up abruptly. 'Goodbye then, Cora. I'm sure you can make your own way home.'

She watched him through a blur as he walked across the bar and left without looking back.

Chapter Ten

It was considered very bad form for men of the Pottses' ilk to break down and cry. Such feminine indulgences were not acceptable for males once childhood had passed. But Geoff wept in his sister's arms when he got home that night, much to his deep shame. His despair was so overwhelming that, when he saw Mollie's warm-hearted concern for him, his self-discipline crumbled completely.

'It'll do you good to let it out,' she said, when he had recovered slightly. 'You men should give in to your emotions more often.'

'It isn't considered manly, you know that,' he said thickly.

'Yes I do but I don't know who makes such ridiculous rules.'

'Me neither,' he said. 'But that's the way it is so not a word to anyone.'

'My lips are sealed,' she promised. 'But I'd like to know what brought you to such a sorry state.'

He told her everything.

'So I suppose it was a sort of test for her,' suggested Molly.

'It wasn't intended to be,' he said. 'It never even occurred to me that she wouldn't want to move in with me. I was so besotted with her, I was blind to reality and thought she felt the same way. But obviously not. Yet we talked about getting a place together all the time and she knew I was trying to find somewhere. That's been our plan ever since we realised how strong our feelings were for each other. Well, it was just mine I now realise.'

'She's always been comfortably off,' said Mollie. 'It's bound to have an effect on her behaviour. Not that it's any excuse. It's terrible, what she's done to you, and I'm furious with her about it. She shouldn't have let things get so serious if she wasn't prepared to let them move on.'

'At least I know where I stand with her now,' he said miserably. 'You could say it's my comeuppance for trying to steal another man's wife.'

'Yes you could say that but I'm not going to because you already know how I feel about her poor husband in all this,' she said. 'You don't need to have it rubbed in at this point.'

'Cora doesn't seem to be bothered by conscience at all,' he remarked. 'She even suggested that we carry on seeing each other as we have been doing. I took that as an insult; talk about having your cake and eating it.'

'Mm.'

'She's the first woman I've loved in such a passionate, life-changing way,' he confided. 'There have been crushes and girlfriends, of course, but never anyone like her. I feel absolutely shattered that it's over.'

Mollie listened without much comment while he unburdened himself and she could tell that he was utterly devastated. She knew from experience just how painful a broken heart was and hoped he had the stamina to rise above it after the initial shock. She was fairly certain that he did. Like her, he was a fighter.

Mollie arrived at the Parkers' house at her usual time the next morning and noticed how pale and heavy-eyed Cora looked. She obviously hadn't slept well.

'I haven't come to work,' Mollie informed her. 'I've just come to collect the wages you owe me for his week. Three days it is.'

'Why?' asked Cora.

'I should have thought that was obvious,' she replied.

'You're finishing as my cleaner, is that it?'

'I'm finished with you in every way,' she said, hurting as she said the words but compelled to do this out of loyalty to her brother. 'I won't be cleaning for you again and neither will you be welcome at my classes. I want nothing more to do with you. I shall avoid your company when I see you at Rose's class and rehearsals for the show.'

Cora was clearly shocked. 'Surely there's no need for such drastic measures,' she said.

'There's every need,' said Mollie. 'You didn't think our friendship could survive after what you've done to my brother, did you? He's in pieces because of you.'

'But that's between Geoff and me,' she said. 'It has nothing to do with you or our friendship.'

'Maybe not by your standards; I know that Geoff isn't blameless in this and I have told him what I think as regards that,' she said. 'But he is my twin brother and we are very close as you well know so my loyalties lie with him. Not content with cheating on that lovely husband of yours, you do the dirty on Geoff as well.'

'It's none of your business.'

'No it isn't,' she agreed. 'But when you hurt Geoff you hurt me. It's as simple as that. I don't want to be around you anymore, and that is my choice, my business.'

The other woman winced and Mollie felt a stab of pain because she wasn't a vindictive person and she liked Cora. But she had to make a stand about this because Cora's treatment of Geoff had hit him so hard.

'If that's what you want, I suppose I don't have a choice in the matter,' she said.

'Not really, no. So if you could get me what I'm owed I'll be on my way.'

Cora was ashen with just two spots of colour on her cheeks. 'I'll go and get it,' she said and turned and disappeared into the house leaving Mollie waiting in the hall near the front door.

Cora's hands were shaking as she unlocked a drawer in the bureau to get some cash for Mollie. She had lost the man she loved and her best friend in one fell swoop.

Now she had no one she really cared for and nothing to look forward to. She had enjoyed having Mollie in her life and had lived for her meetings with Geoff.

Was it too late to tell Geoff that she had changed her mind and beg him to take her back under his terms – *under any terms* – tell him that she would live anywhere as long as they were together? Her spirits lifted at the thought of feeling him close to her and hearing his deep, warm voice again.

But in her heart she knew that she didn't have the courage to leave behind the comfort of her middle-class life without ruining what she and Geoff had with discontent and resentment. As much as she loved him she didn't have that sort of moral fibre. So she wiped away her tears with a handkerchief, put Mollie's cash into an envelope and made her way back to the front hall to see Mollie out for the last time.

As Mollie walked home, the fury that had inspired her to end her friendship with Cora drained away leaving her hurting inside and miserable. She would miss the other woman enormously – their tea-break chats and their shared interest in the keep-fit movement. But she had been driven by devotion to her brother and she knew a clean break had been the only way. To carry on would only result in snipes and little digs which would have eventually exploded into a serious argument.

She remembered once thinking that people from different sides of the fence could never truly be friends and it gave her no pleasure to realise that she had been proved right.

Oh well, it was done now and she had to live with the consequences of life without Cora. The first thing she must do was to look for another job.

Ironically, Geoff was given promotion a few days after his parting from Cora. His first thoughts were of her because his new status came with a significant pay rise which meant he could afford better accommodation for them. He was full of it; not that he had done well and his hard work had been recognised; not that maybe he had talent. Only that he had more to offer Cora. Still not quite what she was used to but something better than the rooms she'd hated, and for which he had managed to get back some of his deposit. He couldn't wait for his lunch break so that he could go to the telephone box to call her. Grant would be at work so it would be safe.

He was almost running to the nearest kiosk when his break finally arrived but when he got there the box was occupied. As he stood there shifting from foot to foot in his eagerness to speak to her, he got to thinking and realised with a heavy heart that the extra money didn't really alter anything. Cora hadn't loved him enough to be with him for what he was and that wasn't going to change just because he could afford accommodation with a slightly better class of wallpaper.

The issue wasn't about money; it went deeper than

that and was about strength of feeling. Cora's for him didn't match his for her so any reconciliation would be pointless because they wouldn't stay the course without mutual love and loyalty. Feeling more dejected than ever because of his brief hope, all the pleasure of his promotion spoiled, he made his way back to work.

Reaching the hotel, he stood across the street looking at the elegant old building with its impressive entrance and feeling a sudden rush of pride that he was a part of it. Maybe only on the other side of the class divide to Cora, who might dine there while he was below in the kitchens. But he was a valuable member of the team. He couldn't have Cora but he still had his ambitions.

Mollie had a stroke of luck as far as employment was concerned. She was chatting to Rose after her class a week or so after leaving Cora's and just happened to mention that she was looking for a part-time job.

'They want someone at head office for routine clerical work because someone has left unexpectedly,' Rose mentioned. 'I think it's part-time and there's no typing or shorthand involved. I was there last week and they happened to be talking about it. They'd prefer to have someone with an interest in what we do so you might be just what they are looking for, especially as they haven't advertised the position yet. I don't know what the pay is like but it wouldn't hurt to make some enquiries.'

'Thanks Rose,' said Mollie. 'I'll look into it as soon as I can.'

Rose gave her an inquisitive look.

'I had a phone call from Cora,' she said. 'She isn't coming to class any more and she's pulled out of the show. She didn't give a reason.'

'Oh.' It was a fist in Mollie's chest.

'I wonder if you happened to know anything about it,' she said. 'I know you are friends.'

Mollie was cornered. 'We have had a falling-out as it happens,' she said.

'I thought you might have when you mentioned that you are looking for work,' she said. 'I know you normally help her out on the domestic front.'

'Yes I did but that's finished now,' she said but offered no further information and Rose, having excellent manners, didn't ask.

The keep-fit offices were in the back streets near Victoria station in a big old house that had once been a private dwelling. Mollie started work there the following week after attending an interview soon after Rose had told her about the vacancy.

The job was four mornings a week and the pay was the same as Cora had paid her so she was delighted. By the end of her first session she knew she was going to enjoy the work. It felt like an extension of her teaching, being all about the association and therefore of interest to her.

Her duties were routine and clerical; she was actually a bit of a dogsbody but she didn't mind. Among other things she printed notices and envelopes on the duplicating machine and sent them out to teachers, ran errands, waded through piles of filing and made tea. Her colleagues were all women, this being a female organisation, and they all attended at least one class so there was a good atmosphere.

'So much nicer for you than cleaning someone else's house, dear,' remarked her mother one night over dinner.

'Not half,' added Nora.

'Both my children are going up in the world,' said Madge proudly. 'You with your classes and your office job and Geoff being given promotion.'

'Mine is just a part-time office job,' said Mollie. 'And I'm only doing the work of an office junior. The reason I got the job is because of my connections to the association. They like their staff to be members too.'

'That's as maybe,' said her mother. 'But it's still quite a step up.'

'Only a very tiny one,' said Mollie modestly. 'But nothing like Geoff's. He really has had promotion.'

'Geoff's very quiet lately,' said Len, taking advantage of the fact that his son was still at work to mention this. 'And he doesn't go out so much as he did. I reckon whoever it was he was seeing has given him the elbow.'

'It does seem that way,' said Madge. 'Has he said anything to you, Mollie?'

'No,' she lied because she wasn't prepared to divulge Geoff's secret. 'I think he's putting all his energy into the job.'

'Probably,' muttered her father.

It seemed incredible to Mollie that such a huge drama had been played out under their noses and none of the family made the connection between her leaving the Parkers' employ and Geoff's romance ending. To Mollie it had been so all-consuming and vivid in her life, she felt as though they must know everything. But why would they? The two things weren't linked as far as they were concerned. It just went to show that it was possible to have some privacy even in a close-knit family like theirs.

After breaking down in her arms, Geoff had been resolutely strong, his pain only visible in unguarded moments when she could see in his eyes that he was hurting. The job promotion had boosted his shattered confidence but not mended his heart. He hadn't mentioned Cora again and neither had Mollie. Ostensibly it was as though she had never been in their lives. But her absence was a powerful force and Mollie knew that they were both feeling it.

The day was bright and sunny and the crowds poured into the Albert Hall for the Women's Keep-Fit Display one Saturday in June. Despite being substantially toned down and a much less spectacular show because of the political situation abroad, it was still an elegant affair and the costumes were colourful and pretty. Rose's team were wearing white satin blouses with emerald green pants and wide black sashes around the middle. They performed a graceful piece using coloured ribbons which received rapturous applause. Mum, Gran and Esme came to the afternoon performance and Mollie met them at the end for tea. As she had to stay on for the evening show they made their way home.

Every moment of the special day had felt like magic to Mollie but there had been something not quite right for her throughout. At the end, when all the performers from far and wide assembled for the National Anthem, Mollie knew that the missing element had been Cora. All the excitement, the hilarity, the stage fright and the camaraderie should have been hers too. As the singing came to an emotional conclusion Mollie felt sad that she had missed this wonderful experience.

There was a curious feeling of finality here; as though this would be the last show, probably because of the war fever that gripped the country. It was impossible to ignore the rumours now that they had been issued with gas masks and Mum had made blackout curtains. Dad and Geoff had even erected an air-raid shelter in the back garden.

Now the show was finally over and she made her way to the dressing rooms with Rose and some of the others.

'Thank you, everyone,' said Rose, gathering her team together before they got changed. 'You were terrific. None of you so much as missed a beat so very well done.'

They gave her three cheers then started to change into their ordinary clothes, the dressing room full of happy female voices.

★　★　★

Although war had been a threat for a long time and had become increasingly inevitable during the summer as news of Hitler's terrible acts in pursuit of world domination became known, it was still a shock when Neville Chamberlain told the nation on the wireless on the sunny first Sunday in September that this country was now at war with Germany. Mollie felt emotional but tried to be strong because both her mother and grandmother were in tears.

'I'm sure it will all be fine,' she said determinedly. 'We're very well prepared with our gas masks and air-raid shelter and everything. We'll be as safe as houses.'

Geoff was at the window. 'The neighbours are all out in the street,' he said. 'So why don't we go out and join them.'

'Good idea, son,' agreed his father.

It was very much a time to be with people so they all trooped out and joined in the chatter. There was mutual bewilderment. Everyone had known it was coming but now that it was here nobody knew what would happen next.

Apart from the siren sending them all into the shelter for what turned out to be a false alarm, life went on as normal except for the blackout. People went to work as usual on the Monday and those children who hadn't been evacuated went to school. All places of entertainment were closed by law so people couldn't escape into a film or a show at the theatre. Fortunately this didn't last long; when these places reopened many people braved the blackout in search of light relief in the evening. Not everyone felt so inclined though.

'Attendance was well down at my class the other night,' Mollie confided to Rose when she saw her after her own first wartime evening class. 'Some members would rather stay at home because of the blackout I suppose. I'm wondering if I should move the class to daytime if I can get the use of a hall.'

'I think you should wait a while and see what happens,' Rose suggested. 'Once people get used to the blackout they'll start coming to class again, I think. The cinemas and dance halls are doing well again and I think our classes will follow suit in time. I'm not going to change my evening class to daytime yet anyway.'

Fortunately she was proved to be right and as the Christmas term proceeded and drew to a close, many of Mollie's regulars had returned to class. People found comfort in company and Mollie could see them unwinding during the course of the lesson. Most were smiling when they left.

As Christmas approached Mollie found her thoughts turning to Cora, who hadn't been seen since their friendship ended. Mollie had thought she might join another class but she asked around at a teachers' meeting and no one knew anything of her. While Mollie still disagreed with what she had done to her husband and Geoff, this country was at war with Germany which was a dangerous situation to be in and it was no time to harbour grudges. Although she wasn't planning on re-establishing their friendship to any large degree, she did want to know if Cora was all right in these worrying times.

So she decided to go to the Parkers' house and went directly after her Tuesday morning class while her grandmother went straight home. A stranger opened the door, a well-dressed woman of middle years.

'Yes,' she said questioningly.

'Is Mrs Parker in please?' Mollie asked.

The woman looked surprised by the question. 'Well no. The Parkers don't live here now,' she explained.

Mollie was astonished. 'Oh,' she began, 'I didn't know they'd moved.'

'Some time ago actually. We bought the house from them back in the summer.'

'Do you happen to know where they've gone to?'

'I don't I'm afraid; they'd already moved out when we first came to view the house and there was no forwarding address. They left in a hurry apparently.'

'Oh, I see,' said Mollie, puzzled. 'Sorry to have bothered you then.'

'That's quite all right,' said the woman and closed the door.

So Cora had disappeared completely. Mollie wondered if the Parkers had left the area or were still local. Maybe they had moved to the country because of the threat of war that was around at that time and had sent many of the well-off to safer regions. But she couldn't imagine that because they were both Londoners through and through. Of course she could go to the store and ask Grant. He would probably still be working there wherever they lived unless he'd been called up into the forces. But she knew she wouldn't go to see him. He might ask questions about why her friendship with Cora had ended and she didn't want to lie about it, which she would be forced to do because she couldn't tell him the truth.

Oh well, that was the end of the Parkers as far as she was concerned. They had always been outside of her usual circle but had somehow found a place in her heart. Now she would never see them again and that made her feel sad.

When she got home something had happened which pushed the Parkers right out of her mind.

'They've come,' said her mother tearfully, clutching an unopened envelope. 'Fancy sending them before Christmas. That's plain cruel.'

'Your brother's call-up papers have arrived,' explained her grandmother helpfully.

'Oh blimey,' Mollie burst out. They had known that Geoff would have to go into the services, of course, but it was still a shock now that his leaving was a reality. 'Are you sure that what's in the envelope?'

'It's from the military so what else would it be?'

'I suppose you're right.'

'We won't know when or where until he gets home from work and opens it,' said Madge shakily. 'And no, we are not going to steam it open because we can't wait to know.'

'The very idea,' said Nora disapprovingly.

'They go to a training camp at first apparently,' said Mollie. 'Some of the women in my class have husbands who have been called up.'

'To train them up to send them overseas to fight, I suppose,' said Madge miserably.

'He'll be all right, Mum,' encouraged Mollie though she was feeling worried too about her brother. 'You know Geoff, he's indestructible.'

'Course he is,' added Nora. 'Anyway, I'm just popping down to the shops.'

Madge looked at her in a questioning manner. 'But we've been shopping, Mum.'

'So I'm going again,' Nora snapped, colouring up. 'Can't I leave the house now without explaining myself?'

Madge and Mollie stared at her because she was rarely bad-tempered. 'Mum, what's the matter?' Madge asked.

'Nothing,' she said. 'All I want is to be able to go out without a flamin' interrogation.'

'We'll see you later then, Gran,' said Mollie.

'Won't be long,' she said, heading for the hall stand to get her coat.

'I wonder what's up with her,' said Madge when they heard the front door close.

'Perhaps she just wants a bit of independence,' suggested Mollie. 'We are quite protective of her.'

'If you can't be a bit protective of your own mother in her later years, it's a poor show,' said Madge. 'She got precious little help or support from my father. I was glad when she moved in with us after he died so she could have some kindness after the life she'd had with

Dad. But she's got such a strong character she doesn't take kindly to being looked after.'

Mollie hadn't known her grandfather well but she remembered him being a grumpy and distant figure. She supposed she and Geoff must have been kept away from him because of his bad temper and it was common knowledge in the family that he had been horrid to Gran.

'Maybe she just wanted some fresh air,' suggested Mollie.

'Don't make me laugh,' said her mother. 'It's December and she hates the cold.'

'I'm sure she won't be gone long,' said Mollie diplomatically.

Nora had felt compelled to get out of the house because she hadn't wanted her daughter to know how upset she was about Geoff's call-up papers. In fact, she didn't want any of them to know how frightened she was of every aspect of the war. She was ashamed of herself. She'd lived through one world war and she was damned sure she could live through another but, for some reason, the whole thing had shaken her terribly. Madge would need her support with her boy going away so somehow she had to pull herself together. She didn't want people to think she was some frail old biddy who couldn't take things in her stride. The younger family members should be able to look to her for courage.

'Blimey Nora, you look as though you're about to go to the gallows,' someone said as she turned into the High Road.

'Oh, 'ello, Wilf,' she said and promptly burst into tears.

'Ooh dear,' he said, surveying the situation and putting a friendly hand on her arm. 'I think you need to come with me.'

So it was that Nora found herself sitting in a café with Wilf Robbins drinking a cup of tea and, for the first time in her life, smoking a cigarette.

'They're not too bad these fags, are they?' she said, having pulled herself together. 'It's the first time I've ever tried one. They taste awful and make you cough and feel sick but they do have a calming influence. No wonder so many people smoke.'

'Even more since war broke out,' he said. 'They help to calm your nerves.'

'This is just a one-off for me,' she said. 'I won't be taking up the habit.'

'That's what I said until I'd had my second or third but you'll do well to steer clear. It can be an expensive habit if you smoke too many.'

'I'm sure it must be.'

'If you feel like telling me what's made you so upset I'll be happy to listen.'

'I suppose I just got panicky because my grandson's call-up papers arrived,' she said. 'It made the war seem real and it scared the hell out of me.'

'You're not the only one who's afraid, Nora,' he said. 'It's nothing to be ashamed of.'

'Not you . . .'

'Of course me,' he said. 'I think most people are if the truth be told except perhaps the young ones who are too busy going out dancing to think much about it.'

'But you're not the sort to be scared of anything. You enjoy your ARP work,' she said.

'That doesn't mean I'm not afraid of what might happen while I'm doing it,' he said. 'I'm just better at covering it up than you are.'

'I can usually; the family have no idea,' she said. 'They think I'm a tough old bird who takes everything in her stride and they look to me for reassurance. So they are not going to hear about what happened today.'

'Certainly not from me,' he assured her. 'Even if I did know them, which I don't. Except of course for your granddaughter who I met briefly that time.'

It would have been the most natural thing in the world for Nora to invite him round to meet them, especially as Mollie had expressed a wish for her grandmother to do so, but Nora just said, 'Thanks, Wilf.'

'Well you know where I am if you need a shoulder to cry on at any time in the future, or even if you just fancy a chat,' he said in a friendly manner. 'You've got my address.'

'Thanks, Wilf,' she said again, genuinely touched by his kindness and feeling a lot better.

Geoff was due to report for duty a week after Christmas which could have put the damper on the festivities if they'd allowed it to. But they didn't because of Esme who was old enough now to get into the spirit and loved the whole thing.

Normally Esme wasn't an overindulged child but on Christmas Day the rules were relaxed and she was spoiled by everyone because she was their reason to celebrate. By Christmas night she was overexcited and overtired and went to bed in tears.

'Children always do it, don't they?' said Madge when Mollie came downstairs after putting her daughter to bed. 'You and Geoff were just the same. Always in tears by Christmas night.'

'It's probably just as well it only comes once a year,' said Mollie.

Without Esme's lively presence the mood fell flat. They had all kept up a front for her but now that the day was over there was only one thing on their minds: Geoff's departure.

'It'll be the first time you and I have ever been parted,' said Mollie to Geoff later when the others had gone to bed. 'We'll all miss you but I expect it'll be worse for me, us being twins. I hope you don't feel it too much. You'll have enough to cope with.'

'I'll be fine,' he said. 'It's a bit of an adventure in a way, meeting new people, doing different things. I'm hoping that I get the chance to travel abroad.'

'There is that about it, I suppose.'

'I think I need a break from round here, anyway,' he said. 'I've never been further than Southend.'

She fell silent, wondering if she should mention her shock discovery just before Christmas. She decided it might be a good thing; just in case he still thought he might see Cora around the town.

'The Parkers have moved away,' she said and explained how she knew. 'Sold up and gone; just like that.'

'Oh,' he said and she could see from the look in his eyes that he still had feelings for Cora. 'In as much as you went to the house, have you decided to forgive her then?'

'I'm not sure about that but I don't think it's a time for bad feeling,' she said.

'I agree with you about that.'

'Does that mean you would take her back if you knew where she was?'

'Oh no, not that,' he said. 'I don't wish her ill and I hope she stays safe but I don't want to see her again.'

He lapsed into thought after that so Mollie went to bed, regretting that she'd mentioned the Parkers as she had obviously stirred up memories for him. Still, he would be away in a few days with plenty to take his mind off Cora.

The bleakness of January wasn't helped by the absence of Geoff and the introduction of food rationing on bacon, sugar and butter with more items expected to become rationed very soon. They all missed Geoff but for Mollie his going away left a terrible feeling of loneliness because he'd always been a best friend as well as a brother.

Fortunately there was a new joy in her life: her children's class which she took on Saturday mornings in a hall over a local row of shops. It was her daughter who had given her the idea. Seeing her copying the steps and moves that Mollie practised around the house made her decide to start a class for little girls. There were already some junior classes around so she wasn't starting a new trend but it was something different to the traditional tap and ballet classes available for children in the area.

With Gran at the piano, Saturday mornings quickly became the highlight of the week for both her and Esme who was already showing signs of her mother's talent.

Geoff had a weekend pass after his basic training, which brightened things up considerably and they all thought he looked handsome in uniform. Mollie got the impression that he had settled well to army life. He said it wasn't too bad and he'd got some good mates which helped a lot, that and the fact that he hadn't been put in the Catering Corps.

'I should have thought you would be a natural for that as cooking is your profession,' said his father.

'The army obviously don't think so,' said Geoff. 'They probably want me where the action is as I'm young and strong. I don't want to be stuck in a kitchen somewhere and having people taking the mick because I'm not in the thick of things. Plenty of time for cooking when I come home after the war.'

★　★　★

Wartime life on the home front was normal life with increasing rationing and shortages, frightening warnings of a German invasion and worrying war news from abroad such as the Allied troops' evacuation from Dunkirk and German soldiers marching through Paris with the swastika flying from the Eiffel Tower. But the war still seemed reassuringly distant. Until September when all hell was let loose on London.

After the terrible raids on London docks that left many East Enders dead or homeless, the nightly air raids spread to other parts of London and Mollie and the family spent almost every night in the air-raid shelter. Mollie's evening classes were cancelled for the time being but she still went into work at headquarters every morning even though she'd had very little sleep. Her daytime class carried on as normal and she was determined to resume the evening ones as soon as possible after the raids eased off. People needed them more than ever now; something to take their mind off things.

She decided against having Esme evacuated, though her daughter had now started school so she could have gone on the government scheme.

'She's too little to be away from her family,' said Mollie. 'I know there is bombing around here but it isn't as bad as in the East End. If it gets too dangerous I shall have to send her but she's staying here with us for the moment.'

'We need to be together at a time like this,' said her mother. 'We'll face whatever comes as a family.'

'Hear hear,' agreed Gran.

What they faced was more of the same: air raids,

increasing shortages, the blackout, power cuts and cold weather. But somehow they carried on and still managed to hang on to their sense of humour.

Despite all of the chaos created by the air raids, essential services still kept going albeit less efficiently than in peacetime. The post was sometimes late but it usually arrived eventually. One day in December an official-looking envelope was delivered to Mr and Mrs Potts. It was to inform them that their son Geoffrey was missing, presumed dead, in France.

Chapter Eleven

It wasn't that Mollie stubbornly refused to entertain the idea that her brother might be dead; more that she was convinced that he wasn't.

'I think I would know if he'd been killed, Mum,' she said to her pale and tearful mother. 'And I'm sure he's alive.'

'Oh Mollie, love,' said her grandmother worriedly. 'I know you mean well but you shouldn't raise your mother's hopes over something as serious as this. I know you are Geoff's twin but you can't possibly know a thing like that.'

'It's what I believe, Gran,' she told her. 'I've no idea how but I am certain that he's still alive.'

'They do say that some twins have a sort of a sixth sense, don't they?' put in Len, who was on late shift so hadn't yet gone to work. 'I never rule anything out because you just never know.'

'I only know how I feel,' Mollie told them. 'It's up to you all what you believe but I'm going to go with my instincts and stay positive.'

'But if he is missing, where is he?' wondered Madge.

'I don't know but I expect there was chaos out there in France during Dunkirk,' said Mollie. 'He could have missed getting on one of the boats but escaped over land and is trying to get back somehow.' She didn't add that he might have been taken prisoner because she knew it would upset her mother.

But the same thought had already occurred to Madge. 'I hope he hasn't been taken prisoner,' she said.

'At least he'd be alive,' said Mollie.

'But they might be cruel to prisoners of war,' suggested Madge anxiously.

'There must be some sort of rules about the way they are treated,' said Mollie. 'Anyway we know nothing beyond the fact that he is missing. I wish I hadn't said anything now. I thought my feelings on the matter might cheer you all up.'

'They have, of course,' said her mother but she wasn't very convincing. 'So let's all try to stop speculating and wait until we hear something more.'

'Why are you crying, Grandma?' asked Esme who was eating porridge at the table.

'She's feeling a bit off colour this morning,' said Mollie quickly. 'You just finish your breakfast or you'll be late for school.'

The atmosphere in the house was fraught with emotion, which was understandable given the contents of the letter. But Mollie couldn't help wondering if, perhaps, she'd been tactless and made matters worse. In future she would keep her intuitive feelings to herself.

★　★　★

Mollie had a class that morning and Rose came along as relaxation from her own teaching. The two women got along well, having a mutual interest, and always had plenty to talk about. Nora joined them for a chat afterwards. Now that Esme was at school Mollie wasn't in quite such a rush to get home and it was nice to be able to linger, especially this morning with all the tension at home. After a few minutes Nora said she had some shopping to do so she would see Mollie at home and she was to tell her mother she might be a bit late back.

Mollie and Rose carried on and were discussing the keep-fit classes in general.

'Not only are we losing members, we are losing teachers as well,' Rose mentioned. 'Some are going on to war work. One teacher I know is thinking of joining the forces.'

'I suppose if you're single and have no kids that might be worth considering,' said Mollie. 'It could be an interesting experience.'

'My husband won't hear of me going out to work, let alone enlisting in the services,' said Rose.

Mollie looked puzzled. 'But you do go out to work,' she said. 'You teach keep fit.'

'He looks on it as a hobby, a bit of pocket money and my own business,' she explained. 'He'd soon put his foot down if I went out and got a job in an office or a factory. He failed the medical so isn't in the services.'

'He's there to keep an eye on you then,' said Mollie in a jokey manner. 'No joining up for you.'

'Exactly,' smiled Rose. 'He's a lovely man, though. Just a bit set in his ways.'

'The money I earn from my classes means a lot more than just a bit of pocket money to me,' said Mollie. 'I subsidise it with what I get from the office job but it's vital to me, which is one of the reasons I shall start up my evening classes again soon, though it isn't the only reason of course. I think the classes are needed too.'

'It must be hard work bringing up a child on your own,' Rose suggested.

'The financial side of it is a bit of a worry sometimes but I get bags of support from the family in other ways so I'm very lucky.' She was thoughtful. 'It would be nice for Esme to have a dad though, of course.'

'Still, I'm sure you make it up to her,' said Rose warmly. 'I would have loved a family but we haven't been blessed that way. We've been married for twelve years so it would have happened by now if it was going to, I reckon.'

'You never know,' said Mollie, positive as ever.

'It isn't meant to be,' she said. 'I accepted that ages ago, and Ken and I are very devoted, maybe more so than some couples because there is only the two of us. We've never had anyone else to consider but each other so we are very close.'

Mollie nodded and steered the conversation back to the original subject. 'So the teachers who are still taking classes will have to take on the members from the centres that are left without a teacher, I suppose.'

'Yes, I think that is what will happen,' agreed Rose. 'Once the air raids ease up, and let's hope to God they do soon, I think members will be prepared to travel further for a class. Most of us are getting used to the blackout now.'

'It's a nuisance but yes, it doesn't seem as bad as it was at first,' agreed Mollie.

Rose seemed thoughtful. 'Why don't you and I do a keep-fit evening between us to raise money for one of the war charities,' she burst out excitedly. 'We could hire a hall for two hours and take one hour each and not charge for our services so that the money we take will go to charity. We'd get the hall cheaper, might even get it free if we say it's for charity. People could do both hours or just one or a bit of each, as they wish. We could try to cobble some refreshments together or tell them to bring their own because of the rationing and have a half-hour of socialising at the end. What do you think?'

'Sounds like a good idea to me,' Mollie approved.

'Can we rope your gran in on the piano, do you think?' asked Rose. 'It's all for a good cause. I could put the idea to my pianist too and they can share the two hours.'

'I'll ask her but I'm sure she'll be willing,' said Mollie, enthusiasm growing. 'She's a very charitable lady and she loves playing the piano.'

'We could make it into a fun evening,' suggested Rose.

'And we can all do with some fun,' agreed Mollie.

'So when things quieten down a bit we'll get it organised.'

'It will be something to look forward to,' said Mollie.

'I'll speak to Gran about it at home as soon as she gets back from the shops.'

The two women were smiling as they went their separate ways.

'Well this is a nice surprise,' said Wilf Robbins when he answered a knock at the door to find Nora standing there. 'Come on in. I'll put the kettle on.'

'No, don't use your precious tea ration on me,' she urged him.

'Don't worry I'll make it very weak,' he said, showing her into his living room which was tidy and uncluttered in comparison to the Pottses', something she put down to his living alone. 'Sit yourself down. Tea won't be a jiffy.'

When he reappeared with the tea, he asked, 'Does this visit mean that you are upset about something and you want a shoulder to cry on or is it that you have finally decided to trust me?'

'Neither really. I just fancied a chat with someone of my own age outside of the family.' She sipped her tea. 'I hoped you might be in but guess you are busy with your civil defence work with things as they are at the moment.'

'Not half,' he said. 'I'm out there most nights and I have to go to meetings during the day as well but I've always got time for an old friend.'

'That's what I need, a friend,' she confided. 'You see, Wilf, I'm with the family all the time and I love them all to bits. They mean the world to me.'

'But sometimes you need a break from them,' he guessed.

'Exactly.' She told him about the bad news they had had in the post that morning. 'We're all worried and tempers get frayed and I sometimes say the wrong thing. I need to get away; just for a breather.'

'You've come to the right place,' he assured her warmly. 'You're welcome here any time.'

'I don't have any women friends, you see,' she went on. 'My husband was a difficult man and he wouldn't allow me to have friends. I didn't say so before when you asked me about him but to be honest he was a bully. After he died I moved in with my daughter so I get plenty of company at home, but sometimes you need to be with your peers.'

'I can imagine. Sadly, though, I don't have kids so can't speak from experience.'

'By the very nature of things you are always Mum or Gran; they only ever see you in that role no matter how much they love you. Sometimes you want to be a person in your own right and with your own views to be taken seriously, not just a member of the older generation.'

'So you came round here to be with another old codger,' he said, smiling.

'No, well yes, I suppose I did but you're not just any old codger are you?' She grinned. 'You and me go back a long way.'

'We certainly do,' he said in a serious manner.

'I don't mean like that again,' she said quickly. 'I mean I just thought . . .'

He chuckled. 'Don't panic. I'm not going to jump on you. I'm a bit past that . . . well, almost.'

Her eyes widened.

'Just teasing. You didn't have a good marriage then,' he went on in a serious manner.

'It wasn't a bed of roses, that's for sure,' she said. 'But I was used to it and I managed though it wasn't always easy.'

'You deserved better than that.'

You don't know the half of it, she thought, but said, 'I never know what people mean when they say that sort of thing. I've never done anything special so why would I deserve better?'

'You're a good woman, Nora, and I bet you are a cracking mother,' he said. 'In my book that means you deserve the best.'

She felt rather hot-cheeked. 'I do get the best now, though. My family are wonderful to me.'

'Yes, I'm sure.'

'They'll be worrying about me if I don't get home soon,' she said. 'I've been playing the piano at my grand-daughter's keep-fit class and I told her to tell them at home that I've gone shopping. I had this sudden need for a chat.'

'Couldn't you have told them the truth; that you were going to visit a friend?'

'Not without an inquisition,' she replied. 'They would want to know all about you, especially as you're a man.'

'Surely you're entitled to do what you want at your age,' he told her.

'I am, of course. But they would be concerned about me so would give me the third degree,' she said. 'It's as though our roles have been reversed and they are in charge now, instead of the other way around, and just now and then I want to do what I want without having to account for it.'

'In that case why not go home and tell them where you've been and that you'll be visiting me again whenever you feel like it. Tell them that I am a friend of long standing. I'll come with you if you like,' he suggested.

'No,' she almost shouted.

'All right, Nora, keep your hair on,' he said, looking hurt. 'I'll keep away if that's what you want.'

'Don't take it the wrong way, Wilf, please,' she urged him. 'I'm just trying to avoid a lot of mickey-taking, that's all.'

There was more to it than that but she couldn't tell him.

'Oh I see,' he said. 'Well, you come round here when-ever you fancy a bit of company and I won't breathe a word to anyone.'

'I'll bring my own tea next time,' she said in a jokey manner to ease the tension caused by her wish to be secretive.

'There'll be no need so long as you don't mind having it weak,' he said. 'I think I probably allowed you two or three tea leaves, that's all. Make sure you finish it before you go. Tea is far too precious these days to waste.'

She actually stayed another half-hour or so chatting and thoroughly enjoying herself. When she left she said she'd call again soon and she was already looking forward to it. For the first time in years, she felt like the woman she had once been.

As Nora pulled the string with the key on the end through the letter box to open the front door, it opened sharply and Madge was standing in the hall looking furious.

'There you are at last,' she said, her face and neck suffused with angry red blotches as she ushered her mother inside. 'I've been worried sick about you. Where the hell have you been?'

'I told Mollie to tell you—'

'She said you'd gone shopping,' Madge cut in. 'But you've been gone for ages. You wouldn't have been round the shops this long, not in this cold weather.'

'Gran's entitled to go out, Mum,' put in Mollie, defensive of her grandmother. 'She doesn't have to tell us where she's going or where she's been.'

'Your grandmother is a widow turned sixty and she needs people to look out for her, which is exactly what I've tried to do since my father died.'

'I know you mean well, dear,' said Nora, taking off her coat and hanging it on the hall stand. 'And it's very good of you to worry about me and I appreciate it but I'm not in my dotage yet. I am still quite able to look after myself outside of this house.'

'Course you are, Gran,' said Mollie supportively. 'Nobody thinks of her as old at my class, Mum. She's just one of us, a part of the team.'

266

'Oh, so I'm in the wrong for worrying about my own mother, am I?' said Madge, looking peeved.

'Of course you're not,' Nora assured her. 'But for goodness' sake, let's go somewhere warmer – it's freezing out here in the hall.'

There was a stew simmering on the stove and an apple pie in the oven so it was warm in the kitchen when Nora, Madge and Mollie sat at the kitchen table.

'Right, now that you've calmed down a bit, I'll tell you where I've been. I went to visit a friend,' announced Nora.

'You haven't got any friends,' said Madge. 'Dad made sure of that.'

'Mum,' admonished Mollie. 'Don't make Gran feel as though people don't like her because they do. She's a very popular lady.'

'I know she is but she doesn't have any close friends and she doesn't need them because she has us.'

'I'd rather you didn't talk about me as if I wasn't here. But it's a childhood friend actually,' explained Nora. 'Recently moved back to the area.'

'Oh, that's all right then,' said Madge sounding slightly reassured. 'What's her name?'

Nora took a deep breath. 'It's a man and his name is Wilf Robbins.'

'Oh,' gasped Madge.

'The man who was kind to me by the river?' said Mollie.

'That's right,' Nora confirmed.

'That's nice, Gran,' approved Mollie. 'A spot of male company will be fun. And he's a lovely man.'

'We grew up in the same area,' Nora explained. 'He's a widower.'

'Mm,' pondered Madge. 'So are you in the habit of going round to his house?'

'No. Today was the first time,' said Nora. 'But I've seen him around the town a few times, not that it's any of your business.'

'You're my mother so of course it's my business.' She looked at Nora and her tone softened. 'Mum, you and I have always been so close, especially since Dad died. I don't like the idea of secrets between us.'

Nora reached over and rested her hand on her daughter's. 'Madge, no one could have a more caring daughter than I have and I really appreciate it. All of you are very good to me. But I need a friend as well and Wilf is a nice bloke.'

'Bloke being the operative word,' Madge pointed out.

'It's all perfectly innocent.'

'I should bloomin' well hope so at your time of life,' exploded Madge.

'You don't stop being a person with feelings just because you've got a good few miles on the clock, you know,' said Nora.

'Oh well, I wouldn't know about that,' said Madge. 'But why couldn't you pal up with some old lady and do your knitting together.'

'Because I happened to run into Wilf and I enjoy his

company,' said Nora. 'But as you're so keen to remind me of my great age, that works both ways. I am old enough to see who I want without your approval.'

'Humph. Well I suppose technically that's true but surely you're going to bring him home, let us get to know him.'

'Certainly not,' said Nora with emphasis.

'Why? Is there something peculiar about him?'

'Not at all,' said Nora.

'You're ashamed of us then, is that it?'

'Of course not; he's just someone I knew a long time ago who I happened to run into again,' she said. 'It's no big thing. I might not see him again for a while.'

'Oh well it's up to you but he's always welcome here,' said Madge. 'Any friend of yours is a friend of ours, as they say.'

'Thank you, dear,' said Nora. 'If I do see more of him it's nice to know that.'

Nora and Wilf had a good laugh about the altercation with Madge when Nora next went to see him.

'Honestly, it was like being fifteen again,' she said. 'Being told off for being late home.'

'I'm glad you told them about me though.'

'You're as bad as they are,' she said. 'There's nothing to tell them. You're just an old friend who I visit now and then.'

'Oh,' he said dully.

'Wilf, what's the matter? What have I said?'

'We did have something special back then.'

'Yeah we did,' she said. 'I wasn't the one who ruined it by going away.'

'I suppose I asked for that.'

'Maybe I was a bit sharp,' she said. 'But it's all in the past, Wilf, and we were just kids. We didn't have any control over our lives back then.'

He nodded. 'We certainly didn't.'

'But we do now, to a certain extent anyway given Hitler's power over our lives. So let's just enjoy the fact that we met up again and are friends.' She paused. 'All right, if we all manage to survive this awful bombing maybe you could come round to the house sometime.'

'I'd love to meet them all, especially not having a family of my own,' he said.

Suddenly she saw the whole thing from a different perspective and realised that she was being rather selfish for keeping her family to herself. After all, his coming to the house couldn't do any real harm . . . could it?

She didn't wait for the bombing to end and invited him for a cup of tea one Saturday afternoon; he was an instant hit with the whole family. He struck up a rapport with Len because they were both football fans, Madge took to his easy-going ways, Mollie was thrilled to be able to thank him in person for his kindness the day Syd had snatched Esme and the little girl thought he was great fun because he made a fuss of her.

'Fancy you two meeting up again after all those years,' said Madge. 'Childhood friends, Mum said.'

Nora and Wilf exchanged a glance and he said, 'Something like that.'

He explained why he'd moved away and they talked of other things, including the war and the worrying news about Geoff, the conversation flowing easily. When he said he had to go because he was on duty that night, Madge said, 'Well don't be a stranger. Now that you know where we are, call in at any time. You'll always be welcome here.'

When Nora saw him to the door, she said, 'You seem to have got your feet well and truly under the table.'

'You are very lucky to have them,' he said. 'Thanks for letting me share them for a couple of hours.'

'Any time,' she said. 'I'll pop round and see you in the week sometime. Mind how you go tonight.'

'Will do.'

She watched him as he strode down the street in his overcoat and trilby hat. He was still a striking figure, even now.

It was January before the air raids showed any sign of abating and that was mainly because provincial cities were having their share of the bombing. Here in London the streets were looking war torn and shabby with bomb craters, rubble and brick dust everywhere. But people had been going out again in the evening for a while now and by all accounts the pubs, dance halls and cinemas were packed every night.

Mollie and Rose decided to follow the trend and go ahead with the charity fun evening; they booked a hall for a mid-week date in February. The word was spread by the members and other teachers and there was a lot of enthusiasm for the event which was to raise money for war orphans.

'We'll have to head for the street shelter if there's a raid,' said Mollie as she and her grandmother walked to the hall in the bitter cold.

'We've had a good few quiet nights lately,' said Nora. 'So perhaps we'll be lucky.'

'It'll be interesting to see how many people actually turn up,' said Mollie.

'Plenty by the look of it,' said Nora as they turned the corner and saw a crowd of women waiting outside the hall.

Not only did the members come, some also brought coal and wood with them and lit a fire in the fireplace at the far end of the hall while Mollie was helping Rose to take the money and Gran getting her music ready.

'This is going to be a good night, Rose,' predicted Mollie, heartened by the thoughtfulness of some of the members and the enthusiasm of them all.

'I do believe you're right,' agreed Rose.

She was; very much so. The hall was packed and everyone seemed cheerful, especially when the class got under way and they started to get warm, the fire adding a cheery glow to the atmosphere, everyone grateful that coal was one of the few items not yet on ration.

Mollie and Rose took turns with teaching and each joined in the class when not on stage. They swayed and stretched, lunged and marched. From top to toe, every part of the body was exercised, even fingers and toes.

'What a lovely night it's been, Mollie,' said one of the members at the end when people were chatting, 'and such a good idea to raise money for charity.'

'It was Rose's idea,' Mollie told her. 'She's the one you have to thank for all this.'

'It was a joint effort and Mollie is giving her services free as well as me,' said Rose in her usual modest way. 'And don't forget our pianists. I reckon they deserve a cheer.'

There were three rousing cheers for the piano players and then for the teachers. Everyone agreed that it had been a real tonic to get out and have some fun. The hall resounded with warmth and friendliness. When the siren sounded there were a few groans but most were glad it hadn't come earlier and spoiled their evening. People headed towards the shelter across the road.

Mollie and Rose waited until everyone else was out before making their way to the exit, Mollie clutching the money in an old shoe bag and Rose looking after the register. They didn't quite make it to the doors before a bomber roared overhead and the terrifying whistle of the bomb caused them to lie flat on their fronts on the floor until the explosion, which sounded quite close and made the hall shake, was over.

Mollie was worried about her grandmother; terrified she hadn't got to the shelter in time. When the bomber moved away Mollie and Rose scrambled to their feet, Mollie running towards the exit in search of Nora. Before she reached the doors there was a creaking, crunching sound and, looking up, she saw that one of the rafters had been dislodged by the blast and was moving downwards.

'Rose, look out,' she yelled. 'Get out of the way.'

But the wooden beam was long and heavy and it crashed down, hitting Rose and knocking her over. She lay motionless on the floor with her eyes closed.

'Oh my God,' gasped Mollie seeing blood seeping from her head which must have been struck by the rafter and was bleeding so heavily Mollie felt bile rise in her throat.

She ran to the door and screamed for help at the same time as the All Clear sounded.

One of the first people to the rescue was Wilf who was on duty and had basic first-aid training.

'The medics will be here in a minute, love,' he said to Rose, on his knees beside her, looking for a pulse and telling Mollie that the unconscious woman was still alive.

'I need to find Gran,' she said.

'I'll stay with your friend while you go to look for her,' said Wilf. 'The medical team will be here soon.'

'Thanks, Wilf,' she said and made her way through the debris in the hall to find her grandmother, whom she met in the street on her way back to the hall, the bomb having exploded nearby. Nora was frantic with worry, having heard that one of the teachers had been hurt and thought it was Mollie.

'Oh thank God, Mollie,' she said, ashen-faced and trembling. 'I thought you'd been injured.'

'And I was worried about you,' Mollie told her. 'But it's Rose who's copped it. Let's get back inside and see if she's come round yet.'

Everyone had drifted back into the hall but the air of gaiety had been replaced by a kind of hush and people were talking in low voices.

Mollie and Nora weaved their way through the crowds towards where Mollie had left Rose.

'I'm very sorry, ladies,' said Wilf in a solemn manner as the medics walked by carrying a stretcher with a sheet covering it. 'She'd gone by the time they arrived.'

'Oh.' It was as though all the breath was sucked from Mollie's body. 'Oh my God!'

'Heavy things, rafters,' he said unnecessarily. 'It's a wonder the whole roof didn't come down. Rose wouldn't have been the only one to cop if that had happened.'

Mollie knew that men always saw the technicalities in every situation and that Wilf was only trying to be positive but it didn't help. Rose had died and it couldn't get worse than that as far as Mollie was concerned.

'I'll have to make a formal announcement,' she said. 'I need to end the evening properly.'

'I think you both ought to go home straight away,' suggested Wilf. 'I'll walk with you to your door to see you safely inside.'

'I must do this first, Wilf,' said Mollie. 'I can't just leave after what's happened. It won't take long.'

He nodded and turned his attention to Nora who was visibly trembling. 'What you need is a double brandy,' he said, taking her arm.

'I wouldn't say no to one of those,' she said. 'But fat chance of that.'

'I know you are all as shocked and saddened as I am by what's happened but I'd like to offer a quick thank-you to you all for coming,' said Mollie from the platform. 'It's such a pity it had such a tragic ending. But Rose was the sort of person who would want us to remember that it was a good night before the disaster and that we raised money for a good cause, so thanks to all of you for turning up. I know what happened to Rose will make some of you want to stay at home at night in future, close to the shelter. Nevertheless I am going to resume my evening classes over the next few weeks and any members from Rose's class who would like to come are welcome. I will do it as a tribute to her. I know that she believed that while we all carry on regardless Hitler can never truly destroy us.

'So thank you all again for coming and I hope to see you all soon. Have a safe journey home. Goodnight.'

There was a ripple of applause but many of the

members were in tears. It had been a frightening as well as tragic incident. Rose had only just turned thirty.

Mollie came off the platform and went straight to the toilets and sobbed her heart out. Then she quickly composed herself and went back into the hall which was now empty apart from her grandmother and Wilf.

'Come on then, Gran,' she said. 'Let's go home. We'll be all right on our own, Wilf, if you need to get back to your duties.'

'I'll see you to your door then I'll go back to base to see what's doing.'

'I hope they're all right at home,' said Mollie.

'There was no damage in your street when I passed on my way up to the hall and the All Clear went soon after that.'

'Thank God for that,' said Mollie. 'What happened to Rose makes you feel so vulnerable.'

The three of them walked arm in arm, with Wilf in the middle, through the smoky streets, passing new bomb craters and men working behind cordoned-off areas.

'I shall be with you at the piano when you start your evening class again,' said Nora.

'I'm not sure that Mum will be too pleased about that and you mustn't feel that you have to. Obviously I'll use my common sense and not do the class if bombs are raining down,' said Mollie. 'But I would love to have you on board.'

'Good, that's settled then.'

'What about you, Wilf?'

'I don't think I'd look too grand in a white blouse and black knickers,' he said.

'You fool,' said Mollie, appreciating his attempt at humour to cheer them up. 'I meant do you approve of Gran going out of an evening to play the piano?'

'I'm sure she wouldn't take any notice of me if I didn't,' he said. 'But we can't let ourselves be trapped indoors by the Jerries. I think it's a question of carrying on regardless and taking cover when necessary. I think Nora is sensible enough to get to a shelter when the siren goes.'

'I shall make sure she does,' said Mollie.

As they approached the house they could see that the door was open.

'Oh you're safe, thank God,' said Madge. 'A neighbour said the hall had been damaged and I've been going mad with worry but I couldn't leave Esme to come and find out because your dad is on late shift and is at work.'

'G'night all,' said Wilf and disappeared into the dark as Mollie and her grandmother went gratefully into the house. What a night it had been!

There was a large contingent of keep-fit members and teachers at Rose's funeral, which showed how well respected she'd been. Her husband was whey-faced and sad as he stood with family members during the service and at the graveside. Mollie remembered what Rose had said about them being devoted and couldn't begin to guess at his suffering.

Oddly enough Mollie found herself feeling very alone even though she was with people she knew and liked. So many people she'd been close to had gone from her life. First there had been Syd, who had once meant a lot to her, then Cora had vanished, her beloved Geoff was still missing in France and now Rose was dead.

Gran had come along to pay her last respects and was standing by her side at the cemetery. Suddenly Nora felt very dear to Mollie and she put her arm around her grandmother and gave her an affectionate hug.

'What was that for?' asked Nora.

'Just because you're you and I'm so glad to have you as my gran.'

'Oh, that's nice,' said Nora emotionally. 'Same thing applies to you. There's nothing like a funeral to make you appreciate your loved ones.'

'Losing Rose has made me feel as though I can't carry on but I know I have to,' said Mollie.

'That's all any of us can do,' said Nora as the burial came to an end and the mourners began to move away.

Mollie and Nora walked arm in arm towards the people they knew.

Chapter Twelve

Mollie resumed her evening class a few weeks later by which time the air raids were much less frequent in London. If the siren sounded the class was automatically cancelled but she didn't have to call off many.

One evening in May, however, the bombing was so bad that Mollie and the family, along with most other Londoners, were in the air-raid shelter for most of the night cramped together in the damp, tomb-like interior. Esme slept for some of the time and when she was awake, they sang songs with her and played I Spy. Mollie saw it as her duty to hide her own fear so as not to pass it on to her daughter and knew that Esme had complete faith in her. The bombs just kept on coming and it seemed like a miracle that they didn't fall on them.

They felt even more blessed when, in the early light of dawn, they climbed out of their cold and damp prison into the smoky atmosphere and saw the damage nearby; as close as the next street. It seemed selfish to be jubilant that you were still alive when other people weren't so lucky but Mollie guessed that it was only human nature.

As it happened that terrible night – during which every London mainline train terminus was hit along with many other important buildings including Westminster Abbey and Scotland Yard – proved to be the last of the raids. Nobody knew how long the respite would be so they just lived from day to day, enjoying the absence of the siren and being able to sleep in their own beds.

As a result of the health benefits of keep-fit classes being generally recognised, Mollie was invited to some nearby factories where she took a shortened version of her class into the canteens and offices during the lunch hour. A friendlier bunch of women she had yet to meet and she looked forward to these hilarious classes enormously. With these additions to her usual teaching schedule as well as her part-time job in the office, she was kept very busy.

As the mother of a young child, she was exempt from the new government law forcing women without dependants to go out to work but as she was working anyway the legislation didn't affect her. She felt as though she was doing her bit because she knew her work was beneficial, especially in these testing times. Her mother joined the army of wartime home workers and sewed military uniforms.

'I'll be going out to work if the war goes on for much longer,' said Nora one day in the autumn of 1941. 'If they keep needing more workers, the over-sixties will soon be drafted in.'

'It won't come to that, Mum,' predicted Madge.

'I wouldn't mind,' said Nora cheerfully.

'You do your bit playing the piano for me,' said Mollie who now absolutely insisted on paying her grandmother for her services as there were more classes and she could afford it.

'There you are, Mum,' said Madge. 'So let's not hear any more about you getting another job. I think there would be an outcry if they sent grannies out to work.'

'If we're needed I'm sure we'll rise to the occasion,' said Nora. 'I will anyway.'

Nothing about this war would surprise Mollie. She had noticed a grey-haired female conductress on the bus the other day. Presumably she'd got the job of her own accord, but being given your ticket by an elderly woman would have been unheard of in peacetime.

Mollie travelled on public transport in London a lot because of her classes and she noticed that the town was crowded with servicemen, especially the mainline stations in central London. She was walking through Victoria station on her way to the tube one day in the spring of 1942, after her shift in the office, and she seemed to be in the midst of a sea of khaki, navy blue and air-force grey.

An airman with a familiar look about him almost collided with her as she hurried across the concourse.

'You're still rushing about then, Mollie,' he said and she realised that it was Grant Parker.

'Grant,' she said, beaming at him with genuine pleasure. 'How lovely to see you again after all this time. I thought you and Cora had disappeared forever. I've not seen a sign of either of you for years. I know you moved house, though, because I went round to your place in the early stages of the war to see if you were both all right.'

'Have you got time for a cuppa?' he asked. 'I think we have some catching up to do.'

She looked at the station clock. 'I can manage half an hour or so,' she said. 'Now that Esme is at school I do have a little more leeway.'

'Good, let's head for the station buffet then.'

He showed a friendly interest in Mollie and had lost none of his affable charm. Over a cup of insipid, luke-warm tea she told him about her classes and how she'd adapted them for wartime, and brought him up to date with news of her family. He was very sorry to hear that Geoff had been reported missing but seemed quite opti-mistic about it.

'War causes such disruption; letters can get lost and take years to get through. People can be missing for ages and turn up eventually.'

'Yes, that's what I said to my mother. Because Geoff is my twin I sense that he is still alive and I'm hanging on to that,' she said. 'But that's enough about me. What about you and Cora. Where did you move to?'

There was a brief hiatus then he said, 'Cora moved out to Ruislip to live with her aunt and I now live across the river in Barnes, though I'm away at camp most of the time. I'm stationed in Norfolk at the moment.'

She stared at him, puzzled.

'Cora and I split up nearly three years ago,' he explained. 'I divorced her.'

'Oh . . . I'm so sorry,' she said.

'It's always sad when any marriage breaks down but ours was never a particularly happy one so it was probably best that it ended, though I know that divorce is very much frowned on by a lot of people.'

She looked at him. 'I don't know about that but I was under the impression that it was a very long and complicated business.'

'It is and ours took a while but I did have genuine grounds, which helped, and a very good solicitor,' he explained.

'I see,' she said politely.

'Cora had committed adultery and she admitted it so the divorce was eventually granted,' he went on. 'There was a lot of legal paraphernalia, of course, but we got there in the end.'

Mollie's mind was racing. Three years ago was about the time of Cora's affair with Geoff. Was that the adultery that broke up the marriage?

She must have looked confused because he misunderstood the reason and went on to explain.

'Cora was pregnant and I couldn't possibly have had anything to do with it. She wouldn't say who was

284

responsible but she admitted that she'd been having an affair and said it was over between them. But there was no way she and I could stay together after that, and she knew it. She moved out more or less straight away after she'd made a clean breast of things. I don't think she wanted to be with me any more than I wanted to be with her though she'll be missing the comfortable life she had with me, I expect.' He paused, sipping his tea. 'She had a little boy apparently.'

Mollie reeled from the shock. What was she to do? Should she tell Grant that she knew about the affair and the man was her brother, and the child, unless Cora was extremely promiscuous, was her nephew and Esme's cousin?

Somehow she couldn't bring herself to utter the words. What good could it possibly do? 'So it's been all change for you then,' she said lamely.

'Very much so. But I joined up early in the war so life has been different for me anyway as I've been away most of the time. Because I'd had a grammar-school education I got into the RAF, which pleased me.'

She looked towards his sleeve at the wings emblem. 'A pilot too, I see.'

'Yeah, that's right,' he said, making light of it and changing the subject. 'You and Cora used to be quite friendly at one time didn't you?'

'Yes, that's right.'

'I never did know why you broke up,' he said. 'I assumed it was because you stopped cleaning for her and she took umbrage over it. I know she wasn't happy about it because it's hard to find someone you can rely on for that job.'

This was the perfect moment to tell him the truth but she said, 'Something like that.'

The clock was ticking and Mollie said, 'I'll have to go soon. I have a class this afternoon.'

'Oh.' He looked disappointed. 'Would it be possible for us to meet again or are you with someone now?'

'I'm still single.'

'I'm on leave for a week then I'll be away for a good while,' he said. 'I really would like to see you again before I go back.'

No woman in her right mind would say 'no' to that. But she had a child to consider and was wondering about getting her looked after. While she was out working was one thing. Asking someone to babysit when she was out enjoying herself, quite another.

Misunderstanding her hesitancy, he said, 'I am divorced, all legal and above board, so I have no ties.'

'I realise that.' She smiled at him. 'I would like to see you again but I am not quite as free as you are because I have a child so if I'm going out I have to arrange to get her looked after. Mum and Gran are very good when I'm working but I'm not so sure about . . .'

'If you are meeting a man, especially a divorced one,' he finished for her. 'What about during the day when Esme is at school?'

'That would be all right,' she said. 'I thought you meant the evening.'

'Any time would suit me as I'm on leave. My time is my own,' he said.

'What about after I finish work tomorrow,' she suggested. 'About twelve noon here. The office is just around the corner and I have the afternoon free. Until my daughter gets home from school anyway.'

'Lovely,' he said and his smile really was quite something. 'There's a Lyons not far from here so perhaps we could meet here then have a wander over there.'

'Sounds good to me,' said Mollie.

All the way home on the train Mollie was debating with herself as to whether or not she was breaking any kind of moral code by arranging to meet the ex-husband of a one-time friend. She decided that as both his marriage and her friendship with his ex-wife were in the past she couldn't possibly be doing anything wrong.

Another thing on her mind was the possible existence of a nephew and she needed to know for sure. If Esme had a cousin Mollie wanted to know. No matter what had happened in the past, if Geoff had a son he would want to know about it. So at some point she was going to have to ask Grant for Cora's address.

She didn't know if the meeting tomorrow was actually a date or just a continuation of the chat they'd had today but it was the first time since she'd first met Syd that she had felt such a buzz of heady anticipation.

★　★　★

'So, Grant and Cora are divorced and you are meeting up with him,' said her mother disapprovingly, later on when Mollie explained that she would be out tomorrow afternoon and the reason for it.

'There's no need to make it sound so disreputable, Mum,' admonished Mollie. 'We're both single.'

'It's about time you had some male company,' Nora put in. 'You've been on your own for far too long.'

'But he's divorced,' said Madge as though it was some sort of a distasteful disease.

'Exactly,' said Mollie. 'He isn't with Cora any more so he's free to see who he chooses. Anyway, it's just one meeting. He probably only asked me because he's on leave and has time on his hands.'

'You be careful, my girl,' Madge warned. 'We don't want you getting hurt again. You've had your heart broken once.'

'Why would Grant hurt me?'

'He's a man of the world,' replied Madge. 'A divorced man at that. We don't know any divorced people. Our sort can't afford such things. We stick at marriage no matter what. You need someone without complications.'

'Don't judge him too harshly, dear,' advised Nora. 'He seemed like a very nice man to me when we met him when Mollie was friendly with Cora.'

Mollie's mother looked thoughtful, as though remembering something. 'We never did know why you and Cora fell out,' she said. 'One minute you were as thick as thieves, the next you'd left your job and Cora was completely gone from your life.'

Mollie could never tell the family the reason she had parted company with Cora. Mum wasn't even comfortable with her daughter spending time with a divorced man so it would break her heart to know that her beloved son had been sleeping with that same man's wife and was actually the cause of the divorce.

Mum and Dad lived in a world where right and wrong were clearly defined and it was shameful to stray from the straight and narrow. Oddly enough Gran, who could be expected to be even more deeply entrenched in that kind of attitude, was more broad-minded. Mollie got the impression that if divorce had been available to people like them, her grandfather would have had his marching orders long before he died.

'Cora and I were never really suited to be friends,' said Mollie, because she couldn't tell her the truth. 'We were from different worlds.'

'So is he but you're still meeting up with him,' her mother pointed out.

There was no answer to that so Mollie just said, 'I'm meeting up with him, not agreeing to marry him.'

'I should damn well hope not.'

As much as she loved them, a close family could be very restricting at times, especially for Mollie who was of an age to have flown the nest but was forced by circumstances to still live at home. Looking back on it, it was nothing short of a miracle that Geoff's secret had remained hidden.

'Well, I am actually looking forward to it,' said Mollie with an air of defiance. 'I always found him to be a very nice man.'

'Good-looking too,' put in Nora with a wry grin.

'I'll say,' agreed Mollie.

Within minutes of being with Grant, Mollie felt happier than she had in a very long time. Without being unrealistic in her expectations she knew they were right together. The chemistry was good and she enjoyed his company, a tingle of desire adding a touch of excitement.

They found a Lyons nearby and had small, wartime portions of braised steak and mash followed by steamed jam pudding and custard.

'We've no need to feel guilty about tucking in since the government want the public to eat out now and again to save the rations at home.'

'I don't have those sort of problems as it's service food for me dished up regularly.'

'Are the stories about food in the forces being awful true?' she asked with interest.

'Well, it's never like this,' he said, looking down at his plate, 'probably because they are catering for such large numbers. But it's all right most of the time. We eat it anyway because we are so hungry.'

'You're looking good on it anyway,' she said, casting an eye over him. 'Uniform suits you.'

'Thank you,' he said. 'That's nice to know, especially as I have no choice but to wear it.'

She asked him how things were at the store in these testing times.

'Dad's managing to keep things ticking over despite

the shortages and lack of staff due to war work,' he told her. 'I do call in there when I'm on leave but I don't stay too long because Dad has taken someone on to do my job, an older man past enlistment age, and he might see assistance on my part as interference. So I keep my distance but Dad knows I would be there in an instant if I was needed.'

'So do you know what you'll be doing next in the RAF?' she enquired. 'Or if you'll be moved?'

'Oh no,' he said quickly. 'They never tell us anything until the last minute. Everything is always very hush-hush. The barracks is usually teeming with rumours, though, about what's going on. I'll just have to wait and see.'

After lunch they walked to St James's Park and strolled among the trees in the sunshine.

'I need to be home just after four o'clock,' she mentioned. 'Esme walks home from school with her friends now but I like to be in when she gets home. I'm out working such a lot I try to be in when I can if she's around.'

'We'll keep our eye on the time then.' He looked at her. 'Talking of your work, do you not have to go out cleaning at all now?'

'No but I'd do it again if I had to. It brought money in when I needed it,' she said. 'With a child to support I couldn't afford to be fussy about how I earned a living after Syd left. Later I was lucky enough to find a way of earning money that I really enjoy, my classes. I continued with the cleaning to make up the difference and the job in the office at headquarters just happened to come along when I needed it.'

'So that's why you stopped cleaning for Cora.'

Oh dear, that wasn't how it was at all. She'd got the job in the office after she'd stopped working for Cora. But if she told him that she'd have to tell all the rest and it would spoil their afternoon. So she just nodded.

Eventually they walked back to the station. He said he would go back to Chiswick with her then get the bus to Barnes or walk.

'No posh motor car for you these days then,' she said lightly as they sat together on the tube.

'That's right,' he confirmed. 'The car is stored in the garage for the duration of the war. Only essential use of private cars is allowed; doctors and so on. It certainly won't hurt me. It's nothing compared to some of the things people have to put up with these days, loss of life and injury. I'm away most of the time anyway so wouldn't use it much if it was allowed.'

When they got to Chiswick Park and alighted from the train, he offered to walk home with her.

'No, that's all right,' she said, not wanting the afternoon spoiled by her mother's disapproval being beamed in his direction. 'I'll be fine on my own.'

'As you wish.'

There were a few heart-stopping moments when Mollie wondered if he was going to ask to see her again. But all was silent and she felt racked with disappointment. Then he smiled and said, 'I've so enjoyed being with you, Mollie. Can we do it again? I only have a few days' leave left so the sooner the better if you can manage it.'

'I'm working for most of the day tomorrow,' she said. 'I'm in the office in the morning and I have a class in the afternoon. I could see you in the evening if I can arrange to get Esme looked after.'

'Lovely,' he said. 'I'll call for you.'

'No, there's no need,' she said. 'I'll meet you somewhere.'

'I insist,' he said. 'It's only right and proper that I should.'

She had no choice but to agree.

Mollie pre-empted the quizzing she knew would come by saying to her mother and Gran as soon as she got in, 'I've had a lovely time. I really like him and I'm going out with him tomorrow night if you will look after Esme for me.'

'Course we will, love,' said Nora. 'Won't we, Madge?'

'Yeah, no trouble about that,' said Madge, looking worried. 'But I do think you should be very careful, dear.'

'I don't see why,' said Mollie. 'Grant is a decent sort.'

'As I've said before, you'd be better with some nice boy without complications.'

'I'm twenty-six, Mum,' Mollie reminded her. 'I have a dependent child and a marriage behind me. Why would an uncomplicated boy want me when he can have an eighteen-year-old girl with no history?'

'She's right, dear,' said Nora.

'Don't sell yourself short, Mollie,' said her mother. 'You are a very attractive and intelligent young woman.'

'And Grant is a very good-looking and clever bloke,' said Mollie. 'He won't be short of offers. Anyway, I like him and I'm hoping something comes of it though he's going back off leave in a few days.'

'Exactly,' said Madge. 'There's no point in getting too attached when he's going away.'

'That applies to every eligible man in the country,' said Mollie. 'They are all in the forces so if everyone took that attitude romance would end until the war is over.'

The conversation was halted by the arrival of Esme home from school, her hair flying out of the bunches Mollie had so carefully tied with ribbon that morning, the belt of her gymslip untied and her top blouse buttons undone.

Mollie hugged her, asked her about her day and then said, 'I'm going out tomorrow night so the grannies will look after you.'

'Where are you going?'

'She's got a date with a handsome man,' said Nora.

'Is he a prince?' asked Esme, who was very keen on fairy tales.

'Not exactly,' said Mollie. 'But he is very nice. You can see him when he comes to call for me.'

'Is he coming on a horse?' asked Esme.

'I hope not,' laughed Mollie.

'Princes are always on horses in my books.'

'He isn't a prince, darlin', so he'll be coming on his own two feet,' said Mollie, hugging her and enjoying the feel and smell of her. She was scented with the freshness of youth and pencils.

Mollie couldn't get to sleep that night; partly because she was excited about seeing Grant again but also because she had decided that if their friendship showed any sign of continuing or developing into something more she would have to tell him that she had known about Cora's affair and all the details.

Maybe he would judge her silence on the matter to be a betrayal but it was only two days since she'd met up with him again. Anyway, whatever the consequences he would have to know.

There was such a fuss about his arrival the following evening, he might as well have been the royalty Esme was so keen on.

The little girl was at the window, along with Madge and Nora, the three of them speculating about every male who happened to walk along the street.

'There's a man in uniform coming,' squealed Esme.

'That's him I reckon,' said Nora. 'Quick, get away from the window.' She stood at the bottom of the stairs and shouted to Mollie, 'He's here. So get down here sharpish.'

Looking lovely in a summer frock and sandals, her hair shiny and loose, Mollie opened the door.

'You've got a welcoming committee,' she said with a laugh and ushered him inside.

He was the perfect gentleman, Mollie noticed, greeting the family in a polite but warm manner and making a great fuss of Esme.

'I haven't seen you for a very long time, young lady,' he said. 'You were just a tiny little thing when I last saw you. Now look at you.'

'I go to school now,' she said, beaming at him. 'Would you like to see the picture I drew today?'

'I would love to see it,' he said.

'Go and get it, Esme,' said Madge, who had been absolutely determined not to like him but, although not completely won over, had to admit that he had a very nice way with him. We'll see, she thought. Time will tell.

'I hope you weren't too overwhelmed by them,' said Mollie as they walked down the street, heading for the river as it was such a lovely evening. 'I can't afford my own place.'

'I thought they were lovely,' he said. 'You'll never be lonely with them around.'

'It comes at a price though,' she said. 'I love them all to bits but my business is theirs too. I'm twenty-six now and of an age to have left home but I don't see how I'll ever be able to afford it. Don't get me wrong, I'm very happy living at home, but sometimes I think it would be nice to strike out on my own, just Esme and me.' She laughed. 'As long as the family were just around the corner of course. I would never want to be far away from them.'

'I wouldn't want to live far from my dad either,' he said. 'There's only us two and we are very close.' He grinned. 'But I don't think I'd want to share a place with him now.'

'Exactly,' she said. 'It's natural to move on when you're an adult. It's just my circumstances that have mucked up the system for me. But I'm very lucky, I know that. Many women in my position don't have the family support that I have.'

'There are many more young widows about since the war,' he said. 'Dunkirk would have created a good few.'

'We are morbid tonight,' she said. 'So let's not talk about the war this evening.'

'We can try not to but it always seems to creep in, probably because it's here, all around us even though the air raids have stopped for the moment,' he said, glancing towards a nearby bomb site. 'You can give me a slap if I mention it again.'

'I wouldn't dare,' she said, smiling, and the mood lifted.

'What do you think about divorce, Wilf?' asked Nora when he called at the house for a chat on his way home from a civil defence meeting that evening.

'I can't say I've ever given it much thought, if any,' he replied. 'Why do you ask?'

'Mollie has a boyfriend who's divorced,' explained Madge; she was sitting in an armchair knitting a sweater for the navy.

'Oh. That's all right, isn't it?' he said cautiously because he sensed disapproval. 'It isn't as if he's married or anything.'

'Madge doesn't like the idea,' explained Nora.

'Oh I see,' said Wilf.

'I'm not the only person who doesn't agree with divorce; most people don't like it,' declared Madge in a sweeping statement about which she had no kind of proof. 'Marriage is supposed to be for life.'

'Well ideally, yes, but it doesn't work out like that for everyone,' put in Len.

'They should try harder then,' pronounced Madge. 'Personally I think divorce is sordid. All that business about providing evidence of adultery and people being photographed pretending to have done things they haven't.'

'That's because divorce is very hard to come by I think, and they have to have grounds,' suggested Wilf mildly. 'I don't know much about it but that's the impression I have.'

'I think you're making too much of it, Madge,' said Len. 'Divorce is outside of our world but this chap Mollie has gone out with seems very decent to me. He and his dad are well respected around here because of their store. I speak as I find and I like him.'

'So do I but that isn't the point,' insisted Madge. 'The fact is, he's had one wife and got rid of her, so who's to say he won't get rid of another.'

'That's an awful thing to say,' admonished Nora. 'We don't know what the circumstances of his marriage were.'

'It is a bit extreme, dear,' added Len.

'He's from a different world,' said Madge.

'Is that such a bad thing in this instance?' suggested her husband. 'At least he'd be able to see to it that Mollie and Esme don't want for anything.'

'Unless that isn't what he wants with Mollie,' said Madge. 'Not many men are prepared to bring up another man's child, are they? He might just be out for a bit of fun.'

'Oh for Gawd's sake,' said her husband irritably. 'The man is going back off leave in a few days. He's a pilot. That's dangerous work. He could get shot down and killed. He won't have time to do her much harm.'

'It doesn't take long as you very well know, Len Potts,' she came back at him.

'You're reckoning without Mollie,' he told her. 'I'm sure she can look after herself if she needs to. So let's all be glad that she's having a night out. If anyone needs a break, it's Mollie. Stop thinking the worst, Madge.'

'All I'm doing is being concerned for my daughter and I'm being made to feel as if I'm in the wrong.'

'I'm not suggesting that at all,' he said. 'But try to take it easy on yourself. Mollie is an adult and long past the age when we have a say in what she does and who she goes out with so stop worrying and be pleased for her.'

'He's right, Madge,' added Nora. 'I think we should give him the benefit of the doubt and hope it goes well for them. It's a long time since she split up with Syd and high time she had a man in her life again.'

'Hear hear,' said Len.

'I think I'd better be on my way,' said Wilf, not wishing to intrude on family matters.

'The news will be on the wireless in a minute, mate,' said Len. 'You won't want to miss that. Madge will be making some cocoa later on too.'

'Oh, that will be nice, ta very much,' he said, settling back in his chair.

Since the war had been on the nine o'clock news had been an absolute must for most people.

Mollie and Grant were sitting at a table outside the pub, absolutely absorbed in each other. She hadn't felt like this since she'd fallen in love with Syd, which seemed positively juvenile in comparison. The sun was setting, the air was warm and moist and she was on her second gin which she had with water because the pub didn't have anything else to go with it, such were the wartime shortages. He said his beer tasted watered down but they didn't care because getting to know each other was enthralling for them both.

'I was attracted to you the very first time I saw you,' he confessed when they had moved on from the initial chit-chat. 'Which probably wasn't the most honourable thing as I was married at the time.'

'You didn't do anything about it, that's the important thing, you are far too much of a gent,' she said. 'I don't know if I would have shown restraint if you had because I fancied you too.'

'Now she tells me,' he said, laughing.

'You would still have been the perfect gentleman if you had known,' she said. 'It's in your bones.'

'Unlike Cora I respected marriage,' he said. 'But you seem to know a lot about me.'

'Not really,' she said. 'But I trust my instincts and they tell me that you are a man with principles. I expect all married men fancy other women sometimes, it's only natural, but the decent ones don't do more than that.'

'Quite a philosopher.'

'Actually I know nothing about it. It's all just talk to impress you,' she laughed.

He enjoyed the joke too and they were both smiling.

'Has there been anyone else since Syd?' he asked.

'No,' she said. 'I never go out except to work. Esme has been my whole life.'

'Until now, I hoped you were going to say.'

'Maybe I was thinking that,' she said, her eyes sparkling. 'But my daughter will always come first whoever else comes into my life. She's everything to me.'

'Any man worth his salt would understand that. I certainly do,' he said.

'That's nice.'

'I won't beat about the bush, Mollie,' he began. 'I fancied you the first time I saw you and now that I know you a bit better I want to know more.'

'Likewise.' She smiled again.

'I'd love to spend time with you during the rest of my leave. I know you're busy with work and Esme but might you find some space for me?'

'I would love to go out with you again,' she said. 'And I'll find the time somehow. I'll have to have a word with my babysitters though and I'll warn you now that my

301

mother is suspicious of divorced people. Well, person, since you're the only one she's ever met. But Gran will do it if Mum isn't willing.'

He beamed at her and she almost melted but she knew she had to tell him something before things went any further. He might change his mind about her when he was in possession of the facts. That was a risk she had to take.

Chapter Thirteen

'But why didn't you tell me you knew about the affair?' Grant asked the next evening when he and Mollie were having a drink at a pub by the river and she had made her confession. 'Surely it would have been the natural thing to do when I mentioned it.'

'Yes, it should have been and I'm sorry. I think I must have been so shocked about your divorce and there being a child, my judgement was impaired. Anyway you seemed to have put the whole thing behind you and I didn't want to bring it all back and upset you. Obviously I didn't tell you what was going on at the time because you were little more than a stranger to me then. Anyway, it wouldn't have been right to interfere in someone else's marriage, especially as Cora was a friend of mine.'

'Of course, I understand that,' he said. 'I was thinking more of recently.'

'Mm, well I've told you now so I hope you'll forgive me for being a bit slow about it.'

'Why tell me now?' he asked.

'Because I would like to go on seeing you and you have to know it all if we are to stand a chance of getting on,' she said candidly.

'There's more?'

'I'm afraid so,' she confirmed. 'But first I want you to know that I hated what she was doing and begged her to stop. She wouldn't listen though.'

'Is that it?'

'No, I was involved in another way.'

He raised his brows. 'Oh?'

'The man she was having the affair with was . . .' She paused, hardly able to utter the words they were so painful. 'It was my twin brother Geoff.'

He flinched noticeably. Silence fell. All around them was the clatter of a pub: conversation, laughter and the clink of glasses, the volume seeming louder in contrast to the agonising quiet between them.

'I found out quite by accident,' she went on hurriedly, eager to get the whole story out into the open. 'I saw them out together on my way home from a class one evening and I can't tell you how shocked and upset I was. My brother is the last person you would expect to get involved in anything like that. I tried to persuade him to stop but he'd fallen for her in a big way. He even found them somewhere to live together but she backed out at the last minute; she decided not to leave you and her comfortable life and broke his heart. He was absolutely besotted with her. I don't think he'd got over it when he went away to the army but it was never mentioned between us again after that terrible night when it ended and he poured out his heart to me.'

He sat still, as though waiting for her to continue.

'The next day I called on Cora and told her I never wanted to see her again,' she explained. 'That was why I ended our friendship and stopped working for her.'

'I see.'

'The whole thing was very painful for me at the time but I eventually managed to put it to the back of my mind. Then when you told me that Cora had a child I realised that it must be Geoff's and therefore a blood relative of mine. I can't ignore it, Grant. Geoff is entitled to know that he has a child if he does make it back after the war. So I am going to ask you if you have an address for Cora so that I can write to her and get her to confirm that her son is Geoff's.'

Grant took a deep breath. 'Well, it's quite a story,' he said and Mollie felt any remaining warmth drain out of the atmosphere between them. 'And I do have an address for Cora and of course I will let you have it.'

'Sorry, Grant, I know I've upset you and ruined the evening for us both but I had to tell you. Geoff being my brother and my twin, I'll always stand by him no matter what he's done and whether I approve of it or not. So, like it or not I am still involved because of the boy. I'll understand if you'd rather not continue to see me. It could be awkward for you. You must feel that you hate Geoff and I'll probably feel compelled to defend him even though he has done wrong. I might not be able to help myself and that will cause bad feeling between us. But, honestly, I didn't intend to deceive you these past few days. I think I'm still in shock about Cora's baby even now. It isn't every day you find out that you have a nephew you knew nothing about.' She paused, leaning forward. 'Mum and Dad know nothing about any of it,' she went on to explain. 'It would break my mother's heart to know that her son had had an affair with a married woman.'

'They won't hear about it from me.'

There was unease in the atmosphere and Mollie wasn't sure where to go next with the conversation so she just blurted out, 'All of these carryings-on happened before war broke out. I think we've all had other things on our minds since then.'

An awkward silence ensued. 'I wasn't here for the London Blitz,' he said, as though the earlier conversation hadn't happened. 'Did you lose anyone in the air raids?'

'We didn't lose any family but I lost a friend,' she said. 'She was a keep-fit teacher; killed when the hall where we were doing a charity event was damaged by a bomb.'

'So you were there?'

'Yes and I didn't get so much as a scratch, which doesn't seem quite fair. But I'll never forget that awful night. It certainly made me realise how lucky I am to be alive. It is just a matter of luck in wartime, whether you live or die.'

He nodded.

'But we can't just let ourselves believe that being alive is the only thing that matters, can we, or we'd all turn into savages,' she said. 'We still have to uphold certain standards, which is why we can't just write off what Cora and Geoff did as acceptable because people are dying.'

'I suppose not.'

'We're doing it again,' she said. 'We're talking about the war and it was me who brought the subject up.'

'So do I get to slap you, which is what you were going to do to me last night if I started it?'

'Help yourself,' she said jokingly.

But he didn't do it as she had known he wouldn't and as she knew that all the fun was lost. They were both making an effort at conversation but it had lost all its spontaneity.

'I would go and get us some more drinks but it's one round only for every customer tonight because of the shortages and we've had our ration.'

'I'm sure we'll manage without it,' she said with a dry laugh. It would take more than alcohol to revive the evening; that much she was sure of.

Mulling it over that night in bed and reliving her disappointment when he hadn't made any further arrangements to see her but had just said he'd be in touch, she thought back on how the evening that had begun with such hope and potential had deteriorated into a cold and dismal failure. They had managed to keep up a dialogue of sorts but all the sparkle had gone.

She wondered if Grant still had feelings for Cora and if perhaps her own mention of the affair had brought her back into his mind and made him realise how much she meant to him; hence no more arrangements to see Mollie. Or would it have been different if her brother hadn't been the other man? Something like that could definitely cause problems but she'd had to tell him how devoted she was to Geoff no matter how badly he had behaved. It was inherent in her.

Whatever the reason, she was feeling gloomy because of it. She was a young woman and wanted the sort of love that Esme and the family couldn't give her. Grant had stirred her the minute she'd first set eyes on him and having got to know him a little better these past few days she'd known he could have come to mean a whole lot more to her.

What else could she have done but tell him about her involvement? It would have come up later because of the child and then he really would have felt deceived. Still, if he didn't feel able to put all that in the past, it was best that they went no further so as to avoid finding that it came between them later on.

None of this sensible reasoning helped much though. What was it with her and men? First there had been Syd, who had let her down so spectacularly; now Grant, whom she *really* liked, obviously didn't reciprocate to the same extent or he wouldn't have let complications stand in their way. Oh well, it's time to get some sleep, she thought, turning over on to her side and curling up.

Fortunately for Mollie she greatly enjoyed her work. Her classes were a joy and her office job kept her in touch with what was going on in the association; which new shows and demonstrations were being planned, which organisations and businesses had asked for classes to be held on their premises. She was only an office dogsbody but she still had access to inside information, and felt a part of things.

The day after the disappointing evening with Grant, she had a shift at the office in the morning and a class in the afternoon so she didn't have much chance to brood. It wasn't until she was walking home from class with her grandmother that a feeling of gloom descended. If things had been different, she might have been going out with a handsome airman tonight. Instead of which she would do what she always did when she wasn't teaching: she would stay home and listen to the wireless while knitting socks for servicemen.

True, it would soon be time for her darling daughter to come home from school; something guaranteed to cheer her up. But even the thought of that didn't do the trick this time.

When she turned the key in the lock and opened the door, the murmur of conversation drifted from the living room; the high-pitched sound of Mum punctuated by a deeper male tone.

'Dad must be home, Gran,' she said.

'Sounds like it.'

Mollie tensed. Dad never took time off work. Was he ill?

She burst into the room which seemed to glow with the sight of air-force grey. Grant was here, sitting on the sofa next to her mother who was positively beaming.

'What are you doing here, Grant?' she burst out.

'Excuse my daughter's manners, Grant, I don't know what's come over her,' said Madge, sounding very matey. Turning to Mollie she added, 'He came to see me as it happens. There's some tea in the pot if you and your gran want a cup. It can take a bit more watering down.'

Bewildered, Mollie turned and went into the kitchen while her grandmother stayed in the living room chatting.

'I'm sorry I was a bit off with you last night,' he said to Mollie later when she was seeing him out at the front door after he'd enchanted the senior members of the family as well as Esme when she got home from school. 'I think it was the shock of knowing that you were involved in all that horrible business with Cora. I thought of you as a new start and then suddenly back pops my ex-wife into my life again. The whole thing, the marriage as well as the divorce, is something that I want to forget. It was a big mistake.'

'It isn't as though I was in cahoots with them or anything,' she reminded him. 'I only got to know about it by accident and they were both well aware of my disapproval.'

'I know and I shouldn't have reacted as I did,' he said. 'Cora means nothing to me now and the father of her child is irrelevant. The boy is a nephew of yours and if I get to meet him because of that, I'll try not to let it be a problem.'

'So why come to the house when you knew I would be out. Did you forget?'

'No, I came deliberately,' he explained. 'You mentioned that your mother wasn't happy about the fact that I'm divorced so I thought I would reassure her that I am respectable, just an ordinary bloke whose marriage didn't work out. I thought I could probably do it better if you weren't there.'

'You seem to have won her over.'

'I hope so, Mollie, because I want to be with you and that means getting along with your folks.'

Mollie's smiles always warmed his heart and this one was no exception. He kissed her and it felt so right she knew he was the man for her.

'I only have three days of my leave left so let's spend as much time as we can together and have fun at the same time, shall we?' he suggested.

'I'm all for that,' she agreed.

'Let's start the ball rolling by going out dancing tonight,' he suggested. 'If you can get Esme looked after.'

'I'm pretty sure that Mum and Gran will oblige now that you've managed to get them eating out of your hand.'

'All you have to do is get your best frock on then,' he said. 'I'll call for you about half past seven. Is that all right with you?'

'That's perfect,' she said.

The next three days passed in a whirl of fun and romance. They experienced the warmth and gaiety of the

311

Hammersmith Palais where they tried to master the jive and jitterbug from the Americans who were there in large numbers and they danced cheek to cheek at the Lyceum in the Strand, both venues full of colour and sparkle in contrast to the grey, war-torn streets outside. It was so long since Mollie had actually done anything carefree and she enjoyed it immensely, though it was bittersweet because their time together was limited.

But they made the most of every second and Grant was always there to meet her when she finished work. At the weekend when Esme wasn't at school Grant took time to get to know her. Many pre-war outings for children such as the zoo were closed because of the war but they took her to the London parks and played ball and other games with her.

Organised entertainment wasn't necessary for her enjoyment anyway; loving attention was enough for Esme who, like her mother, was very athletic and the star of Mollie's Saturday morning juniors' class. It was something that was intrinsic in both of them. She loved nothing more than to do cartwheels, handstands and backbends and she did a great many of them in Hyde Park on that last Sunday afternoon before Grant was due to go back to camp on the Monday.

'I think she likes me,' he said to Mollie when Esme had gone to hide during a game of hide-and-seek.

'I'm sure she does,' said Mollie. 'So you're well in with four generations of Potts women. I hope this doesn't mean you have a way with the ladies.'

'You'll have to wait and see, won't you?' he said jokingly

just before the dulcet tones of Esme calling 'Ready!' rang out from behind some bushes.

Grant was catching a train on Monday afternoon and Mollie went to King's Cross station to see him off.

'I know we've only had a few days together, Mollie, but it's long enough for me to know that I'm in love with you,' he said as they found a corner on the concourse which was crowded with servicemen, the stream hissing from the engines. 'I knew the first time I saw you that you were special and I was right.'

'I love you too, Grant,' she said.

'I don't know when I'll be back again,' he said, holding her close. 'I might get a weekend pass in a few weeks or I might have to wait longer. I have no way of knowing at this stage.'

'Whenever you come back I'll be waiting for you,' she assured him.

'I'll write as soon as I can,' he told her. 'I won't be able to tell you much about what I'm doing though.'

'That doesn't matter,' she said. 'I'll be pleased to hear from you whatever you have to say and I'll write to you whether I get a letter from you or not.'

'You've got the address that will find me, haven't you?'

'Yeah, don't worry. I won't lose it.'

The hands of the station clock were moving inexorably forward. They only had a few seconds left. There were no words to describe the depth of their feelings.

'You take care, Mollie.'

313

'And you,' she said.

'I'd better go,' he said picking up his bag and slinging it over his shoulders.

'I'll come on to the platform with you.'

'Thanks.'

They moved with the crowds on to the platform and he boarded the train and leaned out of the window. One last kiss and the train began to rumble forward with a grinding din, steam clouds hanging over everything. She stood there waving until the last glimpse of him had disappeared, unashamed of her copious tears. She wasn't the only tearful woman around; there were plenty of girlfriends, wives and mothers here to see their boys off.

Drying her eyes with a handkerchief, she walked back along the steamy platform, heading for the underground station. She loved and was loved in return. Knowing that would help her to cope with his absence. In fact she could get through anything with the comfort of that fact to sustain her.

Mum and Gran were clearly concerned about her when she got home.

'Did he go off all right?' asked her mother.

'Yeah, he'll be well on his way by now,' she replied.

'We didn't have our four o'clock cuppa,' said her gran. 'We thought we would wait for you. But I'll put the kettle on now that you're back.'

'That's kind,' said Mollie. 'Thank you.'

'Your gran and I have been having a chat and we've decided that you need cheering up tonight, with Grant going back off leave, so one of us will go to the pictures with you and the other will look after Esme.'

'It's sweet of you but . . .'

'No buts,' said her mother. 'We've decided. A good film will take your mind off things.'

'I've got an even better idea,' said Mollie. 'You two go to the flicks and I'll stay in with Esme.'

'But . . .'

'I've been out having fun every night for the last few days so now it's your turn.'

'I never go out of an evening without your father,' stated Madge.

'I know you don't and it's time you started,' suggested Mollie. 'Have a girls' night out for a change.'

'What about you?'

'I want to stay at home and be with my daughter tonight,' she said. 'And a bit later on when she's in bed I'll enjoy some quiet reflection.'

'Thinking about Grant.'

'Naturally,' she confirmed. 'I've got a couple of letters to write as well.'

Nora was already rummaging in the pile of newspapers on the sideboard until she found the weekly local paper. 'I wouldn't mind going to the flicks, Madge, if Mollie really does want to stay in. So let's see what's on around here.'

'All right,' agreed Madge. 'I'll come if there's something good on and Len doesn't mind.'

'I don't see how he can object seeing as he goes to the pub to see his mates whenever he feels like it,' said Nora.

'There's one rule for men and another for women, always has been,' said Madge.

'Not so much these days, Mum, with so many women out working,' remarked Mollie. 'Anyway, Dad won't mind; he's an easy-going sort.'

While the two older women huddled over the paper, discussing the choice of films, Mollie went to find the ration books. On Monday afternoons after school she took her daughter to the sweet shop to buy her the sweets she allocated for the week out of the month's ration. It was a treat they both enjoyed.

Esme did rather better than most children because Wilf was one of those rare beings who didn't have a sweet tooth so he gave his coupons to Mollie for her daughter. Wilf was such a good sort.

Cora answered Mollie's letter suggesting that they meet and recommended Marble Arch as a rendezvous as she could get into town easily on the tube. Mollie had suggested some days and times and Cora chose one that best suited her.

Now Mollie was waiting for her outside a Lyons tea shop in Oxford Street at the agreed time. When she did turn up Mollie almost didn't recognise her. The lavish clothes and coiffed hair were gone. She still looked tidy but ordinary; her hair was taken up at the sides as was the fashion but she wore very little make-up and her summer frock had seen better days.

'Sorry I'm a bit late,' she said.

'Only by a few minutes,' said Mollie in a friendly manner. 'You have further to come than I do.'

'Everything is such a rush when you are working and you have a child, as you know only too well,' Cora said when they were finally seated at a table after queuing at the self-service counter for ages for a wartime sausage with a strange bread–like filling and mashed potato. 'I work in a shop which is why I chose a Wednesday afternoon to meet you, that being half-day closing around our way.'

'I see,' said Mollie, still trying to get used to this unglamorous version of Cora.

'It's so good to see you again, Mollie,' she said with enthusiasm. 'But why the change of heart? I thought you never wanted to see me again.'

'I didn't when I said that but the war is no time to cling on to old arguments,' said Mollie. 'I still hate what you did to Grant and my brother but it isn't my place to judge. I do, however, have a couple of things I want to talk to you about in particular and they aren't the sort of things best discussed by letter.'

'Ooh,' said Cora, cutting into a sausage. 'That sounds ominous.'

'Not ominous,' said Mollie. 'But serious.'

'You'd better get started then.'

'As I said in my letter, I ran into Grant and he told me that you are divorced and that you have a little boy

317

who isn't his,' she explained. 'I won't beat about the bush, Cora. I want to know if my brother Geoff is his father.'

Cora flushed angrily. 'Of course he bloody well is,' she replied. 'How many lovers do you think I had? I didn't come all this way to be insulted, to have you making accusations. Life is hard enough without that.'

'Sorry if that's how it sounded,' said Mollie. 'I knew he must be . . . I was just making sure.'

'He's Geoff's son all right,' she said. 'The spitting image of him as well.'

Despite the circumstances, Mollie experienced a surge of pleasure at the idea of a new member of their family and a cousin for Esme. 'So I'm an auntie for the first time.'

'That's right,' she said. 'Though because of the way things are I don't suppose he'll ever get to see his relatives. My own family don't want to know, except for Aunt Beth who we are living with. She always was the only member of the family who had any time for me at all.'

'My family know nothing of what happened between you and Geoff, and they'd be very shocked and disappointed in Geoff so I can't very well spring a grandchild on them while he is away.'

'Especially not one born out of wedlock to a woman who was married to someone else.'

'Exactly,' said Mollie. 'But why didn't you tell Geoff when you realised you were pregnant and at least give him the chance to do the right thing?'

'He'd said he never wanted to see me again so I didn't want to go after him just because I was in trouble.'

'He would have said that because he was so deeply hurt,' suggested Mollie. 'He was in a terrible state when he got home after you told him you wouldn't move in with him. I stayed up with him for most of the night.'

Cora dug her fork into the mashed potato on her plate and pushed it around. 'Yes, I know he was very cut up about it,' she said. 'And I have regretted it ever since. I wasn't just playing around with him, Mollie. I really did love him, still do. I just didn't think I could live without all the trappings I was used to. I didn't have the guts to try. Of course, I now know that I can because I have to do it all the time.' She paused and gave a wry grin. 'It's ironic really. I was the rich one and you were struggling to bring up a child on your own; now I'm in the same boat as you were. I work behind the counter in a grocery shop and my aunt looks after James while I'm at work.'

Mollie smiled. 'You called him James, that's Geoff's second name.'

'Yes, I wanted him to have something of his father's.'

'That's nice. And talking of his father,' Mollie began. 'He's been missing since Dunkirk.'

Cora winced. 'Oh no,' she gasped.

Nodding, Mollie added, 'I do have this twin feeling about it and I think he's still alive but it is just a feeling so don't bank on it.'

'Your parents must be frantic,' said Cora.

'We all are,' said Mollie. 'But as time goes on with no word you learn to live with it.'

'I know what I did was wrong but I can't regret what happened between Geoff and me, except for the ending of it,' Cora said. 'I really did love him and I can see his father in James every day.'

'If Geoff does come back will you tell him that he has a son?' asked Mollie.

'I won't be going after him looking for financial support if that's what you mean.'

'That wasn't what I meant,' she said. 'Not at all.'

'What do you mean then?'

'He has a right to know that he has a son.'

'Blokes usually sweep that sort of thing under the carpet, don't they?'

'Not Geoff,' said Mollie with conviction. 'He would want to know. What he does about it is up to him but he needs to be put in the picture.'

'You'll have to let me know if he makes it back so that I can write and tell him then.'

'Has there been anyone else since?'

'A divorcee with a child that isn't the ex-husband's, don't make me laugh.'

'Mm, there is that.'

'I wouldn't want anyone even if I did get any interest,' she said. 'Geoff was the only man for me.' She paused thoughtfully. 'I think I must be one of these people who have something in them that makes them self-destruct. I always seem to muck things up. I had it all with Grant except love. Then I find love with Geoff and I ruin that and lose your friendship in the process. I don't have much to lose now. I live quietly out in the sticks with my aunt, I work in a shop slicing cheese and bacon and weighing up tea and sugar all day but somehow I don't mind because I earn enough to keep James and me. It isn't much but I've proved I can do it. If only I'd known that I wouldn't have lost Geoff. But there's no point in looking back and agonising. So James is my life now.' She paused for a moment. 'Grant's a good sort and he didn't leave me absolutely destitute even after the way I'd treated him. There was a small settlement and I know that if I was really up against it he wouldn't see James and me starve. He has made that clear. That's the sort of man he is. But even I wouldn't sink so low as to ask him. Anyway, being independent isn't so bad once you get used to it.'

'I never thought I would hear you say that,' said Mollie. 'You're like a different person.'

'The old Cora is still in there though; the woman who wants her own way and craves for the good life. But then I see my little boy and I know that I have everything I need. All I want now is to be able to earn enough to give him a decent life. One thing the war did was make more jobs available to women. With so many shop girls leaving to go on to war work or in the forces there are jobs for people like me. I couldn't face a factory and being a mum with a young child I'm not forced to go on to war work. Everybody has less than they did since before the war so my life would have changed anyway.'

'What about your little dog?' asked Mollie. 'Now that you're a working girl and a mum, I don't suppose you have so much time to spoil her.'

Cora smiled. 'Don't worry about Peaches,' she said. 'She's doing just fine because she has three of us devoted to her now. My aunt and James love her too so she has more than enough cuddles and fuss.'

'Good.' Mollie smiled too.

'How about you, Mollie?' asked Cora. 'What have you been doing all this time?'

Mollie told her about her wartime classes and her job at head office. She brought her up to date about Esme, who was now seven years old.

'So you've come a long way from being my cleaner,' she remarked.

'It's just a different sort of work, that's all. As you now know from personal experience, a mum will do anything to feed her child. You're the one who has changed,' said Mollie. 'I like the new you much better.'

'Glad you approve,' she said. 'I hope I don't go and do something to muck it up again.'

'You've matured a lot since I last saw you, Cora,' observed Mollie. 'You might slip a little now and then but I don't think you'll go back to how you were. Besides, you've got James to keep your feet on the ground.'

'We'll see,' she said. 'But let's get down to it. Is there a man in your life?'

'That's the other thing I wanted to talk to you about,' Mollie said, biting her lip. 'Yes, there is as it happens.'

'Ooh do tell,' urged Cora eagerly. 'What's he like?'

'He's wonderful.'

'What's his name, what does he do and is he away in the forces?' she asked.

Even though Cora was divorced from Grant and had never loved him anyway, Mollie still had qualms about telling her but knew she must.

'It's Grant,' she said at last.

Studying Cora's face she saw surprise and thought she spotted a moment of regret.

'Well, that's a bit of a shaker,' she said at last. 'I would never in a million years have expected you two to get together. But, thinking about it, you're quite similar. Both very positive and self-sufficient.'

'I know that you're divorced and not in his life now so I was hoping you'd be pleased for me.'

'I am. You deserve a decent man after what Syd put you through.'

'But I thought for a second I saw regret in your eyes,' Mollie mentioned.

'Maybe just for a moment I might have wished it had worked out for us but only so that I had a settled, easier life now, not because I want him back,' she said. 'Any connections I had with Grant are long gone so I really hope it works out for the two of you.'

'I'm glad about that.'

Cora asked about the family.

'They're all fine, except for Geoff and we don't know about him.' She paused then moved on. 'Gran's got a sort of boyfriend,' she said. 'A lovely man called Wilf. He's like one of the family.'

'Only a sort of boyfriend?' queried Cora.

'We think he's just a friend,' she explained. 'He comes to the house a lot and she goes to his place. They go to the pictures together but they are probably just friends at their age.'

'Nice for her to have someone though.'

'Yes, it's lovely,' agreed Mollie. 'She's got someone of her own to talk to. If we are driving her mad at home she can go round to his place and pour her heart out to him.'

They talked more and it felt to Mollie just like old times only better because Cora wasn't so self-centred now. Mollie told her the sad news about Rose and after they'd talked about it for a while, she asked Cora if she went to a keep-fit class.

'No, I'd like to but it would mean asking my aunt to have James and she already minds him while I'm at work. I don't think it would be fair to her.'

This really was a very different Cora to the one Mollie remembered. The old Cora wouldn't have considered her aunt's feelings for a second. Motherhood was a great lesson in learning to put someone else first. That, and her reduced circumstances, had done wonders for her.

When it was time to leave, they both wanted to see each other again but agreed that they couldn't do it very often because of other commitments and the distance between them. Mollie was keen to see her nephew but knew she couldn't acknowledge him as such and welcome him into the family until her brother had accepted paternity. If the worst happened and he didn't come back then she would do it anyway. But for the time being they agreed to correspond by post and meet up with the children later on.

Going home on the train Mollie felt richer for the meeting. It was good to have a woman friend in her life again. It was a pity they lived at such a distance from each other. Oh well, you can't have everything, she thought, as the train drew into her station and she hurried along the platform.

Cora was thinking much the same thing as she travelled home on the train. She was thrilled that she and Mollie were friends again and wished they lived in closer proximity. But Cora knew she hadn't changed as much as Mollie seemed to think she had. She still had her selfish side and was very envious of Mollie having got together with Grant. Not because she wanted him for herself – absolutely not – but because Mollie had someone special in her life and she didn't. The only man she wanted was missing, probably dead, and he wouldn't want her anyway after the awful way she had treated him.

Being green-eyed towards Mollie was nothing new to Cora. Even when Mollie had been hard up and forced to work as a cleaner, Cora had been envious of her self-assurance and popularity. Now she was jealous of her for having something Cora thought she herself would never have again: a man in her life. She would never let it show, though, because she valued Mollie's friendship and was very fond of her.

Cora felt homesick for Chiswick too and wished she still lived there. But the only reason she could afford to support James decently was because her aunt let her live rent free. So there was no possibility of her moving back. Oh well, such is life, and she did actually have someone very special to love who loved her in return unconditionally: her beautiful son.

Chapter Fourteen

When the Potts family did finally get news of Geoff early in 1943, it wasn't the worst but it was bad enough to reduce the women of the house to tears.

'A German prison camp,' wailed Madge and they each in turn examined a crinkled card which looked as though it had been in the postal system for a very long time. 'My boy a prisoner of war. Oh my Lord!'

'At least we know that he's alive, Mum,' said Mollie but she was upset too.

'But what will they be doing to him?' Madge fretted.

'As I've said before, Madge, there must be some sort of code of conduct in those places,' suggested Nora. 'A rule of war or something so that countries on both sides aren't allowed to mistreat prisoners of war, though obviously they are not going to roll out the red carpet for enemy soldiers.'

'There's something called the Geneva Convention,' said Len. 'I think that sets the standards.'

'But there's no one to check on them, is there, so they can do what they like,' Madge pointed out.

'But he's alive, love,' said Len, putting his arm around his wife. 'And where there's life there's hope.'

'I know,' she said, sniffing. 'But I can't bear to think of him locked away and at their mercy. I bet they don't give our boys much to eat.'

Len had heard all sorts of imaginative speculation about the way prisoners were treated in German prison camps among men at work and in the pub but he wasn't going to upset his wife by telling her, especially as nobody actually knew what went on in those places. 'Look, I've got to go to work but keep your chin up, love. Geoff can tell us all about it when he comes home after the war which surely can't go on for much longer.'

'I suppose you're right,' she said and pointed to her heart. 'But it hurts here.'

Mollie was worried about Geoff too but she concentrated on supporting her mother. 'All we can do is keep him in our thoughts and look forward to him coming home. At least now there's a chance he will make it back. We can write to him too though there might be restrictions. We'll have to find out. I think you address letters to the GPO with the soldier's name and unit when they're abroad.'

Esme came into the room in her school gymslip. 'What's happened?' she asked. 'Why is everybody crying?'

'Nothing for you to worry about, love,' said Mollie, recovering quickly so as not to worry her daughter. 'So sit down and have your breakfast.'

As a general rule Mollie tried always to be honest with her daughter but she did feel it was in the child's best interests to protect her from certain things in these harsh times. Esme had had her childhood stolen by the war so if there was any way Mollie could spare her certain details she would do it. Esme was a little girl who knew her uncle was away at the war. That was all she needed to know for the moment.

There was nothing like a new project for diverting the mind and lifting the spirits and the idea for one occurred to Mollie soon after they'd had the news about Geoff. Actually, it was Wilf who suggested it when he just happened to be at the house one afternoon while Mollie was talking about trying to please all ages and levels of ability at her classes. Her mother was working on the sewing machine in the other room so there was just Wilf, Nora and Mollie.

'If I make the class too slow and gentle, the younger members get bored but if I step it up too much some of the older people and those with minor disabilities can't keep up so stop coming to class altogether,' she told them. 'It's a pity because the exercise often helps with aches and pains. It isn't easy to please everyone.'

'Why don't you do a separate class for the older people and those less able,' suggested Wilf, who was quite knowledgeable on the subject having done a lot of sport as a young man and was still a keen walker. 'Then you could slow everything down and make the exercises less taxing for that particular group.'

'Mm.' Mollie pondered on the subject. She did know

how to adapt the exercises and the idea appealed to her. 'But there wouldn't be enough people to make up a whole class. There are only a few who struggle.'

'Get some new ones then,' he suggested. 'But you'll need to spread the word.'

'It was hard enough getting youngish women to do anything outside the home until recently,' she said. 'I reckon it will be nigh on impossible to get older ladies to come. They've never been used to anything like that. They seem content to stay at home.'

'Oi, do you mind,' objected her grandmother. 'Some of us aren't in our dotage.'

Mollie laughed. 'Of course I don't mean you,' she assured her. 'You're a super gran though you wouldn't be able to do the class because I'll need you on the piano.'

'I reckon I get enough exercise with Wilf dragging me out walking with him whenever he can,' Nora said. 'But there is one thing you haven't taken into account and that's the cost. A lot of pensioners can't afford that sort of thing.'

'Mm, that's a good point,' agreed Wilf.

'I could do a reduced price for them,' she suggested, enthusiasm growing. 'If I could get the hall for a second hour after the Thursday morning class, we would already be there and could just have a ten-minute break then start the second session. It would save us setting up twice.'

'Good idea,' approved Nora.

'I could try it and see how it goes,' said Mollie.

'That's the spirit,' said Wilf. 'I'll be interested to know how you get on with it.'

'I'll give you a full account,' she laughed. 'But I'm not sure what I'm letting myself in for.'

When Mollie first set eyes on her curly-haired, brown-eyed nephew James, she found herself overcome with emotion.

'He's the image of Geoff,' she said to Cora when the boy had moved out of earshot and she'd recovered from the shock of looking into a pair of eyes that were very similar to her own. 'An absolute dead spit.'

'Yeah, he is,' Cora agreed. 'He's sweet-natured like his dad too. I'm really glad. Geoff could never be forgotten while James is around.'

It was the Easter school holidays 1943 and the two women and their offspring had met in Hyde Park for a picnic and to spend time together. Spring sunshine beamed down from a clear blue sky and there was just enough of a breeze to move through the trees and make ripples on the lake. They found a spot on the grass near the water and set out the picnic which was basic wartime fare of fish paste sandwiches and a few jam ones.

Fortunately the children took to each other more or less straight away and went off to play as soon as they had finished eating. Esme was at an age to enjoy younger children and she took on the role of big sister, rolling the ball to him and making him scream with laughter. The likeness between the two cousins was so startling, Mollie couldn't take her eyes off them.

'If you brought him to the house Mum and Dad

would know immediately what you and Geoff had been up to.'

'Do you think so?'

'I can't see how they wouldn't see the resemblance,' she confirmed. 'It's stunning to me and I don't think it's just because I know that I can see it. He really is like Geoff.'

Cora nodded. 'Talking of Geoff, I was relieved to know that he's alive.' Mollie had written and told her the news about her brother. 'But worried about how they might be treating him.'

'I think we all feel like that,' said Mollie. 'Mum is positive he's being tortured. We've told her that there are rules about that sort of thing but I don't think she's convinced.'

'Now that I'm a mother, I'm more able to understand how she must be feeling.'

'It seems never-ending, this bloomin' war,' Mollie remarked. 'We haven't had any air raids for ages so you get all hopeful then you hear about a school getting bombed somewhere near London and hopes are dashed.'

'I didn't get to hear about that which is probably just as well,' said Cora.

'Anyway, I've got something new to take my mind off things,' Mollie told her. 'I'm starting a new class for older and less able women.'

'Ooh you're a glutton for punishment,' Cora joked.

Mollie grinned. 'Yeah, I don't know why I let myself in for these things. I've more than enough to do as it is.'

'A busy person always finds time, so they say,' remarked Cora.

'It might be a lark,' said Mollie. 'You have to try these things, don't you?'

'You do; I don't. I work because I have to. I wouldn't do it from choice and I have no plans to take on anything else. I know you think that I've changed but I'm still bone idle at heart. I'd love to be a lady of leisure again but those times are long gone.'

'For everybody else too,' Mollie pointed out. 'The days of domestic servants are over, or at least hugely reduced, for the moment anyway. So even if you were still rich you'd probably have to do your own cleaning.'

'That's true,' Cora agreed. 'Anyway, how are things with you and Grant?'

'Fine. He had a long weekend pass recently and it was lovely.' That last leave had brought them even closer together and she'd loved every moment. He'd even taken Mollie to meet his father. 'But now I have to make do with letters again. Still, he writes to me quite often.'

'Have you written to Geoff?' asked Cora. 'Or are prisoners not allowed letters?'

'They are allowed them but whether they actually receive any is another matter as there are terrible delays. The letters are heavily censored and have to be lightweight airmails limited to one page because they photograph them and send them abroad by plane then print them for delivery. Sounds like a real palaver,' she said. 'But yes, we've written to him.'

Cora looked rather sad.

'If you want to write to him, Cora, you could give it a try though there is no guarantee that he'll receive the letter.'

'I'm the last person he'd want to hear from after what happened between us.'

Mollie was deliberately noncommittal about this because it was such a delicate matter and personal to Cora and Geoff. 'I don't know about that, Cora,' she said.

'Actually, ever since I heard that he was alive, I've been wondering if I should write and tell him about James,' Cora went on to say. 'I have definitely decided that I am going to tell him anyway when he comes home because I think he has a right to know, not because I want any sort of help from him. Whether or not he wants contact with James will be up to him. I won't be putting on any pressure.'

'If you do decide to write and tell him, it must be your decision,' said Mollie. 'It wouldn't be right for me to advise you on something so personal.'

'On the one hand it could cheer him up and give him something to look forward to when he comes home but . . . he might see it as a burden and he has enough to put up with.'

'I don't know how he'll react to knowing he has a child. I should think he'll be pleased but I'm not so close to him as to be able to predict his reaction to something like that, especially as it will come out of the blue.'

'No. I'll wait until he comes home,' decided Cora finally. 'It's too huge a thing to find out about in a letter that might not even reach him and will have already been read by the censors.'

Mollie couldn't possibly speak for her brother on a matter as personal to Geoff as this. He had once said he didn't want children until he'd made something of himself but that had been years ago and the war had ruined his career anyway. Mollie was instinctively defensive of her brother and if Cora hurt him again she would have her to answer for. She still hadn't forgotten the terrible state he was in the night they broke up. But they had all matured a lot since then. The war had seen to that.

The children came back, James in tears because he had fallen over.

'No peace for the wicked,' said Cora lightly, inspecting her boy for injury and finding nothing more than a slightly scuffed knee but giving him a cuddle anyway.

'I thought the peace and quiet was too good to last,' said Mollie, grateful for the interruption because the subject of Cora and Geoff was an emotive one for her.

Mollie's new class wasn't a success in terms of attendance. After a month they still had only eight members and two of them had been injured during the Blitz so had to exercise while sitting on a chair. But as far as fun and bonhomie were concerned it was top rate. There was a great deal of laughter and singing along to the music, especially during favourites like 'Lily of Laguna' and 'Moonlight Becomes You'.

'I only came to get out of the house,' said a woman of advanced years. 'But I reckon you're making a new woman of me, Mollie. That'll please my ole' man. I reckon he's sick of the sight of the old one after all the years we've been married.'

'I've been feeling better since I've been coming too,' said a woman called Lily who was only in her thirties but had sustained a leg injury during the air raids so was slightly disabled. 'I'm a lot more confident than I was before I joined and I'm sure I'm walking better.'

'I only came for the company originally,' said another. 'But I really enjoy the exercise now.' She grinned. 'I do enjoy a natter too. Pity we can't have a cuppa afterwards.'

'We used to at the other classes but tea rationing put a stop to that,' Mollie explained.

'Oh well never mind,' said someone. 'We still have a chat after the class anyway.'

'Thanks, Mollie,' said a woman who was ready to leave. 'I enjoy your class very much and I'm so glad you started it but I must dash. See you next week.'

'Please tell your friends if you enjoy it,' she said to another satisfied customer. 'Get them to come along. We could do with more members.'

'They probably think it's all bending down and touching your toes, that's why people don't come,' said Lily. 'They don't realise it's lovely music and gentle routines.'

'It says gentle exercise on the notices I spread around,' said Mollie.

'Perhaps they think they're past it then,' said someone.

'You'll have to convince them that they're not then, ladies,' said Mollie. 'We need more people.'

'We'll see what we can do,' they agreed.

'Seriously Gran, I'll have to close this class at the end of term if we can't get more people,' she confided to Nora as they walked home together. 'It's costing me money at the moment. The cheap price and low turnout means I'm not covering the cost of the hall. I don't mind breaking even but I can't afford to put money into it in the long term.'

'It'll be a shame if you have to close it because it's such a good thing.'

'I agree and it's the last thing I want to do but I just don't have the cash to fund it indefinitely,' she said. 'Besides, we need a fuller class to get the atmosphere. As it is now we're using just a corner of the hall and the rest is empty.'

'Mm, you're right,' agreed Nora.

'I know it's never going to be as big as the other classes,' said Mollie. 'Because it's confined to a certain section of the community and some older women think that sort of thing is only for the young ones.'

'The more mature are not so set in their ways as they were before the war, Mollie,' Nora pointed out. 'Many of them are out doing voluntary work.'

'That makes them feel they are helping with the war effort and rightly so,' said Mollie. 'I suspect they think keep fit is self-indulgence and a waste of time, or out of their range.'

'Or it could just be that not enough people know about it,' suggested Nora.

'But I don't know what else I can do to spread the word,' said Mollie. 'I've got notices in the shops, including Parker's store. I don't need a huge amount of people. Just enough to cover my expenses. We need at least double what we have now. I don't mind working for nothing for a good cause, and I'll always support a charity, but I draw the line at working at a loss on a regular basis. I have a child to support and I need to be earning, not giving money away, much as I enjoy teaching the class.'

'I understand, dear,' said Nora. 'I don't know what we can do to save it.'

Wilf came up with a suggestion.

'Why don't you have an open morning,' he said. 'Invite people to come and watch the class for free to see if they might like it; as long as the existing members don't mind being gawped at, of course.'

'I should think they would be happy about that,' said Mollie. 'They know I need more people to be able to continue and they don't want the class to close down. They might like to be involved in a scheme to save it.'

'If we could offer the visitors a cup of tea that would help bring them in and once they see what we do they might join even if they only came in for a nosey and a cuppa,' said Nora.

'Where do we get the tea though?' asked Mollie. 'Rationing being as it is.'

'Ask everyone for a small contribution,' suggested Nora. 'And we'll give our share. It will be a joint effort to save the class.'

'Ooh, that's a bit much to ask of anyone with the tea ration being so meagre.'

'Only a few leaves each,' said Nora. 'And it would just be a one-off.'

'Mmm,' pondered Mollie. 'I'd have to put that to the class and tell them that they aren't obliged to part with any of their precious tea ration if they'd rather not.'

'I think an open morning would be well worth doing even if you can't get hold of any tea. It won't cost you anything because the hall will already be paid for,' Wilf pointed out. 'All you need is a few notices around. I know paper is in short supply but you could use the other side of the notices you already have out.'

'Good thinking, Wilf,' responded Mollie. 'We'll give it a try. I'll get Esme to help to make the notices. She writes beautifully now and loves to do anything a bit creative.'

'Good luck with it then,' said Wilf.

'What would we do without you?' said Mollie because Wilf had become such a valued part of their family.

'You won't have to because I'm not going anywhere,' he said, grinning.

Wilf's suggestion proved to be a winner. They weren't inundated with takers for the 'open morning' but a good few turned up and seven of those joined. At least now

Mollie broke even and could continue with the class in the autumn term. She suspected that it was never going to be as well attended as the other classes but she considered it to be very worthwhile because the members enjoyed it so much and she knew it was good for them.

The population as a whole was in need of something to cheer them up as winter closed in, the war dragged on and everything got even shorter.

'What about this plan they are supposed to have to drive Hitler's troops back and bring an end to the war,' said Nora one bitterly cold evening when they all had to wear their outdoor coats and hats and gloves indoors because they were waiting for their coal ration to come and deliveries were slow. 'When is that going to happen? I reckon they'll have to do something drastic or this flippin' war will go on forever.'

'The Second Front, they call it. There is talk about that,' said Len. 'But nobody seems to know when it will be.'

'Perhaps Mr Churchill will have some news for us in the New Year. Meanwhile we'll just have to do what we always do, grin and bear it,' said Madge.

'I'll be glad to go out to my class tomorrow night,' said Mollie. 'At least exercise keeps you warm.'

'I hope our coal ration comes before Christmas,' said Madge worriedly.

There was a general murmur of agreement.

'Is there anything cheerful on the wireless tonight?' asked Madge. 'We could do with a laugh.'

'I think *Variety Bandbox* is on later,' said Mollie. 'That will cheer us up.'

The programme was on and spirits were raised but they all went to bed fully dressed and with hot-water bottles.

By being very careful with it when they did get a coal delivery, they did have a roaring fire on Christmas Day and that in itself was enough to please them all and they made an occasion of it for Esme. Festive food was sparse but they had saved their sweet rations and that was a treat. So they enjoyed themselves, singing round the piano, playing games and just talking, loving the warmth and cosiness they had been missing.

Wilf spent the whole day with them, contributing to the food as was the custom in these times of rationing and shortages. Grant didn't manage to get home but, despite everything, Mollie could honestly say they all had a happy Christmas.

Many people including the Potts family had high hopes that the New Year would bring news of the much vaunted Second Front. Instead, after three bomb-free years, in January, they found themselves under attack from the air again.

'I thought we'd finished with this lark,' said Madge as they all collected their gas masks and blankets and climbed down into the cheerless shelter which seemed even colder, damper and smellier after being unused for so long.

'I suppose Wilf be in action again out on the streets tonight,' mentioned Len.

'Yeah, I expect he will be,' agreed Nora.

'That will raise their popularity,' mentioned Len. 'Civil Defence workers have had a bad time with the public while we've had no air raids; people have been saying that they're getting paid for doing nothing which is most unfair since a lot of them like Wilf do it on a voluntary basis and don't get paid for their service.'

'Yeah, Wilf has had the odd nasty remark when he's been wearing his uniform if he's been attending meetings or lectures,' said Nora. 'If the offenders are strangers and don't know that he's unpaid. It's pure ignorance but Wilf is a tough old stick. He can take it.'

Mollie wrapped her daughter in a blanket and held her close as they settled down for the night in this ghastly hole, talking, singing and making jokes to take their mind off things. She concentrated on thoughts of the future when Grant and Geoff came home, but it was hard to imagine it with planes roaring overhead punctuated by terrifying explosions. Get a grip, girl, she told herself.

The next morning after Nora had helped with the break-fast washing-up she said she was going round to Wilf's. 'It's a long time since we've had a raid so I want to know how he got on last night. I'll see you later.'

'All right, Mum,' said Madge. Len had gone to work and Mollie had gone with Esme to the school to make sure it was open. 'See you later.'

The smell was back, Nora noticed as she walked through the streets to Wilf's, the harsh, smoky smell that was so pungent after a night of air raids. There was no damage in Pearl Road or the streets around it but her heart lurched when she turned into Wilf's road to see one of the houses turned to rubble. It wasn't his building but it was quite near on the other side of the road. She ran the rest of the way and rapped his knocker hard.

The front door of the adjacent house opened. 'He's not there, luv,' said the neighbour, a woman in a cross-over apron.

'Why? What's happened to him?' asked Nora anxiously. 'Where is he?'

'They took him away in an ambulance,' she replied.

'Why? What's the matter with him?' Nora was frantic now.

'He was helping out over the road before the rescue people got there.' She pointed to the damaged house. 'He went to get try to get someone out who was trapped and part of the building collapsed on him.'

'Do you know if he was badly hurt?' asked Nora.

'No I don't, I'm afraid, dear,' she said. 'We were down in the shelter. I heard about it this morning from another neighbour. Wilf was unconscious when they took him away apparently. Somebody said he was dead but I don't know if it's true.'

'Do you know which hospital they took him to?' asked Nora desperately.

'Sorry, love, I don't,' she said. 'Hammersmith I should think. That's the biggest round here.'

Nora hadn't run anywhere for years but she tore through the streets now, almost colliding with Mollie on her way back from the school.

'Blimey, Gran,' she said. 'Are you training for the next Olympic Games or something?'

'It's Wilf,' she explained breathlessly. 'He's been hurt and is in hospital.'

'You'll be in there with him if you don't slow down.'

'I'm on my way home to tell your mum then I'm going to find him,' Nora explained.

'I'll go with you,' said Mollie promptly. 'You wait here and get your breath back while I pop home to tell Mum.' She pointed to a low garden wall. 'Sit down there. I'll get some money for the bus too.'

'We can walk, love,' said Nora, anxious to be on her way.

'He may have been taken somewhere further afield. The hospitals might be overcrowded after a night of air raids.'

Nora didn't have any choice but to do what her granddaughter said because she was out of breath.

They found him in a crowded ward with screens around him, heavily bandaged, unconscious and frighteningly pale. Nora collapsed into tears at the sight of him.

'It doesn't look like him lying there,' she sobbed. 'What was he thinking, going into an unsafe house? He's an air-raid warden not a bloomin' rescue worker.'

'He did a first-aid course and basic fire fighting as

part of his training, I remember him telling us,' said Mollie. 'So I suppose he thought he should have a go.'

'A man of his age going into a bombed building,' disapproved Nora because she was so worried about him. 'It's downright irresponsible.'

'He's very brave, Gran,' said Mollie. 'The sort of person who wouldn't stand back if he thought he could help.'

'Stupid man,' she said, tears streaming from her eyes. 'Giving us all this worry.'

'I suppose if you know someone needs help and you are trained to deal with it to a certain extent you would act and not think too much about the consequences,' suggested Mollie.

'I suppose so,' Nora agreed at last.

When the doctor finally appeared, after Mollie had asked the nurse repeatedly to see someone, they enquired about Wilf's condition.

'He's been badly knocked about,' he said. 'He has a broken arm and heavy bruising in various parts of his body. He sustained a blow to the head which is why he is unconscious. We'll know more when he wakes up.'

Something about his tone caused Nora to say, 'If he wakes up, is that what you are afraid to tell us?'

'He did receive injuries to his head so is in a serious condition,' the doctor said. 'When he comes round we will know more.'

'Is he going to die?' asked Nora.

The doctor looked serious. 'We will do everything we can to avoid that happening.'

'Thank you for being so honest, doctor,' said Mollie.

'Can I stay with him?' asked Nora.

'Yes indeed. While his condition is as it is visiting is unlimited,' he told her.

'Ooh, Mollie,' wept Nora after the doctor had gone. 'They only allow visiting at all hours when the patient isn't expected to live.'

Mollie knew that this was true and was very worried but she said, 'Wilf is tough; you said so yourself, so don't even think of looking on the black side. The doctor didn't say we should prepare ourselves for the worst and that's what they say when there's no hope at all. I remember that from when Syd died.'

'That's something I suppose.'

In a moment of insight Mollie sensed that her grandmother wanted to be alone with Wilf and, as worried as she was about leaving her, she knew that she must.

'I'm due to do a class this morning, Gran,' she said. 'I don't know if anyone will turn up after last night but I'll have to go just in case anyone comes. We can manage without music for once so you stay here. Will you be all right while I'm gone? Mum will come when I tell her anyway.'

'She's got a lot of sewing work to do,' said Nora. 'I don't need anyone to stay with me.'

'Is there anyone I should tell about Wilf? Any relatives perhaps?'

'There's only his nephew and he's away at the war,' said Nora. 'He only has us. He never had any children.'

'How sad.'

'Yes, I think that was one of the biggest disappoint-ments of his life. Still, we are here for him.'

'Indeed.'

'There's the ARP people,' said Nora, remembering. 'I suppose they ought to be notified.'

'I'll tell Bert next door,' said Mollie. 'He's in the same group so he'll pass the message on.'

'Thanks, love,' said Nora.

'I'll be back as soon as I can and Mum will be along soon,' said Mollie.

'Don't worry about me,' said Nora. 'You get off and do what you have to.'

As the door closed behind Mollie, Nora heaved a sigh of relief because she so much wanted to be alone with Wilf and her thoughts. She needed to make a decision. In that moment she decided that if Wilf was spared she would tell him something he should have known a very long time ago. He had a right to that. If he died without knowing she would never forgive herself.

Mollie had almost a full class which delighted her.

'Thank you all for coming,' she said from the platform before she got started. 'I know none of you will have had much sleep so well done for turning up.'

'The class makes us feel human after a night in the shelter,' said someone.

'Yeah, it gives us a feeling of normality,' said another.

'I'm afraid we'll have to work without music today,'

she told them. 'A close family friend was injured last night so my gran is at the hospital with him.'

There was a sympathetic outpouring from the class.

'Anyway, let's get started on the warm–up before you all freeze to death,' said Mollie. 'Let's have some good brisk walking around the hall.' Mollie came off the stage and walked with them. 'That's it. Heads up, shoulders back and arms swinging. Keep those tummies in. Lovely. Well done! Now turn round and walk the other way.'

The class was as much a therapy for Mollie as the members even though she was working. Although no one could guess, and she would never let her anxiety show to her grandmother, she was actually desperately worried about Wilf who hadn't looked as though he'd stood much of a chance at the hospital. Throughout the class Mollie had been agonising about leaving her gran but had been sure that was what she'd wanted.

Wilf had become a dear family friend as well as a close companion to Gran. It was the first time she had known her grandmother to have a special friend and she could hardly bear to imagine what she would do without him.

'Right, ladies,' she said, pushing her own worries to one side. 'Please get into your lines and we'll continue with some nice lively moves to keep you warm.'

Madge insisted that her mother came home to eat a hot meal that evening, having taken her a sandwich for lunch at the hospital. But as soon as Nora had finished eating her meal, she excused herself, got up from the table and put her coat on.

'Oh, Mum,' said Madge. 'Do you think you ought to go to the hospital again? You've been there all day.'

'Of course I must go back,' she said. 'Surely you don't think I'm going to abandon Wilf at a time like this. He doesn't have anyone else.'

'I'll go down there,' said Len. 'Then you can stay here and put your feet up.'

'While Wilf is at death's door,' she burst out. 'Not bloomin' likely.'

'At least stay and have a cup of tea,' said her daughter.

'All right, just a quick one.'

'I'll go with you, Gran,' said Mollie, 'if Mum doesn't mind looking after Esme.'

'Of course I don't mind,' said Madge. 'But can you see to it that your gran doesn't stay too long please?'

'Will do,' agreed Mollie.

'Honestly, all this fuss. It's Wilf you should be worrying about not me,' objected Nora.

'I am worrying about him,' said Madge. 'But you are my mum and it's my job to look out for you.'

'All right, I'll forgive you,' she said, managing a smile.

In the event the three of them went to the hospital: Nora, Len and Mollie. There was a surprise waiting for them. Wilf had woken up. He was still very weak and the doctor advised them not to raise their hopes too much because he wasn't quite out of the wood yet even though it was a very positive sign.

'Would you mind if I had a few minutes on my own with him,' asked Nora after some greetings and chit-chat had been exchanged.

Mollie and her father looked surprised.

'No. Of course not,' said Mollie quickly, giving her father a look. 'Come on, Dad. We'll wait outside in the corridor.'

As the doors closed behind them Len asked of Mollie, 'What's that all about then?'

'They are close friends, Dad, naturally she wants a few minutes on her own with him.'

'At her age.'

'Of course at her age,' said Mollie. 'You like to chat to your mates at the pub without us there, don't you?'

'It's hardly the same thing.'

'It's exactly the same thing, Dad,' said Mollie. 'Friends say things to each other they wouldn't say to other people. Besides, having us there is tiring for Wilf. I think we were about to get chucked out anyway by the nurse. As his condition has improved they'll probably put him on to restricted visiting.'

'Yeah, you're right,' he said, sitting down on a chair in a row in the corridor outside the ward. 'I really hope he makes it through. He's a nice old boy.'

'He's lovely,' agreed Mollie. 'I'm keeping my fingers firmly crossed for him.'

Chapter Fifteen

With infinite gentleness Nora covered Wilf's hand with her own. 'I hope you can stay awake for long enough to hear what I have to say,' she said in a soft voice. 'I know that you're very poorly and I shouldn't be talking to you about serious matters but what I have to tell you can't wait any longer; it's that important. It must stay between us, though, Wilf.'

'Gawd knows what you're on about but you'd better get on with it so that you can stop looking so worried,' he said, his voice surprisingly strong considering what he'd been through.

She bit her lip, knowing this wasn't going to be easy. 'Well,' she began but faltered and the words petered out.

'Spit it out, love, before we both pass on,' he said with a weak grin. 'All this hanging about is getting me worried.'

'Well . . . you know how disappointed you've always been because you didn't have a family of your own.'

He gave her a studious look, his brow furrowed. 'Yeah,' he said in a questioning manner.

'You do have a family.'

'Yeah I know I'm like one of the family at your place, and I'm very grateful, but—'

'You are actually related, Wilf,' she cut in.

He narrowed his eyes on her, looking puzzled. 'Don't be daft Nora, that isn't possible.'

'It is because my daughter is yours too,' she blurted out emotionally, relieved that the words had finally been uttered. 'You are Madge's father which makes Mollie and Geoff your grandchildren and Esme your great-granddaughter. They all have your blood, Wilf. You really are one of the family . . . in the real, biological sense.'

His lips trembled, he flushed up then turned ashen. She was terrified that the news was going to cause a relapse. Perhaps she should have kept it to herself as she had for so long it had almost been forgotten. But she'd wanted him to know the truth before he died and if that was the outcome of his injuries at least he would have been told.

'Perhaps you'd better explain?' he suggested.

'There's nothing very complicated about it,' she said. 'After you moved away, I discovered that I was pregnant.'

His eyes bulged. 'Oh Nora, I wish I'd known,' he said.

'I had no way of contacting you,' she told him. 'You left so fast and no one knew where you'd gone.'

'As you know, we did a moonlight flit because Dad couldn't pay the rent and was in arrears so we had to disappear sharpish,' he reminded her.

'Yeah, you told me that,' she said. 'But you could have kept in touch.'

352

'Us kids were told that we mustn't contact anyone from our old neighbourhood in case they found out where we were and the landlord got to know and came after us to get the rent we owed,' he explained. 'Dad said we had to make a new life.'

'Oh, now I see.'

Wilf seemed to become distressed; his eyelids fluttered and all the colour drained from his face which sent Nora into a panic and in search of a nurse.

'Mr Robbins needs to rest now and I'm going to ask the doctor to come and have a look at him,' the nurse told her hurriedly, after briefly examining Wilf whose eyes were now closed. 'So I think it would be best if you were to leave now.'

'Is he going to die?' Nora asked.

'The doctor is the one to speak to about that,' said the nurse. 'But the best thing you can do for Mr Robbins and yourself is to go home and take it easy. The siren hasn't gone yet so perhaps the Germans are going to stay away tonight.'

'All right,' Nora agreed with a sigh of reluctance. 'I'll come back tomorrow.'

Walking home with Mollie and Len, Nora was convinced she had brought about Wilf's demise by giving him such a shock when he was so vulnerable. What had she been thinking? She'd been so convinced that he must know the truth she'd blurted it out at the worst possible time. It had seemed so vital then. But was it really that important?

'Surely the nurse wouldn't have told you to go home

353

if she'd thought Wilf was about to breathe his last,' said Mollie, who knew her gran was worried but couldn't possibly know the extent of her distress. 'She would have asked you to stay, as there are no relatives around.'

'Yeah, that's true,' added Len.

'Maybe you're right,' agreed Nora, slightly cheered.

But she still had fear in her heart. Losing Wilf would be bad enough. But having his death on her conscience would haunt her for the rest of her days.

The next morning when she arrived at the hospital to find someone else in Wilf's bed, Nora was beside herself. Finding a nurse, she blurted out, 'Where's Wilf Robbins? He's not in his bed. Has he, did he? I mean is it bad news?'

'Quite the opposite, my dear,' said the nurse. 'He's been moved to another ward now that he's on the mend.'

'On the mend,' she echoed, trembling with relief. 'But he seemed to take a turn for the worse when I was here yesterday.'

'Yes but it was only a temporary thing and he perked up later on; he's better than ever in fact. We thought he might have had some sort of a shock that put him back. But as he's recovering now, it doesn't really matter.'

'It's such a relief.'

'I'm sure,' said the nurse. 'The bad news is, you can't see him now. Official visiting times apply now that he's off the danger list. Three till four this afternoon or seven till eight tonight. So you've had a wasted journey.'

The journey was far from wasted. She would do it happily a dozen times over to hear such news. But she just said, 'I'll come back this afternoon then.'

Now sitting up and looking much better, Wilf was eager to know all the details of Nora's bombshell. 'You must have been worried sick; a young girl pregnant and unmarried.'

'I think I cried a lot; in secret of course because of the shame,' she said. 'I was in a mess and didn't know which way to turn. So when this boy who lived in my street and had always been sweet on me offered to get me out of the scrape I was in by marrying me I jumped at the chance. It was a bad marriage but at least I got to keep my reputation and Madge was able to grow up without a stigma.'

'You told me once that your husband was a bully,' Wilf mentioned.

She nodded. 'He never let me forget what he'd done for me,' she told him. 'He wanted me to be grateful all the time and I did that by being obedient to him.'

'That couldn't have been easy for a live wire like yourself,' he said.

'It wasn't easy and I couldn't always manage it,' she said. 'When I stood up for myself he would have one of his rages and become violent.'

'Did he hit you?'

'Oh yes,' she replied. 'But he never touched Madge. I would have left if he had and he knew that. I've no idea

355

where I would have gone but I know I wouldn't have let her be at risk. She hated him because she saw his violence towards me. After she left home to get married she only came to see me when he was out at work or I went to her place. He never had much to do with the grandchildren. He wasn't interested in them.'

'What a shame,' he said. 'Why was he like that with them as his argument was with you and they were just innocent kids?'

'Because they weren't his flesh and blood and he couldn't forget that. Also I didn't love him as I should and that ate away at him and made him sour with us all,' she said. 'I was very grateful to him for helping me out when I needed it and I tried to be the best wife I could be in return but it was never enough for him. I remained grateful until the day he died but I couldn't manufacture the love he wanted so badly.'

'I left quite a mess behind me when I went away, didn't I?' he said. 'Had I known I would never have let my father drag me off like that.'

'I must admit I did hope to hear from you in the early days after you left.'

'I should have got in touch but the circumstances were such that I couldn't. I thought about you a lot but I had to concentrate on trying to find work to help support the family. I was young and immature and living for the day I suppose, like we all do in our youth. Suddenly time had passed and I thought you would have forgotten all about me.'

'I never did.'

'Why were you so keen to get away from me at first when we met up again in the town more recently?'

'I'd lived with the secret for so long I'd managed to make myself believe that the past hadn't happened and that Madge really was my husband's. Then, there you were out of the blue, bringing it all back, and I felt threatened. I was terrified that Madge might get to know the truth now that you were around. Of course, there was no way you could tell her because you didn't know yourself. Eventually I realised I was being overly cautious and eased up and let you back into my life.'

'And now the cat is out of the bag,' he said.

'Only between us though,' she said firmly.

He looked disappointed. 'So you give with one hand and take away with the other.'

'I thought you might die, Wilf, that's why I told you,' she said. 'I didn't want you to end your life not knowing.'

'You must have realised that I would want them to know the truth,' he said.

'I didn't think past the moment,' she told him. 'I acted on impulse.'

'Are you ashamed of me is that why you don't want them to know?'

'Don't be silly, that's the last thing!' she assured him. 'It's just that I would be really embarrassed for them to know what I'd done when I was a girl. I brought Madge up very strictly in that respect when she got to an age to be interested in boys. What sort of a hypocrite would she think I am if she were to find out that I didn't practise what I preached? Besides, the younger generation

357

hate to think of us doing that sort of thing. It makes them uncomfortable. They know we must have done for them to be here but they don't want to be reminded.'

'I can understand why you might feel like that,' he said. 'But I would love to be Dad to Madge and Granddad to the others, especially as your husband wasn't any good in that direction. I think they might like it too.'

'I know how you must feel, Wilf, and I would love it too, but can you keep quiet about it for me please?' she asked. 'I mean, it isn't as if you've ever been a part of their lives until recently and they think the world of you in your present role as family friend. They don't need to know the rest. You can still love them in the way you want and see a lot of them.'

'If it means that much to you I'll keep quiet,' he finally agreed. 'I'm very glad you've told me though. I feel as though my life has changed.'

'Yes, I thought you would be pleased, you not having any other kids,' she said. 'It's a shame you weren't with me to bring Madge up.'

'Yeah. I'm to blame for that. Had I known I'd have found a way to be with you. But sometimes fate takes a cruel twist and there's nothing you can do about it.'

She nodded. 'Still, with a bit of luck we both have a few good years left so let's enjoy what time we have. You can be as involved as you like with Madge and the grandkids. They love having you around.'

He took her hand. 'I'll look forward to it,' he said, a smile lighting up his pale face.

★　　★　　★

Cora still had no intention of keeping quiet about her secret if Geoff did make it home after the war.

'He's got a right to know that he's a father,' she said to Mollie. 'And James deserves to know who his dad is. It will be up to Geoff what he does about it. If he chooses not to be involved I will respect that but he's going to be told.'

'Give him a chance to settle down though,' suggested Mollie. 'It'll take him a while to adjust I should think. Don't go throwing it at him as soon as he gets in the door.'

'Of course I won't,' she said. 'Do you think I'm mad or something?'

'Not mad. But you are impulsive and you seem very keen for him to know.'

'I'm not even allowed through the door at your place with James anyway,' sad Cora.

'Only because I'm afraid Mum and Dad would see the likeness to Geoff and guess the truth and I don't want them to know before he does. Once it's out in the open and my brother makes his decision you have an open invitation to our place. Even if he doesn't want you in his life you can come to the house as my friend. It won't matter then. I don't want Geoff to come home to find everyone else knows about James except him.'

'Have you heard from him lately?'

'No. Not a word. Apparently there are still terrible delays with the troops' post,' said Mollie. 'I haven't heard from Grant recently either and that really is unusual. I suppose the hold-up must be due to the heavy volume of mail with so many people moving around. I hope he's all right, though.'

'The letters will be held up because of the general chaos caused by the war, I expect,' said Cora. 'So try not to worry.'

'At least the end is in sight now that we've had the Second Front,' said Mollie.

'Mm, thank goodness. The war has gone on for far too long,' said Cora. 'Everybody has had enough now and I should think our boys overseas are fed up with the whole thing.'

It was early June 1944 and the Allied invasion had taken place a week ago so there was a lot of optimism in the air. Cora had made a rare visit to Chiswick to see her mother, who was ill, and had left James with her aunt because her mother wasn't up to having a child around. Esme was at school so the two women had been able to get together for some adult conversation. They had met in the town and walked to the riverside as it was such a lovely day. They were sitting on a bench overlooking the river in a shady spot in Duke's Meadow.

'How are the keep-fit classes going?' Cora enquired.

'Fine. The attendance isn't what it was before the war but enough for us to keep going,' said Mollie. 'The factory classes help too.'

'Are there any big shows planned?'

'Not big national ones but a few of us have been doing a spot on the programme of a show put on by a theatre group who provide entertainment to raise money for war charities; in church halls and so on,' she said. 'It's nice to feel the excitement of working to an audience and to know you are doing something to help.'

'Sounds like fun.'

'We enjoy it and it's all in a good cause,' said Mollie. 'They have some dates booked at hospitals and convalescent homes in the autumn too.'

'All very worthy,' said Cora.

'I know that you're taking the mick but it actually feels rather good to know that you're cheering people up and raising money at the same time.'

'I wasn't taking the mick,' Cora told her. 'I do a bit of voluntary work myself these days. Only collecting for the Red Cross but I feel as though I'm doing something to help and it's rather a nice feeling.'

'Blimey, Cora, what next?' laughed Mollie. 'I still can't get used to this new, nicer you.'

'She's here to stay so you'd better get used to the idea,' she said, grinning. 'But there's still a lot of the old me hanging around, especially my determination to get what I want. This is probably a good time to tell you that, as well as telling Geoff about James, I also want Geoff back and I'm going to do everything I can to achieve that end when he comes home, if he wants it too. I want us to be a family but I realise that his feelings for me might have changed after all this time, especially because of how much I hurt him. Letting him go was the biggest mistake of my life and I've regretted it every day since. I'm planning on putting it right as soon as I can. I thought I ought to be honest with you about it as you are so over-protective of him.'

'I am not over-protective of him,' objected Mollie.

'Ooh, not much,' said Cora lightly. 'Anyone who crosses him does so at their peril.'

'Honestly, you don't half exaggerate,' said Mollie smiling.

'No exaggeration. I thought my end had come when you found out I'd let him down. You scared the hell out of me.'

'It's because we're twins I suppose,' Mollie suggested. 'I'll be the same if you let him down again.'

'That's one thing I won't be doing,' said Cora. 'I can absolutely promise you that.'

'The war isn't even over yet,' Mollie reminded her. 'Let's wait until there is a realistic chance of getting the boys home before we have this sort of discussion.'

'We'll be getting good news soon,' said Cora. 'I bet you.'

As it happened she couldn't have been more wrong. Within days of that conversation, parts of London and South-East England found themselves under attack from peculiar aircraft which dropped out of the sky and exploded on the ground at all hours of the day and night. Nobody knew what they were and there was a great deal of speculation – some people thought they must be German bombers that had caught on fire and crash-landed – until eventually the rumours were brought to an end by a government announcement explaining to the public that Hitler was now using pilotless aircraft on the British Isles and when the engine stopped the explosion would follow within a matter of seconds.

Although these evils beasts caused a huge amount of damage and loss of life, especially as they fell at all hours and were not confined to the nights as earlier bombings had been, somehow people got used to them and took them in their stride. Naturally they were afraid but most went about their business during the daytime in the normal way and dived for cover when they heard the dreaded drone followed by a silence. The siren wailed so often it was largely ignored.

'Doodlebugs' became the favourite term for them. Mollie thought perhaps calling them silly names took the terror out of them for some people.

'They're causing plenty of havoc,' said Wilf, who was now out of hospital and visiting the Pottses one afternoon. 'Lots of work for the Civil Defence.'

'I hope you haven't got any daft ideas about going back, Wilf,' said Madge.

'I'd be more of a hindrance than a help at the moment with my arm still in plaster,' he said. 'But I shall go back as soon as I can once it comes off.'

'Maybe they could give you a job on the clerical side or something,' suggested Nora. 'You've done more than your share out on the streets.'

'Think I'm past it, do you?' he said lightly.

'If you are, so is she, mate,' put in Len. 'But she's still out playing the piano of an evening, bombs or no bombs.'

'It's hardly the same thing, Len,' said Nora. 'I only meant he might like to take a break as he's been injured.'

'If I was dead or permanently disabled I would give it up but as I'm neither of those things I shall carry on,' said Wilf.

'Good for you, Wilf,' approved Madge. 'As long as you don't go back before you're properly recovered. You did give us a scare I must admit. We don't want any more of those.'

'Still, all's well that ends well,' he said, touched by her concern. 'I'm still around to tell the tale and clutter up your living room.'

'You're not cluttering it up. You're one of the family, Wilf,' said Madge, completely unaware of the potency of her words. 'We miss you when you're not here.'

'That's nice of you, Madge,' said Wilf and no one noticed a look pass between him and Nora.

Soon after that Esme came in from school full of energy and chatter and hungry as usual. She was given bread and fish paste and a fruitless rock cake and a glass of milk. When she said she was gong out to play, her mother reminded her that it was Friday and therefore bath night and she would have to come in early.

'Can I have a bit more water in my bath tonight please, Mum?' she asked.

'No, sorry love, you can't,' said Mollie. 'Five inches is the most we're allowed. Government orders.'

'How would they know?'

'They wouldn't but I would so it will be five inches,' said Mollie. 'But after the war when things get back to normal, you can have as much hot water as you like and even some soapy bubbles.'

'Cor, really?

'Yes really,' said Mollie, reminded of the ordinary pleasures this generation of children were missing. 'I certainly hope so anyway.'

'There's a girl in my class called Patsy and her mum lets her have as much bath water as she likes,' announced Esme.

'I'm sure she doesn't, dear,' said Madge. 'She wouldn't do that.'

'Patsy says she does anyway,' insisted Esme. 'She has lots more things than me. She's got a sister, two grandmas and three granddads.'

'She can't have three granddads, Esme,' said Mollie, smiling. 'Even Patsy can't manage that.'

'She has,' said Esme ardently. 'She has her mum's dad, her dad's dad and one of their fathers.'

'Oh, that's her great-granddad,' said Mollie.

'That's right,' said Esme. 'But it's still three granddads and I only have one because I don't know the other one.'

'Well I can promise you sweets and soapy bubbles after the war but a grandfather is beyond me I'm afraid.' It had saddened Mollie that Syd's parents had chosen not to take any part in their granddaughter's life after Syd died. They'd eventually left the area and hadn't kept in touch.

'Still, I'm better at handstands and cartwheels than Patsy,' Esme chirped. 'And she can't even do a back bend at all. Miss says I'm very good at gym and she doesn't say it to her.'

'There you are then,' said Mollie. 'You have a gift and that's much better than more water in the bath and lots of granddads.'

There was a communal chuckle. Esme smiled but she didn't really see the funny side.

'You get your talent for gym from your mum,' said Madge. 'She's always been good at that sort of thing. Well, you know about it because you go to her Saturday morning class.'

'I want to be a gym teacher when I grow up,' said Esme. 'If I can't be a ballet dancer that is.'

'Ooh, big ambitions for a little girl,' said Nora, who couldn't help reflecting on the origin of the athletic inclinations that came from a couple of generations back.

'Can I go out to play now, please Mum?' asked Esme.

'Yes, off you go, but you're not to go out of range of this house and you are to come straight in if the siren goes.'

'Yeah all right.'

'And you are to come right away when I call you,' said Mollie. 'No making a fuss and begging me for more time to finish your game. Promise?'

'I promise,' she said and hurried out of the door leaving everyone in the room smiling.

'I know it must be hard for you, Wilf, but you mustn't take anything Esme says too seriously,' said Nora the next morning when she was at Wilf's place. 'She's just a little girl. Having fewer granddads than the child at school is just like having fewer marbles or spinning tops. It's a competitive thing. She'll have forgotten about it by now and be on about something else. It's the way kids are.'

'She will have forgotten it. I won't,' he said.

'Look. How can we tell a child that a man she knows as a family friend is actually her grandfather? Even if we were to tell Madge and Mollie we'd have to leave it to Mollie to decide when she wants her daughter to know.'

'My brain tells me you're right, my heart says otherwise,' he said. 'But I'll respect your wishes and keep quiet.'

'It's just a word anyway,' she said, but she knew it was much more than that to him. 'You wouldn't see any more of her if the truth came out would you?'

'Probably not.'

'So let's try and live with it,' suggested Nora but she was beginning to feel really bad about denying him the right to make himself known to his descendants. She tried to tell herself it was nothing more than a biological hiccup caused by the recklessness of youth. But in her heart she knew that Madge had been conceived out of love. Fate had parted her and Wilf and brought them back together again after all those years for a reason. They were meant to be together. She didn't need to ask Wilf if he shared her feelings. It was all there in the way he was with her.

But for all that, she still couldn't face the thought of the family knowing the truth. She'd never be able to look them in the eye again if they knew that she'd committed a girl's ultimate sin.

★ ★ ★

367

It was an autumn night and Mollie was on a train with a group of keep-fitters. They were on their way home from a show in which they had taken part at a convalescent home for servicemen just outside Harrow. It had been a long walk to and from the station and several changes on the tube with long delays. But they were well on their way now.

There was a lot of chatter among the women about the show and how they thought it had gone

'You're quiet tonight, Mollie,' said Eileen, who was sitting next to Mollie. 'That isn't like you. Are you all right?'

'Yeah, I'm fine,' fibbed Mollie; it had actually been the most awful day for her. 'I'm listening to you lot doing the usual post-mortem on the show.'

'I was so busy looking at the soldiers I missed a step or two,' said someone.

'I know you did,' said another. 'You nearly put me off a couple of times.'

'I think we did all right though,' decided Eileen. 'The boys seemed to like it anyway.'

'I think they probably like the fact that we were showing plenty of leg in our black pants.'

'They probably enjoyed the chorus girls better. They are more glamorous than us in their fishnet tights and clingy costumes.'

'I don't know so much about that,' said one of the women. 'I got my share of looks when we came off stage.'

'I thought the other performers were really good, especially as they are all amateurs,' said Eileen. 'But the stars tonight for me were our lovely soldiers. Some of them were very badly wounded but they entered into the spirit and were generous with their applause even though it'll take a lot more than entertainment from people like us to make them feel better.'

'My heart goes out to them, it really does,' said one of the team. 'I mean, we think we are hard done by with the doodlebugs and the rationing but we've got it easy compared to the fighting troops.'

They were all in agreement about this and busy discussing it when the train slowed down, juddered then stopped which wasn't unusual; the tube drivers often had to wait a while for technical reasons.

'I hope we're not going to be held up for long,' said Eileen. 'I'll miss my last bus if we are.'

'I'm sure the train will move in a minute – they usually do,' said Mollie, forcing herself to take an interest. 'As we were just saying about the troops, a train delay is nothing compared to what they've been through.'

Everyone agreed about that and tried to be patient as the train remained stationary. The guard came into the carriage with the news that there was a delay due to an explosion on the overground part of the system. It wasn't actually this line that was damaged but trains were being diverted, which was causing problems.

'Still, I suppose we're in the safest place if there's a raid on,' said one of Mollie's group after the guard had moved on to the next carriage, leaving them the news that he would keep them informed about progress.

There was a sudden disturbance further along the carriage. A woman was screaming for help.

'I'm suffocating,' she said, clawing at the doors. 'I have to get out. Please help me, someone.'

Mollie got to her feet and hurried to the woman, who appeared to be travelling alone. 'Don't worry; you won't suffocate even though you feel as though you will. It's just a feeling.'

'You don't understand,' she said, gasping for breath. 'I need air.'

'You'll be all right, I promise.' Mollie took her arm and could feel her trembling. 'Why don't you come and sit with us.'

The passenger nodded and allowed Mollie to lead her along the carriage to her friends where Mollie offered her her seat. 'How about a song to take your mind off it?'

The woman, who was middle-aged, was clearly suffering. She was ashen-faced, her skin suffused with sweat, and she was trembling all over and panting. 'I can't breathe, let alone sing,' she said, looking stricken.

'You can listen to us then,' said Mollie and turning to her friends and the other passengers launched into 'You Are My Sunshine'.

It was a slow start but gradually people began to join in and those who didn't seemed to enjoy listening. The passenger with claustrophobia still looked pale and worried but she was calmer. They got through a lot of songs because it was more than an hour before the train moved by which time the passenger's panic attack had done its worst and burned itself out.

When they finally emerged from the station into the blackout and all went their separate ways, Molly's thoughts turned back to her own problems and her spirits took a dive. It had been the most vile day and she'd be glad to crawl into bed and pull the covers over her head.

When she got home she was surprised to find everybody up as it was almost midnight.

'The windows have been blown out by a damned doodlebug,' her mother informed her, meeting her in the hall as soon as she heard the key in the door.

'Oh Mum,' gasped Mollie. 'Is anyone hurt? Esme . . .?'

'She's fine. We're all are and we've managed to keep the draughts out with newspaper and an old sheet inside the blackout curtains,' said her mother. 'Luckily it isn't all of them; just the back of the house.'

'We'll need to get on to the bomb damage people first thing tomorrow,' said Len. 'But I reckon we'll have to wait even for a temporary repair; they're bound to be snowed under because of the bombings.'

'We made a pot of tea to cheer ourselves up,' said Nora, appearing in a dressing gown and hairnet. 'It's still warm so shall I pour you one, Mollie?'

'Yes please, Gran.'

She went into the living room to see Esme sitting in an armchair looking pleased with herself. Her daughter seemed very precious and Mollie held her tight.

'Isn't it exciting, Mum?' she said when Mollie drew back. 'I bet Patsy has never had her windows blown out. You wait till I tell her at school tomorrow. She'll be green with envy.'

'That isn't nice, Esme,' admonished Mollie but it was only a perfunctory objection. Her daughter had been brought up in war and children boasting about bomb damage was no different to collecting shrapnel. They made playthings and competitions from what they knew.

'Patsy would boast if she'd had it,' claimed Esme.

'That doesn't mean you should do the same,' said Mollie wearily. 'Anyway it's time you went back to bed.'

'Can I wait until you've had your tea? Then you can tuck me in. Please?'

As a responsible parent she thought she should probably take her up to bed right away as it was late but it had been one hell of a day and she was desperate for a cuppa so she said, 'All right then but straight to bed when I've drunk my tea. No messing about. You need your sleep.'

'All right, Mum,' she agreed, smiling.

Mollie sipped her tea, her mouth parched as it had been all day.

Mollie tucked her daughter into bed gently, kissed her goodnight, then turned the light off but left the door open slightly so that she could see from the landing light to get undressed. The others had all gone back to bed now so when Mollie had been to the bathroom to wash she climbed into bed and pulled the covers up around her.

Now there were no diversions from what had been weighing her down all day; no job to get on with or child to look after, no show to do or train passengers to cheer up. Just her and the thoughts that had been tormenting her ever since she had met the postman at the gate that morning on her way to work and torn open the envelope containing the letter from Grant excitedly. She was relieved to have heard from him at last.

As she read the words her energy was drained away. Certain sentences screamed out at her:

> I'm sorry to be saying this and the last thing I want to do is hurt you but I don't feel able to settle down, with you or anyone, so I must ask you to consider our relationship at an end and feel free to go out with other men. I wish you well in the future, Mollie, and hope that Esme and the rest of the family are well.
> All the best, Grant

Going over it in her mind now in bed, all the misery and sense of rejection that had haunted her all day as she went about her business culminated in violent rage. Bloody cheek, how dare he tamper with her feelings so cruelly? It wasn't right. The anger burned itself out quite soon and left her aching emotionally. It cut so deep it was almost physical. She wanted to scream but curled up into a ball and wept quietly so as not to disturb her daughter, who was sleeping peacefully at the other side of the bed.

Chapter Sixteen

'Can you honestly, hand on heart, tell me that you are not just the tiniest bit pleased that Grant has given me the push?' Mollie asked of Cora on the following Sunday afternoon when the two women met in Hyde Park with the children. Mollie was still feeling raw from the effects of the letter but forced herself to talk about it in the hope that facing up to it might help to ease the pain. She was not being spiteful in asking the question; just curious. Such an emotion on Cora's part would be perfectly understandable.

'I certainly can say that, yes, Mollie. Maybe I was a bit jealous when you first told me that the two of you had got together; not because I wanted Grant for myself but because you had someone and I didn't,' she admitted. 'But I surprised myself by getting over it quickly and I can truthfully tell you that I really am sorry that it didn't work out for you.'

'Thanks, Cora.' Mollie thought for a moment. 'It didn't not work out exactly. How could anything go wrong between us when I haven't seen the man for ages? We were getting on like a house on fire when I last saw him which is why it's such a shock.'

'Mm,' pondered Cora. 'It isn't like Grant at all. He's fiercely loyal and hates to hurt anyone unnecessarily.'

'That's the impression I had,' said Mollie. 'I'm wondering if he's met someone else. That's the most common reason for this sort of thing.'

'I suppose it's possible but not very likely,' opined Cora. 'Grant is the type who wouldn't get involved if he's already with someone.' She mulled it over. 'He is a man, though, and only human.'

'Oh well, all the discussion in the world isn't going to change anything,' said Mollie. 'He doesn't want to be with me and I have to accept that.'

There was a sudden interruption. 'Mum, can James and I have somethin' to eat,' asked Esme, running up to the bench where the two women were sitting with the boy close behind her. 'We're starvin' hungry.'

'You can't possibly be starving because you had your dinner before we came out but I've got some apples here,' said Mollie, rummaging in her bag. 'Your gran always stores them at this time of the year for Christmas and she let me have a few before she put the box up in the loft.'

All four of them munched into the sharp tangy taste of a Cox's Orange Pippin.

'We'll go and see if we can get a wartime bun and a cup of tea a bit later on,' suggested Cora. 'We'll probably have to queue for ages but that doesn't matter.'

It was a glorious day with a low autumn sun shining from a hazy blue sky, the trees ablaze with colours as the leaves began to turn, the scent of the season so sweet you could almost taste it. Being a Sunday afternoon there were people in the park even though the doodlebugs were still making their presence felt from time to time. Most of the benches were occupied; there was a steady stream of strollers and children playing on the grass.

The general response to the wail of the siren was to glance up at the sky until the missile came into view then carry on regardless when it had passed over.

'Have you had many of the dratted things over your way?' Cora enquired.

'Not too many but enough,' replied Molly. 'We had our windows blown out a few nights ago and there are one or two bomb-damaged houses close by but no one we know has been killed, or even hurt.'

'Have you thought of having Esme evacuated?'

'That is my daily dilemma,' Mollie confessed. 'Should I send her or shouldn't I? I vowed at the beginning of the war that I wouldn't send her away no matter what. But these damned flying bombs are still around so I wonder if I should. I keep thinking they'll stop soon but they don't seem to be easing up at all.'

'Well, James is staying put with Auntie and me no matter what anyone says,' said Cora. 'He's too little to go away.'

The All Clear sounded and a sense of relief was noticeable in the air, though people were keen not to show it. Although the populace took these robot bombs in their stride, no one was in any doubt as to how lethal they were.

'Come on, kids, let's have a game of hide-and-seek,' suggested Mollie with a heartiness she wasn't actually feeling. 'Then we'll go and see if we can find a cup of tea and a bun. You two go and hide and we'll come and find you.'

Watching Esme take James's hand then turn towards him and say something, probably using her seniority and issuing orders, Mollie couldn't help noticing the striking resemblance between them and thought that they could easily be taken for brother and sister. They were so achingly lovely together it saddened Mollie that they were cousins but that circumstances prevented them from knowing the fact.

'How is Cora keeping these days?' Madge asked Mollie when she got home.

'She's very well,' replied Mollie.

'It's about time she came to see us,' stated Nora. 'We haven't seen her for years. I know the two of you lost touch for a long time but now that you see each other again we'd like to see something of her too.'

'We've never even set eyes on her little boy,' added Madge.

'She lives at a bit of a distance,' Mollie said. 'So it's easier for us both to meet in the West End. She goes out to work now too so she doesn't have so much time as she used to.'

'Oh well, give her our love when you next see her and tell her we'd love to see that boy of hers before he starts work,' said Nora drily.

'I'll tell her,' said Mollie, evoking a mental image of Esme and James together in the park, looking so much alike; she was even more convinced that if the family saw him they would immediately see the likeness.

Looking back, it was astonishing that they had known nothing of the dramas unfolding so close to home a few years ago. If they saw James the secret would surely come out so she couldn't take the risk until Geoff was put in the picture and could tell them himself, if that was what he chose to do.

When the government finally admitted to the public that the new crop of explosions in and around London were being caused by another German missile called the V2 which was preceded by no warning and exploded after a flash of light causing even more extensive damage and loss of life than the earlier robots, Mollie finally decided she would have to send Esme away to safety.

The little girl thought it was great fun to be embarking on an adventure in the country with her pals from school. It was Mollie and the other Potts women who were in tears after seeing her off.

Without her daughter's cheerful and vibrant presence and no letters from Grant to look forward to, life felt bleak indeed for Mollie. After the Second Front in June, hopes of peace had been high. But here they were with Christmas approaching and they still had bombs raining down, even more severe rationing, cold weather and a coal shortage.

Mollie thanked God for her classes which were still her escape and salvation. They blotted everything else out while in progress and lifted her spirits for quite a while afterwards. She was delighted also to be invited to take part with her team in a few special Christmas shows that were being put on by the concert party they worked with occasionally, at various hospitals and convalescent homes.

The first of these performances was on a Saturday afternoon in a mansion that had been converted into a military hospital just outside Richmond. Seeing the effort that had been made with paper chains, tinsel and a Christmas tree, the latter apparently having been donated by the Americans, Mollie couldn't help but cast her troubles aside and enter into the spirit wholeheartedly. The show was held in the dayroom, a large lounge with big sash windows and endless wood panelling. Some of the patients had had their beds wheeled in for the show; there were a few in wheelchairs and the others sitting in rows.

Seeing the condition of some of them, Mollie wondered how she'd ever had the nerve to complain about being cold and hungry. At least she had her body intact; many of these poor souls had terrible injuries yet they could still smile and enthuse about the entertainment.

Everyone was in high spirits as the show opened with some dancing girls, then a comedian and female singer and a man playing the accordion.

The keep-fit item was scheduled to take the show into the interval and Mollie and her team went on full of heart, the music provided on this occasion by the concert party pianist. The secret to staying in step was to concentrate totally on what had been learned and rehearsed and not be distracted.

Mollie's mistake was to glance at the audience who were in full view, this not being a theatre with stage lights and the facility to black out those watching. That was when it all went hideously wrong for her. She lost her concentration and her place in the routine. Her feet took on a life of their own and all because of the person she had seen in the audience. Sitting towards the back was Grant Parker, looking different but unmistakably him. He was a patient here in this hospital!

'Sorry everyone, to have messed up and put you all off,' Mollie apologised to the team as soon as they came off stage, she having finally managed to get back into step. 'I'll explain later. But now I have to see someone.'

Slipping her coat on over her costume, she hurried in search of him. Patients and performers were mingling as they took refreshments but there was no sign of Grant. Desperate to speak to him she asked a nurse where he might be, telling her that she was an old friend.

'He'll be here somewhere,' said the nurse, looking

into the gathering. 'If he isn't around here he must have gone back to the ward which means he wants to be left alone.' She gave Mollie a close look. 'These men have been through an awful lot and they don't always feel sociable. The very least we can do for them is to respect that.'

'Yes, of course,' said Mollie. 'What is the usual visiting time for tomorrow?'

'Three until five tomorrow as it's Sunday.'

'Thank you,' said Mollie and hurried back to join her friends who were mingling with the patients.

After lunch the next day Mollie set off on her bike to the hospital. Because she'd needed to get Esme minded she'd felt obliged to tell the family about seeing Grant, which she would rather not have done at this stage, but that was how it was when you lived within a family. They gave her a home and support with Esme so the least she could do was let them know what was going on in her life. They'd been most concerned about Grant.

'The poor man,' her mother had said. 'Of course you must go and see him. Esme will be fine with us. We'll let you off the washing-up too.'

Nothing, as far as she and Esme were concerned, was ever too much trouble, and Mollie never stopped being grateful to them. An inevitable lack of privacy was a small price to pay.

★ ★ ★

When she arrived at the hospital she was told that Grant wasn't seeing visitors.

'But I've come all this way,' Mollie told the nurse at the reception desk. 'I really am ever so keen to see him.'

'I'm very sorry,' said the nurse. 'But those are his instructions.'

'I won't stay long, I promise,' said Mollie. 'I'm a really close friend of his.'

The nurse shook her head.

'Just five minutes, please,' begged Mollie.

The nurse leaned towards her and said in a confidential manner, 'If I were to get distracted in some way and didn't notice you going past me, he's in Howard Ward, second on the left down the corridor.'

'Thank you,' Mollie whispered to the nurse's back as she ostensibly busied herself with some files.

Wearing a dark blue dressing gown, he was sitting on a chair beside his bed reading a book. There were only a few men in the ward, she assumed because those who were able were seeing their visitors in the dayroom. He looked up as she approached, his expression one of shock.

'Mollie,' he said. 'I gave the nurse instructions. I'm not seeing anyone.'

'I managed to slip past the nurse so don't be angry with her,' she said, her gaze drawn towards one side of his neck which was distorted by ugly red scarring. Her heart went out to him but she deemed it wise to make no comment. 'My fault not hers. I was . . . well, just really desperate to see you once I realised that you were here.'

'It's good of you to come but I'm not feeling very sociable,' he told her.

'It's just me you don't want to see, I think, not visitors in general?' she suggested. 'You knew I'd spotted you last night during the show, despite hiding yourself away at the back, and you must have guessed I would come.'

'Not much point denying it, I suppose,' he said.

'Not really,' she said. 'You can imagine the shock I had seeing you so unexpectedly.'

'Sorry.'

'No need to apologise,' she said, trying to avoid the unsightly scarring but finding herself drawn to it. 'So how are you, or is that a silly question?'

'I'm doing all right, considering,' he said. 'They are very good to us here.'

'I'm pleased about that.' She cleared her throat nervously. 'The reason I am here, as well as wanting to know how you are obviously, is because I want to know why you broke up with me. I think I deserve that much.'

'It's as I said in the letter . . .'

'If that really is the reason, I will leave now and you'll never hear from me again. But I find that hard to believe; I mean you don't just fall out of love with someone when you haven't even seen them to feel bored or irritated by them, unless of course you have met someone else.'

'There's no one else.'

'Oh Grant, I was so hurt when I read that letter,' she blurted out emotionally.

383

He looked sheepish but didn't reply

'I was absolutely devastated because we'd been so happy together,' she said. 'What makes you think you can break my heart without a second thought and not give a decent explanation? Am I so worthless you think I can be discarded at will?'

'Don't be ridiculous,' he said, looking shocked by her interpretation of the event. 'Surely you must know that isn't true.'

'How am I supposed to know when you send me such an awful letter?'

'Was it that bad?'

'It was horrible.' She gave him a studious look. 'So, since I am here, please tell me why I was given my marching orders.'

'As you are here I should have thought it was obvious,' he said, turning slightly and pointing to his neck. 'The burns go right down the side of my body and the neck is the least unsightly part. I don't like to look at it myself so I certainly wouldn't want to inflict it on anyone else.'

'What happened?'

'My plane was hit and burst into flames.'

'Oh Grant, that's terrible.'

'Yes, it wasn't an experience I'd like to repeat but I'm luckier that many of the chaps who didn't make it.'

'How did you survive a thing like that?'

'I managed to parachute into the sea and was eventually picked up.'

'Eventually. Does that mean you were in the water for a long time?' she asked.

'It felt like forever.'

'It must have been awful.' She gave him a studious look, seeing the dark shadows under his eyes that seemed to have lost all their sparkle. 'So you ended it with me just because of your injuries?'

He lowered his dressing gown to reveal more of the burns. 'Do you think I want you to have to look at that every time I take my shirt off, to have to touch it when we make love?'

Mollie had instinctively given a sharp intake of breath and regretted it. 'Oh Grant,' she said again with tears in her eyes. 'I'm so sorry.'

'You're sorry.' His voice was hoarse. 'That is precisely my point. Do you think any man wants pity from the woman he loves?'

'No of course not,' she said. 'It was an instinctive human reaction, I suppose.'

'Exactly,' he said. 'You'd either be revolted by it or sorry for me and I don't want either of those things. That's why I ended it between us.'

'Grant,' she began in a gentle tone. 'I don't know how I will cope with your injuries because I have never experienced anything similar so have never been tested. But I know that I still love you so please will you give me a chance to try?'

'You're sorry for me.'

'Of course I am, since I'm not made of stone, but that doesn't mean I don't still love and fancy you like mad.'

'Oh,' he said and the bleakness in his eyes lessened

385

slightly. She knew she had done the right thing in mentioning the physical aspect.

'Do you think an injury would make you less desirable to me?' she asked.

'Well, yes . . . it must do, surely.'

'It doesn't, not for me anyway. I reacted when I first saw the burns, of course, but I'll soon get used to them,' she said. 'So can we forget all about the letter and face this thing together?'

'If you're sure.'

She leaned over and kissed him in the way that a lover would. 'Has that convinced you?' she asked.

He smiled and the effect on her was as devastating as it ever was. 'I'm so pleased you came to see me, Mollie. Thank you,' he said. 'I've missed you so much.'

'Likewise,' she said softly.

For the rest of the visit they talked about other things though he did tell her that he was being moved the next day to a special burns unit somewhere in Sussex where they carried out surgery on burns victims.

'The treatment is quite new and experimental apparently but they think I might be suitable and it could improve the scarring to a certain extent,' he said. 'Some poor devils got their faces burned off. They can reconstruct them with plastic surgery, though it takes many operations. Mine is nothing compared to theirs.'

'I'll come to visit.'

'No. It's a long way so don't even think about it,'

he said firmly. 'We'll keep in touch by letter. I'll be there for a while too because it's a complicated procedure and the recovery takes a long time. So I'll see you when I get back. Now that we are together again it will be bearable and we'll have letters to look forward to.'

'If you're sure, we'll do it that way then.'

'Good, that's settled so let's move on to other things,' he said. 'How is Esme?'

She made a sad face. 'I don't really know because she's away in Somerset. When the V2s started coming over I felt I must have her evacuated. But I'm bringing her home for Christmas. As soon as the schools break up I'm off to the country to get her. It would break her heart to be away from home at Christmas, though we'll have our work cut out trying to make things festive with everything being so short but I'm sure we'll manage somehow. Mum is a whizz at creating something nice out of anything she can get hold of.'

'I'm sure.'

'Another wartime Christmas eh,' she said regretfully. 'We really did think there would be peace by now.'

'I know it's a cliché but, from what I've heard on the news, it really won't be long now,' he said.

Cycling home in the dark, though some lighting was permitted now that the blackout restrictions had been modified and she could have her bicycle lamp facing ahead instead of down, Mollie was both happy and apprehensive. While she was ecstatic to have Grant back in her life, at the same time she knew that the immediate future for them wasn't going to be easy. Grant was in physical pain and emotionally fragile. The last thing he wanted was sympathy and that was the natural emotion his condition evoked at the moment. So she was going to need lashings of patience and a hearty sense of humour until his health improved.

More than anything she wanted it to work out for them. She hoped she had it in her to do what was right and necessary over the next few months.

After Mollie had gone, Grant's thoughts were all of her and he relived the visit over and over again in his mind, such was his joy at having her back in his life. She was lovely inside and out and he felt undeserving of her. It had been different before the burns; he'd felt worthy of her then and confident he could keep her. Now he was insecure and moody. It wasn't self-pity exactly; more a feeling of inferiority. He certainly didn't feel able to ask her to marry him at the moment and that was what he wanted most.

But he must make an effort to be more positive and less sensitive or he really would lose her. There were many people here much worse off than he was and Charlie in the next bed was one of them. He'd lost both legs in an explosion during the Allied invasion of Europe. Grant went over to his bed.

'How's it going, Chas?' he asked.

'Not so bad, mate,' he replied, predictably cheerful. 'How's yourself?'

'Pretty good as it happens,' replied Grant, smiling.

'I thought you might be,' said Charlie. 'After having had such a gorgeous visitor.'

The best part about Christmas for Mollie this year was having Esme home. Her youthful exuberance filled the house and was a tonic to them all. She did more to create the Christmas spirit than any amount of tinsel or alcohol ever could. With a great deal of hard work and ingenuity they managed to make things festive. Presents were queued for or homemade and nobody asked what was in the Yuletide food. They were all too glad to have it to bother about such trivialities as the content.

The windows still hadn't been properly fixed so the house was cold and draughty, but they had managed to get some coal and they had a fire, which was blissful. One decision Mollie did make over the holiday was not to send Esme back to the country. There were still a few rockets about but the general opinion was that the war was drawing to a close so she was to stay home with the family where she belonged.

When news came through in March that Montgomery's forces had crossed the Rhine, people really began to believe that the war was coming to an end and when in April the Americans and Russians, advancing from different directions, joined together and cut Germany in two, there was jubilation on the home front. It still wasn't quite over, but almost.

Everyday life went on. Mollie still worked and took her classes. Grant came home from hospital after surgery with news that the treatment had been a success. There was an improvement in the scarring. It was still quite noticeable but seemed slightly less ugly and easier for Mollie to look at, though she would never tell him she had found it difficult at first.

'It's amazing what can be done these days,' he said. 'One chap is having his face rebuilt. It will take lots of operations and it will never be quite the same as the original but there's a noticeable improvement already. It's all due to a surgeon who is a pioneer in this field. Burns victims were disfigured for life and discarded until quite recently. I'm lucky that the flames missed my face.'

'Yes, I suppose you are.' It wasn't easy to see anything lucky in having burns covering so much of his body but she knew what he meant.

'I couldn't have got through it without you,' he told her. 'Getting your letters, knowing that you would be there when I came home gave me confidence.'

'You would have coped anyway,' she told him. 'I haven't done anything special.'

But she knew in her heart that she had come through some sort of a test on the winning side. There was no romance for Mollie in watching someone she loved suffer and having to learn to love an ugly scar. But it didn't trouble her at all now; it was simply a part of him.

When on VE Day, with a sea of Union Jacks waving in Trafalgar Square, he asked her to marry him, her answer was a resounding yes but she did ask if they could wait for the wedding until her brother Geoff came home.

'Absolutely.' He beamed. 'I'll probably be demobbed by then too.'

She couldn't throw her arms around him because his wounds were still a little sore but she did embrace him carefully and seal their future together with a kiss. They weren't completely out of the woods but they had come through the worst times and the war was over so the future was bright.

Cora took James into central London to join in the celebrations because it was an historic occasion and she wanted him to be able to say he had been there. But although the atmosphere was unbelievable and the outpouring of joy unlike anything she had ever experienced before, she felt horribly lonely all day.

Her aunt had gone with them but found the crowds too much and James got overexcited and tired after a while so Cora was glad to come home and join in the local celebrations. At five years old James was a darling boy. With a thatch of curly hair and round brown eyes he was a good-looking child like his cousin Esme. He had inherited his father's gentle nature too; Cora could never see anything of herself in him, except occasionally perhaps when he wanted his own way about something and really dug his heels in. Then she knew he had inherited something from her. She adored him and he was her raison d'être.

Loneliness was inevitable, she supposed, with no partner in her life. She was still a young woman and needed more than the love of a child. Many women had lost their men to the war but plenty would be welcoming them home. Mollie and Grant were back together now too. But for Cora there had been no one since Geoff. Her enthusiastic attitude towards his homecoming when she had talked of telling him about James and trying to get him back had faded as the event became a distinct possibility.

He needed to know about James, of course, but her confidence about trying to persuade Geoff to have her back had drained away. The arrogant woman she had been when she had been married to Grant had vanished along with the money and status that came from being a successful businessman's wife, at least when it came to herself though she would stand up to anyone on her son's behalf. She was all he had, at the moment anyway. But she was much more cautious about approaching Geoff now. It was a very delicate matter.

After she tucked James up in bed and VE Day drew to a close she went to the window and looked out at the peaceful sky, no longer afraid to let the light be seen. Nothing could spoil the joy of knowing that there would be no more bombs and that her boy would grow up in peace.

She had a sudden urge to see Mollie and wished she lived nearer so that they could meet more often. But even if there were any places available to rent in this terrible housing shortage she couldn't afford one. The only reason she could manage to feed and clothe James and herself on a shop girl's wages was because her aunt didn't charge her rent because she owned the house and therefore had no rent to pay herself.

Cora shared all the household expenses with her aunt; without rent to pay every week she could manage, and she was very grateful. But a move back to her hometown was what she really wanted. Still, the war was over so life would be better whatever her personal circumstances.

She moved away from the window and listened to James's even breathing indicating that he was already asleep. It had been an exciting day for him, she thought fondly, as she left the room and went downstairs to join her aunt.

'No, I don't feel in the least bit upset about you and Grant being engaged,' said Cora in reply to Mollie's question one fine day in July when the two friends met as usual at Marble Arch and headed for the park with the children. 'Why would I when I never loved him myself. Anyway I'm used to the idea of the two of you being together now; have been for ages. I'm glad one of us is fixed up in that direction. How is he now?'

'He's coming along really well now,' replied Mollie. 'He's demobbed so he's going back to work at the store soon. The surgeon who did his operation thinks his patients should get back to work as soon as they feel able because it's good for their morale. During the war some of the burns victims went to work in the RAF offices and control rooms between operations if they had to have more than one.'

'Good, I'm glad he's all right,' said Cora, holding James's hand tightly as they crossed the busy road. 'Any news of Geoff?'

'No. We've put a welcome home banner up but it's a case of we'll expect him when we see him, I think,' she said. 'It will take a long time for the military to get all the boys home so we'll have to be patient.'

'That applies to everything I reckon,' said Cora. 'Rationing is worse than ever and they say it will be years before it finishes altogether.'

'Yeah, I heard that too,' said Mollie. 'It's the same with building work and repairs. Everything is very shabby but since there are all sorts of restrictions we'll just have to live with it. We've all looked forward to the end of the war for so long, I suppose we had the idea that everything would be back to normal right away.'

'Still, there are no more bombs and that's enough to keep us happy,' said Cora.

'Exactly,' agreed Mollie.

They entered the park and strolled for a while then sat down on a bench while the children went to play on the grass, the sun spreading its light over everything.

'I was thinking, Mollie, about Geoff,' began Cora cautiously. 'I'm wondering if it might be better for you to tell him about James when you think the time is right.

It's too important to be done by letter and my turning up at the house and blurting it out might be a bit much for a man who has been a prisoner of war for five years.'

'Yes, perhaps it might be best if I break it to him,' said Mollie. 'He'll know very soon that you and Grant split up because of my engagement to Grant so I'll probably tell him about James sooner rather than later.'

'Oh dear. I feel really nervous,' admitted Cora. 'I so want him to be a part of James's life but I'm afraid to get my hopes up.'

'We'll just have to wait and see,' said Mollie. 'But it could be months yet. I should try and put it out of your mind.'

'Easier said than done,' said Cora with a wry grin.

One evening in November Mollie was rinsing the shampoo out of her hair with a cup at the kitchen sink when she heard screams coming from the other part of the house. The kitchen door was closed to try to lessen the draughts so the noise was muted. As the screams died away her mother was shouting for Mollie come quick.

'What the matter now,' she muttered under her breath as she wrapped a towel around her head and rushed into the living room to find her mother and her gran crying and her father not far off.

'He's here, he's home at last,' said her mother through her tears.

At first sight of her brother Mollie didn't recognise him. Five years older and a whole lot thinner, his eyes seemed to bulge in his slender face. But then he smiled and said, 'Hello, sis,' and she was hugging him and they were all crying.

Wondering what the fuss was all about Esme got out of bed and came downstairs.

'It's your Uncle Geoff, Esme,' said Mollie. 'He's home.'

It was his turn to look puzzled. His niece had been a cute little five year old when he'd last seen her; now she was a leggy young girl of ten.

'Hello, Uncle Geoff,' she said politely and Mollie was proud of her lovely manners. 'Welcome home. I helped the others to make the banner.'

'Thank you, young lady,' he said. 'You've grown up so much I don't know whether to hug you or shake your hand.'

He settled on a hug anyway and everyone was talking at once. Len went to the off-licence to get what he could in the way of bottles and there was a party feel to the evening. Naturally the subject of Mollie's engagement came up.

'Grant Parker,' Geoff said, astounded.

'He and Cora got divorced years ago,' explained Madge.

'Oh really. Well, congratulations, sis,' he said. Mollie could see that he was shocked and guessed he was wondering about the details but the conversation moved on to other things. Geoff was very keen to know all the home news although not so eager to talk about what had happened to him.

'You're so thin, son,' said Madge with typical motherly concern.

'I'm not so much now, am I?' said Geoff. 'The army have been feeding us up ever since we got out.'

'Gawd knows what you were like before then,' she said.

'I'm glad you didn't see me like that but it's all water under the bridge, Mum,' he said. 'The war is over. Time to look forward. Not back.'

'That's the spirit,' said Mollie.

Mollie and her mother used the week's cheese ration to make sandwiches and they all had a glass or two to drink and chatted until Esme almost fell asleep in the chair and was helped up to bed by her mother. Gran said she was off to bed, Madge and Len soon following her.

'It's just like old times, Geoff, you and me having a natter after everyone else has gone to bed,' said Mollie. 'I can't tell you how much I've missed you.'

'Likewise.'

'Why didn't you write?'

'I did.'

'We didn't get one letter.'

'I'm not surprised,' he said. 'We suspected that our mail never even left the camp. They probably burned it to save the bother of sending it or were scared something might get out about their treatment of us POWs. But that's enough about that. I'm home and I want to put all that behind me.'

'Fair enough.'

'So you and Grant Parker,' he said. 'How on earth did that come about?'

She knew now was the time for whole story to be told. 'After you and Cora split up, she discovered that she was pregnant with your child,' she began. 'That was the final nail in the coffin for that marriage. Grant divorced her on grounds of adultery and they went their separate ways. I knew nothing about it until I ran into him unexpectedly years later and he told me. He and I hit it off and one thing led to another.'

'And Cora?'

'She and her little boy James live with her aunt out at Ruislip,' Mollie told him. 'She works in a grocery shop. She needs an income with no husband to support her and the boy. He's five now.'

'Blimey, Mollie,' said Geoff. 'Things have changed around here. Me a dad. That's a turn-up for the books.'

'A ghastly shock or a nice surprise?' she asked.

'I don't know yet,' he said. 'It hasn't properly sunk in.' He thought for a moment. 'Why didn't she let me know?'

'That's what I asked her when I met up with her again after a break of several years. She said she didn't think it was appropriate after the bitterness of your break-up; it could have seemed as though she wanted financial support. War had broken out anyway and she knew you'd be away. So she set about bringing him up on her own and she's making a really good job of it.'

'That doesn't sound like the Cora I remember, the woman who was so spoiled she let me down because I didn't have the money to keep her in luxury.'

'She's changed, Geoff; she's had to with no husband to support her.'

'People don't really change.'

'They do if their circumstances demand it and they have no other choice but to adapt,' said Mollie. 'I'm not saying she wouldn't sometimes like all the trappings of her other life back, that's only natural, but she's got used to a simpler life and she's a good mum to James.'

'Well well. Who would have thought it?'

'Because of the situation between the two of you and your having been away for so long, she asked me to tell you about James so that you can think about it in your own time with no pressure,' Mollie explained. 'And she says you are welcome to be involved in his life as much as you like but only if you want to be. She'll leave it to you to decide.'

Up went his brows. 'She really must have changed,' he said. 'That's very decent of her.'

'Yes, it is,' she agreed. 'James is the image of you, Geoff. So much so that I haven't dared let Cora bring him here in case Mum and Dad see the likeness and put two and two together. It will be your decision if you tell them they have a grandson. I didn't want to pre-empt that.'

'Slow down, sis. I haven't got used to the idea of being a dad yet, let alone telling Mum and Dad that I have provided them with a grandson.'

'Take your time to think about it and I'll give you Cora's address if you want to do anything about it.'

'Do you really think I need time to decide if I want to see my son?' he asked.

'But you and Cora parted so bitterly.'

'This isn't about Cora and me,' he pointed out. 'It's

about me and my son. So I'll have that address as soon as you like please.'

It was so long since he'd seen Cora and life had been so brutal for Geoff since they had parted, the pain he had suffered when their affair had ended had been lessened by time and extreme hardship in the prison camp.

As a result he didn't really know how he felt about Cora now. Travelling on the train to Ruislip two weeks later, he wasn't sure if the feeling of nervous excitement he was experiencing was because he was going to see his son for the first time or the thought of seeing Cora again.

They had arranged by letter to meet at the station and as he went up the steps he was inwardly trembling. When he got to the top he saw a woman and a small boy standing just inside the entrance. He hardly recognised Cora at first, she looked so different, her hair worn simply and make-up at a bare minimum, unlike the lashings he remembered.

'Hello, Geoff,' she said, looking at him with a wary smile and then he saw those magnetic eyes that he had never forgotten. 'Welcome home. This is James. James, this is your daddy.'

Geoff could barely speak for emotion. 'Hello, son,' he said, going down on to his haunches to him.

'Hello,' the boy said shyly. 'What was the war like?'

'Not very nice,' he said hoarsely. 'But it's all over now so we can forget about it.'

They went to a nearby café which only had one rock cake left and the tea was weak and tasted stewed. They gave the cake to James and made do with a cup of the awful tea.

'He's a fine boy, Cora,' said Geoff. 'You're doing a really good job.'

'Glad you approve.' She sipped her tea while James played with a small car he'd brought with him. 'He's my life.'

'There's no one else then.'

'Absolutely not,' she said, not afraid to let the emotion show in her voice. 'You were, and still are, the only man for me. I'm so sorry I hurt you, Geoff. I caused myself pain too. I've never stopped regretting it. It was the biggest mistake of my life.'

Their eyes met and it was as though the clock rolled back to the time of their love affair. Even after all these years he still felt the same about her. That rush of love, the ache of desire that he'd experienced the first time he'd set eyes on her when she'd come to the house to see Mollie. She was the only woman he'd ever wanted with such a passion and he had no time for looking back. She was sorry she'd hurt him and that was good enough for him. The other stuff belonged in the past along with his experiences in the prison camp.

'Maybe we could give it another try,' he suggested, reaching over and taking her hand. 'The three of us.'

'I would really love that, Geoff,' she said with tears in her eyes. 'And I'm sure James would too.'

★　★　★

Finding out she had a grandson she knew nothing about and the circumstances of his conception was a huge shock for Madge when Geoff explained everything that had happened to the family that evening.

'I can't say I approve because I don't,' she said, her face and neck flushed with emotional blotches. 'You shouldn't have got involved with another man's wife. You were brought up better than that. We taught you to know the difference between right and wrong and you go and do a thing like that.'

'People can't always stick to the rules, Madge,' said Nora. 'Human emotions aren't that simple.'

'There is such a thing as restraint,' Madge retorted.

'Well, I think it's wonderful that Geoff and Cora are going to try again and bring James up together,' Mollie put in.

'You would say that as you are engaged to be married to her ex-husband,' said Madge. 'Why couldn't you both have found someone without complications?'

'Syd didn't have complications and he didn't do me much good, did he?' Mollie reminded her.

'Mm, there is that I suppose,' Madge conceded.

'Anyway the complications are all in the past. Both Cora and Grant are free to be with whoever they wish. Personally, I think it will be lovely having another child in the family,' said Mollie. 'Esme will be thrilled to know that James is her cousin now that it's all out in the open. He's a darling little boy, Mum. I know that you'll love him.'

'I'm sure I will. None of it is his fault anyway,' said Madge, beginning to warm to the situation. 'I just wish you'd told us before so that we could have seen something of him, Mollie.'

'Geoff didn't know anything about it until he got home and I didn't think it would be right to tell you until he'd accepted James into his life.'

'Mm, I can understand that,' said Madge, smiling as the idea of having another grandchild took hold. 'What's done is done so the sooner you bring your intended and your son over to see us the better, Geoff.'

'I'll organise it as soon as possible,' said Geoff, beaming. There had been times in the prison camp when he'd thought he would never have cause to smile again. He never dreamed there was such happiness waiting for him at the end of it all.

The next morning when Len and Mollie had gone to work, Esme to school and Geoff had gone to see Cora, Nora and Wilf confronted Madge.

'We need to talk to you,' said Nora.

'Carry on,' said Madge, who was polishing the furniture. 'I can listen while I work.'

'It's important, Madge,' said Nora, 'so we'd like you to sit down and listen.'

'Oh.' Madge looked at them, her brow furrowing. 'You're both looking very serious. I hope you aren't going to give me another shock. One of those is enough for the moment.'

'I'm afraid we are,' said Nora sheepishly. 'We wanted to wait until Geoff was home before we told you.'

Madge looked from one to the other. 'You'd better spit it out then and put me out of my misery,' she said.

'Well the first bit of news is that Wilf and I have decided to get married,' said Nora. 'I know it might seem a bit silly at our age but what time we have left we want to spend together.'

'It doesn't seem silly at all and I'm very pleased for you both. But there's nothing very shocking about that,' Madge approved. 'So can we have the other thing before the congratulations please? Don't keep me in suspense.'

Nora and Wilf looked at each other.

He turned to Madge. 'I'm your dad,' he said nervously.

Madge's face worked and she looked about to cry. Then she beamed at him, tears falling. 'I've had my suspicions about that for a while and wondered if it could possibly be true,' she said, her voice distorted by tears. 'I'm so glad it is. Welcome to the family.'

Nora was shocked. 'What made you think he might be?' she asked.

'The strong family likeness,' Madge replied. 'We all have his eyes, me, the twins and Esme. You mentioned the fact that you knew him before you married Dad and I knew I came along quite soon. It didn't take a genius to work it out.'

'You're not shocked about your wayward mother then.'

'You're a woman too, Mum, and these things happen,' said Madge.

'You don't seem angry.'

'Why would I be angry to find out that I don't have

any of the man I knew as Dad in me? No, I am relieved and very happy. You know how much I hated that man and how much I think of Wilf. I'm only sorry it took the two of you so long to find each other.'

'We found each other in the end, that's the important thing,' said Wilf.

Madge went over to Wilf and hugged him. 'I'm so pleased you are my dad,' she said. 'I won't call you that until I've told the others. Mollie and Geoff that they have a granddad and Esme that she has a great-granddad.'

'Don't forget Geoff's boy James,' said Nora.

'No, I would never do that,' said Madge. 'Once we get to know him he'll be included as a matter of course.'

Nora nodded.

'So I suppose you'll be moving out after the wedding then, Mum,' said Madge.

'Yeah, I'll be moving in with Wilf.'

'Mollie will be moving out too when she marries Grant and Geoff seems intent on making a go of it with Cora,' said Madge regretfully. 'The place will seem empty.'

'It's time you and Len had the place to yourselves,' said Nora.

'I suppose I'll get used to it.'

'We'll all be back visiting so often you won't notice we've gone,' said Nora.

'Maybe,' said Madge wistfully.

'You've no regrets about moving back to Chiswick, have you, Grant?' Mollie said to her husband of two months

405

one Sunday afternoon in the early summer of 1946 when they were walking by the river at Chiswick. Esme was skipping along ahead of them looking at the boats.

'None at all,' he said. 'I only moved to Barnes because I wanted a change of neighbourhood after the divorce. I knew you wouldn't be happy being a long walk or bus ride away from your mum's and you've got your classes in and around Chiswick. Esme would have had to change schools, which would have been unsettling for her. I wanted us to start our married life in a place where you and Esme want to be. It's convenient for work for me too now that I'm back at the store.'

'I was pleased when you suggested it and so was Mum,' said Mollie. 'But she didn't have an empty nest after all when Gran and I moved out because Geoff and Cora got married and have moved in with James until they can get a place of their own. I expect they'll stay there for a couple of years, at least, with housing being so short in London, but now that Geoff has got his job back at the hotel they should be able to save a bit, especially as Cora's got a part-time job in a sweet shop while James is at school.'

'I still can't get over how much she's changed,' he remarked.

'Yeah, it is a transformation. That's what comes of being with the right person I suppose.' She turned to him. 'As long as you don't change. Not one little bit because I love you just the way you are.'

'This included?' he said, turning to her and pointing to his neck.

'Absolutely,' she said, leaning up and gently touching the scars which had been much improved by surgery but were still quite visible and not particularly nice to look at. 'They are part of you and remind me of why you were awarded a medal for bravery.'

'I don't want to be reminded of any of that now that the war is over,' he said. 'I'd rather think about now and our future together. The three of us.'

She linked her arm in his. 'Life is good, Grant, and we are so lucky,' she said and they quickened their step to catch up with their adored Esme.

07.905357552